INTERRUPTED...

Reggie Lewis stood in front of the cabinet, hand over the pull, but still hesitated.

"Damn it. Just get it over with. It's always easier to just pull the bandage off." She yanked the middle drawer open and it rattled in her hands. In the dim light of the workshop, it was just a square of slightly darker shadow. Empty, as Lila had said, as she'd seen. She hooked her wheeled stool over to her and sank down, finally having to face what for the past forty-eight hours she'd allowed herself to keep denying.

All her files were really gone. It didn't get much worse than this. Of course, maybe it wouldn't be a problem. Everyone in the Okanagan knew her designs. Frankly, everyone in BC who was involved with jewelry probably did, and even a few of the big American shows on the west coast. She should be fine. Better than fine with the show coming up in Milan.

But all the reassurances in the world didn't stop the queasy feeling in the pit of her stomach.

A sharp rap of knuckles on door frame sent her stumbling to her feet. She banged into the open drawer, caught her hip on the corner, and stubbed the toe of her work boot on the leg of her workbench, almost fell again because her left leg had somehow fallen asleep. A hand on her arm steadied her.

The scent of cut grass and verbena filled the shop and she stopped dead, the bracelet throbbing on her arm. She swung around. Cesare Angelucci stood too close, his palm under her elbow, his tiger eyes thoughtful, his lips curved in a nearly devastating grin that made her mouth go dry and sour because he could be laughing.

At her.

BOOKS BY THE AUTHOR

Romance
Ashes and Light
Shades of Moonlight
Judas Kiss
Second Spring
A Different Nightmusic
Shadow Play
Unlocking Her Heart
Unlocking Her History
Unlocking Her Grace
Unlocking Her Dreams
Unlocking Her Chance (January 2016)

Mystery
Through Dark Water

Fantasy
The Cartographer Universe **series:**
The Warden of Power
Impossible
The Cartographer's Daughter
Afterburn
Aftershock
Aftermath
Afterimage

Terra Incognita
Terra Infirma
Terra Nueva

Also by the Author
Mutable Things
Emberstone
Ice Dragon
Crystal Courtesan

UNLOCKING HER DREAMS

Karen L. Abrahamson

To the Peachland that was.

UNLOCKING HER DREAMS

Prologue

The mid-afternoon traffic of Berlin's Grunerstrasse and Karl Leibknecht-Strasse streets moved in a rhythmic pulse between the leafy confines of the sidewalks. The Fernsehturm, the bulbous Berlin television tower, glittered and fractured the sunlight as it poked out of the grey expanse of buildings like a periscope searching for prey. The thing that dwelt in Johan Fehr felt the same way.

All his plans so far had come to naught. But he had charted a new course when his pure frontal assault had not worked on the three women. Now he just had to make his new plan work.

Down below, the summer streets of the city were crowded with shirt-sleeved Berliners rubbing shoulders with the constant stream of foreigners who came to the city. Tourists, students, artists, businessmen crowded into the Mitte area with the glittering, golden chariot above the Brandenburg Tor, the grey arch of the Brandenburg Gate, the parliament buildings, the gray concrete and glass towers and modernity of PotsdamerPlatz. Humanity, all of it, and all nothing more than fodder for him.

Swirling his chilled crystal glass of scotch, he turned back from the view of the puny lives, the puny efforts to prove that humans were a great boon to the world. His apartment, repaired since his latest temper had led to his destruction of much of its contents, had a new, white, lamb's leather couch that formed a corner in the center of the room like a body curled on the floor, the huge, chrome-legged, zigzag-shaped glass coffee table set into its angle like an ancient tool of torture. The white wool rug that the couch and table sat on was like a field of new snow awaiting the destruction of footsteps. The two-story white walls held bold new paintings, red as splashed blood.

He sipped the whiskey and considered the largest painting of white background with vivid orange and red streaks down the canvas as if something had been disemboweled and hung there. One of the damnable women would be his preference. Who would think that four women from a place with the imbecilic name of Peachland could stymie him? *HIM.* The place was a scattering of houses, barely deserving of the name town, and he was—he was as old, as inexorable, as time. Had always taken what he wished from the puny humans—always until that fatal last time that had left him no more than a shade of himself, wandering the world, searching for what had been stolen from him. Yes, stolen.

Johan Fehr's fist tightened around the crystal glass, the knuckles white.

The silver bracelet was his. Though he might not have made it, it contained too much of his essence, too much of his power. All these years it had been lost, his power confined in its links, but so long as it existed he was safe.

Now, though, the bracelet had come to light and the ancient curse he had placed on the thing was coming undone, link by link, his power dissipating. If he did not reclaim the thing soon, he would be left with no more power than was within this body, and he had spent so much of that strength to reclaim the bracelet that if he was not successful, he could be left with nothing.

The body inhaled to quell the anger his emotions bred in the flesh and bone. He and this body had been together so long that they were almost one. They controlled the *Schwarzenacht Corporation* empire, which was another kind of power and one that he would use now to get what he wanted. He had been a fool to try frontal assaults on the women. As long as they were together—bound together in friendships so strong—they would defend each other. And he could not succeed. Or at least not without expending more power than he could chance.

So another approach was necessary. One that would break them apart. One that would destroy their friendship and everything it had built. One that would leave the bracelet wearer alone and easy prey.

The phone rang and he stabbed the receiver on. Listened.

"Good," he said and hung up.

It was four thirty in the morning in the place called Peachland and his plan was in motion. Now to see it through to completion.

This time he would succeed.

Chapter 1

The early morning hung brooding grey over the Okanagan Valley of south-central British Columbia; a storm off the Pacific Ocean had sent thick clouds streaming eastward over the coastal mountains and over the long valley that contained the eighty-mile-long Okanagan Lake. As a result, the rising August sun barely glowed in the clouds that filled the eastern sky, though the air was still warm—the thermometer on the porch post said it was almost seventy-eight degrees.

Ponderosa pine covered the folded mountains of the western shore above the town of Peachland, while on the eastern shore, fire had scoured the trees from the mountains. But life returned. Life always returned—grasses, the wild poppy and black-eyed Susan, fireweed and lupine would have been the first. Even the pines had started to grow again, their long-fallen seeds kindled to life by the flames that had killed the forest. At least that was what Lila Weber told herself, when a tingle of ill-ease had awakened her with the dawn this morning.

And with the new growth had come the wild mountain goats that, to Lila standing on her porch far across the lake, looked like tiny white flecks on the distant mountainside.

She smiled at the sight. It had been years since the herd had been on those rugged mountains. She stood, nursing her first cup of coffee of the day and hugging herself against her nerves, on the broad porch that spanned the front of the beloved red and white, two-story heritage house that she had inherited from her grandparents. It sat like a stately old dowager across Beach Avenue from the beach and the usually blue lake where she had whiled away many a summer as a child. But the lake was uneasy today and reflected how she felt. A cool wind from the south stirred the usually pleasant lake into a mass of whitecaps that only the most madcap boater would chance. On shore, even though it was August, the beach was empty of its usual flock of summer people, though the diehard, Lycra-clad joggers and the silver-haired, Birkenstock-sandaled walkers still made their way along the promenade that paralleled the beach beside the road.

The wind smelled of heat and dry places and tasted of iron on her tongue. Heat lightning, maybe, but it reminded her more of dark, like the smothering dark in caves, instead of the dry desert hillsides of the Okanagan. No, something was unnatural about this wind. It soured her smooth, hazelnut-flavored coffee until it tasted only of chemicals. She wondered what Chloe, her friend, business partner, and resident 'psychic' would make of this change in the weather from her condominium down around the point.

A shiver ran down Lila's spine and she pulled her pale blue pashmina shawl around her shoulders, her light, three-quarter-sleeved shift of blue Indian cotton suddenly severely inadequate for the weather. After the attacks on three of her friends over the past three months, it really was no wonder that she feared the worst when the air was like this. Each of her friends had worn the same silver bracelet that she had brought into this house from an estate sale, so in a way, it was all her fault. And now the bracelet of seven perfectly-fashioned silver doors was on Reggie's wrist—Reggie Lewis of Regulus Designs, who was now winging her way home from Europe and Milan from her first in-person meeting about jewelry planned for the fashion runways of Europe.

It didn't bode well that she was due back today. This wind, this scent, made Lila's stomach clench and her scalp prickle despite her long auburn hair. Something was coming, and given the experiences she and her friends had had over the past three months, nothing that came on a wind like this could be good.

Lila roused herself and went inside, through the shop called *This and That*, the fashion jewelry store that she ran with her friends. They specialized in silver and gold jewelry of semiprecious stones that she found all over the world, as well as the astoundingly beautiful pieces that Reggie fashioned in her workshop out back. At this hour of the day, with lights turned off and only the light through the front windows that gave onto the lake, the shop had a misty feeling with its lavender walls and dark wainscoting filling the space with a lovely light.

It was a good shop, with its glass cabinets and flowing displays of pashminas. They were selling well and making their mark with the marketing genius of Kylee, the latest addition to their little enclave of women.

And yet here she stood, actually sweating with—well—fear. Yes, that was what it was. She held out her coffee cup one-handed and tremors disturbed the top of the liquid. Definitely shaking. Definitely fear.

Well, enough of that, because she had nothing to fear. Her life was simple. It was good just being here with her friends and her business.

And a bracelet that brought danger into all their lives. Even Ally's. Her friend Allison McVay had come to town for a visit and had been the third woman nearly killed while she wore the bracelet.

Lila closed her eyes. She was not going to think about what could have happened. She pushed through the beaded curtain to the rest of the house and left it clack-clack-clacking softly behind her as she returned to the kitchen to flush the ill-tasting coffee down the drain.

The kitchen was her favorite room of the house and always had been. From her grandmother's domain of strictly functional summer kitchen, she'd remodeled the room into a thing of beauty and light. The rear wall gave onto the backyard through a French door, and a string of windows stretched over a long counter and sink. Pale yellow walls were offset by white cupboards. Stainless steel appliances had pride of place, with the gas range set off in its own alcove under a copper range hood. Bright accents of turquoise and tangerine were present in a turquoise-faced wall clock, a utensil jar, and salt and pepper shakers shaped like small orange tropical fishes. In one corner of the room she'd kept her grandmother's cozy kitchen nook, but had changed the cushions to tangerine and turquoise to go with the décor.

She pulled her darkest roast coffee beans out of the cupboard and set to making herself an espresso. Get rid of the chemical taste and get her day started, because along with the fear came a kind of lethargy at the inevitability of whatever was coming.

Her little espresso pot had just started its gurgling when the bell above the front door jingled. Hadn't she locked it behind her? Darn it, why was she so nervous?

"Lila?" came the melodious voice of Chloe Main, but the voice cracked. "You're up. I know it."

"Kitchen," Lila called and pulled a second cup from the cupboard.She turned around as Chloe entered the room, dangling her key from her fingers.

Chloe Main was a long-time friend and one of the most serene people that Lila knew—except when she'd gone through a bout of wearing a certain bracelet. But today, straggling into the kitchen with one of the three sets of shop keys dangling from her fingers, she looked almost as shaken as she had after a man had attacked her during that horrible time. Yes, her hip-long, lustrous brown hair was done up in its usual thick braid and she wore her usual thigh-length caftan and leggings—these in deep purple—but her deep blue eyes had a glazed, shocked look. Most of the color had drained from her cheeks, as well.

"Chloe! Are you all right?" Lila left the stove and caught her friend's arm to lead her to the kitchen table.

"I'm fine. Really. I am." Chloe pulled loose as she sank down into the nook. "I just had a bad dream and then—well—I woke up and went out onto the patio to get some air and calm myself but..."

She shook her head, the jet beads clicked and rattled amongst the silver cavalcade of necklaces she wore.

"Then you felt it, too, and I'm not imagining things. Something's coming." Lila went back to the stove where the little silver espresso pot bubbled and spluttered. "Latte all right?"

Chloe nodded. "Just make it strong." She bowed her head as if seeking strength.

Lila pulled milk out of the fridge and measured it into a pot to heat.

"Something's coming. Some new disaster. Or danger." Chloe said, clutching at the string of jet. According to Chloe, they were protection against evil spirits. "I dreamt about a black wind, laden with sand. It blew through Peachland, tearing everything down. The sand ate away the red and white paint and the wood of the store. It tore down the marina and my condo. It stripped flesh from bones, and the worst of it was, the whole time I heard horrible laughter as if whatever sent the wind reveled in what it had done."

She looked up at Lila as she whisked the heated milk to a froth. Chloe's lovely, deep blue eyes had gone violet with emotion.

Lila pressed her lips together and nodded, then turned back to the coffee. She'd known Chloe long enough to know that Chloe's dreams should be listened to. She poured the thick black coffee into two off-kilter shaped mugs reminiscent of something out of *Alice in Wonderland*, then poured in the the steaming milk with a little flourish so small flower designs blossomed on the top. She brought them over to the table and slid in beside Chloe.

"So what's coming? Any idea?"

Chloe shook her head. "You know me. I get impressions—emotions. I don't get details. When I realized that it wasn't just a dream, I got dressed and came right over. I was scared something had happened to you. Or the others."

"I'm fine. I heard from Reggie that she'd gotten on the plane. Everything was fine—great, even. She should be home this afternoon."

Chloe nodded. "That's a good bit of fortune, but it brings the bracelet back here while something's happening. Have you heard from Kylee?"

Lila smiled thinking of her high school BFF, who was now fully ensconced in the life of Peachland and the store. "Undoubtedly she's with your baby bro. Brett'll keep her safe if anyone can."

From the store came another bright jangle from the bell above the door. "Please tell me you locked the door behind you." Lila said.

"I did." Chloe looked toward the hallway where the bead curtains clicked behind somebody.

"Lila?" Kylee Jensen's bright voice travelled down the hall. The third person to have shop keys.

"Right here in the kitchen. If your ears were ringing, Chloe and I were just talking about you." Lila stood to greet her diminutive friend with a hug. "You okay?"

Kylee's bright blonde cap of hair was disheveled as if she had just gotten out of bed. She wore a pair of capris and a bright red blouse with an overlarge men's black hoody clutched around her neck. She nodded.

"Just flipping freezing. I woke up scared to death so I got up. Brett's still sleeping. So what's happening?"

"We're having a coffee and trying to figure it out. Want one?"

"Sure." Kylee headed for the table, then stopped. "Have you checked the house?"

Lila paused in refilling the espresso pot's water reservoir. "Why?" She filled the filter with fresh, finely ground coffee.

"In case anything's wrong. The store looked fine, from what I saw."

Lila screwed the top on the pot and placed it on the stove. "A good idea. I'll check upstairs. Maybe you two can check down here. Any idea what we're looking for?"

"Anything that could spell trouble," Chloe mulled. "We'll know it when we see it."

Lila took the espresso pot off the burner and headed for the stairs. As usual, Kylee's idea was a good one, but Lila couldn't see where someone breaking into *This and That* could bring on this disastrous feeling. She hadn't felt this way even when the shop *was* broken into and all of Reggie's prototype pieces made for Milan had been stolen. But those pieces had been recovered and were all safely with Reggie. From what Reggie had said, the pieces had been a triumph with the clothing designer.

Lila checked the guest room, recently vacated when her friend Ally had left for East Africa and now ready for its expected next guest, the assistant designer who'd be arriving home with Reggie. The bed with its patchwork lavender duvet was made, the chalk-painted dresser standing primly against the wall complete with a vase of white lilies and baby's breath. The window blinds were open onto today's grey view of the lake. Nothing here. She headed for her office and had just poked her head inside when a shout came from the rear of the house. She clattered down the stairs again and back to the kitchen.

The back door was open and Kylee and Chloe both stood outside on the patio deck paving stones. The yard wasn't large— just room for the flagstone deck, barbeque, patio chairs, and a small flower garden—because most of the area was taken up with Reggie's jewelry workshop. Initially she had worked at home in a smallish shed. That had changed when *This and That* had opened and she'd needed more space. So she'd moved all her equipment here and had bought more until she was able to produce the jewelry that met her inspiration and vision. At the moment the door to the workshop hung open.

Chloe stood frozen in the middle of the patio, her arms wrapped around herself. Kylee stood at the door to the shop as if afraid to enter and glanced back at Lila when she stepped outside.

"The door was open when I came out. You better see this," Kylee said and motioned Lila forward.

Lila crossed the flagstones and peered inside.

It was a long, narrow room, with a workbench surrounded by smoke-dimmed windows at one end and counters with kilns and grinders and other equipment that Lila would prefer not to know about stationed neatly along the walls. Regardless of the general grime that came from the heated work of jewelry making, Reggie always kept the place tidy, with jeweler's tools in neat racks up above, cupboards for supplies, and a cabinet where Reggie kept files on her pieces—molds and processes used, the provenance of stones, etc., for each of her designs. At least that was how the place was supposed to look.

At the moment it was more like a hurricane had passed through it. The room reeked of spilled chemicals and kiln charcoal. Lila wrinkled her nose and cautiously stepped inside. The large pieces of equipment still stood where Reggie'd left them, but the small anvil and tools that Reggie kept close to hand at her work bench had been scooped off the table top into a pile on the floor. The cupboards, too, had been emptied, spilling small plastic bags of semiprecious and precious stones through the mess. Here and there the dark gleam of ruby, garnet, topaz, and sapphire caught the gray light from the door. No one was here.

She picked up a pale moonstone at her feet. Everything was devastation. It would take Reggie to make sense out of this mess. But Reggie wasn't here.

Lila swung around, her gaze falling on the yawning filing cabinet drawers.

Empty.

The sense of disaster flooded in once more.

Chapter 2

The Boeing 727 jerked slightly as it rolled to a halt on the tarmac. Its engines powered off and from outside the plane came the welcome hum of the staircase being driven up to the aircraft's cabin door. Fresh air would be a godsend after the long haul of connecting flights from Milan to Paris to Vancouver and now to the blessed tarmac of Kelowna International Airport in the heart of the Okanagan. The circulated air seemed to carry a sour pall of sweat and bad coffee that just underlined Reggie Lewis' fatigue.

Out the windows the low mountains surrounding the Okanagan valley gleamed summer-brown—sunburned grasses and sage mixed with the dark green of ponderosa pine and the fluttering green-gray leaves of poplar that followed the seams of the land where there was running water. The afternoon sky was brilliant, cloudless blue and the afternoon sun would be like an old friend on Reggie's shoulders. She might be returning triumphant from Milan, but she sighed with relief and cast a glance at her travel companion as the passengers beat the clicking off of the seatbelt sign and stood to deplane.

"Let's just let the others push and shove and we'll gather our things after the crush," Reggie said. Around them the overhead bins were releasing carry-on luggage large enough to be lethal if one fell on their heads. Her single suitcase was similar in size because she'd only been away for five days and it was packed in the overhead bin, but Victoria Angelucci didn't travel quite so light so they'd be waiting for the luggage arrival anyway. No reason to hurry.

Victoria nodded and sat back down.

The woman was the epitome of a fashionable Italian, even though she wasn't what you immediately thought of as Italian. Victoria was a honey blonde, with hair in thick soft curls à la Brigitte Bardot, and with the voluptuous curves to match. She wore what had to be a custom-fitted Armani suit of navy, with red piping along the collar of the peplum jacket and a pair of flowing trousers over towering, stacked red heels that Reggie was in awe of. Even after the sixteen hours of travel, Victoria looked just as wonderfully put together as she had at the start of the trip, while Reggie's grey-blue knit pants and tunic felt like rags and her makeup had probably melted on her face. Oh, to return to her usual garb of camo pants and sleeveless top and the comfort of her workshop.

Five days in Milan had felt like forever. She missed her space, her friends at the shop, and most of all her daughter, Thalia.

The cabin door opened and the smell of jet fuel, heated tarmac, pine, and lake water filled the cabin. Reggie inhaled like a hungry woman. Home. She was home. How the heck had Kylee and Chloe managed to stay away so long? How did Lila stand those long buying trips? The Okanagan was home and, at the moment, she didn't want to leave it again. Ever. Well, maybe not ever, but at least not until Milan fashion week. Then she'd go back to see her jewelry grace its first European runway. If the response of Erminio, the designer, was any indication, she might be seeing a lot of fashion weeks in the future. A little frisson of excitement ran through her.

Maybe next time she could take Thalia with her. Thalia would love the adventure of it.

Finally the other passengers had mostly shuffled past and she stood to hand Victoria down her various and sundry belongings—three bags from duty free, a coat, a hat, a briefcase and small suitcase to go with the larger suitcase she had checked through as luggage. With Reggie helping juggle Victoria's belongings, they trailed between the empty passenger seats, said their goodbyes to the cabin crew—in Victoria's case it was *"Ciao, bella"*—and then descended the long set of stairs to the tarmac and the painted walkway to Kelowna's small, one-story terminal.

"This eeze charming," Victoria said as she scanned the hillsides. "It eeze very dry. My skin will feel this very quickly." She plunked on a wide brimmed hat that matched the peplum on her jacket, placing her classic features in shadow. "The mountains are—how do you say? Rugged? Is that the word? And not so green as Lombardy. There are no tall, snowy mountains, either." She pouted her disappointment.

"The tall, snowy mountains are along the coast or east of here. The entire province is ridges of mountains, but this is one of the folds of valley in between the worst of them." Reggie tried to parse whether Victoria was really serious. Reggie still hadn't been able to figure the other woman out, though Victoria had been with her throughout her time in Milan. She was a wonderful host and had made sure Reggie saw the best of Milan and nearby Lake Como during her brief stay, as well as chauffeuring her around from her hotel to Erminio's design studio so that she and the Great Heir to Italian Fashion—as the fashion pundits were calling him—could discuss his vision for additional pieces of jewelry for this season and the next. The meetings had left Reggie just a tad ecstatic and a heck of a lot terrified. There was so much work to be done.

"Come on! There'll be people waiting for us."

Trundling their bags, they followed the last of the passengers up the ramp into the low-slung glass and concrete terminal. The gaggle of passengers had stopped there like a flow of silver, congealing in the mass of welcoming family members. Reggie and Victoria stalled at the door, Reggie craning her neck for a familiar face. Then she spotted welcoming auburn curls. Lila Weber waved over the heads of the crowd.

"Follow me." Like inserting a jewel into a delicate setting, she started easing them through the chattering families until suddenly Lila was there, looking lovely and cool as ever in a sky-blue sleeveless three-quarter-sleeve shift and white ballet flats with a cascade of silver chain and seed pearl necklaces. But her large hazel eyes had a hint of worry in them.

"You're home safe and sound and thank goodness for that." Lila tugged Reggie into a hug and then clasped Reggie's right hand to inspect the bracelet around her wrist. "Still got it on, I see."

Reggie shrugged. "Was there any alternative?"

Lila grinned. "I thought maybe one of those Italian studs might have swept you off your feet." She held out her hand to Victoria. "Hi. I'm Lila Weber, Reggie's friend."

"And co-owner of *This and That*, a little jewelry store we have in Peachland," Reggie added.

"Welcome to the Okanagan," Lila finished.

Nodding graciously, Victoria shook. It was like the two women were inspecting each other; both seemed to like what they saw and both relaxed.

"Victoria came back with me to help me with the final designs for the fall show and to discuss concepts for next spring."

A hesitation and then Lila grinned. "Are you telling me that they want your designs for a second season?"

Reggie could barely contain the need to shout it to the moon that had been bursting in her chest since her last meeting with Erminio. Now it bubbled up and she squeezed her eyes shut. "This is one of those squee moments, where I want to dance like a kid, but I'll leave that to Thalia."

A congratulatory hug from Lila, but then the baggage carousel buzzed and they went with the crowd to retrieve Victoria's other bag.

While Victoria went carousel-side, Lila turned serious. "I want to hear all about your trip, but first, about the bracelet— there were no problems?"

Reggie held up her wrist for inspection. It was, without a doubt, the most intricate piece of jewelry she had ever laid her eyes on—more so than anything she had ever attempted. Yes, the Italians might have their way with jewel-encrusted torques, rings, and bracelets, but this bracelet was solid silver and very old—at least she'd put her money on it being old given the patina and the signs of slight corrosion.

It was made up of the most intricately cast and created doors she had ever seen. Seven doors—each unique—formed the bracelet. One was a tiny arched door with a gargoyle, one an iron-strapped heavy wooden door, another of wood and edged with ivy. Still another had what looked like scrolled fairy hinges, while another had hinges shaped like leaves. The sixth door looked like a Dutch door that would split at the middle so the upper area could be open to the air.

The final door had heavy, square-carved lintels above the door as if it had been removed from a place of some pomp and importance. A tiny silver Fatima hand hung as a door knocker. One of the doors had a tiny padlock on a miniature chain holding it closed. Reggie didn't know the provenance of the bracelet, only that it had been amongst the jewelry of an estate sale. She and her friends had found an old diary belonging to a British colonel who had owned the bracelet. He'd written that he had found it in the North African desert during the Second World War. Said colonel had always considered it lucky, but Reggie wasn't so sure, given the danger that the bracelet's other wearers had gone through.

She ran her fingers over the linteled door—the one she found her fingers straying to over her time with the bracelet. She raised her eyes to Lila's. "Problems? Only the fact that the darn thing won't come off and I had to choose my jewelry around it. People like Victoria notice things like that."

She nodded at the Italian woman who was hefting her bag off the rotating carousel with surprising strength. Victoria might look like an exotic bird in this environment, but she clearly had no expectation of being waited on. But fashion—all aspects of it down to the tiniest of details—was clearly important.

"But no attempts on your safety?"

Reggie shook her head. "I felt safe as a baby. Victoria was the perfect hostess," she said as the other woman rolled luggage almost as big as a smart car toward them. Reggie grinned. "Now

I just hope I—we—can be as gracious. They set a pretty high standard, Lila. They set me up in the Hotel Principe Di Savoia and I felt like a princess." She turned to Victoria. "We could still set you up in a hotel in West Kelowna. There is a nice place down on the water."

"No, no, no." Victoria held up her hands. "I came because I want to see where the magic of your jewelry comes from. If your friend is kind enough to let me stay in her home—please, it will be enough. And Reggie tells me it is near the water— like the villas of Lake Como? How can I turn such a pleasure down?"

"Well..." Lila said. "You're very welcome. Just don't be expecting a villa. It's my home—was my grandparents' and the place I always came to in the summer. Now it's also our shop. But you are more than welcome."

Lila led them out to her little Ford Escape SUV and Reggie thought of the limo that they had used to whisk her away from the Milan airport. Welcome back to the land of working folk. They loaded the luggage—no minions to do it for them—and climbed in. Reggie took the back to allow Victoria to have the better view. Then they headed to Peachland.

The highway took them through the sprawl of Kelowna's strip malls and hotels and then up and over the floating bridge over the narrow waist of the lake before winding up through West Kelowna's light industrial and commercial areas, all the while catching glimpses of the lake and the mountains and hills that at this time of year were tinder dry.

"Still no rain, huh?" she asked Lila.

"A thunder shower the other day. We all held our breath, praying there'd be no lightning strikes."

"We've had a couple of bad forest fires near Peachland," Reggie explained to Victoria. "A few years back they had to evacuate half the town. Luckily we weren't affected."

"This must look very different from Milan," Lila said as she guided the SUV down the long, steep slope that was known as Drought Hill and turned toward the lake.

"Here it is very dry—compared to Lake Como. There it is all trees and flowers and streams pouring down from the mountains. The mountains are taller, too."

"Well, the Okanagan is technically a desert, but just add water and you can grow anything. We have lots of flowers and orchards and more and more very good wineries."

The familiar lapis shimmer of the lake lay ahead and all the tension of the five days of meetings and trying to be fashionable enough to get by in a city like Milan—in other words, trying to be something she was not and would never be—faded from Reggie's shoulders. This was her turf and Victoria was just going to have to accept it. She grinned a little, certain that Reggie Lewis in camo and singlet was going to be a bit of a shock for fashionable Victoria. Lila, now—she was the fashionable one.

Lila turned down the lane that ran behind *This and That* and the other houses and businesses that fronted the lake.

"We have many wineries in Lombardy, as well. My family owns one."

"Really? Well then, I know someone who'd love to chat with you. Our friend Chloe's brother is part owner of Elkhart winery here in Peachland. You'll meet him, I'm sure."

Lila turned into the carport of the large, two-story, red-trimmed white house and turned off the engine. Reggie opened her door and inhaled the moist heat of the lakeshore. Roses and honeysuckle from Lila's rear garden, heat off the patio paving stones, and the permanent, slight under-taste of kiln charcoal from her shop. She closed her eyes and realized she'd missed the sweat and the heat and the ecstatic god-struck feeling that she always got in the midst of creation. Milan had been good for discussing ideas with Victoria and Erminio, for Victoria was a designer in her own right, but this—the fire, heat, and hard metal tools of her shop—this was creation. As if she was one of the mythical silversmiths of the dwarves or an apprentice of Vulcan, the god of the volcanoes.

"Reggie? You all right?"

Lila had unloaded the luggage and was leading Victoria toward the house.

Reggie shook herself. "Yeah. Sure. Fine. Just tired from the trip, I guess. And itching to get back to work in my shop. My head and my notebook are full of designs that I need to get to work on."

"Well, let's get Victoria settled and then I'll give you a run back to your place so you can get a shower and some rest before your start everything. Thalia called here three times this morning asking if you were back yet. She must be driving your parents crazy."

They crossed the patio—scorching hot in the afternoon sun, regardless of the shady maple tree at the rear of the yard—and went into the air-conditioned cool of Lila's sunny kitchen with its welcoming nook and its bank of windows onto the back of the house.

Reggie sighed, closed her eyes, and could have just planted herself at the table it felt so good to be here, but this was only her home away from home and she wanted to see her daughter. It had been like a constant ache since she left even though they'd talked every night. Lila and her friends might be a big part of her life, but Thalia was her *everything*. She needed to get home and hug that ten-year-old body. Hard.

"You're here!" Chloe's voice came from the shop at the front of the house and the rush of footfall came from the hallway. Two figures pushed into the kitchen: Chloe Main clad in her usual knee-length caftan and leggings, these ones deep purple, with her hip-long hair kept confined in its ubiquitous heavy braid. With her came the blonde sprite that was Kylee Jensen, wearing a pretty little floral sundress that no one in Milan would be caught dead in because it was much too simple and probably too inexpensive. Her cap of bright hair framed her gamine face and large blue eyes.

"Reggie!" Kylee threw her arms around her in a hug. "We missed you."

Chloe grinned and turned to Victoria, who stood in all her finery. Chloe's eyes widened slightly at the larger than life hair, makeup, and suit. She stuck out her hand. "I'm Chloe Main.

Welcome to the madhouse." She leaned in to buss Victoria's cheeks. Trust Chloe to have an Italian welcome for an Italian. She stepped back with a tiny frown.

"I'm Kylee," Kylee said, separating herself from Reggie and shaking Victoria's hand. "You must be exhausted after the trip. Would you like some tea? Coffee? Something to eat?"

"Whoa! Would you whoa?" Reggie said, stepping between her friends and Victoria. "This is Victoria Angelucci. She's Erminio Biondi's partner and she's here to work with me on the designs. But she's been through a heck of a long flight, just like I have, so let's let her have some space, okay?"

She looked from one enthusiastic face to the other. Both nodded.

"Of course. I forgot," Kylee said. "Those international flights can take it right out of you."

"But it is very nice to meet you both. Perhaps a cup of tea would be nice after a chance to freshen up?" said Victoria with a smile.

"Then let me show you to your room and then I'm going to run Reggie back to her place. Chloe, Kylee, I'll ask you to play hostess while I'm gone. Maybe you can show Victoria the shop and help her get settled. I should be back in twenty minutes."

She left, hauling Victoria's largest suitcase up the stairs to the guest room on the second floor. Reggie hoped it would do. It was a lovely room—or at least she'd always thought so until they put her up in what amounted to a suite that had looked like it was something out of a castle when she was in Milan. Totally outside her expectations and she wondered if Victoria would be able to handle the down-home comforts of Peachland. Well, she'd check with her tomorrow and if it wasn't working, she'd get the woman moved into a hotel. But she'd deal with that tomorrow.

"Lonely. That's the word for Victoria. I get the sense she doesn't trust many people," Chloe said, looking thoughtful.

"So how was it?" Kylee asked. "As exciting as it must have been?"

"Sure. It was." But God, she was so tired. She really needed to sleep because she certainly hadn't on the plane.

"So spill, girlfriend. What about the men? Meet anyone?" Kylee tugged her toward the nook's turquoise and tangerine seating.

"No, there were no men. Why the heck would I be interested in an Italian man? They're all hands and leers and rude comments."

"Now that sounds like sour grapes—like maybe someone who's carrying a little disappointment that she didn't get swept off her feet," Chloe crowed.

Reggie batted her arm. "It sounds like someone who had better things to do than moon over a man. I have Thalia. I don't need another person to take up my time—not with all the work I have to do. And don't you two have a shop to tend or something?" she ended as they started tittering. "Get outta here and leave me alone."

She waved them away, but not before they each gave her another hug.

"So glad you're home safe, hon," Chloe whispered in her ear and then they were gone.

Reggie was just pondering whether she'd be able to get up again if she let herself curl up in the nook when Lila came back into the room.

"Victoria's settled. She's talking about taking a shower and maybe going for a walk on the beach. She seems very nice."

"She is. She—everyone—treated me like royalty over there. I just hope our homey little Peachland is enough for her. I mean—well—you saw her."

Lila caught her arm. "Don't worry. A lot of Europeans pine for the simpler life Canada offers them. Now let's get you home. I've got to talk to you about something."

They piled into the SUV again and Lila backed out and onto the lane. Then she stopped and bowed her head into the steering wheel. "I wasn't going to tell you until tomorrow, and then I wasn't going to tell you until you were home, but I guess I'm having a crisis of conscience."

"Just what are you talking about?" Reggie tried to understand, but her jet-lagged brain wasn't quite putting the pieces together. Lila wasn't helping, either. In fact, her auburn curls tumbled around her cheeks effectively blocking her face from Reggie almost as if she'd planned it.

Lila sighed and turned to her. "It happened this morning, I think. I was outside and it was as if the wind blew in change that smelled like hot iron. All the little hairs on my arms stood on end and the next thing I knew Chloe was here, and then Kylee, too. We searched the house looking for something that would match the disaster we were all feeling." She shook her head, her hazel eyes settling on Reggie. "It wasn't in the house. It was your shop. The door was open and everything easily moveable had been thrown on the floor."

Frowning, Reggie shrugged. "That's not so bad. I can sort stuff out again."

But Lila was already shaking her head. "Let me finish. They did that, sure. And it was a mess, but they got into your files, Reggie. They took everything."

Chapter 3

Everything.

Absolutely everything was gone from her filing cabinets, leaving them behind like an empty husk of a nut or a banana skin. She'd seen it when she'd leapt out of the SUV and run back into the yard and into her shop, before Lila grabbed her arm and dragged her back to the car, murmuring that there was absolutely nothing she could do about it at the moment and that she'd function better after she got some rest and saw Thalia. That had been eighteen hours ago.

Still in the thin grey t-shirt and men's pajama bottoms she wore for sleeping, Reggie sat at the oak table under the window in her tiny sun-filled kitchen, inhaling the welcome scents of chicory, dust, and pine that were normal for her house at this time of day with the window wide open. The chicory came from her oddly crooked, hand-shaped coffee cup complete with four, toed feet—a footed cup—that she'd used ever since she received it as a gift from a mightily proud six-year-old Thalia. The dust and pine came from the outdoors—although the dust could be from the lack of housekeeping the place had had over the past few weeks what with everything going on.

The kitchen was a little old-fashioned, with avocado-colored appliances and white, ceramic-tiled countertop, but it went with the brown-painted cupboards. She'd been up since three-thirty from jet lag and was determined to be up for the day, so she was dosing herself with coffee to keep the energy up and the smile on her face in the human equivalent of electroplating. Meanwhile Thalia was upstairs sleeping like only a kid could.

The house was as diminutive as the kitchen, but it sat snug and warm amidst the ponderosa pine nestled in a fold of the hillside above West Kelowna, or what the old-timers still called Westbank. Small house with a warm little living room and a narrow set of stairs leading up to two small bedrooms that had narrow windows that looked out onto trees and forest and the occasional deer that wandered into the yard. One of her favorite photos was of Thalia as a towheaded child playing outside with a fawn. Both had been too young to know that they weren't supposed to be friends. That photo now sat on the miniscule mantle above the living room fireplace, guarded by two brass candlesticks that Thalia's father had bought Reggie as a gift before he died. The photo still had the power to make her smile when she was feeling at her worst.

Except this morning. Ever since she'd seen the yawning emptiness of her file cabinet, her stomach had clenched up and had stayed that way. Just what the theft meant she couldn't say, but that it had been done for a reason there was no question. Random break-and-enter artists didn't leave behind bags of precious and semiprecious stones, not to mention small amounts of gold and silver in favor of a bunch of musty files. Not unless they were planning something.

The question was what. Her hand rubbed the bracelet absently and she sipped her coffee and peered out the window. From here there was no sign of the lake, just the trees and the quiet and the jeweled flash of hummingbirds coming to the feeder just outside the window. The ruby-throated males were out in full force today. They were feeling feisty, too, shoving and pushing to get access to the sweetened water. Beyond them, the seed feeders in the tree were also garnering appreciation—rosy finches, little downy woodpeckers, the occasional gorgeous red-capped yellow oriole. They pecked and grubbed at the seed containers, fluttering away when something larger and showier came down to feed. Sort of like she had spent her life doing until she had partnered with Lila Weber and Chloe Main when Lila had gotten it into her head to open a jewelry shop in Peachland.

The banks had said it was a foolish idea, but Lila had the money to bankroll them to start, and with Reggie's and Chloe's savings thrown in and with all their hard work, all their dreams had come to fruition. And now the missing files suggested everything they'd built could be at risk. At least her part of it definitely was.

"Mom?"

The voice of her daughter brought Reggie back from her ruminations. Thalia stood in the doorway, still rumpled with sleep, her blonde hair a tangle, her coltish legs and arms poking out of her brand-new pink shorty Italian PJs with little lambs on them. Reggie had seen them in a store window and had immediately seen exactly this scene in her mind's eye and had bought them regardless of the atrocious European prices.

"Hey, honey. You're up awful early. It's only six thirty." Reggie swiveled around and patted her lap. Thalia shuffled over to cuddle and Reggie wrapped her arms around the warmth and sweet scent of young girl. If she could bottle the scent, she would, because this was the true scent of home. She kissed the silky crown of Thalia's head, and felt her sigh.

"I went to crawl in bed with you, but you weren't there," Thalia murmured into Reggie's shoulder.

"Guess that's 'cause I was here."

"I thought we'd be able to cuddle like we used to. I miss doing that, Mom."

Of course, less than a month ago this same child had refused to be hugged in the local shopping mall because she was too old and mature for public displays of affection. Reggie smiled to herself and rocked her daughter. She still had her baby. She didn't have to let go yet—but soon. It added a layer of bittersweet melancholy to the tremor of fear that had been there before.

"Mom?"

"What, honey?" Reggie brought her attention back to the here and now.

"I asked you what we're going to do today?"

"We-elll... Do you mean before or after I tickle you?" She poked tickle-fingers in Thalia's sides and the girl squealed and tried to make a leap for safety, but Reggie snagged her around the middle. "Nu-uh. I've been on daughter withdrawal for the past week. I'm getting my fill today. Now come'ere, kid." She planted messy kisses on Thalia's face until Thalia ducked out of her grasp and leapt across the room like a wary colt.

Fully awake now, she turned dark brown eyes on Reggie. They were so much her father's, sometimes he seemed to look out at her from them. Reggie'd loved him—once—though not enough to marry him. Thalia had been a gift he left behind though it hadn't exactly felt like it at the time. Thankfully Reggie's parents had been thrilled at the prospect of a grandchild once they'd gotten over the shock of an unwed mother for a daughter.

Reggie held up her hands in a sign of peace. "Okay. No more tickles. For now. Given you are now fully awake, how about I make us pancakes and then we pull together the beach stuff and head down to Peachland. We can have a picnic together and I can have a quick word with your Aunt Lila. Sound like a plan?"

Thalia hesitated, but then nodded. "Not too long in the store, okay? You're always there."

"And today is all about us—the Team of Two—because we haven't had our team together for awhile, what with me off in Milan and you off with that horse of yours. But I did have a lady come all the way from Italy to help me with jewelry, so I'm going to have to get really busy tomorrow, okay? So for today, how about you go have your shower and get dressed and I'll make breakfast. When you get down here, we'll decide what we want for lunch."

Thalia still hung by the door.

"Sooo? There a problem?"

The girl hung her head. "No."

She turned and left, her shuffle slow and pained down the hall and up the stairs. Reggie sighed and set her coffee down. It was always the same. Thalia craved—and deserved—so much more of Reggie's time, but making a living required more and more of her time, too. She'd been so lucky that Thalia could spend time with her grandparents, and Thalia's best friend lived just down the hill from them and owned the barn where Thalia kept her horse, but Reggie needed to get her act together. Maybe it was a matter of bringing her shop home again so she could be here for her daughter. That would require the money to build a whole new building or majorly renovate the old structure she'd used before. Maybe it would be worth it. It might even be possible if the work for Erminio took off. Of course, even if it did, it just meant that she was flavor of the month unless she put her all into staying in front of the trends.

She pulled out mixing bowls and flour and eggs and milk and decided to try making the Italian apple *frittelle* she'd tasted in Milan. She pulled a couple of apples out of the fridge, peeled and grated them and mixed up the batter, then added the apple to it. In a non-stick frying pan she heated a little oil and then started spooning in palm-sized clusters of the batter. The aroma of fresh apple and pancake filled the room.

She brewed herself another cup of coffee, poured orange juice she'd defrosted last night, and set out syrup and frosting sugar for the pancakes. By the time the pancakes were done, Thalia had wandered back into the kitchen wearing a pair of pink plaid shorts and matching pink t-shirt. She came up and wrapped her arms around Reggie's waist.

"Sorry. I know you work hard for us, Mom. Sometimes I just wish you didn't have to. Maybe if Dad..."

"Your father wouldn't have been with us even if he was alive, honey. You know that. It's Team of Two, remember. The ToTs forever." But it only added to Reggie's melancholy that her daughter felt this longing. "Come on. Tell me these aren't the best pancakes ever."

She brought the platter to the table, while Thalia grabbed placemats and silverware and balanced the full orange juice glasses to the table. Reggie refilled her coffee cup and sat there with her chin in her hand, watching her daughter as she took one pancake, tasted gingerly because what kid likes to try something new? Then her eyes grew round and she looked up at Reggie.

"These are really good! Not chocolate-chip pancake good, but really good, too."

"I know, right? Victoria—that's the lady from Italy who came back with me—she gave me the recipe. It was her nonna's—her grandmother's."

"So I get to meet her today?" said around a mouthful of pancake.

Reggie served herself and decided to try them with just the powdered sugar as Victoria had recommended. Very good. "I guess so, if you're coming to the beach with me. Maybe she'll want to come to the beach with us? Take a bit of a break after the long flight." She could hope, anyway, not that Victoria seemed like a particularly "take a break" kind of woman.

Of course, maybe distracting Victoria at the beach would give Reggie a chance to better assess what was going on with the theft of her files. Reggie needed to file a follow-up report with the Royal Canadian Mounted Police as to what, exactly, had been taken. She didn't want Victoria in the middle of that. Thank goodness Jas Stone, Chloe's main squeeze, was the investigating officer and was waiting for her to get the information to him.

A short time later, having bought a picnic lunch on their way, they headed south to Peachland. Reggie wore a pair of cutoff denim suspender overalls that sat just above the knee and a singlet t-shirt over her bathing suit. They had beach supplies and a couple of lawn chairs loaded into the back of her old, white, beater truck.

The day was perfect for the beach—not that most days weren't during an Okanagan summer. The blustery August morning that Lila had reported yesterday hadn't rematerialized today. The sun was bright, the sky blue, the lake glittering cool under a soft breeze that carried the scent of pine and sage and sun-warmed lake water. Reggie turned off the highway and onto Beach Avenue. She pulled up, just down from *This and That*—close enough she could set up Thalia on the beach and keep an eye while she also talked with Lila and Victoria at the store.

"How's this for a spot?" she asked, climbing out of the truck and opening the side door.

Thalia was eyeing the red and white house warily. "Maybe we should go into the store first and get it over with and *then* go to the beach."

"Crafty girl." Reggie tousled Thalia's thick blonde hair. "Then we'll leave the food in the cooler and do just that."

There were customers in the store, so together they went around the side of the house into the back yard where Reggie's workshop stood. Go in there again? Though Lila and the others had tried their best to mitigate the destruction before she got home, she knew there was still an incredible amount of work to do. At the same time, she needed to be getting to work on the additional designs. But today was for Thalia. Victoria would just have to understand.

She knocked once on the house's kitchen door and pushed into the sunny kitchen.

"Hello? Lila?"

"Hold on a moment. Be right down."

There came a clatter of shoes on the hardwood stairs and then Lila breezed into the kitchen in a pair of bronze-colored leggings and slim-fitting tunic of angled black and bronze bands. She wore black ballet flats and, as usual, looked like a goddess with her lush auburn hair floating around her shoulders.

Behind her came Victoria, in a flowing, floor length white caftan threaded with silver that Chloe was going to covet. The garment might be largely shapeless, but when draped over Victoria's voluptuous body, it couldn't help but have a sensual feel. Of course, Victoria had makeup on, but maybe she was just a little less sculpted in the cheeks, a little less eye-lined, and had set aside the vivid lipstick for something more subtle. It still didn't stop her presence from packing a punch, however.

Reggie felt Thalia stiffen.

"Hey," Reggie started, feeling Victoria's studied regard. "I thought today would be a day of rest and regrouping after the trip home. Thalia, here, has a mind to go to the beach. Thalia, this is Ms. Angelucci, who has come all the way from Italy to help me with the jewelry designs. Victoria, this is my daughter, Thalia."

Reggie wasn't sure what she expected, but it wasn't the delight that crept into Victoria's face as she smiled.

"Thalia? What a lovely name for a lovely young woman." Victoria held out her hands and, surprisingly, Thalia stepped forward instead of hanging back. Victoria bussed both her cheeks. "That is an Italian welcome. I am so pleased to meet you. Your mother talked about you very much. Did she give you a little gift?"

Thalia checked with Reggie over her shoulder. Reggie nodded.

"Pajamas. I slept in them last night. They're very nice."

"Good. Your mother said you would like them."

"Would you—would you like to come to the beach with us?" Thalia asked, her ten-year-old face solemn.

Reggie's heart went tha-thunk with pride because she knew Thalia wanted it to just be a ToT day.

"That is a most interesting offer. We could speak of designs there as well as we could inside, and I did bring a bathing suit."

"Then how about Victoria goes to get her stuff while you, Thalia, go and get our blankets from the car and nab us a spot. Okay?" She dangled her car keys and Thalia grabbed them and headed out and around the house. Victoria retreated to her room and that left Lila and Reggie to converse.

"The police will be here at eleven to interview you about the files," Lila said. "Have you come up with any reason why this might have happened—a motivation?"

Reggie sighed and shook her head. "Only what I mentioned last night. Without the files I've got nothing to document that the designs are mine. Anyone could claim them. I should have listened to you, Lila, and not been so old-fashioned. I should have digitized everything, but it was just such a big job."

Lila slung an arm over her shoulders. "We all put things off. You were busy creating all those designs—especially after the break-in at the shop. I'm sure it was just someone who didn't know what they were doing."

But they both knew that was a lie.

§

Lila exhaled in relief as Reggie banged out through the front door and was gone to the beach. Disaster might be hovering over them all, but there was no reason that Reggie didn't deserve one day of bliss with her daughter before she had to focus on business. Reggie was always about business and worked incredibly long hours to keep her jewelry designs creative and unique.

The kitchen ached around Lila like an empty tooth, the sounds of Chloe's and Kylee's voices amid the murmurs of customers in the store absolutely no comfort when usually it made her smile. The scent of the coffee she'd made this morning added a pungent acridity to the air and the room felt too warm even though the sun was on the other side of the house. Yup. Something was wrong. Something ill was coming and she didn't need a certain silver bracelet on her wrist to know it. Since the darn thing had swept into their lives, it had meant nothing but trouble. She hadn't bothered Reggie with the results of the additional reading that she'd done of the diary of the last owner of the bracelet—a Colonel in the British army. After discovering the bracelet hidden in the wall of a cave in the Sahara desert during the Second World War, he'd tried to find out about the bracelet in the kasbahs and markets of Cairo. All he'd been able to glean was that the bracelet was of a style no one had seen before. Even the Egyptian museum had said that the bracelet showed no sign of being part of Egyptian antiquity. It was something else. The Egyptologists had suggested something more Middle Eastern—Iraq, Iran, or Syria—or possibly even Turkey, Greece, or Italy.

That was a lot of geography. How were they ever going to figure out what was going on with the bracelet when they knew next to nothing about it? How they were going to deal with the evil that seemed to follow it—for something seemed to be able to possess people in an attempt to get it. Even Danny Forester, a Royal Canadian MountedPolice detective, had experienced it.

Whatever it was, it was as dangerous as heck and when it vacated the person it touched, it usually left behind madness—Danny being the one exception for some reason they did not understand. The whole situation had her concerned, and if Reggie could have one full day of light and laughter with her daughter before whatever impending disaster struck—well, then, Lila was going to see that she had it.

The click-click-click of heels on hardwood told her that Victoria was finally done changing and was coming downstairs. Lila roused to greet her and help her find Reggie and Thalia.

At the base of the stairwell Victoria stood in shadow, her golden mass of hair glowing softly as if it contained its own light. She was clad in a navy-blue maillot with a knee-length cover-up of the same color. The only thing was that the cover-up might as well have been made of fishnet, exposing pale olive skin and a set of shapely legs that ended in dainty feet set into wooden-soled platform heels that someone less coordinated could break a leg in. Peachland males were about to get an Italian eyeful today.

Victoria smiled Lila's way. "I'm sorry it took so long. I had a family call to take care of."

"Nothing bad, I hope."

She frowned. "Not so bad, I hope. My brother. He is a *donnaiolo*—how do you say? A playboy? A problem child." She shook her head. "He has been wandering the world and had heard I was in North America. He wondered where. So he called. I told him to keep wandering. That boy—he is trouble." Another toss of curls.

"Then let's get you out to the water where the sun can bake your worries away."

She led Victoria out the back door and around the house, then out onto the promenade along the beach and down to where Thalia stood waving madly to get their attention.

The girl had done well, claiming a broad swath of beach with the two bright red blankets and the couple of folding beach chairs that had seats of bright aqua and purple flowers. The water lapped quietly at the fine pea gravel that made up the beach, and the rounded stones squeaked together at the edge of the water. A soft breeze ruffled the waves and carried the scents of good strong coffee from the café down the beach and the seasonal coconut of suntan lotion. Ah, the years that coconut scent brought back.

"Here we are," she said and held her breath as Victoria teetered down to take a seat on one of the low-slung beach chairs. Thalia went racing into the water, sending up a rainbow spray that the wind caught and sent splattering Lila and Reggie.

Victoria got the worst of it—a full-on spray right in the face.

The soft sound of water and people's sun-somnolent murmurs was cut by her shriek.

Chapter 4

It was the spray off the crystal blue lake that attracted Cesare Angelucci as he strode the quaint promenade along the water. It was not the broad, paved panoply of people found at the California beaches, though the sky was as blue and the air as warm. Nor was it one of the glittering, moneyed boardwalks of the coastal cities of the Mediterranean, with the flock of white yachts tethered to the wharfs in the harbor. Instead, this long, narrow lake was dotted with the occasional white-winged sailboat or small family powerboats pulling water skiers or inner tubes with screaming children. This promenade was no more than a paved pathway and only broad enough that two people walking abreast could effectively block the way for those faster than them. Lucky for him, he had grown up dodging the human and vehicular traffic of northern Italy.

On one side of the promenade, long planters held tall tufted grasses, young trees, and lavender that permeated the breeze, while the other side of the path was decorated by the bathers—many *bella* women with nubile bodies and lotion-slicked skin, their hair tangled by water and lightened by sun. In that, he could like this small town of Peachland. Looking at the lush bodies clad in meager bikinis, he could almost imagine how the town got its name. But after the past three years of wandering to savor all the various loveliness of the world, it was time to resist his urges and put down roots again—not an easy thing to do for the prodigal son of any family.

Harder by far for the eldest son and black sheep of Milan's ancient, noble Angelucci family.

He looked from the piece of paper with the address he sought to the large red and white house across the street. The address was correct, but a jewelry store? His sister was residing at a *shop?* He'd thought perhaps it might be a small boutique hotel as was often Victoria's preference. But to stay above a store like a—*commoner?* His sister might have gone against their father's wishes for her to get married and raise the next generation of Angeluccis, preferring to forge her own career in the fashion industry, but the possibility that she could be living *here* was most definitely *not* what Cesare would expect of dear Victoria.

But when he had called her office in Milan twelve hours ago, her secretary had provided this as her destination. It had been easy enough to hop a plane from Los Angeles and arrive only a day after her. He'd phoned her from the airport to see if she would take his call. She did—barely. But barely was better than not at all, so she clearly had softened toward him even if she would not give him her address. So he'd rented a car and come directly here. Victoria had helped smooth the waters between him and their father many times before. Pray she would do the same now.

It was the splash, the spray, and the familiar scream that made him forget the red and white house. A young blonde girl a few years from blooming into a woman and yet still with the *suggerimento di bellezza*—the hints of the beauty she would become—stood knee-deep in the lake, her hands over her mouth in horror, lake water dappling her skin with sunlight. A dark-haired woman in a black bikini had leapt to her feet and was apologizing profusely to a woman swearing so proficiently in Italian there was no question who had caught the full brunt of the spray.

His dear Victoria sat spluttering, her war paint and perfectly coiffed hair no longer quite so perfect, her navy maillot—now quite soaked—clinging to her skin. Not exactly the best timing to win his way back into his little sister's good graces, but perhaps it would help out the woman who was split between apologizing and scolding the girl in the water. A third woman, dressed in bronze and black with a head of chestnut-colored curls had grabbed a towel and was gently dabbing at Victoria's arms and legs.

From what he could see, the woman in the bikini was definitely worth helping out. If dear Victoria was all about the voluptuous in life—the good food, the most excellent wine, the most beautiful clothing and—dare he say—the most handsome men—then this stranger was her opposite. She was slim, with fine curves, but little of the *carne con l'osso*—the meat over the bone, so-to-speak—that his sister brought to the picture. This one was all muscle and sinew, hip bones jutted, long legs like a runner, and broad shoulders and strong arms with biceps encircled by matching Celtic knot tattoos. She wore a silver bracelet and had small, high breasts and high cheekbones like figures in Egyptian tomb paintings. Shoulder-length hair was the absolute black of the night sky over the open Pacific. When he stepped down from the path toward Victoria, the woman looked up at him and the whole world seemed to shudder for just an instant.

He shook himself and looked away from that almost black gaze and had to steady himself a moment before he grinned down at his sister. He was not one to be subject to the *colpo di fulmine*—the thunderbolt—not at all.

"*Ciao, caramia*. What is the saying? Fancy meeting you in a place like this?"

His sister's brown eyes widened and she blinked as if she did not believe he was here.

"That's right. It is your beloved older brother, come to check on the well-being of his baby sister. Are you surprised, perhaps?"

He eased past the bronze- and black-clad women and knelt beside Victoria to use a corner of the blanket to dab at the water on her legs. In their long history as siblings going to the beach, Victoria had forever been about the sun tanning, but heaven forbid that she might get wet.

"Un po'dacqua non tiuccidere, caramia." A little water will not kill you. He grinned his most winning smile because that had always charmed her as a girl.

Victoria jerked her leg away.

"Che palle!" She waved him away as if he was an annoyance so he almost fell backward. She continued in Italian. "What are you doing here? I just spoke to you and said I did not wish to see you again."

The black-haired woman regarded him intently and suddenly all the Italian swagger and machismo that he had always gotten by on seemed to fail him. He stood.

"I came because I need your help, Victoria. Just as I always need you, no?" he said in Italian.

The little blonde had waded out of the water and now stood beside the raven-haired beauty, because she was beautiful—in a way that had never attracted him before. With the little blonde beside her, he could see the family resemblance. Sister? No, more than that—mother and daughter? Now that was a surprise, because she shared her daughter's boyish shape. But there was something else about her—something that kept him glancing back at her.

He forced his gaze away long enough to grin down at Victoria. "I know, I know. I've run our father a merry chase these past few years when he wanted me tied down in an office learning the business. But there is more to life than that and I wanted to experience it. Now I have. Now I have plans." He shrugged.

"Reggie, Lila," Victoria switched to English. "This *villano* is my brother, Cesare. Cesare, this is my friend, Reggie Lewis, and her business associate and my hostess, Lila Weber." She turned to the little blonde. "And this is Reggie's daughter, the delightful *signorina* Thalia, who has doused me so completely that I must rethink my approach to coming to the beach. It seems I am not just to rest here and be lovely and catch the sunshine." She grinned evilly at the girl and wagged a finger. "I will get you, little one, just you wait and see."

The girl didn't look all that worried until his sister leapt to her feet. Together Victoria and Reggie dragged the younger girl, screaming in delight, into the water. Then they dunked her and left her there to wade back to shore. Thalia came up spluttering and laughing.

"That will happen every time you splash us," Reggie—such a strange name for a woman—said.

In response the girl slapped her hands on the water, sending a good bit of spray in their direction again.

The two women, dark and light, voluptuous and athletic, repeated the dunking, then turned and waded back to shore like Athena and Artemis rising from the water. Cesare, standing next to the third beautiful woman, laughed encouragements at the girl—until Victoria threw her soaked arms around him and gave him a sodden hug and a quick buss on the cheeks. When she released him, it was her turn to laugh as he spluttered down at his wet chinos and polo shirt.

"You see," he said to the little blonde. "One must always be careful of this one." He tapped the top of Victoria's much lower head—she was only five foot six to his six foot two—until she ducked away from him. "She is quick to anger and quick to revenge."

In mock disgust, she waved him away. "So, brother. Where do you stay?"

"Uh... I had thought perhaps with you—that you would have a suite that might have a couch for me..."

"You've run through your money again?"

He glanced at the dark-haired beauty, not liking that Victoria portrayed him as a spend thrift. It was bad enough that she always thought the worst of him. Did she have to taint everyone else's opinion as well? He shook his head.

"The money is fine. I invested a little and have been living off of that. I just—" Just what? Was lonely for family? Missed Victoria and her feminine wisdom after all these years apart? It had been a long time.

"What can I say? I hoped to take advantage of you again," he said with a nonchalant shrug. It was the part his family expected him to play, even though it rankled. He shrugged and shoved his hands in his pockets.

"My brother has been 'trying to find himself' these past five years." Victoria said unkindly, as she hooked her fingers around "trying to find himself." "He broke our father's heart when he finished his law degree and then refused to practice in the family business." There was a hint of disgust in Victoria's voice. "When do you grow up, *cara*? You are not a boy anymore. There are lines around your pretty brown eyes from staring into the sun too long. Perhaps it is time to look back to the earth and reality again." She shook her head and looked back at the one named Reggie. "My parents named him perfectly. Cesare for severed and Angelucci for angelic—our very own fallen angel."

The one called Reggie looked uncomfortable. Cesare bit back an answer, just as he had done for so many years in so many situations. His family—Victoria and his father—had never been discrete with their opinions. It was part of their flamboyance and of the operatic roles they had each been slotted to play in the melodrama of their lives.

"So you live up to your name, then, do you?"Reggie asked as if uncomfortable with the airing of family differences.

Her voice was deep for a woman, as if she might once have been a smoker, but the clarity of her skin and eyes said that wasn't the case. Still, something had deepened her voice into something sultry that sent a shiver through him.

"Perhaps I've tried." He shrugged again. So easy to do when it is expected.

She gave a slight shake of the head as if she did not approve—well, who did, these days?—but suddenly it was important that she understand. "Perhaps you would understand the desire not to lose oneself in a soulless job."

Her dark gaze flickered and she looked away, then met his gaze head-on like one of those Spanish fighting bulls. "Perhaps. But I also understand the worth of a hard day's work."

She was bold, this one. Not about to be wooed or cowed—at least not in the usual ways. Interesting. Very interesting the way the sun caught her angles like a renaissance painting and pronounced her full lips most kissable. "And what is it that you do that passes for soulful work?"

The bronze-clad woman, Lila, had narrowed her gaze at him as if she did not approve, but when had Victoria's friends ever approved? No, they might bed him, but that would not stop them from disapproving—at least in public.

"Aah, our Reggie is the most excellent of artisans," said Victoria. "She makes jewelry, Cesare. Her designs will grace Erminio's show this fall and next spring. She will be the talk of Milan—just wait and see, yes?"

Cesare frowned. "You are still working for that fraud? I thought you would have grown your own wings, begun your own house. You know he has no intention of letting you have your own line."

Victoria rolled her eyes. "Of course you are wrong. He tells me that my designs are not quite right yet, but getting closer. This fall he included a dress almost of my design in his collection."

"And took the credit, no doubt."Cesare frowned. His sister was too trusting. When was Victoria going to understand that Erminio might be talented, but so was she. With the financial resources of the family, she could easily open her own design house instead of being mined for ideas by the likes of Erminio.

"Listen," Lila interrupted."Maybe we should get you two back to the house and settled. Cesare, I'm sure that between Reggie and me we can find you suitable accommodations."

Reggie nodded. "Thalia, honey. This might take a few moments. Are you okay here by yourself?"

"Course, Mom. I'm not a baby."

He winked down at Thalia and she grinned back at him in silent communion. Mothers never understood the maturity of their children. For that matter, fathers and younger sisters weren't that good at it, either.

So the beautiful Reggie was indeed a mother. How lucky her husband was to have a beautiful wife and daughter. The thought saddened him, but he couldn't stop himself from enjoying the view as she bent to retrieve a pair of suspended cutoffs and a t-shirt.

She pulled on the t-shirt and sneakers and led Victoria—teetering on heels—up from the water to where Lila waited. Reggie's long-legged, athletic stride was enough to get him to follow her across the street to the big white house.

Or perhaps anywhere.

§

She was trying to be polite, but darn it all, the day was supposed to be hers and Thalia's—not a day to nursemaid Victoria's long-lost brother. But then, Victoria was *her* guest and she couldn't very well leave Lila to deal with this situation. Reggie checked her watch—and it was almost eleven, when Detective Jas Stone was to show up. She sighed.

It was a perfect day for the beach—clear skies, blue lake with just the lightest ripple of waves brought by a nice breeze that cut the heat. The lake water had been warm and Thalia had really been trying her best—aside from the frankly hilarious misstep of tearing into the water and splashing bathing beauty Victoria. The upside had been Victoria's rising to the occasion to help dunk Thalia. It had been a fun-loving side of Victoria that she—Reggie—liked a whole lot more than the frozen-faced woman who now marched beside her up to the house—even if it was on three inch heels. Clearly, Cesare's arrival was not a happy reunion.

Lila pushed through *This and That's* front gate and led them around the house to the patio, intending to take them inside, but Victoria thumped down in a turquoise-cushioned chaise and turned her face to the sun. "We can discuss you're arrival here, Cesare," she said like a queen.

"Reggie, dear. Could you get us some water and leave us? This is *affari di famiglia*—family business between me and Cesare." She pronounced it *Cease-air*.

What? She was a servant now? Just one of the hired help?

Grinding her teeth instead of saying what really came to mind, Reggie turned on her heel. She rolled her eyes at Lila and together they headed for the kitchen but not before she caught the little smirk on Cesare's face.

Cesare? Who the heck named their child after a Roman dictator who was stabbed in the back? But then again, from Victoria's reaction the guy wasn't exactly an upstanding citizen.

She thumped into the kitchen following Lila. "Nice one, huh?"

"Not exactly how I saw this afternoon going."

Reggie grabbed two bottles of water from the fridge and took them out to the patio where all conversation stopped dead as soon as she opened the door. As if they were talking about national defense secrets or something.

Victoria accepted her water without comment.

"*Grazie,*" Cesare said. His fingers lightly brushed hers as he accepted the bottle.

A jolt ran through her from the bracelet and she stumbled until he caught her elbow to steady her. What the heck? She pulled loose and looked up at him. "Thanks."

"It is nothing. You are all right? Well?" He shook his head. "That is the correct word? Well?"

Those brown eyes of his were almost like tiger eye stones with their flecks of gold. She could set them in a stylized silver tiger's face pendant complete with stripes and whiskers. She swallowed. "Well is fine, and I am. Well. All right works, too. Mostly. I mean, people know what you mean. The vernacular."

Oh, God, she was babbling like an idiot. He wasn't that good looking. And besides, from what Victoria had said, he was a shiftless bad-boy and from the look of him, with that mop of tousled, sun-bleached black hair and those broad shoulders and slim hips and long legs, probably very, very good at it. The kind of man you have a tumble with, but that you never, ever bring into the life of your daughter.

"Well." She smiled."Another meaning of the word entirely. You have your water and I need to talk to Lila about where Cesare, here, might stay."

"I'm not sure that will be necessary, Reggie. My brother is only here for a very short time as he wanders his way off to his next disaster that he must be rescued from." Victoria's lovely face was hard-edged as a radiant cut stone, emphasizing her strong jaw and brow.

Looking from brother to sister, it was pretty clear that being farther away from their discussion was better.

"I'll get out of your hair." She edged back from Cesare and his tiger eyes, standing over Victoria like a supplicant before a queen. Then the kitchen door handle filled her hand and she practically fell inside.

Lila was waiting. "What's going on?"

"Wow! *That* is one tense family reunion." Reggie glanced over her shoulder at the patio. "What happened to the woman who soaked her brother by hugging him?"

Lila studied the scene and shook her head. "Perhaps it's the way it's always been between them. Families can set up expected roles for family members. They get trapped in them."

Whatever was being discussed, the discussion was heated with many violent hand gestures—but then, she'd seen a lot of that in Milan and it didn't always mean what it had meant in her family—that her father's temper was on the edge of exploding.

Rubbing the silver bracelet—warm from the sun—she turned back to Lila. "So what do we do? Is there any place we can put the man up for a day or two where he won't do any damage?"

Lila eyed the verbally sparring pair in the back yard as if she was assessing something. "You really think he'll be staying?"

Reggie shrugged. "No idea, except that I got the sense he's looking for some kind of redemption with his family—sort of the Joseph with the technicolored dreamcoat sort of thing—Thalia's drama club is doing the play. Except Cesare apparently hasn't been the good boy Joseph was." Just where she'd gotten that impression, she couldn't say. He hadn't exactly said it—it was more like something communicated through their brief touch. She glanced over her shoulder at the siblings in the yard. Weird.

"Hopefully he wasn't sold into slavery by his brothers," Lila said dryly.

"I don't think he had any brothers. In fact, I didn't know he existed until he showed up on the beach. Victoria never mentioned any siblings at all. No love lost, I guess." Reggie grinned and glanced back at the yard one more time. The voices were getting more heated. So were the gestures.

Lila was drumming her silver-ringed fingers on her lips. "I don't really have space here, and given the relationship between them, I'm not sure him staying here would be a good idea anyway."

"Well, I can't take him home with me. I don't have a room unless Thalia bunks with me, and I don't know if you've ever done it, but let me tell you that ten-year-olds do not make good bedfellows. They are all knees, elbows, and too-sharp toenails." She eyed Cesare and felt Lila's regard. "Besides, he's not the kind of influence I want around Thalia."

"Good looking, though, isn't he?" Lila twirled one of her curls innocently around her finger.

"Uh—yeah. A real piece of eye candy. Why? You interested?" Because if Lila was, Reggie was going to have to clamp right down on the little butterflies that were tickling her stomach the more she looked at him. Darn it all, there was no way she wanted a guy like that anywhere near her life. She sighed.

"Not me, but I'm thinking you might be. There's a light in your eyes I haven't seen in a very long time." Lila's hazel regard was all too intense. Darn it, the woman was *way* too astute.

"Not the same thing at all. I mean, look at the guy. That is not the kind of man who settles down for anybody, and certainly not for a woman with a daughter who's almost a teenager."

But Lila shook her head, her mane of auburn curls bouncing around her shoulders. "From what I saw in Italy, there were a lot of Cesare-types. If they didn't settle down, where'd all those little Italians come from? The country would have died out."

Reggie looked heavenward, but heavy footfall from the front of the house stopped her response. Chloe came into the kitchen leading Corporal Jas Stone, the tall, dark, and good-looking detective who was none other than Chloe's heartthrob. He wore a pair of brown chinos and a green polo shirt that showed off his swimmer's muscles.

"Look what I found clumping up our front doorstep," Chloe said.

"Hey." Jas nodded. "You guys have got to quit having your own Peachland crimewave. People at the detachment are starting to talk." He grinned, but then his smile faded into concern. "Seriously. It was bad enough with Kylee and Chloe, but the thing with Ally freaked me out. And now this. What the hell is going on?"

"When you figure it out, would you let us know?" Reggie said, sighed, and looked at Lila. "So what do you think? We could either do the interview here or out on the porch. Your house, your choice."

"Why not do it on the porch and that way you can keep an eye on Thalia and she can see you."

Reggie led the way through the shop—thankfully no customers at the moment as she still hadn't pulled on her cutoffs over her still-damp bathing suit. Down on the beach, Thalia popped up at her appearance and waved, ever hopeful. Reggie waved back and pointed at Jas, then sat down on the wicker loveseat with its yellow and aqua cushions. Jas faced her from the lone chair.

"So where's Danny?" she asked after Jas's partner, Danny Forester.

"Tied up with some phone calls with Interpol about Johan Fehr and *Schwarzenacht*." They were two names at the center of the investigation into the mysterious events that had begun when the silver bracelet currently on Reggie's wrist had first turned up at *This and That*. So far, Kylee Jensen had been abducted and Chloe and their friend Ally McVay had both nearly been killed. In each case there were suggestions that *something* had possessed the attackers. There were even some people, like Danny, who claimed it was aliens in their head. Crazy talk, all of it, but the danger to the wearer of the bracelet certainly appeared to be real, and Johan Fehr and *Schwarzenacht* were clearly linked to both Kylee's abduction and the attempt on Ally's life.

Her hand fell to the silver links, her fingers favoring the small door with the ornate lintel.

"Do you think this has to do with the bracelet?" she asked.

"Doesn't everything bad that happens here?" Jas said as he hauled his notebook out of his pocket and flipped it open, his elbows on his knees. "So tell me about it."

"What do you need to know?" she asked.

"I know you've barely had time to get home. Did you see your shop?"

"I saw the disaster they left behind, even though Lila and the others tried to clean up the worst of it and protect the inventory of stones. Some of the chemicals can seriously ruin some of the more porous stones like turquoise."

"Tell me about your business, Reggie. I don't know much about the jewelry business, although Chloe's trying to enlighten me."

That was the good thing about Jas. He'd been around them all summer and something had to rub off when he was dating Chloe. He knew she wasn't just some scatterbrain.

"The jewelry industry is big, Jas. Really big. And competitive. There are a lot of commercial entities that supply stones and sell precious stone jewelry in the stores we see everywhere from the local mall to Fifth Avenue or Rodeo Drive. There are also the hobbyists, who string beads and twist wire for jewelry. I guess I'm somewhere in the middle, in the artisan class, you could say. I've taken it far beyond the hobbyist to—I like to think—the art form. I take stones that come from all over the world and imagine settings for them, or I design a piece of jewelry and then search out the perfect stones for them. Some of them come from vintage pieces that Lila gets in estate sales. Others come from Lila's purchasing trips to other countries, and still others come from gem shows—though we don't use the latter so much anymore. These days you can even order your stones online, though you have to be careful about the quality."

She stopped and got up to go to the edge of the porch to get a better look at the spot on the beach where Thalia was flaked out on one of the blankets reading a book. She should be down there making sure her daughter had enough suntan lotion on her back, not sitting here talking about her business to a cop.

She glanced back at Jas. "Sorry. Daughter." She motioned at the beach, then pointed at herself. "Overprotective mother. Where were we?"

"I asked you about your business."

"Right." She sat down again and caught a glimpse of one Cesare Angelucci coming around the side of the house. He did not look happy. He looked decidedly less happy when he saw her talking to Jas. He let himself out the front gate and started down the street, then stopped and went across to the promenade and down to one of the park benches near Thalia. A little alarm bell went off in her head, but he seemed to be minding his own business, simply staring out at the lake.

"Reggie? The business?"

She shook her head. "Of course. Yes. The business. I'm in the production side of things. God save me from having to deal with customers. I get impatient with indecision—you want it or you don't. I design and make jewelry—everything from heavy-shanked rings to pendants, earrings, and bracelets. On occasion I make beaded jewelry, too, though that's not my first love. Give me the physical process of making something with molds to make and heated metal to shape. I like the physical sensation of it—pounding a hammer, making the mold, filing off rough edges, buffing and shining, the selection and careful setting of exactly the right stone. It's the care that makes the piece. A lot of people have got the skills to make jewelry, but it's the care and attention to details—the love—of taking that extra step in unique details that makes the difference in the jewelry you produce, instead of producing as much as you can, as fast as you can. It makes for long hours, but you get something unique and beautiful as a result."

Cesare hadn't moved, his dark good looks standing out enough three sets of spandex-clad, tanned female joggers made three passes past him, but got no more than an appreciative smile.

"Is unique important?" Jas's gaze slipped down to the bracelet on her wrist, drawing Reggie back to the conversation.

It was one of the most unique pieces she'd seen—ever. A piece that she would have liked to have designed and made herself. She'd even taken a riff from it for a pendant and earrings for her Milan group. She smiled.

"In this day and age of mass produced goods, unique is very important. People will pay a lot of money for unique or one of a kind. In an ever-crowded world of sameness, people want to be different; and when different is also beautiful—well, you can understand how the jewelry might sell, even at a much higher price point than you find on the costume jewelry you can find in a department store. Because along with being unique, this jewelry is real—a real crystal or carnelian or topaz or sapphire, real silver or gold, real pearls. Understand? It's sort of like the fascination with tribal and native art—people want something genuine."

"So your jewelry spans the space between the high-end wedding ring and tiara trade and the hippy selling braided leather bracelets on the sidewalk in the summer." He grinned. "So tell me about your shop—the break-in."

She thought about it. "First off, in a small space like that, I have to be neat. Everything has its place and I take care of my tools. I have to make a living with them, so it's important to me that everything is maintained well. Before I left for Milan, I made sure everything was clean and ready for me to come back and get busy. All my supplies were in cupboards, forge and gas kiln ready. I had updated all my files for the Milan designs, too."

She stopped and shook her head. On the beach Cesare was talking to someone. Then she realized it was Thalia and all her protective instincts kicked in. She stood up and went to the porch rail, her movement catching Thalia's eye. Thalia waved. Reggie waved back. There were words she couldn't hear exchanged between Thalia and Victoria's brother and then Cesare glanced over his shoulder and waved as well. Ignore him, when she wanted to tell him to get the hell away from her daughter? She raised her hand and turned back to Jas.

"I really need to get back to my daughter. Before you ask, the files contained all the documentation and photos about my designs. There are copyright concerns with unique jewelry. I mean, how good would it be if just anybody could take my designs and copy them, right? So each designer—if they are smart—documents their work—early sketches, photographs of the stages of the work. The source of the particular inspiration for the piece—that sort of thing. The content of the files aren't worth a thing—except to prove the designs are mine. They set the making of a piece in time and space and show the processes. I also use them to document the exact chemical solutions, patinas, temperatures, etc., used—like a recipe, sort of. It helps if years later I want to replicate an effect."

Jas wrote in his notebook and then frowned up at her. "So what you're saying is that the only real use for those files is if someone wanted to replicate your work and then claim it was theirs."

He'd said it. What she'd been so afraid to put fully into words. She sank down in her seat, the happy beach sounds of people laughing, iPod music, water splashing, and the low drone of highway traffic from behind by the hillside fading.

"That's what I'm afraid of. I need a chance to figure out how I can rebuild my files, but just getting back I haven't had time yet."

"Can you tell me how many files there were?"

She shrugged. "Somewhere between three and four hundred, maybe. I only create files for the unique pieces. I do a lot of other bread-and-butter work, too, like setting stones in plain pendants, or making bead necklaces like bronze or blue-colored pearls— that sort of thing. They sell well and don't take as much time. Those I don't worry about. But anything with extensive silver or gold work, I create a file."

Jas thought a moment and shook his head. "This sure seems like another one of those strange attacks on you women and the store. Maybe one of the first things you can do is make a listing of those files as best you can remember. Perhaps with a sketch of the design. The fact that you list the files and give them to me for a police file might help your claim if anything happens."

Reggie nodded, but movement on the beach caught her attention. Cesare stood up and shifted over to one of the beach chairs by her and Thalia's blankets. She shot bolt upright to her feet. If that guy was hitting on her daughter, she was going to shoot him.

"I have to go. Or maybe you can come with me and arrest the idiot who's accosting my daughter."

Jas joined her at the porch rail and followed her gaze. "He just looks like he's talking to her. Do you know him?"

Reggie ground her teeth. "He's Victoria's—the woman who came from Milan with me—he's her brother. A cad by all accounts."

"A cad?"

She heard the laughter in Jas's voice at the old-fashioned word. "All right. How about bad boy and black sheep? Victoria as much as asked him to leave as soon as he arrived. That can't be good to have around Thalia."

Jas shrugged. "I suppose, but he doesn't look like he's doing anything untoward."

She looked him in the eye. "And you would know that, how?" She marched past him to the door to the shop and inside. No customers, thankfully. "Lila!" she yelled.

Her auburn-haired friend materialized out of the darkness of the hall and pushed through the beaded curtain.

"What happened with Victoria and Cesare?" Reggie demanded.

"She asked him to leave before I could arrange a place for him to stay. I'd thought about asking Kylee if he could stay at her place because she's never there, but before I could ask, Victoria had turfed him out." Lila grinned. "Our blonde bombshell's much tougher than she seems."

"Great. Now he's out there accosting Thalia." Reggie wheeled around and marched out onto the porch to drag Jas down to the water's edge and preferably arrest Cesare. What well-meaning man would *want* a conversation with a ten-year-old? Nope, he should be chasing the spandex-clad joggers more like. It wasn't as if they weren't interested.

Jas wasn't on the porch.

Nope, Jas Stone was down by the water, standing over Thalia and Cesare and doing his police thing. Well, at least this latest police visit was good for something. Heart racing, she half ran down the porch stairs and through the yard gate to get down to her daughter, who was standing at the water's edge.

"Thalia! Are you all right?"

She inserted herself between Cesare and her daughter and made a show of slipping an arm around Thalia's shoulders.

"Mo-om! What gives? Mr. Stone, Mr. Angelucci and I were just talking." She pulled away and shook her head. "I was just telling Mr. Angelucci about your jewelry. How good your stuff is. Mr. Stone agreed with me."

"Your mom makes pretty fantastic stuff, all right. I've seen some of it—don't understand the half of it, but it's some pretty great stuff," Jas nodded. "You in the jewelry trade, Angelucci?"

Cesare shook his head. "Fashion is more my sister's area." His gold-flecked gaze met Reggie's. "I am between trades at the moment, though of late I've been engaged in—winemaking."

Almost as if he'd pulled that particular industry out of the air. You couldn't be too long in the Okanagan before you recognized the number of vineyards in the area.

"Well, you've come to the right area if you're looking for a job. If you've got experience, I'll bet there's a lot of places that would be interested in a vintner with Italian experience," Jas said. "So what brought you down to the water and young Thalia today?"

Cesare looked from Jas to the water to Thalia to her. Suddenly his face grew concerned and he shook his head and stood up, his hands up as if this was a hold-up. "I am very sorry if I have crossed a line. Signorina Thalia and I were only talking."

"Mom! What are you accusing him of?" Thalia stamped a foot and rounded on her. "We were talking. That was all. I saw him sitting there and we'd met, so I started talking to him. He came over when I invited him. Gee-whiz, Mom, I'm not a little kid. You weren't here, but Mr. Angelucci was. He was telling me about Milan. It sounds really interesting."

"Milan, huh?" She turned an evil eye on Cesare. "Like what?"

"I told her about the great palazzo and the Galleria Vittoria Emanuele, and Sforza Castle and Lake Como."

"A real castle, Mom. And a lake a lot like this one, he says."

Cesare gave her a look of innocence. "It is drier here, though. By far. And perhaps hotter."

Harmless conversations all. Conversations that any adult from a foreign country might have with a young girl and no damage done. Reggie swallowed, trying to slow her heart and shove away the fear she'd been feeling.

"Fine. I'm glad you had a nice conversation. Mr. Angelucci, thank you for keeping an eye on Thalia. Jas, thanks for coming down here. Did I give you enough information at the house?"

Jas considered a moment. "I still have one or two more questions."

"All right." But she really didn't fancy having them asked right here. She led Jas back up to the promenade. "What else do you need to know?"

"The names of anyone who might have something to gain by stealing your designs."

Reggie shook her head. "No idea. I mean, I suppose any artisanal jewelry could profit from my designs, but no one specific and certainly no one local. All I can think of is that this might have something to do with the bracelet, just like the break-and-enter of the store did. That's what scares me."

Jas looked up from making a note in his notebook. "That might be a leap."

"It might not be, too. *Schwarzenacht*. That was the name of the company. Maybe look into their connections to the jewelry business, too."

"Okay. But we're not getting a lot of cooperation from Interpol, I have to tell you. And that was in relation to the abduction of Kylee and the assaults on Chloe and Ally. It's a pretty big, influential corporation."

"Mom?"

Jas flipped his notebook closed as she shifted toward Thalia. "What is it, hon?"

"Mr. Angelucci needs a place to stay. I said he could have my bedroom and I'd sleep with you. Okay?"

Lord-love-a-duck, as her mother used to say. "No, honey. Mr. Angelucci does not want to stay with us." And she did not want to have him there. "I'm sure Mr. Angelucci would be happier in a hotel rather than in a girl's room of pink frills and a too-short bed. Right, Mr. Angelucci?"

A hint of devil flared in his eye. "It was a kind offer. Who am I to be fussy?"

Tell him no way in hell? Panicked, she looked to Jas for help. The good detective's dark eyes met hers and he shook his head. "Angelucci, if it's a spare room you're looking for, I happen to have one. It's pretty Spartan—a bed and dresser and that's all, but you're welcome to bunk there a few days."

Cesare left Thalia on her beach blanket and climbed the pebbled beach to them. "That is a very kind offer. I would appreciate it."

"You got a car?" Jas asked.

Cesare nodded.

"Then how about you follow me and I'll get you settled. One rule, though. No drugs."

Cesare held up his hands as if in surrender. "Drugs are not part of my life."

Well, at least that was something.

"Then let's head out. Reggie, if you think of anything else, give me a call." Jas nodded at her and then ambled off toward his police sedan, leaving Cesare standing with her.

"It has been a pleasure, Reggie Lewis. To meet you and your daughter. Perhaps we will see each other again."

Not if she had anything to say about it. But as he headed after Jas, he glanced over his shoulder. Those tawny glints in his eyes held a wicked promise.

Chapter 5

Bright and early the next morning, Reggie arrived at *This and That*, refreshed and still smiling after a long, lingering afternoon and evening with her favorite daughter. They'd finished the afternoon by the lake, swimming and taking in the sun and talking about all that Thalia had seen and done while Reggie was away. Apparently Gladiator, Thalia's leased Thoroughbred show horse, had cast a shoe and the farrier had had to be called—one more bill to pay, but the stable's brand-new dressage coach, Dietrich, had said that Thalia and Gladiator were ready to start showing at level two before the end of the summer. They'd gone down to the barn so that Reggie could be suitably impressed by Gladiator, though to Reggie's eye, he was just a big brown horse. She hadn't had met Dietrich, however, but she promised to come to Thalia's next practice to do just that. Altogether, it had been a very full day.

This morning the sun still leaned on the top of the humped eastern mountains, turning the top of the lake to molten gold and silver that silhouetted the willows and cottonwoods that grew along the edge of the water. She parked her truck just down the street from the shop.

She'd dropped Thalia off at the barn for her morning mucking job that earned half of her horse board. The moist morning air carried the scent of lake water and pine and from somewhere the scent of burning. She hoped there wasn't a local fire and scanned the ridges above Peachland.

The pale blue sky was clear. So was the sky over Okanagan Mountain across the lake. When Thalia was born a wildfire had started just across from Peachland near Rattlesnake Island, the legendary home of the lake's monster, Ogopogo. Swept on by high winds, the fire had become a firestorm that consumed almost all the trees on Okanagan Mountain, almost 250 homes in Kelowna, and had forced the evacuation of 27,000 residents. She would never forget the fear, the way the air was full of ash, and the stink of fire. The media had been full of images of frantic residents trying to get themselves, their pets, and their livestock out of the firezone.

But there was no sign of fire this morning other than that faint scent of burning—or maybe it was her imagination, but it still sent her heart skittering. There had been other fires since then that were closer to home, but that was the one that had scared her the most. Perhaps it was that she'd felt so alone at the time. Alone and six months pregnant.

Uneasy, she looked up at the white and red house with its hanging copper planters festooning the front porch with red and white geraniums. Purple heliotrope placed a baby powder scent on the air. The house looked pristine in the morning quiet. A few joggers loped past and, out on the smooth water, a single kayaker got his morning paddle in. A few hardy dog owners took their canines along the promenade above the beach and a few dogs splashed at the water's edge in the off-leash area.

Everything placid. Everything as it should be and yet something in her breast was as tight as a piece of silver refusing to come out of its mold.

Absently she rubbed the bracelet's silver door with the lintel and tried to shake off the disquiet. It was likely just the result of her interview with Jas and her worry about the missing files. She let herself in through the gate and followed the path around the side of the house to her shop.

Even with the door open in the bright Okanagan sunlight, the interior was dim. The place was originally built by Lila's grandfather as a workshop, during the days when single-pane windows let in the cold during the winter and the heat during the summer.

The place reeked of the eye-watering combination of borax, nitric acid, and saltpeter, almost masking the forge scent of burned coal and clinker. It had been bad two days ago when she'd first seen the devastation, but an extra twenty-four hours locked in her shop had made the air almost unbreathable. She took a deep breath, darted inside, and turned on all her fans and opened the few windows, then dashed outside again, the pungent stink of chemicals on her heels.

Outside, she lingered five minutes, then entered again. The fans had done their job. Manageable, as long as she could stand her eyes watering. The floor had been swept, but still showed the streaks of chemical spill. Every flat surface in the room had the contents of her cupboards stacked on them. A teetering pile of small plastic bags that held jewels—topaz, sapphire, and garnet— or antique pieces of jewelry that could be inspiration, but were more likely to be melted down and used for more modern pieces. Long cords of silver solder wound in a cat tangle, a small jar of gold ingot. A plastic bag of freshwater pearls dyed various colors. A few old jewelry pieces that were fatally flawed, but that she could never set aside—as if they were rehearsals for something grander to come. She picked up her favorite, a silver crescent encrusted with moonstone. Her vision had been one of a luminous crescent that would glow like the moon. Instead it just looked heavy and awkward, but she still loved it because it was the first piece of her own design she had taken a chance on. It hadn't worked, but what she had learned in the process had paved the way for other pieces that had.

She picked it up and put it on her small anvil as a token that things could get better even in this devastation.

Then she started reestablishing the order of her world.

An hour and a half later, the fans had done their work and she no longer had to take breathers in the backyard. The morning breeze off the lake had lifted the chemical miasma away and left cool, clean air to replace the stink inside her shop. With the door and windows open and the fans blowing, it hadn't taken near as long as she'd thought. With her supplies and her books and tools back in their places, the long narrow shop didn't look anywhere as badly damaged as she had thought. In fact, she could likely get back to work today once she and Victoria had agreed on the designs that were priorities.

Although most of the jewelry design had been agreed upon with Erminio in Milan, there were still a few pieces that the designer had left for Victoria and Reggie to decide upon.

She did a circle of the room: Forge and small brick kiln. Heavy concrete sink for running water. Her workspace of small anvil, mallet, and hammer, mandrels for ring sizing, pliers, nippers, scissors, soapstone for molds, engraving tools, lengths of beading wire, disc cutter, drill, vise, rubber and steel bench blocks. All back in place, their well-worn handles signs of honest effort. Stone-setting bezels and tweezers, various bottles of homemade patinas she used to give her pieces their unique color and shine, the formula of which had been amongst her missing files.

She turned slowly to look at the cabinets she'd been avoiding.

Maybe the files would all be there when she looked this time. Maybe Lila had been wrong and she—when she'd come tearing in here her first night back—had been impressionable and had imagined the yawning drawers as empty.

She stood in front of the cabinet, hand over the pull, but still hesitated.

"Damn it. Just get it over with. It's always easier to just pull the bandage off." She yanked the middle drawer open and it rattled in her hands. In the dim light of the workshop, it was just a square of slightly darker shadow. Empty, as Lila had said, as she'd seen. She hooked her wheeled stool over to her and sank down, finally having to face what for the past forty-eight hours she'd allowed herself to keep denying.

All her files were really gone. It didn't get much worse than this. Of course, maybe it wouldn't be a problem. Everyone in the Okanagan knew her designs. Frankly, everyone in BC who was involved with jewelry probably did, and even a few of the big American shows on the west coast. She should be fine. Better than fine with the show coming up in Milan.

But all the reassurances in the world didn't stop the queasy feeling in the pit of her stomach. Idly she twisted her hair up behind her head and grabbed a mandrel to poke through the resulting knot. Her hair stayed where she'd put it but she felt tired. Closed her eyes, though she'd had a full night's sleep last night.

A sharp rap of knuckles on door frame sent her stumbling to her feet. She banged into the open drawer, caught her hip on the corner, and stubbed the toe of her work boot on the leg of her workbench, almost fell again because her left leg had somehow fallen asleep. A hand on her arm steadied her.

The scent of cut grass and verbena filled the shop and she stopped dead, the bracelet throbbing on her arm. She swung around. Cesare Angelucci stood too close, his palm under her elbow, his tiger eyes thoughtful, his lips curved in a nearly devastating grin that made her mouth go dry and sour because he could be laughing at her.

She quickly pulled her arm away.

"Thank you. I'm fine, thanks. My leg just went to sleep." She looked down at the offending limb and rubbed at the pins and needles in her thigh. Anything to not look at this guy. "So you don't have to hang around here. I'm sure Victoria is up and waiting to have coffee with you."

"My sister does not take her morning coffee with anything or anyone who might annoy her. Mornings are a sacred time for Victoria. Time to commune with the gods, not speak with a troublesome brother." He looked good. A slight patina of sweat glazed his handsome features. He wore a loose pair of running shorts and a damp, sleeveless t-shirt in the red-white-green tri-color of the Italian flag. Long, muscled legs stretched down to expensive-looking Nike trainers. Strong legs, to go with the long muscles of his arms in that nice dusky olive color, but darkened by sun.

She swallowed and found herself straightening her jars of patina, nudging the tools on the wall behind her workbench until they were a line of perfect soldiers. Darn it, this was her space—why did she feel uncomfortable and nervous? The guy wasn't exactly doing anything.

"Then what brings you here so early in the morning? I thought you were bunking at Jas's place in West Kelowna."

"Eh." His long-fingered hands gave a "what can you say" gesture, both cupping empty air. "I grew bored at the detective's home and though I could have run through the orchards there, I remembered this lovely lakeshore and came here instead. I finished my run and noticed a vehicle parked in front of the shop, so I decided to see if someone was up. Someone was." He cocked his head in a most winning of ways. "*Bella* Reggie all alone in a dark place. What is this place?"

He straightened and looked around as if mystified.

Really.

"A workshop, maybe?" She wasn't about to play silly little schoolgirl games with some guy who thought he was a heartthrob.

"It is—more like a castle dungeon, no? Dark, when jewelry should be filled with light." He went to the doorway and flicked the light switch. A line of fluorescent lights flickered on down the center of the ceiling.

She marched over and flicked off the lights. "If I'd wanted them on, I'd have put them on, wouldn't I? I prefer it the way it was, thank you very much." Didn't the man get that he wasn't wanted here, no matter if he was built like a Roman gladiator—or a god. "I have all the light I need over my workbench. Natural." Well maybe not, given all the grime over the bank of windows that surrounded her workbench. She usually had small spotlights focused on her work when she was in the midst of creation.

Cesare, darn him, didn't seem to get the hint. He wandered around the room examining the various pieces of equipment as if taking stock. Then he paused by her workbench and picked up the old moonstone pendant.

"Yours?" he asked.

"A failed early design, worth nothing. I keep it as a reminder that all perfection had to start somewhere."

She felt his regard—those tiger eyes gone amber around the edges. Then he nodded.

"A good philosophy for someone intent on building something from nothing. You have a good shop here. Well equipped."

And how the heck could he know that? "What? You've made jewelry, have you?"

He shook his head. "Far too—how do you say?—finicky? for me. But I spend some time amongst jewelry makers at a commune in Israel and then an ashram in India. Their equipment was not too different." He pointed out and named the kiln, the forge, the stone polisher.

Okay, so he wasn't just a pretty face, but... "Shouldn't you be running back to Jas's place and getting ready to talk to Victoria?"

He swung around to her then, still rolling the moonstone pendant in his fingers.

"You are very determined to get me to leave."

She squared off to face him. "Maybe I have things to do. Did you think of that?"

"I thought—no. I thought perhaps you would go for coffee with me. I noticed a coffee shop down the street." Another one of those toe-curling smiles and this one turned fully on her.

No way, no how. What evil had she done to bring this kind of karma into her life? She held up her hand.

"Stop. Stop now. I don't mean to be rude, but you're not my type. Yes, Signor Angelucci, you are a handsome man who undoubtedly many women would consider a prize, but I don't happen to be one of them. I am a businesswoman with business issues to deal with—not some wanderer vacationing in some exotic locale. I am in the middle of the biggest deal of my life, creating jewelry for fashion week in Milan. That means that I have no time for flirting, so I would appreciate you leaving me in peace."

Maybe she'd been too harsh the way the grin faded from his face. Then he nodded and turned to leave. His shoulders looked stiff compared to the easy slouch he'd affected.

At the door he stopped. "I think my sister has given you the wrong impression. A man can grow out of his foolish ways, Signorina Lewis."

"My pendant, please." She held out her hand. "It—it has sentimental value."

He dropped the moonstone piece in her palm. "It shows promise."

His tawny eyes looked deep into hers so she would have liked to have looked away, but she was not going to let him win. Then his hand came up and, gentle as a feather, he swept a stray hair from her eyes, barely brushing her skin.

"*Ciao, Bella.*"He smiled, turned, and walked away out into the light of the summer morning.

Reggie turned back to the dim reaches of her shop and tried to ignore the stunned feeling in her brain and the rapid beat of her heart.

§

Chepalle! That had not gone well—or at least not as well as he had hoped when he had planned his little run in Peachland. Most of the night and the early morning he had spent on the verandah of the house of Jas Stone. He had stared out past the orchards at the lake and inhaled the sweet scents of pear and apple and pine. For some reason the rich combination of scents and the absolute black of the sky brought thoughts of Reggie in relentless repetition. They had reinforced waking dreams of the woman. Sensual waking dreams.

That was not like him.

No. Usually he could just walk away. If he wanted a woman, he would have her, no problem. They paraded before him like a big Italian meal or a Swedish smorgasbord, there for the taking. In Italy women had swooned for his family name and the wealth behind it. On his travels, once he had given up his identity and called himself Cesare Lucci, it had been for his looks. None of them had really cared for the man inside the body.

The quiet Okanagan night had only reinforced the difference of this place and the difference in himself. So different than the nights in California—whether in Los Angeles, or Napa, or the hills of Monterey—for they were places that truly never slept. Always there were great snakes of traffic shining red tail lights down the highways. Always there was the noise of nightclubs or bars spilling out into the darkness. Always angry yells and gunfire. Too many guns everywhere and everyone more angry than even he had been when he left Milan.

Even living as he had these past few years up in the California hills, the nights had been full of the signs of human habitation. In Los Angeles the field of city lights had stretched forever. Though some people spoke of them as jewels on velvet, or a field of stars, they had been too brittle, too crowded. Even in Napa there were so many signs of habitation.

In contrast, *la notte*—the night—over the lake had been different, the silver disc in the sky truly reflected in the lake. The mountain across the lake a void of darkness like deepest space—like Reggie's eyes.

Space. Room to breathe and grow himself. Wasn't that what he had been seeking when he abandoned his father's entrapping dreams for him in Milan?

Escaped, more like. But yes, space had been part of it. The space to be his own man, instead of only his father's son.

Funny that after wandering so many places, it was this small town that finally held a woman who intrigued him and who, during those brief moments he'd touched her, had sent a jolt through him.

And strangely refreshing that she wanted nothing to do with him.

The morning was perfect—or could have been so—a light haze over the sky and the promise of heat at midday, but now still cool enough to run in. Ruminating on Reggie, he took the path around the house and pushed out the gate. He would not return to Jas Stone's house yet. He had things to work out—physical as well as emotional now that the back-haired beauty had so completely treated him as the crudest of interlopers. But perhaps it was not so completely. She had had the startled dark eyes of a gazelle when he touched her cheek at the end. Her skin had been the softest silk he could imagine, and her expression had been one of yearning—before it firmed into determination to get him out of her space.

That meant there was still a possibility.

With a grin on his face, for he liked a challenge, he started out again at a loose, ground-eating lope toward his parked rental car. He *would* head back to the home of the detective and then he would shower and change and come back to speak with Victoria.

If luck was with him, he might again find a chance to speak with Reggie. Such a foolish name for such an exotic warrior-woman. But even Reggie would succumb to his charms eventually.

The bigger challenge would be getting his baby sister to listen to him after she'd already made it clear she, too, wanted nothing to do with him.

Chapter 6

Four hours later, wiping sweat off her brow, Reggie stumbled out of the shadows of her shop. The midday heat was unbearable, reflected back off the house's flagstone patio, but the heat in her low-roofed shop was worse. Regardless of the steady whine of the fans. They did nothing more than stir the heat and the still-tainted air. She'd been stupid.

She had. She turned around to look at the usually welcoming dim reaches of her shop through the doorway. To prove to herself that a certain visitor had had no effect on her, this morning she'd turned the forge on and had spent the latter part of the morning messing with the design of a tiger head pendant.

Tiger eyes. Tiger pendant.

It was just a piece of jewelry, nothing more. A way to contain her emotions in a piece of silver. When it was done, she could just as easily melt it down again.

Cesare Angelucci might not be good for much, but he'd been good for inspiration. The pendant she'd planned sat unfinished as a stylized, roughed-in, silver silhouette of a cat's face, awaiting polishing, a jewel setting, and the application of patina. The rest of the work she could do at her work table, but the forge work had been required first.

Using the forge with its sweltering heat had seemed like a good idea at the time—it had nothing to do with masking the flush she'd felt after a certain Italian male was gone. She was not attracted to the man. They had nothing in common and she had no time for a fling, what with Victoria waiting and Thalia deserving more of her time.

"Besides, you don't know anything about him except he's trouble," she mumbled. Not about to find anything more out about him, either, the way she'd virtually chased him out of her workshop. But better for everyone involved. She had no time for a relationship and certainly no time for a roll in the hay with anyone, let alone the black sheep brother of the woman who held her future in her hands.

"Who are you talking to?"

Reggie spun around to find Chloe coming around the side of the house.

Reggie sighed and used a rag from her pants pocket to wipe away the sweat threatening to roll off her bangs into her eyes.

"Would you believe no one? The heat's just fried the last of my brain cells, I guess." She went over to turn on the garden hose in the corner and palmed cool water over her face and the back of her neck. "I tell you, it is hot in there. Hot enough this patio is a picnic by comparison."

Chloe frowned, fanned herself, and shifted her heavy braid over her shoulder. "To you, maybe. You want to talk, I'll be in the kitchen. Isn't Victoria waiting to talk to you, too?"

Reggie swiped at the water on her face and straightened. In the heat, the droplets evaporated almost instantly, but sweat still formed crescents under her arms and a deep V between her breasts on her black sleeveless t-shirt. Not exactly how she'd looked in Milan. She hoped Victoria could see past it.

"Yeah. And it's about time I got on with it. I went in to the shop to sort things out, and what with everything that's happened, I ended up frying my brain in the heat." She shook her head. "Tell her I'll meet her on the front porch in five, would you?"

Chloe nodded and disappeared inside, leaving Reggie to reclaim an empty sketchbook from inside the workshop—the used ones having all been stolen along with the files. Then she dug a brush from a work bench drawer, used it on her sodden hair, and tugged her sweat-stained t-shirt straight. It was about as good as she could get in the circumstances.

Hair pushed behind her ears, she went into the kitchen and almost staggered at the cool. The tang of fresh-squeezed lemonade filled the room and she went to the fridge and stuck her head inside. Blessedly cool enough she could just climb in. A glass pitcher filled with pale yellow liquid and floating lemon slices waited on the top shelf. She hauled it out and the pitcher instantly frosted as she poured a tall glass and drained it down. A second glass, the grain of sugar on her tongue as counterpoint to the smooth pucker of lemon and the tinkle of ice. The half-empty pitcher sweated on the counter. She added water and found the lemon juicer in the cupboard, sliced three lemons she found in the fruit bowl and squeezed them, then poured the juice into the lemonade. Tasted.

A little sugar and no one would be the wiser for her gluttony. She piled glasses and the pitcher on a tray, stuck her sketchbook in the back of her waistband, and shuffled down the dim hall for the front of the house. Just inside the beaded curtain she paused. The jewelry shop was empty, but through the front windows she saw the backs of four heads—the women of the house taking their leisure there. She craned her neck to check her wristwatch. Lunch time. She'd been working out back longer than she thought.

She pushed through the beads into the dark-wainscoted shop with its glittering chrome and glass counters and then elbowed her way out the front door. The little bell overhead ding-a-linged her exit as Lila, Kylee, Chloe, and Victoria all turned to look at her.

"Lemonade? I thought we all could enjoy it." She set the tray down on the bright yellow and aqua cushioned ottoman and hiked herself up on the solid porch railing between the hanging copper pots. "So what'd you all do this morning?"

Lila raked her with an assessing frown. "Obviously not as much labor as you. So what were you making?"

Reggie shook her head, but caught how they were all looking at her. Did they know Cesare had been by? She shrugged. "A pendant I had a sudden inspiration for. I figured I needed to work the kinks out before I got to work on the Milan pieces. I thought Victoria and I could sit here in the shade and plan out what else is needed. She knows the clothing and Erminio's style and I can sketch out ideas as we talk."

"Maybe we should leave, then," Chloe said.

"Nah. Stay. Chloe, you know stones, and Lila, you know style, and Kylee, you know marketing better than anyone I've ever met. With a trinity like that and Victoria's knowledge of Milan runways, how can we lose?"

She met each woman's gaze as she spoke, even though Victoria looked a little taken aback. Chloe looked fresh in her flowing tunic of pale coral and bright coral tights, her silver and jet necklaces a tangle down her chest. Lila wore her usual Zen expression and her favorite dove-wing-colored dress with smart gray and cream spectator flat shoes and a single, silver-knot pendant that was an old Regulus favorite of hers. Kylee wore a bright print sundress that went with the day and her bright shock of short hair, while Victoria looked like a Roman goddess in long, draped, white trousers and a loose top reminiscent of a toga,with gathered shoulders and slashed-open sleeves. Her blonde hair was piled on her head with loose curls escaping. The whole group of them were flipping intimidating—or would have been to someone in camo fatigues and a sweaty t-shirt if Reggie hadn't known them so well.

"All right, let's have at it then," Lila said, playing mother to pour five glasses of lemonade, then settling back in her high-backed wicker chair. The others made themselves comfortable on the wicker loveseat and chairs while Reggie balanced on the porch rail, her lemonade beside her. She flipped open her sketch pad.

"First off, I was thinking about that long, gunmetal tunic and trouser outfit. You know the one, Victoria."

Victoria frowned. "Of course. It is an expansion of a design of my own, with ankle-length, oriental panels front and back. It has long draped sleeves, princess neckline, and a side closure that also buttons over the shoulder and down the side, leaving the front as an unembellished grey panel except for the seaming."

"So, very clean aesthetic lines," Lila said.

Victoria nodded. "With slightly structured shoulders, the piece flows marvelously. It deserves jewelry to match."

"My thoughts exactly." Reggie nodded and thought a moment. "What about something long, to match the long lines of the piece. Something modern like the outfit, but with a slightly retro feel. Like this."

She quickly sketched a necklace comprised of a thick double chain that was kept separated by oblong beads that in her mind were of jet. The double chain came around the neck and down between the breasts, where the two sides joined to form a single long chain pendant that continued the beaded separation and ended in a fringe of more silver and beads of various shapes and sizes. She held the sketch up.

"What do you think? It's simple like the lines of the dress."

"But bold and dramatic," Lila said.

"And if you did the design in jet like these," Chloe stroked her chains, "then the stones fit with the strong lines of the necklace and the outfit, sort of a warrior outfit, and this necklace is a new form of armor, and the jet keeps the wearer safe."

"I love that," Victoria said.

"That's the kind of thing you could use in describing the outfit—the modern warrior—soft but strong. It would play well, I think," Kylee said.

Victoria nodded, her smile saying her reservations were quickly evaporating. "Very good. That is one design approved." From her bodice she drew out a tiny, silver-embossed notebook on a chain and made a note of something, then looked up.

"What about the white linen piece. That is similar in design, though the tunic is not so long, but it is far lighter, airier. Does it need any jewelry at all?"

"Does it have the same neckline?" Lila asked.

"It is a V," Victoria said. "The closure is not across the shoulder, but the right front buttons at the left side after crossing under the breast. There are three pearl buttons."

Lila smiled. "It sounds lovely. The kind of thing I might wear. Erminio always provides lovely classic designs. What about something that sits framed in the V?"

Reggie thought a moment, then sketched quickly: a silver chain hung with a large, hammered silver disc with a single pearl set off-center. But maybe not... She tried again. Same silver chain with an open silver circle, inside the circle a smaller circle that might—if she could figure out how to do it—travel around an inner channel in the larger circle.

She held up the page with the two designs.

"Wow," Kylee said, sipping her lemonade. "Those are fashion statements. I like the first one, but the second one... A wheel within a wheel a-rollin'?"

Reggie looked at her sketch. "Could be. Never really thought about it that way. I guess all that time in Sunday school rubbed off or something. I was thinking of the movement of the clothing and the piece would reflect that."

"I like them both," Victoria asked for the sketchpad and set it in her lap. "Will the little wheel turn?"

Reggie shrugged. "That's something I'll have to work on. I can create a small channel on the inside of the outer wheel that the inner wheel could follow, but I'm not a hundred percent sure how that would look. If I got really ambitious, maybe I could put a similar channel on the outside of the small wheel so that it turns itself, too. I just can't guarantee that it'll work."

"Could you make both designs so that we can choose?"

"I can try. I'll make the first as it is for certain. The second one will be more uncertain. At the least I could make the second one with the smaller wheel stationary inside the larger—but that is worst case scenario."

"And if the disc is selected, you can talk about the piece being the daughter of the moon come to earth. If it's the wheels, well then, she's a sun worshipper always rolling along to follow the sun."

Victoria noted those comments and they continued on, discussing the last few outfits of Erminio's spring clothing line and what would be the perfect jewelry design accompaniment. Victoria seemed to relax in the face of the expertise and thoughtfulness of the discussion. Customers came and went and Chloe or Kylee would excuse themselves and go to help. When a small van of women out on a shopping tour arrived, Lila went with Chloe and Kylee to help.

"They are very sophisticated, your friends. I had not thought to find that here," Victoria said, shoving a curl back from her forehead.

"Because Peachland is such a small relaxed town, or because of me?" Reggie motioned to her attire. "You probably already figured that this is me more than the woman in fancy clothes who showed up in Milan."

"Darling, you may look anyway you want if you can make these designs. Your work is *bene*, artful, strong, and elegant as you are. Everyone will sing your praises when the first show runs. Erminio will be called a genius for having discovered you. You wait. You will be hiring people to do the tedious labor so you will be free to design more wondrous things."

She would? Just how would she feel about giving up the sweat and eye-and-muscle-numbing work that had filled her life for so long? There were days when the frantic need to create left her wilted, exhausted, dehydrated, and starving. Lila and the others of *This and That* took care of her then and made sure she made it home to Thalia and rest. Would she be happy to no longer do that? At the moment it was part of her.

"I guess that's something I'll have to think about." Reggie dug for a smile.

"Oh, no." Victoria stiffened in her seat, her gaze locked on something in the street.

Reggie twisted to look over her shoulder. Crap.

Tall, ruggedly handsome in knee-length tan chino shorts, pink polo shirt—now that took a man with confidence—and deck shoes, came Cesare Angelucci. He looked like he should be stepping off the flipping America's cup yacht winner, not pushing through the gate of *This and That*.

Victoria climbed to her feet and went to the shop door. "I do not wish to speak to him. Please keep him here."

She disappeared inside leaving Reggie floundering for something to say. She set her notebook down and slid down off her perch.

"Cesare, hi. Apparently your sister doesn't want to talk to you."

He looked from her to the door. He hadn't missed Victoria's disappearing act.

"*Merda*," he swore. "That woman—she is a coward if she will not talk to her own brother. I am not the man I was before. I have not come begging for money."

He was vehement enough, and upset enough that she almost believed him. Almost.

He shook his head and swung around to her. "And you are also going to tell me to go, is that it? All the lovely women of this town have no time for a poor, sad traveler."

She arched a brow at him. "Don't you think you're laying the drama and the accent on a little thick?"

"Dramatic! I am *Italiano. Passione* is in my blood." The skin around his eyes crinkled a little—most attractive. "I'll show you, if you like." The accent had almost disappeared.

She held up her hands and backed a step. "No, thanks. Besides, I'm grimy from the shop. I'd get that pretty pink shirt of yours all dirty."

He looked down at himself. "I am told it washes and that there are all sorts of cleaners to get out grime." He took a step toward her.

"Hold it right there, buster."

His shoulders sagged and he sighed and almost became an ordinary man. "Please accept my apologies for this morning. I interrupted you in something that was clearly a difficult task. And now I've gone and done it again, have I not? You and Victoria were in the middle of something."

Well, that was a change—the man actually seemed to realize he'd done something wrong, instead of being oblivious to everyone else's needs.

"Yes. We were and you did."

He bowed his head. "Then please accept the apologies of this man. Sometimes he can be an ass."

And surprisingly charming. When he got over himself and quit with the act. Her mouth went dry, but she nodded.

"Apology accepted. It was just—Victoria and I were trying to finalize the last of the designs for the fall show. This morning I'd had a break-in while I was away and I was trying to put things right."

"So I am an idiot that I did not see." He tapped his forehead before glancing toward the shop again. He shook his head. "But she is just as blind. I do not understand her. People can change, but she refuses to even listen. To consider."

"If you like, I can talk to her for you." Now just where the heck did that come from? She didn't know this man. She didn't know what he'd done to alienate his family. Heck, he could be an axe murderer for all she knew. "Why won't she talk to you?"

"Because my sister is the most stubborn, most holy woman in the world."

"Okay, that makes no sense. Most holy?"

He closed his eyes and curled his fists in frustration, then sighed and shook his head. "Sorry. It is the translation. I meant that she is—righteous, is the word—when it comes to me. When I left home, I said and did some things. I left her to deal with our father's anger. She has not forgiven me."

Those darn amber eyes of his had gone soft like—like Thalia's when the kid had so desperately wanted a pony. Reggie knew she was going to hate herself for this, but, "Sit down and tell me what's brought you all the way to Peachland and I'll talk to Victoria. We've had a good morning. She's in a good mood. Or she was until she saw you."

Cesare sat, for once not looking like some Italian Adonis who knew that women couldn't help but fall for him, but like a desperate man—even if he was an incredibly good-looking one.

"So it is like this. I left Milan five years ago. My sister calls it when her brother ran away from home, but she hasn't felt the weight of our father's expectations as I have. She had her freedom to play with her designs and her fashion. I preferred the family lands outside of the city, but our father would not hear of it. I was to be the family's corporate lawyer, but I left after I completed my training."

He scrubbed at his face as if the memories were painful for him. Then he looked up at her, his hands clamped on his knees. "At first—for three years—I just played—until my father cut off my allowance and I was forced to use the money left to me by my mother. Then I grew more serious. I have tried small businesses—a bar in Thailand. A restaurant in Bali. I spent time working at a vineyard in Australia and more time, most recently, at one in Napa. I discovered over the years that I actually like business, but not as my father does it from an office where he, how do you say—stirs the pot—without getting his hands dirty. Perhaps it is that I like the dirt."

A lovely Italian shrug and her heart sped up a little. She recognized in his desire a similar need in herself.

She shoved her hair behind her ears and briefly met his gaze. Gold-flecked as petrified wood, but these were very, very alive—a spark of hellion, a hint of rebellion, a passion to drink life down.

That was so foreign she had to look away. How could anyone live like that? Life—her life—was about responsibilities and working hard to do what needed to be done to get by. That was what happened when you grew up in poverty. Her parents were still poor and seemed to have accepted their fate, but she was determined to do and be more in her life.

She swallowed. "So why are you here now?"

"Because I want to buy a winery. In Napa the cost is so high that it would take every cent I have and leave nothing for the purchase of the vines or to live on as they mature." He smiled and a look of wonder filled his eyes. "To see the vines grow. To shape them and choose the clusters of grapes. To see those clusters you select grow and mature on the vines so that you must pick them at the very most perfect time and then the *magia*—the magic—of making the wine. It is as much an art as fashion or—or the design of jewelry." He caught her hand and the silver door bracelet caught the sun. An electric spark ran up her arm and she went to jerk back, but Cesare stopped her.

"*Chefigata*! This is a beautiful thing," he said, studying the bracelet. "Almost as lovely as the one who wears it."

Reggie rolled her eyes and slid her hand away. Typical—lull her into listening and then, bam, hit on her. Not gonna happen. "When you say crap like that, you sound like the bad boy your sister named you. A moment ago I almost liked you."

He frowned, his dark brows almost touching. "Now that is a terrible thing when a man cannot compliment a beautiful woman. It is something Italian men are trained to do from birth. Italian women expect it."

"Well, I'm not Italian, am I? Canuck through and through, here." She tapped her chest and her head. "As for this bracelet— it's a mystery and, frankly, a pest. It won't come off until it's good and ready." She flipped her hand over and showed him how the tiny silver key would not fit through the lock. "See? It fit fine when I put it on, but it doesn't seem to unlock until the darn bracelet decides it's time."

Without asking, Cesare caught her wrist again and tried to work the lock. His light touch on the inside of her wrist sent electric jolts up her arm so she almost leapt up and ran. But no way in heck was she reacting like that. Cesare was just a man, a darn handsome one, but just a man. She went to ease her hand away when he'd failed three times, but he still held on.

"These are marvelous doors. They remind me of many places." His fingers stroked the silver thoughtfully and her flesh seemed to ignite again.

She pulled her hand away. "See what I mean? A mystery, because it won't come off."

"But surely the maker did not intend for the bracelet to stay forever on a woman's wrist?"

She shrugged this time. "Who knows what the maker intended. We don't know who the maker was or even where it's from. All we know is that it was found in North Africa during the Second World War, and someone wants it badly now. But he can't get it as long as one of us wears it. So there it is."

She held it up in the sun, the light catching on the tiny silver planks and padlocks. Lovely, unique, and, frankly, a pain in the butt because it caught on things and was totally at risk when she was working in her shop.

"So bottom line, you want Victoria to go to bat with your dad on your behalf to help you buy a winery?" So there it was—regardless of what he'd said, he did want his father's money.

He gave an equivocating nod, but his gaze still followed the bracelet and she felt heat rising up her arm into her cheeks. *Just what was that? She was not attracted to this man anymore than she would be to another pretty boy. Certainly not to a pretty boy who was dependent upon his wealthy father to bankroll him. Not even one who made her stomach flutter.*

She stood up and went to the door to *This and That*. "All right, I'll talk to her. Now I suggest you get lost somewhere else and try coming back tomorrow. Hopefully, she'll have had a chance to think about things."

She abandoned him on the porch and pushed inside to the little ding-a-ling of the bell. A nod in Kylee and Chloe's directions and she pushed through the midnight-blue-beaded curtain and down the hall to the kitchen. Lila, apparently finished helping the customers, had found Victoria and brought her into the comfortable nook.

Victoria's carefully cultivated Brigitte Bardot look appeared to have fractured a little, like a stone placed on a too-hot piece of metal. Her artful tangle of curls had sagged, or perhaps it was artifice the way it had begun to tumble around her shoulders. She—Reggie—would never look so good with her eyes reddened from crying.

"I spoke to Cesare. He didn't mean to upset you." Okay, so the guy had said no such thing, but it was still the right thing to say. "Are you all right?"

Victoria shook her head. "I—I'm not sure. It is awful the way he comes into our lives to ruin things all the time. He was so difficult a son. My poor father had an attack of the heart when Cesare left home."

A little thing Cesare happened to leave out, if he'd known.

Reggie leaned on the kitchen counter and peered out at her shop. The back patio and the heat were looking better every minute.

"He said he couldn't be what his father wanted him to be, so he went out to find himself. That he's been trying out businesses and now he wants to buy a winery and settle down."

"Hah! That is what he would say. His string of businesses? *Una taverna—una taverna!* We are Angelucci, growing and selling some of the finest wines in the world—not beer sellers."

Reggie sighed. Stupidest thing she'd done today, agreeing to help the guy. "He said he owned a restaurant, too, and has worked in wineries and vineyards in the US and Australia."

"What? You are *un magnaccia*—a pimp—for him now?" Victoria wiped her eyes and black mascara smeared the backs of her hands.

A cold burn flushed Reggie's face. Her hands formed fists. She left the counter for the table and slid into the chair at the table. "I'm not a pimp for anybody and I'd appreciate an apology. I am a jewelry maker, but you and your brother brought drama into my world. I was hoping to make peace enough between you two so that his presence won't upset you. That way you and I can continue with what we need to do." Her words fell as cold and hard as her hammer. "I thought Erminio needed your attention on the designs, not some family drama."

There. She's said it. Hate it or love it, it was out there and Victoria was just going to have to deal.

"He should just leave me in peace." Victoria pouted.

If she was looking for someone to coddle her it wasn't going to be Reggie Lewis.

"Maybe he should, but he's not going to, is he?" Reggie said.

Thankfully Victoria sniffed once, twice, and nodded. Contrary to the Italian histrionics, the woman apparently was a big girl with big girl panties.

"You are right, of course. I am so sorry you had to deal with this. With him."

"He sounded like he wanted to get his life in order." Maybe.

Victoria shook her head. "He is like that. He has said these things so many times and my father listens and then Cesare disappoints him again. I will not have it happen. I will not be part of breaking an old man's heart again."

Reggie nodded. Being protective of someone she loved, that she could understand. "Will you at least meet with him and talk?"

Victoria's sigh was as deep as a diamond mine. "I will talk, though I do not understand him. Why a winery when we have the finest vineyard in Italy. Father has never been against a hobby."

"Maybe he wants more than a hobby," Lila said. Her quiet voice seemed to cut through the drama and Victoria relaxed back against the cushion.

"Perhaps. We will see. But I fear that it is only that he has run out of money that he comes to me. He does not care for anyone but Cesare."

A damning enough endorsement that even the little flush of heat she'd felt out front made her feel foolish. Cesare Angelucci—definitely not someone suitable for a woman with a daughter.

Chapter 7

With reluctance, Cesare left the porch of the red and white house and returned to his rental Camry for the fifteen minute drive back to the house in West Kelowna. The sprawling length of Okanagan Lake was silver-blue in the sunlight, small pleasure boats cutting wakes through the waves like his father cut through resistance of all but the most stubborn of competitors. It was strange to see the lack of development on the far side of the lake. At Lake Como, the shoreline was filled with villas built around the lakeshore and roads that lined both sides. His father had helped finance it. Here the development followed the thin cord of the highway. Similar, and yet not the same. There was something wilder—less tamed and settled—about this lake. Less genteel as well, given the sawmill and all the strip malls in West Kelowna. He liked that so far it had held men like his father at bay.

He turned off before the main town and travelled down through orchards to Detective Jas Stone's house. A dark sedan sat in the driveway, as did the SUV that was Jas's vehicle. Cesare pulled into the curb and climbed out into the sunlight. The house looked single story and deceptively low slung, with nothing for gardens except for low cedar and juniper hedging and a rhododendron bush whose leaves had gone dark and dusty in the sun.

Using the key Jas had given him, he went inside into cool. A small tiled entryway overlooked a great room down below that had two stories of windows looking out onto a deck with wrought iron patio furniture, and rolling orchards beyond that sloped away toward the deep blue of the lake. The house was silent except that somewhere inside an air conditioner hummed. Keys in his pocket, he padded down the open stairs beside the river-rock fireplace to the living room with its low slung leather couch and chairs that were perfect accompaniment for the large-screen TV on the wall. Not so typical was the huge, iron-banded Zanzibar door hung suspended above the fireplace. Why anyone would do it, he was not sure, but it did seem to fit with the house and with Jas Stone.

A well-equipped kitchen sat under the stairs, while out on the deck beyond the iron patio furniture sat two men on cheap plastic chairs tipped back, the men's sneakered feet resting on the deck railing. One, clad in cutoff jeans and a faded olive t-shirt, was Jas Stone, the other Cesare did not know. He stuck his head out the sliding glass door and the two men looked up.

"Hey, Cesare," Jas said. "I was just telling Danny, here, about you. Danny Forester, this is Cesare Angelucci. I pronounced that right, didn't I? Danny's my partner in crime, you might say. Also a Corporal with the RCMP."

Polizia. Cesare hesitated. It was written in the man's steady green eyes. This one knew what was right and lived by that code. He had dealt with such unforgiving men during his wild younger days.

"Pleased to meet you," he said and shook Danny's hand, reserving judgment.

Danny was a tall, lanky man with hair the red of Southeast Asian soil, and he wore hot-looking khaki trousers and a Hawaiian shirt of dark blue orchid design. Both men had an open beer to hand.

"There's beer in the fridge if you want one. Or we were just contemplating heading up to Betty's Diner for a late lunch. You interested?" Jas asked, then he frowned. "By the look of you, the visit with your sister didn't go any better. What is it with these women?" He shook his head and looked at Danny and Cesare. "Here's another option. I haul out some meat and we barbecue some burgers. That way we can drink our beer in peace and comfort our Italian friend. You game?"

Cesare nodded agreement. "If you tell me where the liquor store is so I can refill your fridge."

"Not necessary, buddy. The fridge is full. So's the wine cupboard, if you prefer," Jas said.

"Listen to him. He *always* has the best-stocked fridge—especially since Chloe started hanging around with him," Danny said.

It was part of the charm of these North Americans; they made people welcome and could change their plans so easily to accommodate others. At least the best ones could, and Jas Stone had proven himself one of that kind when he took an Italian stranger into his home.

Cesare threw up his hands in surrender. "What can I do to help?"

"Get yourself a beer and take a load off and tell us what happened with that sister of yours. Victoria, isn't it? You should see her, Danny—a regular Italian bombshell if there ever was one. No offense, Cesare," Jas said as he stripped the cover off of a stainless steel barbecue.

"No offense taken. She is blessed with the looks of our mother, who was an Italian movie star. Unfortunate for us all, she also got our mother's Italian temper and our father's stubborn nature." He grinned. "In other words, a typical Italian woman. Half lovely, half madness—or she creates it in others." He touched bouquets of fingers to his head, then exploded them apart.

Shaking his head, he retreated to the house, found a long necked beer in the fridge, and returned to the deck, where Jas had pulled up one of the iron patio chairs.

"So what happened today? Better or worse than yesterday?" Jas asked. He lit the grill and closed the lid to turn back to Cesare. "Yesterday the woman as good as kicked him out of Lila Weber's house."

"That's bad," Danny said. "From what I've seen, Lila's a paragon of moderation. You must have really riled your sister."

Cesare shook his head. "She did not throw me out. I left. She would not even listen to what I had to talk to her about. Instead she lectured on how I hurt our father, how I have failed him, and how I bring shame on the name of Angelucci." He shook his head. "When she finished, I was angry. If I had stayed, there would have been war. And who ever recovers fully from war? Today? Today I did not even see her. She saw me and she took refuge in that house—that shop."

He shook his head, feeling mildly pathetic, which was something he was unaccustomed to. "*Chepalle*! The woman has me blocked at every turn and I do not like it! She may leave me no choice but to brave my father's wrath, myself." He stood up from his chair and leaned on the rail. There was no question, the second option would not go well. It never had without Victoria's intercession.

"If it's any consolation, those gals really rally around to support each other, but they're also pretty fair. There's a good chance they'll talk some sense into your sister," Danny said as Jas returned from the kitchen three *molto grande* hamburger patties on a platter. They went onto the grill with a sizzle and the heavenly scent of cooking meat, until Jas closed the lid. The sound of beef juices splattering hot flames filled the verandah.

Cesare nodded. "The dark beauty, Reggie. She said she would speak to Victoria."

The two men looked at each other.

"What? What is there I should know?"

"Not a darn thing—except Reggie is more the kidder and stirrer of pots than helper—at least from what I've seen. She's not around as much as the others—I guess it's the working in her shop and then she has her daughter and the kid has a horse. That has got to take time," Jas said. "Interesting that she offered to help you."

Jas shrugged and checked the burgers. Turned them when they had a nice char. "These are going to be done in about five. There's buns and fixings inside. Every man for himself."

"Reggie said that she was busy." Cesare shook his head.

Another look between the two *polizia*—almost as if he was

sixteen again and once more being questioned about the damage to his father's friend's Lamborghini.

"So what'd'ja think of her—Reggie? Interesting, right?" Danny asked and with a speculative look, took a long swig of beer. He got up and went to the grill to inspect Jas's cooking.

Cesare turned back to the view out at the lake. It was a good question. "An interesting woman—like a young warrior. A creature of silver and steel and a scent of baby's breath and iron, with eyes like staring into the night sky."

"Now *that* is interesting. I never could get past those tattoos of hers," Danny said. "But then she *is* wearing the bracelet, so it's not surprising that some guy comes sniffing around." Danny elbowed Jas in the ribs. "You've been there, buddy. Maybe you should enlighten this poor sod."

Cesare looked from one man to the other, not sure he understood. Certainly Danny was suggesting something. "I find Reggie interesting. We could perhaps have a good time together, no? That is all. Do not read into my interest more than is there, my friends."

Danny gave a lopsided grin. "Sure, man. You keep telling yourself that. You forget, I've seen this before—first with Brett and Kylee, then with Chloe and this heartthrob right here, and then with Ally and Séamus before they left for Africa." He batted Jas's shoulder, almost knocking a finished burger onto the deck as Jas transferred it to a platter. "Three women with that bracelet on. Three men who are planning weddings now. Kiss of death if you're a confirmed bachelor like I am. Gotta keep your distance. But listening to you, I'd say you're already a goner. Don't you Italians have a word for it? Lightning or something?"

"*Un colpo di fulmine* —the thunderbolt. Or l'amore prima vista—love at first sight."

No way. No how. That was the American saying. He was a *confirmed* bachelor. He had proven that time and again. No woman in sweat-stained army fatigues could mean more than a fling—not even one with midnight hair and eyes the color of space between the stars. Could she?

Pondering the question, he looked up and found Jas looking at him intently while Danny scraped the grill with a Cheshire Cat grin on his face.

"Don't listen to Danny. He doesn't have a clue what he's talking about. But if you are interested in Reggie, you need to be aware that each of the women who wore that bracelet had attempts made on their lives. What with her daughter and the jewelry making, Reggie pretty much keeps to herself at her place in town here. She could use someone watching her back, because this whole bracelet thing is pretty weird stuff."

"Reggie said the bracelet had trouble."

"The weirdest shit I've ever seen," Jas said.

That did not bode well. "What do you mean?"

Jas tipped his head at Danny. "I mean first class weird. This one has been knee deep in the whole thing. You sure you want to hear about it? It'll stretch your ability to believe. I know I wouldn't believe if I hadn't seen it myself.

The policeman's words filled Cesare with disquiet. Finally Cesare nodded. "Tell me."

Jas stood there with the platter of burgers in his hands and shrugged. "Your funeral. You see, there seems to be someone after that bracelet. Or I should say, some*thing*, because whatever it is seems to be able to jump into the heads of other people and possess them for a time. They do bad things then, like kidnapping Kylee and trying to strangle Chloe. The last guy, Abel, took Ally diving in the lake. Let's just say, it wasn't pretty."

Leaving Cesare to ponder his words, Jas went into the kitchen, the platter of burgers in his hand. Danny hooked his head at Cesare and they followed.

"This is true, what he says?" Cesare asked. "It sounds like a nightmare—or a movie. Not real."

Danny shook his head, his grin momentarily lost and forgotten. He nodded. "I'm one of the lucky ones. There's a couple of guys still locked in Kelowna General psych ward. Me—

the thing had me for a few days, but somehow what makes me, me, survived. Don't know why, I'm just grateful I did. The damn thing was, I knew I was spying on the women at *This and That*. I also knew that I wanted to hurt them for having the bracelet." He shuddered. "Scariest thing in the world is not being able to control your own body."

It was too much to take in. Too strange to be true. He looked from Danny to Jas, but both appeared normal. Were these two joking? Perhaps toying with the foreigner?

Jas expertly sliced cheese and tomatoes and washed lettuce and soon they each had a plate and assumed their places on the verandah, the burgers running thick with juices, the beer rich and dark—some local artisanal brew that was good even if it was not a good red wine. Overall, the perfect afternoon.

Cesare was still chewing his burger when Jas turned to him. "So did Reggie talk to Victoria for you? You never said."

"She told me to come back tomorrow and that she would speak to her this afternoon. I will hope it goes well."

There were supportive nods all around.

"She really is a talent—at least, so Chloe tells me," Jas said. "Not that I'd know a great piece of jewelry if I fell over it, but apparently women ooh and aah over it. I gather it's a big break for her having this deal in Milan. If someone was interested in her, that'd be the way to get closer to her—help her with that."

"Well, that might work, but for women like her, I'd say the way through the door is to get along with the daughter. Women love a guy who's good with kids," Danny offered.

Cesare rolled his eyes and thought of Reggie's suspicious regard when he'd tried to do just what Danny suggested. "I do not think I need help from you in this. I am Italian. We are born experts in *amare*—in love. Though Reggie may have caught my eye, I would not be looking for a long-term relationship. I found a small vineyard in Napa that I want to buy. I will be returning there once I have Victoria's assistance with my father."

"Hey," Danny held up his hands. "Just trying to help, man. Like I told Jas, get you off the market and there are more ladies for me." He grinned and set down his already empty plate. These Canadians did not seem to know how to savor their food—or their women, for that matter.

"I have already met Reggie's daughter—the little blonde."

"Aah," Danny said. "What'd I say, Jas. No need for our advice. Guy's a natural and moves fast. Some guys have just got it."

"Better watch what he does. You might learn something." Jas popped the last of his burger in his mouth and leaned back in his chair to close his eyes as if he might have a siesta.

"Thalia—that is her name, I believe. She is a most humorous child."

"She's got her mother's sense of humor, all right." Jas inhaled and seemed to go limp in the sunshine. "I hear it's done her well in her riding. Kid's horse crazy like most girls, but she's actually had her photo in the local paper for winning some big prizes at some local horse shows."

Interesting. And humorous, the way they were feeding him information as if he needed their help in the romance department. Still—

"I used to ride jumping horses when I was in Milan. The girls were there—at least many pretty ones."

Danny whistled softly. "What'd I tell ya, Jas? This guy and Reggie—could be a match made in heaven." Then he burst out laughing.

Not the match he was seeking—at all. No, regardless of Reggie's sleek body and raven hair—regardless of the silken touch of her skin and the dark mystery of her gaze, the match he needed was with his father's connection to money, not a woman in a small Canadian town who came complete with a family.

Magari—Maybe.

§

It was four thirty by the time Reggie arrived home that afternoon. She turned into the narrow driveway marked by two tall pines and drove the hundred yards into the yard, where the sunshine caught in the dust sent up by her pickup's tires. She could have stayed longer at her shop, getting ready for the great bout of creation she was about to embark upon, but she'd promised Thalia that she would be home for dinner and that was a promise she was going to keep. She climbed out of the truck carrying a plastic grocery bag into the heated breeze of late afternoon.

The cooling breeze from the water didn't really reach this far back from the lake, so the idling air carried the rich, heady resin of pine and the scent of creosote and sage from the small corral she had built when Thalia was younger and still just riding horses for pleasure instead of to compete. There were times when she yearned for those old days because with Thalia's success in competition came so many more costs and much higher expenses. New horse, new boots, new breeches, new saddle.

Ka-ching.

Ka-ching.

Ka-ching.

The local saddle shop had had a field day and it wasn't going to get any better with Thalia moving up to higher levels of competition and growing like a weed.

Sighing, she headed to the house, pulling her keys out of her pocket to unlock the door. Inside, today's mail lay splayed on the kitchen tiles from the slot in the door. She scooped it up and tossed it on the counter. Bills could be worried about after dinner was ready. Thalia would be home from the barn any time and she always arrived hungry.

The grocery bag gave up fresh broccoli, carrots, green beans and snap peas, and a package of boneless chicken breast. After a good hand wash to get rid of her shop grime, she quickly cut the chicken into strips and set it to marinate in a combination of egg white and sesame oil. Then she chopped the vegetables into bite-sized pieces suitable for stir-frying.

A quick mix of hoisin sauce, chili, garlic, and white wine for the stir fry and a glass of wine for herself and she went to her bedroom for a quick shower and change. In clean, if often patched, jeans and a faded red t-shirt, she returned to the kitchen, tossed her dirty clothes in the washing machine, started the rice, and caught a glimpse of Thalia turning up the drive.

She wore a short-sleeved white t-shirt with the silhouette of a horse head on it, her dark blue breeches and high black boots had to be ridiculously hot on such a warm day. She came trudging up the driveway, looking like she carried a hundred pound weight on her back. Her footsteps clumped up the kitchen stairs as Reggie turned on the heat under the wok, poured in some olive oil—all she would cook with—and pulled the chicken in marinade out of the fridge.

Blonde hair a tangle around her face, Thalia entered the kitchen. Her gloomy face brightened when she saw Reggie. "You're really home!"

"The truck's here isn't it? And I said I would be. I'm making Szechuan chicken for dinner."

"Yum." Thalia used the boot jack in the corner to pull off her dusty knee-high boots. "I thought maybe you wouldn't be here because of all the important work you said you had to do."

Reggie went over to her and, disregarding the dust, gave her a hug. "You're more important. Now what's happened that's got your lower lip keeping your chin company?"

She placed a kiss on Thalia's head and inhaled her daughter's herbal shampoo. Wrinkled her nose at the pungent horse sweat and dust that came through and held Thalia away by the shoulders. "Well?"

The blonde head sagged a little. Thalia shrugged. "Just a bad practice, I keep telling myself. Dietrich kept yelling at me about the flying changes. I kept missing them. And Gladiator was too stiff in his half passes to get anything better than maybe a four in a test. So much for ever being ready for level two competition."

Reggie'd seen it before and was pretty sure she'd see it again: the end of the world with one bad practice. Thalia could bomb in a social situation, she could bomb on a test at school—not that she ever did—and she would sail right through it. But let her have a bad ride and everything came crashing in on her.

"You know it was just one ride, right? And knowing you, you ended with something that did go right, didn't you?"

The tangle of blonde nodded.

"Then you did good and left your horse ready to get it right tomorrow. Isn't that what Liz always said?" Liz being Thalia's coach until a car accident took her out of action and Dietrich moved in a few months back.

"Dietrich wasn't happy. He gave up on me and spent all his time coaching Lindsey."

"And that, my dear, is the silliest thing I've heard today, and I've heard some doozies. Now why don't you go get cleaned up while I whip up dinner and figure out how to cheer up my favorite daughter."

She gave Thalia a little push toward the door and watched her shuffle out sock-footed to schlep down the hall to the bathroom shower. The bathroom door closed and soon the sound of running water came from the rear of the house. She seriously doubted that things had been as bad as Thalia reported, because what coach would say something like that to a kid? Pondering it, Reggie turned back to the stove. The rice was boiling. The wok oil was smoking so she tossed in three tiny dried chilies, stirred until they were browned and had released an eye-watering pungency. Then scooped them out and tossed in the chicken. A burst of steam and splatter and she swiftly stirred them until they were cooked and pulled them out again and onto a plate.

The vegetables went in then: carrots and onions first because they took the most time to cook, a few stirs and then in went the green beans, and finally the broccoli and snap peas. Stirred, then stirred in the hoisin mixture and the sweet, almost licorice scent permeated the room with its undertone of garlic and chili. She stirred more and added the chicken back to the mixture and then some raw peanuts, and basil from her garden.

Barefoot, Thalia came back to the kitchen, her hair slicked back, wearing a pair of denim shorts and a purple t-shirt that was almost too small for her. At ten the darn kid was already as tall as most twelve-year-olds. Thalia put cutlery on the table and poured herself a glass of milk while Reggie was dishing out plates. There was enough that there would be food left over for lunches tomorrow. Good.

Reggie stabbed a piece of broccoli and smiled at her daughter. "Feel better, right? The shower helped?"

Thalia nodded around a bite of chicken and rice coated in the dark, fragrant spicy sauce. "Good Mom. This is good, too." She speared another piece of chicken with a carrot slice. "I love stir-fry. Especially the peanuts."

"That's why we're having it. You might be eating with your grandparents a bunch over the next few weeks as I start making up the designs. I've got a lot of work to do, but I wanted a little more time with my daughter."

Thalia nodded, but kept her head down, her focus on her food. Not a good sign.

"I'm sorry, hun-bun. But you know this is important, right?"

"Yes, Mom." Long suffering resignation.

The sound of car wheels in the driveway interrupted the conversation and Reggie craned a look out the window. A maroon Camry had pulled up behind her truck, a tall, familiar form climbing out.

Holy God, no.

Cesare Angelucci, wearing long khaki trousers and a blue polo shirt, stretched in the gold-dust afternoon light, the sunlight catching in his almost black hair. He looked toward the house and smiled, almost as if he saw her there.

She was on her feet and headed for the door. "Stay here."

She met him halfway to the house. "What the heck are you doing here? How did you even know where here was?"

He gave her a bone-melting grin so she had to fist her hands to remember how ticked she was.

"There is such thing as a computer. I looked you up."

Hands on her hips, she faced him. "And why would you need to do that?"

He frowned and even frowning he was one nice-looking man. "Reggie, it is nothing evil. Truly." He caught her biceps, squeezed gently as if in reassurance, and released them again. "You were going to talk to Victoria, so I thought it made sense to find out what happened."

"I have a phone," she said, crossing her arms over her chest.

"But a phone is such an impersonal instrument." A lovely shrug of his broad shoulders and he shoved his hands disarmingly in his pockets.

Grr. She was of half a mind to tell him what she really thought of anyone who would just show up on her doorstep—at dinnertime, no less.

"Mr. Angelucci?"

Reggie whirled around. Thalia stood behind her, her long bare legs shoved back into her riding boots. "I thought you were going to wait at the table."

"I wanted to say hi," she said, stepping to Reggie's side. "Did you come for dinner?"

Reggie stiffened. No way in heck was this happening. "No. He did not come for dinner. He came to ask me a question."

"We could ask him for dinner. Grandma and grandpa always say that it's better to throw some more bread on the table and make room for one more."

Lord-love-a-duck and too flipping true. Her folks might not have much money, but it was how Reggie'd been raised, too. But it wasn't meant to deal with a man who came with all the wrong kinds of recommendations. For all she knew, Victoria's black sheep brother could have a criminal record to boot.

"Your mother is concerned about inviting a man like me into your home," Cesare said.

Surprised, Reggie looked at him. A sardonic grin lifted the corners of his lips.

"Is that true, Mom? What kind of man is he?" She must have seen the answer on Reggie's face, because her questions stopped and she stepped back.

Just how was Reggie supposed to explain this to a kid who was at that stage in life where fairness was everything? She could just imagine Thalia's recriminations because she wasn't exactly being fair to Cesare Angelucci—she was doing exactly what Victoria was doing. What exactly had Cesar done wrong to her, other than get under her skin a little?

Hands fisted at her sides, she met his too-handsome-to-be-real gaze. If he was any kind of gentleman he'd refuse, because he darn well knew how she felt.

"Are you interested in dinner?" she asked through clenched teeth, knowing she'd been manipulated and not liking herself for allowing it. "It's just Chinese food, but we've only just started."

He looked away to Thalia. "How can I refuse such an open-hearted offer? I will have dinner with you and perhaps you can tell me about those boots that you wear. Will that do?"

Thalia grinned and then swallowed it back when she glanced at Reggie. Reggie felt like a thundercloud as Cesare let himself be led to the house by a chattering ten-year-old. Damned man was an infernal charmer, is what he was, but it wasn't going to work on her. She should have told him she'd talk to him tomorrow. She should have told him to leave. She should have kicked his handsome rear right off her property. Instead she was feeding him dinner.

It had to be the jet lag.

Chapter 8

The house nestled in a fold of the hills above and to the west of West Kelowna. It sat alone, its nearest neighbor down a long gravel road that gave onto a paved street with a riding stable at the corner. It was a small house, but snug, like some of the small stone farmhouses near his grandparents' winery in Northern Italia and, like those homes, this one sat in a copse of trees amid the late afternoon's golden sunlight. Of course, instead of cypress trees, these were long-needled pine with insects buzzing in the heated afternoon. The air was heavy with expectation and there were massive dark clouds gathering overhead. A storm was coming. Would the small, cedar-sided house stand firm?

Un pensiero un po'strano—an odd thought. Better to focus on the small blonde *signorina* chattering beside him and throwing apologetic glances at her storm-faced mother. Thalia told him her boots were for riding her horse Gladiator. So Jas and Danny had been right—like so many young girls, this one was horse mad. But all the while Thalia led him up the driveway and to the stairs, it was the woman who trailed behind him that he felt like an unseen presence.

Reggie Lewis. Regardless of his protestations to Jas and Danny, just seeing her again—even furious—made it hard to deny his attraction. And was that not a natural thing of a man to a woman—especially for *la belladonna*—a beautiful one. The amazing thing was that she did not seem to know it.

Neither should he, for that matter. For in her patched jeans and t-shirt, she was far from his type. His history was littered with women who wore the perfect hair, the perfect clothing, the perfect makeup, all to be tossed away during *una cosine voloce*—a quickie. Even these past five years, the women he had been with had been the artful ones, the local beauty or the traveler who carried her makeup and curling iron with her. Not a woman like this who wore a t-shirt so faded to mud it was hard to determine exactly what color it might have been. Still, she wore that mane of raven hair like a crown, and even with no makeup showed a natural beauty with upturned eyes, a patrician nose, and full lips that needed kissing. And then there was her scent of baby powder and iron, like tenderness and strength. He wondered what her tattoos meant.

He followed the girl up the stairs and inside into a small, tidy kitchen of yellow and blue, a table set for two, and heavenly-scented food reminiscent of that he had eaten in Asia. Thalia didn't wait for her mother, simply grabbed a plate from the cupboard and cutlery from a drawer and set a spot for him at the table on the side between her and her mother.

"You can sit here, between us," Thalia said.

A cool-eyed Reggie took his plate and stiffly filled it with rice and a stir-fry from a wok on the stove. Vegetables and meat. White. Chicken, most likely. Beside it she plunked down a goblet of white wine with no comment. This was not going well. In fact, he did not think it could go worse, unless Victoria were there coaching Reggie against him.

She settled in the chair at one end of the table and gave him the evil eye while Thalia continued talking. He sampled the wine—surprisingly good.

"Thalia, enough questions. There's food on the table and I'm sure Mr. Angelucci would like to eat in peace so that he can get going."

"I'm just telling him about my boots, Mom."

"Boots that you did not remove at the door, if I'm not mistaken."

Cesare put down his fork before he had tasted anything other than the sourness of regret. His usual modus operandi of charming his way into places he was not wanted had turned this opportunity to be with Reggie into something far less. Something ugly, and he did not want that between them. "Please. Let me leave. I am sorry. I push in where I'm not wanted and cause friction in this house. I do not wish to." He pushed away from the table, but Reggie stopped him with a shake of her head.

"You're our guest. Now. You have food before you. Now eat. This is a mother-daughter thing." She nodded her head at the door. "Thalia, the boots."

With a world-weary sigh, Thalia went to remove her boots at the door and then, barefoot, padded back to the table and resumed eating.

"So where did you spend your afternoon?" Reggie asked as she forked a piece of the meat into her mouth. Her dark gaze was intent, angry, and cloudy, with barely masked contempt. So she had listened to Victoria's stories and clearly did not trust him.

"With the *policia*—the police. Jas and his friend Danny—we had lunch on the patio."

"All afternoon?" Reggie asked.

"Eh... A little lunch, a few beer, and discussion. It was not so bad. A good time with other men."

"Better than duking it out with your sister, I'll bet."

Cesare cocked a brow at her. "What is 'duking'?"

At that she smiled for the very first time and it was like a light momentarily blinded him as she held up her fists and feinted a one-two jab at him, her fist barely missing his nose. "That's duking—except a real fight would hit the mark."

"Then, yes, far better than duking it out with my sister." He smiled back, but her grin faded and she sat back in her chair as if avoiding him. "But this is better than the hamburger Jas made for lunch and that was very good." He tapped his fork on the plateful of vegetables before him.

Reggie shrugged. "Better or not, it's all you'll get around here. We try to eat healthy."

"And you do well, as you do well in your jewelry." He finished his plateful and laid his fork and knife across the plate. It *was* tasty.

A slight flush of color flowed up her neck and placed points of color in her high cheekbones. *Bella.*

"I suppose I should say thank you." She finished her last forkful of food and munched thoughtfully, then stood up to remove their empty plates. "I can offer you coffee, or tea if you prefer, but it's plain old drip. No espresso or cappuccino here."

She moved around the kitchen with a strained self-consciousness, as if she knew too well right where he was. She stacked the dishes in the sink, poured in dish soap, and started the water. Steam rose from the sink and she was about to start washing when he came up behind her and caught her arms right over the bands of her tattoos. Her skin was soft even as her muscles tensed.

"It seems to me that you cooked the meal, therefore Thalia and I will clean up. It is only fair, correct?" He turned back to Reggie's daughter, who sighed and nodded.

Thalia came up beside him. "Those are the rules, aren't they, Mom?"

Reggie's hesitation went on too long as if she wasn't sure what to do. Then finally she held up her hands in surrender and stepped aside. "Far be it from me to block two eager dishwashers."

Half-bowing, she handed Cesare the sponge, grabbed the stack of mail, and plunked back down at the table as Thalia cleared the surface and Cesare started washing.

It was the most domestic scene and something he had never experienced, growing up as he had in a household with servants. But he had cared for himself these past five years and one batch of dirty dishes was not beyond him. He would show her that he was more than what his sister named him.

"This is interesting," Reggie said as if to herself.

He glanced over his shoulder to where she had opened a vellum colored envelope and was reading a letter.

"What is it, Mom?" Thalia dried her mother's wine glass and put it away.

Reggie didn't look up. Her brow furrowed as she read the letter. "Something from UBC's metal analysis section. I sent them a scraping from the bracelet and this is the result of their analysis."

She held up her wrist and shook the silver bracelet so its links jingled softly in the kitchen.

It looked like such a simple piece of embellishment, and yet from what Jas and Danny had told him, it was the most diabolical of things. And it was on Reggie's arm. What would happen if someone came after her as they had done to the other wearers of the bracelet? What would happen to young Thalia if something happened to her mother?

There was something about the two of them—something private, intimate, and mutually protective that he doubted anyone, let alone a man, could ever hope to be accepted into. To be expected, perhaps, given the fact they were alone, but the *isolamento*—the isolation—of her house gave him pause. How would he or anyone know if danger came here?

"What does it say?" He asked, feeling his stomach tighten.

"It says it's old—at least the metal is. They've provided the metal composition, and the reason it took so long to get the results is that they sent the sample results to their art history department for further identification of the region of origin. The chemical properties of the alloy can narrow that down." She looked up from the letter, her face suddenly guarded, eyes gone watchful.

"Thalia, honey, would you leave the dishes and head to your room? I have something I need to discuss with Mr. Angelucci." She held the arm with the bracelet across her body as if to shield it.

"But I need to dry the dishes, Mom."

"Since when has missing out on drying dishes ever been a problem?" Reggie's gaze never left his, like a small rabbit regarding the prowling cat. "Now scat."

Thalia still hesitated and Reggie stood, caught her daughter's shoulders, and pushed her gently toward the door from the kitchen.

"Mo-om? What's going on?"

"Thalia, for once in your life, do as you're told. Scat now!"

Thalia's face flushed and her eyes filled, but Reggie couldn't have seen, because her gaze never left his face as she eased herself between him and the now-empty doorway.

"Is there a problem, Reggie?" Her expression said there surely was. Almost as if she was afraid. He held up his hands, palm open. "I do not want there to be."

"I'll ask you one more time, Cesare. Why are you here? Is this little visit of yours about the bracelet?" She had hidden her wrist behind her back.

"No." He frowned. "Well...perhaps. Jas and that Danny. They told me about the danger it brings."

"A handy excuse to come up here and get into my home. Chloe and Kylee said that they had bad feelings about the person who attacked them, and I have bad feelings about you. And you're too attractive—just like the last guy."

"Reggie, no! You want me to be honest? It was not the bracelet that brought me here—it was you. I came to see you. You are so different than anyone I know." Let her see that he was being honest with her, for all he sounded like a lovesick fool.

She snorted—actually snorted her disbelief.

"I'd like you to leave. Now." She pointed to the door.

He was a proud man, but he was not about to remain only to feed her suspicions and anger. He wiped his hands of dish water and strode to the door, then stopped.

"Reggie, this is too bad. I hoped to be your friend, at least. What is in that piece of paper that sends me away?"

"Just. Get. Out." Her lips were thinned and white, her eyes hard as the marble floors of the Galleria Vittorio Emanuele II in Milan.

"This is not over, Reggie Lewis." *Sciocco*—a foolish thing to say, for by her eyes, it was.

With a shake of his head, he pushed out the door into the cooling air of evening and headed for his car. From behind him came the click of the door's deadbolt. At his car, he looked back at the house. As he watched, someone yanked the kitchen curtains closed.

§

In the ticking silence of her blue and yellow kitchen, Reggie leaned against the counter, head down, waiting for her heart to quiet. She had let that man into her house against her better judgment. She had placed Thalia in danger by doing so... just what kind of a mother was she?

She straightened and turned to look at the kitchen. He had sat *right there* in that wooden chair at *her* kitchen table, talking and laughing with her *daughter*. Hands shaking, she turned back to the window, shifted the yellow gingham curtain a little. The damned maroon Camry was still there.

Why was he just sitting there, staring up at her house with his tiger eyes that had just about eaten away her resolve to stay angry? His presence was a potent corrosive. The letter had come at just the right moment for her to realize the danger she was putting Thalia in.

Outside, in the golden light of evening, a car engine started, followed by the grumble and crunch of tires on gravel. She peeked past the curtain again as the Camry's taillights flashed as he navigated the driveway down to the road. She pulled the curtain open and watched him go. The sunlit bands through the trees flared in the dust raised by the car tires, beautiful, but just a reminder of what she had done.

She had brought that man into her home.

To think of something else, she picked up the sponge and began washing the rest of the dishes, then realized she stood exactly where he had, held the sponge just as he had, when she had opened the letter. The letter that still sat on her table that said that the bracelet silver matched most closely with what the silversmiths of northern Italy in the first millennium A.D. had been using. Had Cesare come as an emissary from Johan Fehr?

But if he had, why hadn't he done something? He'd left when she asked, almost like a gentleman.

Dammit, her hands were shaking. Clutching the edge of the sink, her hands still sudsy, she closed her eyes and drew in deep breaths of the hoisin-sauce-scented air. It was too cloying. The room was too small. And oh, God, she'd yelled at Thalia, too.

Abandoning the half-washed dishes and the claustrophobic kitchen, she went upstairs and found Thalia's door closed.

"Thalia, honey? Can I come in?"

Silence and then: "Do whatever you want. You're going to anyway."

Ouch, because it was probably true.

Easing the door open, she poked her head inside. Thalia sat on her bed, the pillow behind her back, her knees drawn up, and a book in her hand. Her blonde hair was still a tangle and she did not look friendly.

"I'm sorry, okay? I was wrong to say what I did, but I had to get you out of there."

Thalia just looked down at her book and started reading.

Reggie opened the door further and stepped inside. "I know this needs some explanation, but I—I'm not sure what to say except that I'm not sure Mr. Angelucci is a safe person to be around."

Thalia snapped her book closed. "He seems nice enough to me. He liked talking about Gladiator. He wanted to see him. He liked talking to *me!*"

"Why? Think about it, Thalia. Why is he trying to get into our lives? We don't know him. We don't need him."

Thalia glared up at her mother and shook her head. "Gee. Maybe because he likes horses? He used to ride, Mom. In Europe. Weren't you even listening? He used to compete in Italy and Switzerland and even in France. I wanted him to see Gladiator and watch me ride, maybe help me a little. But no, you have to chase him away like he's a danger or something. I don't think he's a pedophile, Mom—if that's what you're thinking. Not given the way he looks at you." She crossed her arms over her chest in preteen disgust.

"What are you talking about?"Reggie had been there. She hadn't missed the conversation, had she? But then, maybe she had. She'd been pissed off enough at his arrival that all she'd been focused on was getting him to leave.

"He was looking at you all the time—as if he couldn't get enough, or something. He kept smiling at you, but you never smiled back. At least not with your eyes. I've never seen you like that, Mom. You always tell me to be pleasant, even with people you don't like. You weren't even nice—at all."

"O-kay." She blew out a deep breath. "I was rude—but for a reason. I wanted him out of here to make sure you were safe. But I apologize." Her hand worked around the bracelet, her fingers settling on the lintel door.

"It's not me you need to apologize to, it's Mr. Angelucci."

Whoa. Since when had her daughter become the manner keeper? How had she gotten this old at age ten?

"Maybe. We'll see." She looked down at the bracelet. Maybe she did.

She'd thought the bracelet was old, possibly a couple of centuries—but over a thousand years? That had spooked her enough. But the fact that the bracelet's origins were likely Italy and she had a so eminently male Italian in *her* kitchen, just brought all the dangers that Kylee, Chloe, and Ally had faced right into focus. All of the danger had involved men they didn't know well.

Like she didn't know Cesare.

She thought of the look on that handsome face of his as he left—almost injured. If he'd wanted to, he could have killed her and taken the bracelet. He hadn't.

Maybe, just maybe, she had overreacted.

After an evening trying to make things up to Thalia by taking a walk down to feed apples to Gladiator, she woke the next morning with the certainty that she *had* indeed let Victoria's opinion of her brother cloud her personal dealings with the man. Darn Thalia for being right. This kid was altogether too bright for ten.

Showered and dressed, she went down to the sunny kitchen to put on the coffee and make breakfast and found Thalia had left a note that she was headed down to the barn. Okay, so the kid was still miffed at her mother. The trouble was, the kitchen still seemed filled with Cesare's presence. There was even a hint of his cut grass and potent verbena scent beneath the smell of fresh coffee. That was the trouble with the man, he filled up a room—optical illusion, of course, but he left her feeling foolishly threatened. She made herself a piece of toast, slathered it with homemade strawberry jam, made a thermos of coffee because there was no way Lila would be up this early, and headed out for her shop via the riding stable.

Earl's Stable sat on a piece of irrigated benchland, with weeping willows towering over the front gate that welcomed you into verdant, white-fenced, green fields where expensive horseflesh lounged. The place was far more expensive than she could ever afford, no matter how determined she was, except that Thalia worked part-time, before school and on weekends, cleaning stalls and feeding horses to offset the skyrocketing stabling costs. With farrier and vet costs, she could just barely cover everything and keep a roof over their heads on her artisan's earnings. The Milan deal would make it all much more sustainable.

She pulled in at the side of the blue-paneled indoor riding arena and climbed out into the sweet-scented early morning. Well, maybe not that sweet scented, as Thalia came out pushing a wheelbarrow laden with manure and soiled horse bedding that the kid swore didn't smell at all.

"Hey," Reggie climbed out of her truck. There was no one else around—too early for rich folk to ride, apparently. "How's Gladiator this morning?"

"Good. He's good." Thalia resumed pushing the wheelbarrow toward the manure pile at the far end of the building.

"And how about you?" Reggie followed behind, feeling a lot foolish.

"Fine." Thalia set down the barrow and turned back to Reggie. "Why are you here, Mom?"

"Well…I could fib and say it was to check up on my favorite daughter." She grinned. "But really it's because I wanted you to know I feel bad about last night and I'm going to invite Cesare over for dinner—if you like."

Thalia dug the scuffed toe of one black-booted foot into the dust and then looked up through her tangle of blonde hair at Reggie. It was a look that melted Reggie's heart every time and the dratted kid knew it.

"Sounds great, Mom. Maybe he can come early enough we can bring him down here."

"Would four o'clock be early enough?"

"Sure."

Her daughter was growing up so fast—faster even given she was an only child of a single mother. With the dinner arrangements agreed upon, Reggie gave Thalia a hug and headed for her shop, making plans for dinner—maybe pork chops done on the grill with garlic and rosemary and chopped mushroom stuffing, and potatoes and vegetables cooked in olive oil and herbs on the side. Another of Thalia's favorites and one Reggie could cook in her sleep—important after a full day at the shop.

It was barely six thirty when she drove down the long slope of Drought Hill and turned into Peachland proper, past Taste Bakery Café that oozed luscious scents of fresh-brewed coffee and freshly baked bread to park down the street from *This and That*.

It was another of those crystal blue days at the lake, summer-cool at the moment in her sleeveless singlet, but destined to be another scorcher as the sun rose over the lake. Forest fire weather. The mountainsides were parched from the long summer with little rain. Already a few hardy boaters were unloading gear and backing their boats down the boat ramp into the gentle blue waves. At this hour there was rarely any wind. That would come as the day progressed and the weather blew up from the coast.

The air was sweet with water and the pansies planted in the house yard, but there was a hint of smoke as well. She sniffed and scanned the hillsides, but there were no telltale trails of smoke against the blue. Frowning, she walked down the sidewalk to the white house with red trim and let herself in through the gate. She went around back and unlocked her shop and went inside. This early the room was dim, so she left the door open, still eschewing the fluorescent lights Cesare had tried the other morning.

The first time he'd accosted her.

Well, not exactly. Sure, he'd pushed himself into her space and she'd felt uncomfortable, but actually, when she thought about it, he'd been charming—and those eyes of his. Her gaze fell on the half-finished tiger head pendant. Yes, they looked like tiger eyes—haunted and hunted and full of wild mystery. That was the thing about Cesare—he was something wild and he didn't want to be tamed. There was something about him that really was cat-like—the loose way he moved, the fact that—at least according to Victoria—he refused to do what anyone expected. He was his own man.

And yet he had come to see her last night—or so he'd said.

She settled the unfinished sterling pendant on a charcoal block on her workbench and sat down on her stool. The tiger eye cabochon should go right—there. She marked the sterling and then brought out the stone and checked. Yes, it gave the impression of a single, tilted eye staring out from between tall grass. That determined, she used the sticky edge of a post it note to measure the circumference of the stone, then cut sterling silver wire to the same length. She corrected the edge of the cut piece of wire using a soft rubber mallet until one edge was flat and then filed the two ends to make sure they were flat enough to make a good match to each other.

Satisfied, she used needle-nose pliers to shape the oblong bezel that would hold the stone and crimped the ends so that they met perfectly. Then she brought out her torch, painted the seam with flux, and added solder before she turned on the torch. The charcoal block under the stone would reflect the heat so she ran the flame around the edge of the bezel, watching for the shift in flux color that preceded the flash of the solder. The room filled with the scent of burning propane, and heat reflected off her hands and face. The charcoal stone reflected red and then came the small, mercurial flash of the solder on the silver bezel. It filled the space between the two ends to create a single ring. She used pliers to shift the metal to a basin of water to cool.

When it was cool, using the finest file and sandpaper, she erased sign of the solder and then checked the fit of the stone. Perfect. The bevel height just allowed the curved top of the stone to display its showy face. She placed bezel and stone on the tiger silhouette's sterling back and adjusted until the tiger eye looked the most mysterious and marked the sterling. After removing the tiger eye, she painted flux on the silver and on the bottom edge of the bezel and then placed the bezel in position. A few tiny flecks of solder around the inside edge of the bezel and she was ready for heat again.

After the heat and the mercurial flash of the solder, she again cooled the metal, but it looked white and dull as any heated silver would. She carefully brushed the silver with a brass brush, then used a jewelers rouge to rub the silver clean and bright. The stone went into the bezel with a light tap of her fingers and, held perfectly in place, the tiger's eye now peered out at her. A last shine of the silver with a jeweler's cloth and she added a long silver chain and laid the piece on a cloth of black velvet to admire and poured herself a cup of coffee from her thermos. She stood back and sipped the nutty flavor cut with cream. The pendant really was a lovely abstract piece, from the wavy edge of the tiger's half-face, to the large mysterious eye and the hint of etched whisker.

And a total waste of time given all the work she needed to do.

She pushed away the satisfaction that came with a piece of well-made jewelry. She had jewelry that she was under contract to make, so why waste her time on something that was no more than a whim, a lark, a bit of whimsy?

Not wanting to think about the answer that stared out at her from that tiger eye stone, she set her mug down and turned back to her bench. It was ridiculous. Totally ridiculous. The only reason Cesare Angelucci was on her mind was because she had to see the man today and ask him to dinner as an apology.

Teeth clenched, she turned her back on her creation and pulled out her designs. This one—the large hammered disc with the single pearl setting. That should keep her busy for a while. Get her hot and make her work, too, given it would require forge and hammer work. Better to do it in the cooler hours of the morning—of course, she'd mostly wasted those on a totally frivolous effort. Perhaps not totally wasted. The pendant would surely fetch a good price in the shop and help to pay for Thalia's expensive riding lessons. She'd have to show Lila.

She carefully cut the disc of silver. Then, leather apron and gloves on, she used tongs to get an overall heat in the silver and began the careful process of hammering it into the slightly concave shape that she wanted. It was careful work, like an ancient tinsmith. She'd worked with a man who had shaped copper and tin by hand in India to learn the careful craft of shaping that left perfect dimples patterning the metal. It was painstaking work, each hammer blow positioned exactly to lead to a naturally fluid appearance of the metal. This she then brushed, buffed, and shined until the silver looked like it was a fluid bowl of quicksilver that filled the palm of her hand. Good.

It still required the shank link for the chain and the pearl embellishment—either white or blue, she would need to discuss that with Victoria, but otherwise the piece was done. She lay the silver disc on the velvet display and went back to work—focused this time on the creation of a crescent moon pendent that was to be made of three hinged pieces that Erminio had selected as one of his signature pieces.

She had just started with a template sketch that she would use as a pattern to cut out the silver crescent when a soft knock came at the door. She glanced back over her shoulder—Lila stood there, the sunlight catching on her auburn hair. She wore a pair of navy capris and a boat-necked navy and white striped top that was somehow reminiscent of old Audrey Hepburn movies. All she needed was a scarf tied jauntily around her neck. But Lila eschewed the scarf for a long silver chain with a seagull pendant and plain silver hoop earrings.

"Hey, partner." Reggie swung around on her stool and took a sip of now cold coffee. "You're looking fine this morning. What's up?"

Lila wasn't smiling. In fact, the little worry line she got between the eyes was back and she glanced over her shoulder and stepped inside as if she was afraid of someone hearing. She held an open paper in her hand.

"It's not morning anymore, Reggie. It's ten past twelve. A man just came to the shop asking for you. For some reason I told him I hadn't seen you. It wasn't quite a lie, but I figured you'd be in your shop. Anyway, he's looking for you, but that didn't stop him from giving me this." She held out the document.

Hot and sweating and wishing for a bottle of water—she always forgot to drink when she was working and she hadn't restocked the small fridge she kept in the corner to fill the need when she took a break—Reggie got up and took the paper from Lila. Angling it in the light through the door, she realized it wasn't just a letter.

This was something formal—legal.

Notice of Action, it said in the subject line. *Cease and Desist.*

She raised her eyes to Lila's feeling a little weak in the knees. "Is this what I think it is?"

Lila nodded, her hazel eyes grave.

"It's in Italian, but they provided a translation. It's a Cease and Desist letter. It alleges that you've stolen your jewelry designs and that the store and its staff are parties to creative copyright violation—to wit the sale of items that are the result of stolen intellectual property. Bottom line, we can't sell your jewelry until the suit is dealt with or else they take us to court and sue us. We could lose everything."

Reggie's legs folded under her and she staggered back to her seat on her stool. "But how can that be? You know I design everything myself. Does it give the name of the person accusing me?"

She couldn't breathe. Was going to be sick—at least her breakfast felt like it was poised just back of her tongue.

Lila crossed the shop to her and put her arms around Reggie, regardless of the workshop grime on her clothes.

"It's someone causing trouble for us, Reggie. That's all it is."

"But why? Why would someone do this? Why steal designs that are already sold?" Reggie pulled back to look up at Lila.

"To cause us trouble, of course."

The situation sank in and she felt like she was somewhere deep in the middle of the lake or at the worst time of her life when she didn't know how she was going to make ends meet.

"This—this was planned, wasn't it? That's why my files were stolen. I've got no proof that my designs are my own."

It felt like she'd lost just when she thought she'd won. No one would want her designs in this kind of situation. She wouldn't be surprised if people returned her designs to the store. Erminio would be canceling their association pronto. She'd be *persona-non-grata* at all gem and jewelry shows. She wouldn't be able to compete at jewelry competitions. Everything she designed would be suspect. She'd be back to square one.

And that was just her career.

With no jewelry sales, she'd have to get a job; and with no other skills, she'd be taking something low paying. That would mean barely enough money to live, and that would mean no money for riding lessons or saddles or—or a horse.

"Oh, God, Gladiator. Thalia will die if we have to cancel the lease."

"Whoa, there. Whoa. I'm sure we can get this sorted out quickly enough that Gladiator's safe."

But the worry in Lila's eyes said she was just trying to be supportive. This was trouble—big trouble. She looked at the paper Lila held and frowned. "Why is it in Italian?"

Lila paused. "I don't know. That *is* strange. Maybe the complainant is Italian?"

Reggie shook her head. "There're entirely too many Italian connections at the moment. Cesare, Milan, Victoria. What do I tell her? There's no way Erminio is going to want my designs. He won't be able to use them. He won't take a chance if this isn't sorted out." Reggie scrubbed her fingers back through her sweat-sticky hair. Her thoughts were awhirl. How was she going to deal with this? She took the documents from Lila, but they simply named a big legal firm that, from the footer, had branches internationally. Could she even trust Victoria, let alone her scoundrel brother?

"It doesn't say who's making the claim, just that the legal firm is filing on their client's behalf."

Lila took the translation back and read them once more. "I'm going to get my lawyer on it. Presumably one lawyer will talk to another and we can get some advice. You should probably think about who could be doing this, but the lawyer should be able to answer our questions."

Reggie nodded, feeling as weary as if she'd worked for a week instead of a morning. "I need to see what I can dig out that proves the designs are mine. I had some sketch pads at home that I doodled on."

Standing, she looked around the shop. It was hot as only forge work could make it hot, and the air carried a combination of propane sour and the female sweat that was running down between her breasts. "Let Victoria know there's been an emergency. And if you see Cesare..."

What? What was she going to say to Cesare? Nothing would be best, because she couldn't imagine facing that handsome, mocking face under these circumstances.

"So what did you want me to tell Cesare?" Lila asked.

Shaking her head, Reggie went around the shop checking that everything was turned off and grabbed her wallet and keys. At the door, she stopped. "Don't tell him anything. I was going to invite him for dinner as an apology for last evening. He showed up at my place and I was rude."

The skyward tilt of Lila's brows spoke volumes.

"So what did he want that he came to your place?" she asked.

Reggie shrugged. "How the hell do I know? To irritate me all to hell. To charm my daughter with his apparent expertise with horses. To see me. Who knows? He just showed up and got under my skin until I threw him out."

Somehow Lila's brows rose higher. "You kicked him out? What'd he do?"

Her hands were on her hips, her expression one of speculation.

Reggie blew out a deep breath. "I don't know. Nothing, really. But—well—remember back when Kylee was wearing the bracelet I took a scraping and sent it in to the University for analysis. The results came to my place yesterday. It said the silver composition is similar to that of the archaic silver worked in the area of Europe that is now northern Italy." She swallowed. "Doesn't it seem kind of weird that just when I'm wearing the bracelet, a man shows up from that part of the world and then this comes, written in Italian?"

"Maybe." Frowning, Lila shrugged and eased Reggie out the door and closed the door behind her. The lock clicked shut. "Just get out of here and see what you can find at home. I'll take care of things here, and keep Victoria at bay, but I'm going to pull your jewelry from the shop for the time being. Sorry, sweetie."

Catching Reggie's shoulders, Lila turned her toward the path down the side of the house and gave her a little push. "Go. Take care of yourself and your daughter. I'll let you know what my lawyer says."

Numb beyond believing, Reggie nodded and schlepped around the house, using the rough siding to steady her unsteady legs. The blue sky felt too distant, the sun hot as her forge, and her whole life was melting like silver into an amorphous puddle good only for pouring; but the only mold she had was broken. What was she to become if her jewelry was taken from her?

She made it to her truck, a roar filling her ears that she realized had to be the sounds of summer fun on the beach. The breeze off the lake felt chill on her bare arms and chest, her singlet too flimsy. She'd feared something like this when her files were stolen, but nothing had prepared her for the reality. It was still sinking in. And her failure to digitize the files was going to leave Lila, Chloe, and the shop, and therefore Kylee, all in jeopardy, too.

Fumbling her keys out of her pocket, she climbed behind the steering wheel into the familiar scent of saddle leather, horse sweat, fast food wrappers, and spilled milk that she had never seemed to quite completely clean up. She sat there, just trying to breathe, to calm her heart, but she needed to be doing something—not sitting here feeling sorry for herself.

Not sorry for herself—more like shocky—like she'd just been run over by a truck.

In a way, she probably had been—all her dreams and hard work turned to nothing in the flick of a piece of paper. A paper served on Lila and the shop. She—Reggie—hadn't even received hers yet. Well, they could find her at home.

She got the keys in the ignition and started the van. It rumble-grumbled under her as she checked her mirrors.

Just down the street, a maroon Camry pulled in front of *This and That* and out climbed Cesare looking handsome and fit in knee-length khaki shorts and a livid Hawaiian print shirt in red and orange that only he could pull off. She could apologize in person, but at the moment she didn't think she could string the necessary sentences together. Easing the truck out from the curb, she pulled a quick U-turn on the quiet street and headed home.

Cesare obviously saw her, for he stopped and raised a hand.

She didn't wave back.

Chapter 9

The noonday sun placed hard shadows on the heated pavement as Cesare climbed out of his rental car in front of the large white house with the red trim. From the house's front porch hung opulent, overflowing baskets of matching red and white flowers with a hint of purple thrown in. The breeze off the lake rustled the ornamental grasses along the promenade and provided welcome relief from the burning weight of the direct sun. Children splashed in the lake, while their elders lay comatose on their beach blankets. Out beyond the buoy-marked swimming area, powerboats towed water skiers and screaming hordes of children on inner tubes. The scent of tuna sandwiches and potato salad reached him from picnic tables set up just up from the water's edge and brought back memories of the times he, Victoria, and their nanny had gone for picnics when he was very young. Of course the food had been different, but the feel was the same—the freedom to explore out from under the overwhelming expectations of his father, whom he could never please.

Down the street, a familiar, older, cream-colored pickup pulled out and did a U-turn before cruising past Cesare. He raised his hand in greeting, but the night-haired driver showed no sign of seeing him. No, Reggie Lewis sat bolt straight, her hands clutching the wheel, her eyes straight forward, her face white as a sheet. Not even a turn of her eyes toward him. A complete refusal to even admit he existed.

His jaw worked as he watched the truck down the block. It was better, perhaps, than being chased off her property like the night before, but not promising and he was an *idiota* for thinking there could be anything between them. The difficulty was that he could understand her reaction after having thought over what Jas and Danny had told him. It could be reasonable to suspect an almost-stranger of nefarious intent when the bracelet had apparently been associated with so many strangers who brought dire events. But if the *infernale* woman would just listen to him, she would realize she was mistaken.

Of course, what woman *ever* listened? It seemed totally foreign to their gender, if Victoria was any example.

"*Chepalle,*" he mumbled his disgust under his breath. Reggie Lewis was nothing if not a pain in the ass—at least for the way he couldn't get her out of his mind.

But there was time for that later, depending upon his visitation with Victoria. If only Reggie had truly spoken to her.

He shoved through the gate and strode around the house, letting himself into the rear patio in time to hear rising voices from the kitchen—or at least one rising voice. Victoria's.

"What do you mean, she is gone? I had no issue with a day of rest, but this? There is too much to do—too many designs. There is no way they will be done in time."

A quiet murmur that he could not make out, and through the kitchen window he saw Lila try—in vain—to lead his sister to calm. Of course it wasn't working.

"Victoria, you must listen!" Lila finally raised her voice to get noticed.

That was the thing with Victoria, she could steam roller right over you if you did not make your own needs known. Passionate to a fault—that was his sister. If she ever truly believed in her own fashion designs and went off on her own, she would be *formidabile.*

Lila held up a piece of paper. "This came today. Someone has claimed that Reggie has copied someone else's designs."

Victoria grabbed the paper and read.

But the idea of it, given what he had seen in her shop yesterday, was *ridicolo*. The woman was an artist and devoted to her work. Even what she considered her poor pieces had a singular beauty to them.

Cesare knocked once on the door and entered without waiting for an invitation. The yellow and white kitchen gleamed around them, Victoria seemingly a part of the scenery in a bright yellow smock dress with a square neckline and bared arms. She swung toward him, but at least she seemed to be thinking instead of yelling. He nodded in Lila's direction.

"*Ciao*. I heard you from outside. What has happened to Reggie?"

The room smelled brightly of oranges and a carafe of freshly squeezed juice sat on the counter with two glasses. He looked from one woman to the other.

Lila shook her head. She wore a navy outfit that he might see in Capri or on any yacht in Cinque Terre.

"Apparently a client of the firm Smithers, Bruge, Hopfgarten & Strauss claims that she stole their designs. They've filed papers demanding that the shop stop selling her work or we'll face a lawsuit."

"But that cannot be true!" Victoria stopped reading. "I met with her before she came to Milan. I saw her designs. We worked together on her designs the other morning. She is an artist!"

"She is." Cesare slipped the document from his sister's fingers and scanned down. His years of legal training settled around him. "They are demanding that all her works be turned over to the legal firm unless proof of her own design can be provided." He looked up at Lila. "Surely she must have records."

"That's just it." Lila shook her head. "The morning that Reggie and Victoria arrived home, Reggie's workshop was broken into. I called the police. Whoever did it caused a bunch of minor damage—spreading everything over the floor—but the only things taken were Reggie's files. They didn't even take the jewels or silver or gold she has in the place."

Lila sighed. "I just sent her home, because she's hoping she might have something at home to help her case and she's worried about Thalia and affording her horse. I mean, if she can't get out from under this, it could mean her jewelry and her name would be next to worthless. She won't have any income."

She scrubbed at her face. "Oh God, I need to talk to a lawyer. I want to support her, but if this thing has legs, the scandal could ruin the shop, too. I can't let my grandparent's house be put at risk. Can you excuse me a few minutes?"

Lila left them. Victoria, her eyes wide, stood with her back against the wall as if she feared she might fall without its support. "I recommended her to Erminio, Cesare. What will he do if her pieces are all stolen? I found her. I will be tarred with this same brush. I will have ruined his show. Where will we find another jewelry maker on such short notice?"

Cesare grabbed her arm and led her to the table and helped her into the yellow and turquoise cushioned nook. Then he went back to the counter for the juice. Poured her glass. "Drink. You are talking craziness. Do you really think Reggie would do such a thing? You said yourself you have seen her create."

Victoria sipped her juice and he poured himself a drink, slid into the nook across from her.

She set her glass down. "It was on the front porch. I would describe one of the outfits for the Spring show. She would sketch something and we would comment on it. But what if she had already stolen someone's designs in preparation for such a discussion?"

He caught her hands, still damp from the cool of the glass. "Think. Her files were stolen. I saw her in her workshop. I saw early things that she had made. There is something unique about her—her art."

Victoria looked up at him at his hesitation. She pulled her hands free and had another sip of juice, her dark brown gaze studying him.

"You defend her when, if she has done this, she will ruin me. Why?"

What could he say? That he found himself infatuated with a woman he barely knew?

He shook his head. "I am thinking as a lawyer. It is too convenient that her files are stolen and then this happens. It fits too well with what has been happening here."

"What do you mean?"

In quick Italian he told her the story of the bracelet that was currently on Reggie Lewis's wrist: found in an estate sale box, how each wearer had faced difficulties such as Reggie faced."

"And you believe this?" Victoria's expression said she did not.

"I am not a fool. These were police officers who told me this. And you have seen the bracelet on Reggie's wrist. She wears it always, does she not?"

Victoria shook her head and shoved the orange juice aside. "Clearly you have not studied women with a favorite piece of jewelry. We will wear a good piece with everything and never take it off." She went to shove out of the nook, then stopped. "I suppose you wish to speak to me about your situation, but this is not the time. I have Erminio and the show to think of."

"And I have Reggie to check on. She will need a friend as this moves forward." He drank back his juice and pushed to standing. Victoria was watching him.

"You are strange today. Usually you would demand that I listen to your case."

An unfair statement—but then perhaps it wasn't. "People change, Victoria."

She cocked her head and shrugged. "Maybe. Maybe not. But come talk to me tomorrow and we will see."

She swept out of the room like the true diva she was and he was left alone in the kitchen with only the ticking of the turquoise wall clock and the scent of oranges for company. He knew it was out of character for him to take care in the kitchen, but he put the carafe in the fridge and rinsed out the two glasses before leaving.

Reggie. He needed to find her. She needed a friend and he planned on being one.

§

In the afternoon light through the kitchen window, she sat at the scarred maple kitchen table, an untouched cup of coffee at her elbow, amid the heaps of old doodle pads that she always kept next to her chair in the living room in case inspiration struck while watching television. There were a few early drafts of designs here that might help her. At least the notebooks—all dated in her fastidious handwriting—were a testament that she had been designing jewelry for a long time. It even showed the progression of her ideas. But thinking of these things in comparison to her files, this was nothing. The meandering imagination of a wannabe artist. Her mouth soured at the thought.

The room was filled with the bright afternoon light, softened by the blue calico curtains over the sink and the table. The white tile counters gleamed even though she hadn't disinfected the grout for weeks given all her attention had been on making up her designs and then her trip to Milan. The floor needed washing as only a house with a girl with horses needed it. She'd get to that, too, one of these days.

Movement outside and the crunch of gravel, and then a maroon Camry came up through the trees dragging a tail of dust and pulled in behind her truck, just like last night. Cesare.

She slumped in her chair. Could this day get any worse? She'd totally forgotten about the invitation she was supposed to deliver, so what was the man doing here? Even worse, when she'd come home, her head had been so full of her predicament that she'd totally forgotten to pick up the makings for dinner. Thalia was going to be less than impressed and Cesare—well, he didn't have to know what she'd planned for the meal. She had to have something in the house to feed him.

The chair squealed across the floor tiles as she stood and went to the fridge. Leftovers and not much else, though the staples were there—milk, cream, eggs, butter, broccoli. Yeah, like that was going to make a dinner for three. She hauled the freezer drawer open and cast around through the remains. Hallelujah. Chicken breasts, even if it meant chicken two days in a row. Back to the fridge. She had Dijon mustard. She could make chicken with a Dijon cream sauce—if she could get whipping cream—and have rice and broccoli on the side. She checked her watch. Still early enough that she might catch Thalia. She hauled out her phone and dialed, praying that Thalia's mad had blown over.

"Mom?"

Thank you, powers that be. "Thalia, there's been a change of plans for dinner. Cesare has shown up before I got a chance to get out to the store." Forget the fact she hadn't even invited him, but Thalia expected it. "I need some whipping cream. Can you check with Mrs. Earl and see if she has some she could spare? Tell her I'll replace it tomorrow. 'Kay?"

"I'll ask. What if she doesn't have some?"

"Then I'll improvise, won't I? We won't starve."

She hung up just as a manly rap sounded at her door. She looked down at herself. A mess, that was the only assessment. She hadn't bothered taking a shower after her morning in the shop. She was a mess of dried sweat and the grime that came from working with kiln and heat and—well—rocks. Dark lines of grime ran up the underside of her forearms from steadying her arms on the edge of her workbench while adhering the tiger eye bezel and doing the fine hammering of the silver disk. All for naught as it turned out. Victoria and Erminio sure weren't going to want her work after this.

Another knock at the door.

"Just a minute!" She ran for the kitchen sink, scrubbed her arms and doused her face and confirmed that she hadn't rid herself of half the dirt when the tea towel she used to dry herself off came up grey from grime.

Nothing she could do at this point. Ran her fingers through her tangle of hair—realized it was still twisted up with the help of a long ring mandrel she'd affixed it with this morning and hauled the offending tool out of her locks. Certain that releasing her hair probably hadn't helped her sorry state of affairs much, she went through the mud room and opened the door.

Afternoon sun backlit Cesare so he seemed caught in a corona of dust-filled light. He wore the same khaki shorts and atrocious Hawaiian shirt she'd seen when she left Lila's, his legs long, lean, and muscled just like his arms. His face was lean, too, ascetic with its high cheekbones, but with the arched patrician nose and the full lips and tiger eyes that were one hundred percent bad boy. He stood patiently at the top step of her porch, carrying a couple of plastic shopping bags.

"Hi. So. Cesare." She checked her watch at a bit of a loss for something to say and then motioned to the bags. "What's all this?"

"What do you think?" he hefted the bags. "This is dinner. I heard what happened from Lila. I thought perhaps a nice dinner would make you smile on such a hard day."

He brushed past her into the house and placed the bags on the counter. Frowned.

"What is this?" He motioned at the broccoli and the chicken fast defrosting in a bowl of warm water.

As usual he seemed to take up too much space and air. She swallowed back her immediate reaction to get annoyed. "Dinner. What do you think? I—I saw you in the driveway and thought I'd offer dinner. As a peace offering, maybe?"

She sighed. "I wanted to apologize for being so unpleasant last night, so I was going to invite you for dinner tonight."

It was hard meeting his gaze. Those eyes of his could about swallow her up. She forced herself to look at him and felt her neck and shoulders color at the infernal heat of the man. Damn.

"Um. Thalia really likes you and was hoping maybe you'll be able to go down and meet her horse later. She thought you might give her some pointers." There. She'd clarified that it wasn't her interested in him at all.

He shook his head as if he didn't believe her.

"It is a good thing I thought to come by," he said.

Her mind went blank for a moment. "It is?"

He cocked a brow. "If I did not, you would have cooked the meal for nothing. Besides," He took one step and was across the too-small room and she had no room to back up from him. His hands came around her arms, neatly covering the knotted coils of her Celtic tattoos. "You look like you have had a very bad day—all work and no laughter. You arrive at your shop early, you work so hard, and then you get news that someone else takes credit for your work. So you come home to try to find a way to save your designs. Now why don't you go have a bath or a shower and let me worry about the dinner? I am a very good cook."

I'll just bet you are.

But she swallowed up at those mesmerizing eyes that seemed to be searching deep inside her and nodded.

"*Bene*. Then you go do what you need to do and I will get started here."

She roused herself away from his regard. "It's kind of you to offer, but you don't know where anything is… Besides, I just thawed the chicken."

"And I am an adult and this kitchen is not so big. I will find whatever I need or I will fake it, no? And the chicken will keep in the fridge until tomorrow."

It was so close to what she had just told Thalia that she had to smile.

"You're sure?" The thought of a shower was compelling.

"*Certo*. Now go. You will feel better after a shower. Things are always better when you feel refreshed and I will cook you a meal. After that everything will be *perfetto*—perfect."

His grin broadened, showing his model-perfect white teeth, and he was standing in her kitchen offering to cook her dinner after she had been a perfect bitch the night before. Without thinking, she stood on tiptoe and planted a brief kiss on his cheek that brought a rakish smile in response.

"Thank you." She got out of the kitchen and up the stairs to grab clean clothes from her closet and doffed what she had on as she went into her bathroom, all the while too aware of the sounds of his movements in the kitchen. The man was too big for the house, let alone the kitchen.

Feeling slightly strange doing it with a man in the house, she turned on the shower and climbed in. Blessed warm water sluiced over her skin as the clatter and clang of pots came from her kitchen, then a steady pounding as if he was remaking her kitchen. God alone knew what he was doing. Heck, she didn't even know if he could cook. She could imagine the disaster her kitchen could be, but it was a small price to pay for the shower. The warm water beat at her anxiety like a massage. Cesare was right—the shower did help. She shampooed her hair to a lather and soaped the dirt off her body and was just rinsing when through the wall came the sweet notes of a deep bass voice singing in Italian.

She didn't know the words, but as they flooded in at her, she was pretty sure they were a love song. She smiled.

Chapter 10

Singing, Cesare bustled around the kitchen, a dishtowel tucked into the front of his trousers as an apron as he prepared dinner for Reggie and her daughter. It was a small space, well lit, with natural light and the white tile counters helping to illuminate the workspace. Thankfully, though the room was small, Reggie had somehow managed to organize everything so what he needed was always to hand. It shouldn't surprise him, he had seen the underlying orderliness of her workshop. Why would her kitchen be any different?

At the moment, in the fridge he had the prosciutto wrapped around sweet green melon. He had found an Italian delicatessen thanks to Jas and a wonderful Italian woman named Elizabetta di Maria and had bought good balsamic vinegar, Arborio rice, and fresh bocconcini cheese. From the recommended greengrocer he had bought fresh basil and tomatoes and fresh green beans that snapped when he broke them. From the meat market he had bought tender veal loin for slicing and pounding.

Now, with a bottle of good red wine breathing on the kitchen table, his supplies covered the rest of the flat surface. The bocconcini was sliced and ready for plating with fresh tomato, basil, and a drizzle of olive oil and balsamic. The veal had been pounded out for extra tenderness and sat waiting in milk while he stirred the rice and mushrooms that would become a luscious, creamy risotto. Once more, he thanked his nanny, Maria, for allowing him, as a boy, to escape to the kitchens from his father. The cooks had taken to him and let him try his hand at cooking. He had loved that more than he had loved anything—until he had the chance to try his hand at winemaking. That was why a restaurant was part of his plans for the winery in Napa if the plan ever got off the ground. Part of his wandering had involved collecting recipes, and the time with the restaurant in Bali had been learning the ropes of that endeavor. So had his time in Australia, where destination wineries were all designed around local produce as bountiful as these beautiful vegetables and the pear and peaches he had bought for desert to be served with whipped cream with just a hint of expresso flavor.

The kitchen door opened and, "Mom? I couldn't get the whipped cream."

Thalia stepped into the room, wearing dusty navy breeches and a t-shirt emblazoned with a dressage horse in full extended trot. Her hair was pulled back in a ponytail, but fine blonde strands haloed her classic features. For some reason, at this moment he was struck by just how much her eyes were her mother's, as was the shape of her mouth. He hadn't noticed it before because of the juxtaposition of their coloring. Her eyes widened as she scanned the kitchen and saw him.

"Cesare. Hi! Where's Mom?"

"She is in the shower. Your mother had a very bad day today. I arrived to make dinner so that she wouldn't have to cook."

Thalia's brown gaze narrowed. "She was *supposed* to cook *you* dinner. For kicking you out last night."

"*Figurati.* Don't worry about it. Things were happening. She worries about your safety."

"My safety?" She rolled her eyes. "I'm not a baby."

"You are ten, cara." And still a veritable baby in the eyes of the world. "You could be forty-five and your mother will still worry. She will always be your mama."

Another roll of her eyes but it was followed by a grin as she stepped further into the kitchen. "So what is all this stuff?"

"Dinner, of course. There is prosciutto and melon, and bocconcini and tomato for a start, followed by risotto and mushrooms and then veal marsala and fresh pasta."

He pointed out each dish and grinned as Thalia stole one of the prosciutto-wrapped melon wedges. She bit in and her eyes rounded.

"Good," she said, licking her fingers. "I'm famished. Can you come down to the stable after dinner and meet Gladiator?"

"It would be my pleasure. Now your mother is in the bathroom, by the sounds she has finished her shower, so why don't you wash up here while I set the table?"

Thalia washed hands and face and then together they set the table. When the bathroom door clicked open, he turned to put the water on for the pasta, then poured two glasses of wine and met Reggie at the entry to the kitchen.

"Wow, it smells wonderful!" she said, looking around wide-eyed.

She *looked* wonderful, her still-damp hair a dark fall to her eyes and shoulders. She wore a simple tunic top in red that bared her shoulders, and black leggings that showed the muscled shape of her thighs. Sans makeup, with her arched black brows and lush lashes, she was more attractive than most women ever were capable of. She still wore the legendary bracelet on her wrist and the tattoos on her biceps.

"What can I do?" she asked.

"You can be seated at the table and enjoy your meal." He caught her arm and felt her tense as he led her to the table, held her chair as Thalia slid into her own.

"He made all this, Mom. Can you believe it?"

There was a platter on the table filled with bright rounds of tomatoes topped with tiny white moons of white cheese and sprigs of fresh basil, all drizzled with brown balsamic vinegar and golden olive oil. Another platter held crescents of pale green honeydew melon wrapped in pink prosciutto. Cesare forked a serving of each onto their plates and then held up his wine glass.

"To friends who can help us through the hard times," he said.

She met his gaze and he would not look away, willed her attention and her happiness at his presence. Finally, her lips curved in a reluctant smile. She nodded and lifted her wine glass in toast. Thalia joined them with her glass of milk.

Reggie cut a slice of the melon and prosciutto and closed her eyes as she chewed. A good sign. He was waiting when she opened her eyes.

"It is good? Yes?"

"Wonderful! Like sunshine on a plate." She sampled the bocconcini and tomato. "OMG, this is wonderful, too. And so simple. That was the thing with the food in Milan, it all seemed so effortless, but it was all so good."

And so the meal started with praise and he sipped his wine and watched Reggie and her daughter as they savored their food, the daughter polishing off more than the mother, but both clearly enjoying the meal.

When they had each finished servings of the melon and the tomato, he returned the platters to the counter and served each of them a small bowl of risotto, also decorated with a sprig of basil. At the same time, he turned up the heat under the frying pan where he had previously cooked the mushrooms and garlic. He added some oil.

At the table he sampled the risotto, creamy, the mushroom flavor like a perfume for the tongue.

"Mom! Wow. What is this?" Thalia was forking the risotto into her mouth as if she was afraid someone would steal it.

"Whoa, honey. Slow down. You don't need to bolt your food. Enjoy it. I know I am." She looked at him over her wine glass. Smiled—truly smiled like she meant it.

"This is wonderful. I haven't had risotto in years and I don't think Thalia's ever had it. You really are a wonderful cook."

He basked in the words, but his frying pan was smoking. He held up his hand and excused himself, went to the stove and began to cook his veal scaloppini, flouring and salting each slice before he dropped it into the pan and swiftly seared each side.

Then he pulled them out and poured in marsala wine, scraping the bottoms and sides of the pan, the wine boiling fiercely. He dropped the fettuccini into the boiling water at the same time he poured the demi-glace into the hot wine and stirred them together.

He felt, rather than heard Reggie come up beside him, having cleared the risotto dishes from the table.

He returned the mushrooms to the pan and cooked two minutes longer as the sauce thickened. The pasta done, he drained it in the sink and then coiled a pile on each of three warmed plates, placed two scaloppini on the top of each, and spooned marsala and mushroom sauce over the top. A sprig of parsley and the plates looked perfect.

Reggie picked up the plates to take them to the table and he leaned over and lightly kissed her cheek. She stiffened, but when he pulled back and smiled, her lips curved in response. He followed her to the table where Thalia sat studying them.

"Veal marsala for the dressage rider to keep up her strength," he said as he took one dish from Reggie and set it before her daughter.

Settled again at the table, they took their time over the meal. Cesare savored the wine—surprisingly good for a local vintage, for the wine store Jas had sent him to had not carried Italian wines. He picked up the bottle.

"Elkhart winery, Peachland." He frowned. "This is the same Peachland where your store is found?"

Reggie nodded. "It is. Elkhart is part owned by Chloe's brother, Brett. You probably haven't met him yet. You should. With your interest in food and wine, you two would get on like gangbusters."

Maybe it was the wine and maybe it was the meal, but the tension seemed to have drained out of Reggie Lewis so that she was simply a beautiful, intelligent woman with whom he was having dinner. He liked it.

He sampled the wine again. "It really is very good and goes well with the meal."

"They have some good wines, though I didn't know they were doing much with reds yet. Their viognier is wonderful—when you can get it. Chloe's lucky, Brett's always bringing her bottles of his latest vintage that's ready for the table. I think she's his guinea pig. Lila, too."

Her smile faded a little and she looked away.

"You are worried that this thing today may have ruined your friendship." Without thinking, he reached across the table and caught her hand—it was meant only in friendship, but the ripple of sparking energy up his arm said that is was far more than that. So did the sudden startled look in her eyes.

§

What the heck was going on? Reggie sat at the table knowing something was wrong—or if not wrong, different. Yes, not wrong—*different*.

Different as the man filling up her kitchen, for he did fill it up with his deep voice and his pleasant scent of cut grass and verbena that somehow found her nose even through the luscious scents of the dinner he'd made. His movements were *so* certain as he shifted around the kitchen—as if the kitchen had shifted to fit him. Would it still fit her?

And now his heat flowed from his hand into hers and up her arm and right into her core. Those darn tiger eyes of his seemed to look right into her. Apparently they liked what they saw because his smile broadened, and with his free hand he picked up his wine.

"To friendships. The good ones are always sustained, no matter the ill that befalls them."

She joined him in the toast, though she wasn't ascertain as he was. Everyone had a price they weren't prepared to pay, just as she did. For her it was Thalia. She would move heaven and earth for her daughter. For Lila it was the house and the store. She would never risk losing them—not even for a friend.

She eased her hand free and reached over to stroke Thalia's cheek. So soft yet. She remembered the miracle of the first time she was handed her daughter to cradle. Thalia might be too big for that now, but she was still and always would be Reggie's baby.

"You must be just itching to get Cesare down to the barns. How about you take him down and I'll clean up here and meet you down there after I'm done?"

It wasn't that she didn't want to go with them, it was more that she did want to go—to be around Cesare Angelucci—and that was a little scary given everything that was going on.

"There is still dessert..." Cesare said.

"Then a walk to the barn would be perfect because, at the moment, I'm stuffed. Now why don't you two head out and leave this to me. Believe me, I'm very good at cleaning up." She slid out of her chair and began to clear the table of three scraped-clean plates. "Besides, if I get to clean up, I get to lick the bowls." She grinned.

Thalia stood. "Just let me get my boots on. Gladiator is not going to be happy that I've just eaten all this food."

"I am sure that any horse named Gladiator will handle the weight of a little veal marsala." Cesare stood beside her and waited as Thalia ran to change into clean breeches and then returned to use boot hooks to pull on her high black boots. Then the two of them stepped out into the evening.

Reggie watched them go, the early evening light through the trees dusting them with golden light as they walked down the driveway together. They made a good picture, tall dark Cesare, with his strong shoulders that spoke of safety and protection and the slight figure of her daughter like a new blade of grass venturing into the big, bad world. But Cesare seemed to have gained Jas Stone's seal of approval and he seemed to have changed, too. A surge of protectiveness ran through Reggie that made her knees momentarily weak, but Thalia was okay. Cesare had to know how precious Thalia was. He wouldn't let anything happen to her. Now she, Reggie, just had to find a way to solve this thing with the jewelry.

With that, all the good feelings and relaxation of the meal were blown away like the breeze blew away the dust that rose at Thalia's boots. The light in the kitchen flickered and dimmed.

On automatic, she placed plastic wrap over the remaining prosciutto and melon and the bocconcini platter, too. The last two pieces of veal she placed in a container and slathered the remaining sauce over top. Well, most of it. Some of it, she had to lick from the spoon. It was so good, it left her smiling and thinking of Cesare and the quick, expert way he had in the kitchen.

She'd lay money on him being that expert in other areas as well.

Hmm. Naughty girl. She sipped the last of the wine in her glass as she starting filled the dishwasher and refilled her glass, which emptied the bottle. Going to have to watch her drinking, but it just went down so well.

The dishwasher loaded and she busied herself cleaning the rest of the things off the counter and wiping down the table and stove. When she was done, she checked her watch. Only thirty minutes gone. Gladiator would barely be suitably admired if she knew Thalia. Then would come the grooming and the saddling and then would be the grand production of showing the horse off in the arena. She could afford to finish her wine and then head down there herself.

Which was strange when she considered that she'd just sent her daughter off with a man who a few days ago she thought of as a black sheep of the Angelucci family. Oddly, somehow over the past couple of days, she'd come to trust him.

"And you're a damn fool because you do."

Shit. What the hell was she doing, letting her daughter go off with a man she hardly knew? "Look at what you've just done! Jas Stone knows beans-all about raising a daughter!"

On the white tile countertop she abandoned her wine glass—the most likely cause of her lapse in judgment—yanked on runners and grabbed a jacket before heading out the door.

She half-jogged, half-ran down the hill, the evening full of the sound of lawn mowers and the scents of fresh cut hay and peaches heavy in the orchards. Earl's Stables sat in one of the few flat areas in the series of benchland, plateau, valley, and ravine that made up this side of the Okanagan Lake valley. That allowed the large indoor arena and its companion outdoor ring to be built amid the gently rolling fields and loafing paddocks.

At this time of day, with the shadows extending their reach over the ground and dinner recently eaten, there were a few riders who sought the cooler air. Under the fading sky after sunset, the open doors at both ends of the indoor ring allowed in the breeze—a positive she supposed, given for some reason even on a lovely evening like this the arena inside was still the working area of choice. But as she neared she recognized the big brown horse under the slim blonde rider in the outdoor ring, a lone male figure leaning on the railings.

She slowed and felt her heart slow with her. Nothing wrong. In her anxiety over everything going to hell in her life, about Cesare she'd been wrong.

Totally, utterly wrong.

As she sauntered up to the ring beside him, she was glad she had been.

"Hey," she said as she leaned on the rail.

Out in the ring, Thalia had Gladiator in a smooth forward trot. Reggie didn't know much about horses, but anyone could tell that this horse could move. Even at an ordinary trot, he had a certain lift to his body that left him looking momentarily suspended midair.

"How's it going?" She looked from Cesare to the horse and rider.

"She rides very well for one so young. The horse works well with her." He waved Thalia over. "Try just a little more half halt as you drive forward with your hips and you should have a very nice medium trot. Like this."

He demonstrated small discrete tugs on the reins that would signal to the horse to slow at the same time as she drove from behind. "That will help the horse shift his balance more to his hindquarters and will give you a loftier extended trot all around." The trouble was balancing those signals so the horse understood.

Thalia nodded and rode Gladiator around the end of the ring and came out of the corner headed diagonally across the ring.

Her weight shifted slightly back and her hands worked lightly and suddenly Gladiator appeared to shift his movement, each outstretched foreleg floating on the air, each hind leg reaching farther under him.

When she got to the far side of the ring, Thalia brought Gladiator to a walk and dropped the reins so he could stretch his neck. She let out a whoop of delight and jogged the horse over to them.

"Did you see, Mom? Did you see? I felt it. I got a perfect medium trot. For some reason—and I'm gonna blame Cesare—it worked tonight. I've been trying for weeks to get a difference between a working trot and a medium trot and still have enough for an extended trot. But that was it." Her eyes squeezed shut as she had a squee of happiness moment, then she went serious.

"Would you—would you like to ride him?" she asked Cesare.

"Oh, no." He shook his head. "I could not. You ride him and your mother and I will watch. We have things to discuss."

They did? Reggie frowned.

Thalia's eyes narrowed as if she was assessing just what this could mean, but then she shrugged, tossed her head, and rode Gladiator away on a long rein.

Together they watched her.

"Is she as good as I think she is?" Reggie asked. "I mean, I don't know much about the finer points, but she and that horse..." She shook her head. Sometimes she could almost cry it was so beautiful, the way a blonde-haired kid and a plain brown horse could become something so—graceful.

"She is very good. The horse—it is not so big, but very well balanced. And he wants to please. That is the big thing. But I think Thalia could do even better on a better horse."

"Well, that's not going to happen any time soon, now, is it. Besides, Gladiator is the best horse in the world—according to Thalia." Her throat felt tight as she watched Thalia's easy ride, the way the horse looked so contented under her. A better horse, and she couldn't afford this one. All that good food she'd eaten felt like a lead weight.

"I read the letter that Lila received. It was in Italian. That suggests that the person laying the claim against you is there. Copyright law says that case will always be filed in the plaintiff's language."

"So what are you telling me? That what I thought was going to be a difficult case is going to be damn near impossible? That I'm going to have to fly to Italy to defend myself in a language I don't speak?" The prospect of all the devastating costs made her hold onto the rail for support. Overhead the sky was turning the pale purple-blue of dusk and the robins were trilling in the trees. From the west came towering thunderclouds threatening the silver disc of the moon.

"I will help you, if you let me."

She turned to him, then, so tall, so everything-that-attracted-a-woman that she wanted to take a step away, but couldn't. She'd been fighting for what she wanted for too long. In this fight she'd use whatever tools came to hand. Even one with woman-eating tiger eyes.

"Why? Why help me?"

Those self-same eyes smiled and his mouth curved around teeth made whiter by his olive skin and five o'clock shadow. "Why not help you? You are charming and talented and someone has done you a grave disservice."

"You don't know that. You don't know the case they've got against me. Maybe I'm a cheat and a liar and—and a thief."

He turned from the riding ring then, to face her. His six-foot-plus height towering over her five foot seven, his body so close she had to tilt her head a little.

"That is true? You could be, but I do not believe it." His hands came up and ran lightly down her arms, caught her hands, then released her, but not before this invisible heat lightning flashed through her again.

"Perhaps it is that I like you," Cesare said softly. "You are a charming woman, for all your thorny moments. Exotic and strong. Someone so strong and dedicated to her craft would not stoop to stealing someone else's designs."

"That's a whole lot of assumptions." Because he couldn't possibly know her well enough to make such a call.

He raised a single brow and pursed his lips, his hands now dug deep in his pockets. "When I like a woman, I am prone to assumptions. Actually, I think we all are."

The gold in his tiger eyes brightened like a flare of flux and the flame could just about devour her. She looked away to the riding ring and Thalia, but it was too late. She was already feeling his heat.

"I'm not sure I want to understand what you mean. I—I'm a mother and a jewelry designer whose designs have been stolen and so I'm in the fight of my life for my career—for everything. I don't have time for romance, if that's what you're suggesting." She eased space between them, but the infuriating man—for each step she took away, he followed.

"All I am asking is for you to let me help you. Why? Because I can. I speak the language. I have legal training—in the Italian civil system. And I work for free. Can you think of a better deal?"

She chanced meeting his gaze again. Solemn, so this wasn't a joke to him. Still half-glimpsed gold through darkness, like something surfacing through waves. Still enough to make her skin hot, her body throb.

She swallowed. "I pay my way. I don't like to be in debt to anyone."

Shaking his head, he caught her shoulders. "Reggie, sometimes even the strongest person must eat their pride and ask for help. I have just learned this. After two years of living off my father, I found my pride and learned to stand on my own two feet. I did not need or want his help. I was determined that anything I would become, I would become myself. I have worked hard to do so, but now the California deal requires him to co-sign the loan for the new vines and equipment. It is not what I want, but the banks want his assurance because I have never done such a large deal before in America. So I must swallow my pride and ask, and so I am here. The fact I ask does not mean that I am the man I was three years ago. It does not make me less, just as you accepting help does not make you less."

A long speech, and one she wasn't sure she believed. The way Victoria told the tale was different, but then, there were two sides to any story. Thalia rode toward them, apparently finished cooling out Gladiator. Reggie pulled the ring gate open and horse and rider headed for the shed row that ran along the outside of the indoor riding ring. She let the gate close shut and turned to find Cesare still waiting, with his hands in his pockets.

"You aren't going to take no for an answer, are you?"

A shake of his dark head and a broad grin gave his answer.

"Then I guess I'll be gracious and say thank you. I could use a friend right now."

"*Bene!*" He swung in beside her as she followed Thalia into the barn, his arm casually falling over Reggie's shoulder.

The shed row formed a double line of facing stalls on the east side of the huge indoor riding ring. A broad concrete breezeway with rubber matting ran down between the stalls, the rubber matting effectively muting the clop of hoof falls as Thalia led Gladiator down the breezeway. High fluorescent lights hummed and buzzed above them. From the arena came the thickly accented instructions of Thalia's latest coach, Dietrich, as he coached another student. The gently moving air smelled of saddle leather, horse, and sweet alfalfa—a combination that would forever remind her of Thalia.

Outside Gladiator's stall, Thalia pulled off Gladiator's bridle and put on his halter, then put him in cross-ties that held the horse in place in the center of the breezeway. She stripped off her saddle and rubbed down his back with a dry cloth before giving his glossy coat a brush and turning him into his roomy, wood-sided stall. She found him a flake of alfalfa and fed him, then grabbed her saddle and headed for the tack room just as another rider and a short, bearded man in breeches and boots led another horse out of the arena.

"Dietrich! Hi!" Thalia said and glanced over her shoulder at Reggie and Cesare.

"You are back again? You realize that they do not pay you more for more hours?"

She laughed. "I just wanted to show Gladiator to my friend, Cesare."

Dietrich swung toward Reggie and Cesare. The riding coach was a new addition to Earl Farm. Before him, coaching was done by Thalia's friend Lori's mom. But having a European coach was a big deal apparently, so the stable had brought him in when Liz got hurt in a car accident. Not that Reggie could see any improvements in Thalia's riding, but Thalia thought so and that was what counted.

"Good evening, Dietrich. I'm Reggie Lewis" she said.

"Of course."

She could have sworn he almost clicked his heels and half bowed like some eastern dictator, but really it had to just be a slight condescending nod of the head in her direction. Most of the riders here had European Warmblood horses, but that level of horseflesh was far beyond her price point. He'd figured that out very soon after arriving here and so most of his attention was spent on the riders with more money to spend on his not inconsiderable side businesses of overseas horse agenting and importing German-made tack and custom riding equipment. Reggie missed Liz for her real world approach.

"This is Cesare. He's from Milan," she said.

"Milan, is it?" Dietrich turned to Cesare, gave a nod as if that was all that was needed, and turned back to Reggie. "Thalia has told you that coaching fees have increased? And we are discussing the horse boarding at the stable as well. Unless every horse is paying its way, we may have to look at asking the owners to move them."

In other words, the high tone of the stable could no longer afford a charity case like her daughter.

Feeling truly sick to her stomach, she dug deep and found the strength to nod. "I suppose that makes business sense. I'm sure Thalia will keep me posted."

Dietrich nodded. "There will be individual letters going home to the owners."

His gaze seemed to glint in the harsh fluorescents.

"Reggie, I believe Thalia is done brushing Gladiator. Perhaps we should go pay our respects to the great horse and then take our leave," Cesare said.

He caught her elbow and she let him ease her around and back to the horse. What the heck was she going to do? Her mind sparked and fizzled like steel in a forge, all the impurities showing. She couldn't afford to pay the full board fee, and if Thalia lost her place in the barn there was no close-by place that would pass the requirements in the lease agreement for Gladiator. Any stable farther away would be almost impossible for Thalia to get to after school, and who knew if any other barn would even agree to board in exchange for barn chores.

She felt dizzy and weak as she came even with Gladiator's stall. Thalia was inside having one of those private girl-horse conversations about what a fantastic, talented horse he was and how now that they had mastered medium trot, they really were almost ready for the next level up in shows.

"It will be fine, Reggie." Cesare's voice soft in her ear. "The world is not ending, like your face suggests."

"For you, maybe. To me, it feels like it." She looked up at him and instead of the sexy beast he usually exuded, she found compassion.

The arm she hadn't even noticed come around her shoulders when he guided her away from Dietrich tightened. "You will get through this. We will make sure of it, yes?"

As if they were partners, when the only true consistent partner she'd ever had was Thalia, who was dependent upon her to make the right decisions. Thalia and their Team of Two. She looked up at Cesare again. He'd offered to help.

But was there really room in her life for a—a 'friend'—like him?

Chapter 11

For Lila, the night was just a restless extension of the anxious evening before. At three in the morning, she gave up trying to sleep and paced the night-darkened house, considering her best course of action. She finally settled in the kitchen where she made herself a mug of warm milk with a dash of vanilla by the light of the fridge and the gas range flame. The darkness was better than the jarring overhead lights—at least the darkness was a more accurate reflection of just how she felt. She curled her legs up under her in the nook, sipping the warm milk, her head laid on the back of the bench chair so she could stare up at the night sky and the stars through the broad summer-kitchen windows.

When the sky began to gray, she tugged her apricot silk robe around her and went out through the shop, disarmed the alarm, and went out onto the porch to settle in her fan-backed peacock chair. Her knees pulled up to her chest, she rested her chin on them and stared moodily out at the lake.

The air was fresh this morning; it had rained lightly overnight. Not enough to douse current forest fires, but perhaps enough to deter new ones. She could hope.

She could hope a lot of things as she sat there in the predawn light trying to come to some conclusions when everything seemed to point in one direction.

Everything and everyone seemed to counsel the same thing: for the time being she had to cut Reggie loose. It was the smart thing to do to protect herself.

No Regulus jewelry in the shop and none on the website that Kylee had just set up.

No Reggie Lewis at their jewelry parties. No Reggie in her shop. Her lawyer, after discussing the fact that the plaintiff involved was a German jewelry company named *Lotus* that seemed to have very deep pockets, suggested she should padlock the workshop closed as further proof to the plaintiff that she had no intension of sanctioning the theft of jewelry designs or the making of such stolen goods.

One part of her wanted to tell them to go to hell. Another part was terrified of what they could do to her. She'd actually pulled an old padlock out of a junk drawer.

Could she do that to Reggie?

No way.

At least not under normal circumstances, but the damages figure quoted in the lawyer's letter would not only wipe out any savings she had from her mistaken foray into film stardom when she was a teenager, it would place a hefty mortgage on her grandparents' house. The house they had worked all their lives to pay off.

Bottom line, she just couldn't chance it.

Ding-ding went the little bell above the door to the shop and Victoria pushed out the door with a mug of what smelled like the strongest coffee in creation.

"*Buongiorno.*" She wore pale pink, wide-legged pajamas of brushed satin and had a pashmina scarf of cream with pink stripes that she pulled tighter around her shoulders as she sank into a chair and looked out onto the lake. "You could not sleep, I think. I heard you moving all night."

"I'm so sorry. I never thought... I didn't mean to keep you up. Please, accept my apologies."

"*Figurati*—it is nothing at all. I could not sleep either, so I spent the night thinking. This whole thing, it is *un disastro*—a disaster."

An apt description if ever there was one. Lila looked out over the lake as the sky bloomed pale lavender and apricot and the color reflected in the waves like a bruise. The breeze was cool this morning and laced a light ripple across the waves. Overhead a thin cloud picked up the first sun's rays like a carnelian curtain in the sky.

What was the saying? Red sky in the morning and sailor take warning. Another bad omen and yet she wasn't someone who even believed in omens. Still, she shivered and the scent of baby's breath and heliotrope from the hanging basket seemed oversweet and cloying.

"I think I must return to Milan," Victoria said, disturbing the silence.

There. Another bit of disaster—not Lila's, perhaps, but Reggie's for sure. She looked over at Victoria, but Victoria was avoiding her gaze.

"You're going to give up on Reggie so easily?"

Victoria swallowed and studied her feet—small, feminine, in cream-colored mules with two-inch wooden heels. "I know it is not a sign of faith that I go, but Erminio will need me. He will be—what is the word—in crisis? I must go home until this is over, then we will discuss whether Regulus designs can still provide our pieces for us."

Sighing, Lila nodded. "I see. We're all going to be like rats leaping from a sinking ship when we say we don't think Reggie has done anything wrong. What would we do if we did?"

A deep pink stain ran up Victoria's porcelain shoulders and neck.

"You shame me," she said.

Lila sighed again. "I shame myself. Reggie is a dear friend and has been for years, yet I find myself considering severing all ties with her until this blows over. It—it is evil, this consideration. So evil I couldn't sleep all night."

Turning to Victoria, she caught her hand. "You haven't known Reggie very long, but surely you can see her passion and her artistry. She's been designing for years and every year her material has gotten better. Our store has clients who collect her creations. There's no way she's done what they say she has."

And yet, she, Lila, who had known Reggie for years and knew these things, had, as her first reaction, doubted her friend. Perhaps it was not doubted, but she had circled the wagons and left Reggie to fend for herself.

Her mouth tasted of iron and the sourness of lack of sleep. She stood and let the wind blow through her. It smelled of smoke.

"I'm sorry. I've just realized I've been a very poor friend. Reggie has been here right from the beginning. She's been there for us every time there's been a problem, and yet the time she needs us, we abandon her. No longer."

"You think I should forget Erminio's needs?" Victoria said as she stood. The breeze blew her pink pajamas close to her body as the sun finally found its way over the mountains. Warm light found Victoria's lovely face.

"I think... Victoria, I don't know your life or your business or how much risk you can stand, but I do know my friend. I think you and Erminio could do a lot for her if you stood with her in her defense. You've seen her design process in action here. Surely Erminio did in Milan. Shouldn't that mean something in an Italian court?"

"I—I suppose it might."

"And I've been her friend. I have records of all the pieces she's sold here. If I have to, I'll phone each one of those women so we can show the progression of Reggie's talent. There's no way in heck any decent court can't find in her favor." She caught Victoria in a hug. "Thank you. Thank you so much. You've helped me clear my thoughts so I know what I have to do, even if it means I might lose this house. Grandma and Grandpa would understand—family comes first, and Reggie is family."

With a flourish she hurried back into the house, Victoria at her heels. She locked the door and headed back for the kitchen, poured herself a cup of Victoria's licorice-dark coffee, and headed upstairs to her office. She had five years of personalized receipts.

With that and her mailing list, she should be able to start calling as soon as her clients could reasonably be considered to be awake.

§

It was after ten in the morning when Cesare pulled up in front of the white house with red trim that held the jewelry store. He climbed out of the maroon Camry sedan to stretch and admire the view because regardless of the challenges Reggie Lewis had to deal with, they had ended the evening on a positive note. They'd even arranged to meet this afternoon once—hopefully—she had been served the legal documents intended for her. Her dark eyes had looked up at him trying so hard to hide her vulnerability as they stood in her small kitchen, the clumps and bumps of Thalia's movements in her bedroom upstairs echoing around the room. She had thanked him as he left and when he looked up at her framed in the light of doorway, she had actually smiled at him. Smiled.

He grinned at the memory. Things were going better with Signorina Lewis, whether she recognized it or not. The day had that clear light that he had always loved at Lake Como, the clouds like shredded sails overhead, unable to confine the deep blue sky, the wind lifting the water into small waves that slapped at the confines of the low wharves along the shore. It was, a little, like the way his chest felt this morning—like all that clear light shone right through him and warmed him up when he hadn't even realized he had been cold.

Odd, given the day was warm enough to coax families to the beach and their towels; playing children and sun-somnolent adult bodies littering the pebbles.

On the promenade a few spandex-clad runners went past, their athletic bras not quite up to the task of preventing some lovely female bouncing. He watched them down the street toward the curve of the lake and then turned back to the house. The breeze carried the scent of what North Americans considered good coffee from the little shop down the beach, with the undertone of lake water. Even with the sun warming the surface, this lake looked deep enough there would be cold waters below—just like Lake Como.

It was a good metaphor for his sister, too. Victoria looked all blousy blonde, but she was everything their father had ever wanted in a businessman son—cool, collected, and controlled. Unlike Cesare who chafed at the strictures of that life. Give him the great adventure. He wanted to build his fortune—not inherit it, and the building was the most important part. He would be happy with creating a place that simply paid for itself and allowed him to live. He'd learned over these past five years that all the minutia of wealth was not important.

The people around you, however, were.

Sucking in the butterflies he felt at trying to manage Victoria again, he headed for the house. The store was open, judging by the discrete little sign in the window by the front door. He pushed through the white picket gate and the cedar hedging and up the walk to the porch stairs. He wasn't going to go around the house today like a beggar. Today was a frontal assault because Victoria *was* going to listen to him.

He took the porch stairs two at a time and pushed into the shop, a little bell above the door announcing his entrance.

A light haze of oversweet incense filled the air from a brazier before a small bronze Buddha statue set in a wall alcove above the cash register. The incense stick trailed a sludge-gray line of smoke into the air. His nostrils curled as he took in the details of the room: glass counters with displays in the center of the room— one suspiciously empty. Glass cabinets on the wall filled with silver and stone earrings in an overwhelming number of shapes and sizes. Scarves on a display near an open window, their ends fluttering in the breeze.

Two women stood conversing at the counter, both unique, both lovely. One had a mane of brown hair that she unfortunately kept confined in a braid that reached past her waist. She wore an equally unfortunate loose, flowing top and bundle of silver necklaces that reminded him of the gypsy women that still travelled in caravans around Europe. The other woman was a small, sunny blonde who wore a bright floral dress that set off her huge blue eyes.

Both women looked at him, then at each other. Then, as if some agreement had been reached, the taller woman with the brown braid came around the counter.

"May I help you?" Her eyes were deep blue—almost violet—but the color seemed to shift in the sun.

"I need to speak to my sister."

Her gaze shifted to one of recognition. "Aah. You must be the infamous Cesare."

Her gaze raked him up and down.

"Faithful," she said, and frowned as if she was surprised at something.

"*Scusami*? What are you saying?"

"Don't you pay any attention to her," said the little blonde, coming up beside the dark-haired beauty. "She does that with everyone she meets—comes up with a word that defines who they are, though frankly I'm a little surprised. From what Victoria said, I'd have expected something more like 'scoundrel.' Right, Chloe?"

Chloe, coloring a nice pink, nodded. "My apologies. I believe Victoria is upstairs packing right now. With everything that's happened, I don't think she saw any value in staying. You're lucky you caught her because I think her plane's this afternoon."

So like Victoria, trying to slip away before their promised conversation.

"Which way?" he asked, trying to make it less a demand, though it was.

"How about we call her down for you?" the small blonde asked.

"No. No, thank you. Victoria has avoided this conversation long enough."

He stepped past them, heading for the beaded curtain that could only lead to the rest of the house.

"Excuse me! You can't go back there!" Chloe said.

He shrugged and spread his hands as he did exactly that.

The beaded curtain clacked behind him and he found himself in a darkened hallway with a collage of framed black-and-white family photos on the wall. Halfway down the hall there was a stairwell with scrolled wooden railing leading up to the second floor. He took the stairs two at a time and found himself in a light-filled, cream-walled hallway that must stretch the entire breadth of the house. To his right there were only closed doors, but what appeared to be light tunnels allowed in the ample Okanagan light, filling the hallway with a soft daylight glow. To his left there were two doors—both open.

He headed left. "Victoria?"

The first door gave onto an office where Lila sat on the floor, stacks of what looked like receipts spread around her.

"Cesare?"

She went to get up, but he was already past and to the other door.

Victoria faced him in a room of lavender and gray. Gray-white walls, lavender-toned quilt on the bed, a dark lavender chair under the window, and what looked like an old dresser of white. On the bed lay an open suitcase, fully packed except for a few items still on the bed.

He filled the doorframe. "So. It is true. You planned to leave without a word to me."

His chest felt tight enough it was hard to breathe. Harder still not to cross the room and grab her. The thing was, he wasn't sure what had him madder—that she would avoid their too-long delayed conversation, or that she would abandon Reggie at the first sign of trouble.

She looked up at him, her brown gaze troubled, so at least there was that—a little guilt that she had tried to sneak away.

"I was not avoiding you, if that's what you accuse me of. I simply had no purpose here anymore." She turned back to her suitcase and refolded a blouse before placing it into her suitcase.

"*Merda!*" He crossed the room to her and forced her to look at him. "I know we have to talk and that you avoid me, but you would leave now—when Reggie needs you?"

"*Sì.*" She glared up at him. "What do you think? That I should lie in the sun while waiting for this to blow over? For something to prove that she is not a fraud. Cesare, I am not heartless—I know that Reggie is talented. I have seen her work. But Erminio will need me. He will be in a panic, and this show of his could be my big break with my designs included in his work."

"So you've let him steal your designs again, have you? Don't be a fool, Victoria. Erminio hasn't had an original thought in years. It's you and your predecessors who provide the magic to the Erminio line. He can recognize talent and draws it around him. Then he takes the credit."

"*Vai all'inferno,* Cesare." Go to hell. She pulled away and grabbed the remaining items on the bed, tossed them in the suitcase, and tried to zip it closed. The zipper caught on cloth and she fought it.

"Stay, Victoria. Fight for your friend," he said, swallowing back his anger.

"Reggie Lewis is a business associate, not a friend." Her voice was tight, rigid, controlled—just like always.

"That's the thing, is it not, Victoria?" he said switching to Italian. "Both of us raised by a man who we so desperately wanted to please, but never could. We've cut ourselves off because no one can ever live up to our high standards. And when someone in power over us disappoints us, we accept it because that is all our father ever did to us."

He caught her shoulders and felt her stiffen. "Now is the time. Help Reggie. Help yourself."

She pulled loose and stepped back to look up at him. "This is not like you, all this concern for an almost stranger. I thought you came here to fight for your audience with father."

He stopped, suddenly struck by the fact that he had set that mission aside for the moment.

"I did, but more important was the fact that a woman and a friend has been wronged."

His sister's dark gaze searched his and suddenly her annoyance softened. "You mean this, don't you? You would miss your chance to help yourself to help Reggie Lewis. You like her."

A smile curved her lips so he had to look away. She caught his chin in her hand and met his gaze.

"Answer me, true. You like her, don't you?"

He shrugged, for he had helped a number of people on his long sojourn. He had not just opened a tavern and a restaurant. After an episode when he found his four roommates in Phuket had brought home a fourteen-year-old Hilltribe girl to share, he had used the profits from the tavern to support relief work in the Hilltribe refugee camps and had even helped fund a school for the girls. It still hadn't assuaged his guilt at all that he had had and squandered when so many were in need. But this was the first time his attempt to help someone had intersected with his family.

"I like many people. She is worthy of help."

"That is no answer at all. Now look me in the eyes."

She hauled his head up and around as if she was their old nanny. She forced him to look at her directly.

He shrugged. "She is a beautiful, unique woman. How could I not like her?"

Victoria threw her head back and hooted in a fashion most inconsistent with the image his sister always chose to present. This was more that of the teenaged girl who had taken the greatest pleasure in sabotaging his flings with the servants or the neighbor's daughters. Or wives.

"What of it, if I like her? She is an adult. I am an adult."

"You, my dear brother," she poked him in the chest, "are the rolling stone that gathers no moss—is that not the saying? You run away from every responsibility and yet you take this woman's cause. This is more than a simple 'like'."

He was tempted to tell her about his other acts of kindness, but this was not about him. It *was* about Reggie. He switched back to English.

"If it is, time will tell. In the meantime this thing ruins a woman's life, and she has a daughter to support. If you are bound and determined to go—which is very bad of you, I think—then I will ask you to make Reggie's case with Erminio. Convince him that she is the talent, not this pretender whoever he is, who has hidden behind the name of a law firm. In the meantime I will work with Reggie to document her ownership as best we can."

"That—that is a very kind thing."

Cesare and Victoria both turned in surprise. Lila stood in the pool of sunshine at the bedroom doorway.

"It is nothing. I have a law degree. It is only logical that I mount Reggie's defense."

Victoria snorted. "It is only logical if you are infatuated by her. What does she think, I wonder?"

Last night had been a breakthrough, a gift, though he had done nothing with it other than be her friend. But Reggie Lewis was not the type of woman who would throw herself at anyone. No, if anything was to grow and blossom between them, it would need to be built on a firm base, like building business on sound research, or a winery on good soil. But when had he ever thought about building anything with a woman beyond a night or two?

Chapter 12

It was done. Or undone, as the case may be. Every. Frigging. Good thing in her life was coming unraveled. In the late afternoon, Reggie sat at her maple kitchen table just as she'd sat there since this morning, a doodle pad—unused—on the table in front of her. From upstairs came the sounds of Thalia in her room. Sunlight filled the window over the kitchen sink and filled her driveway outside. A hummingbird with a ruby breast and iridescent green cheeks came zooming in to the feeder she had hung by the kitchen window. The little birds actually seemed to prefer the fuchsia she had hung by the kitchen door and the butterfly bush she had growing out front, but there were still a few who preferred the ease of the feeder.

Thalia's breakfast dishes still sat on the counter because Reggie hadn't had the energy to wash them, though lunchtime had come and gone long ago. She hadn't had the energy to eat anything either, but her stomach had finally given up on grumbling and had contented itself with the cold coffee she sipped from a mug that she had poured that morning and promptly forgotten. Bitter taste for a bitter woman?

That was about right.

She had sent Thalia off to the barn in the morning, praying that she wouldn't come home with that dreaded letter from Dietrich— but Thalia had. Reggie hadn't had the courage that morning to tell her daughter about the fact that their world was coming apart, and once she'd phoned the store to see about coming down to the shop and had found out that Victoria was leaving—well, that just put the icing on the cake and kept her mostly immobile in her seat at the kitchen table. When she came home from a day at the barn, Thalia, thankfully, had been so full of excitement over how well Gladiator was doing at medium trot that she hadn't even noticed the unwashed dishes. She was used to her mother busy sketching at the table in the early throes of creation.

And just what creation would that be, Reggie?

She had no shop, no supplies that she could access, and no designs she could even work on to keep herself busy. She shoved the unused sketch pad away to the far side of the table.

Sure, she had the old, used sketch/doodle pads here at the house. They *were* better than nothing to support her case, but they didn't mean squat in the face of her files if the files were produced against her. And pinning her hopes on a man like Cesare Angelucci—well, that was just plain stupid. He wasn't the kind of guy who helped other people—at least not according to Victoria.

Which all meant that her dreams last night were mostly correct.

She stood high on the mountains above Okanagan Lake, the rocky buttresses of the mountains falling away from her in rolling tapestries of dark ponderosa pine with folds of light green poplar where water ran. Far below stretched the long finger of the lake, crooked northeast and southeast from its pivot point at Peachland. But the lake was different this time, the water draining away southward, the air tinder dry and smelling of sage, pine, and smoke, and yet there was no fire that she could see. The air shimmered with heat under an unrelenting robin's egg blue sky and the hard eye of the sun.

Where the water receded, the lakebed was black, black reeds, dead trees, garbage, and the water fell farther, boiling with fish seeking water, and still the liquid drained away until the deep trench of the lake lay empty except for the dying fish and something huge and black, long neck writhing. Ogopogo, perhaps.

But that water was gone and the draining of life-giving water continued, the trickling brooks in the mountains were sucked dry, the poplar leaves curling gray and falling as if autumn had come in a day. The pine forest around her reeked of pine pitch, and the smoke scent became worse. Pine needles turned red and the air buzzed with cicada sound as the needles began to fall to leave desolation all around. The humming stopped. The birds were gone. The parching sun shone down and she was so thirsty, dying for water, but there was none here.

The roar of fire came from behind her like a locomotive. The wind blew thick smoke that teared her eyes.

She shuddered at the memory. She didn't need a psychiatrist to figure out the symbolism. Everything good was draining away from her and dying and the fire was coming for her, too. Whether in dreams or reality, she was screwed. Her hand went to the bracelet at her wrist and she fingered the little doors, finally caressing the one with the square lintels like some old-fashioned formal doorway.

"So if you could open, what would you let me into? Would you let me escape?"

Thalia poked her head in the doorway. "Escape?"

Reggie started. "I didn't hear you come downstairs."

Thalia plunked down at the table. "So what's for dinner, cause I was thinking that marsala stuff Cesare made last night was pretty good."

"There's leftovers in the fridge," Reggie said and heaved herself up to standing. A good thing there were leftovers, because the thought of cooking dinner about turned her stomach.

On automatic, she pulled the leftover containers from the fridge and a single plate. Began to spoon out a large portion for Thalia, who came up beside her.

"Who are you trying to feed? An army? That's way too much for me."

"It is?" God, her head felt so muzzy and her knees so weak. She looked down at the white plate. A platter of noodles that could feed both her and Thalia. Both slices of veal. She'd been just about to pour all the remaining sauce over the top.

"That does look like a lot, doesn't it?" she said and carefully put one of the meat slices back in the container with some of the leftover sauce.

"Less noodles, too."

"But you're a growing girl and you've worked hard today." She tried to find a smile.

"Where's your plate?" Thalia asked, sliding her arm around Reggie's waist.

Her plate? Eat, when just the scent of food left her feeling queasy? Or ravenous. She wasn't sure which.

"Mom? What's the matter? You're acting really strange."

Strange enough that Thalia noticed—not a good thing. Shaking her head, she tried to pull some shred of normalcy around her. Smiled and ran her palm over Thalia' mop of blonde hair.

"What's this? I thought I had a few years to go before we had our role reversal. I'm just fine, honey. I just have a lot on my mind. I think the Milan thing may have fallen through."

Thalia's blue eyes widened. "Mom! No! That Victoria lady seemed really nice. Everything was going so good."

"Yeah. It was." She shoved the plate of veal and noodles in the microwave while she stirred a small pot of the marsala sauce to warm it. Then she poured the sauce over the noodles and carried it to the table. Thalia had already set their places.

Tucking into her food as only a growing kid can, Thalia looked up at her. "So what happened?"

Here was her chance to tell her daughter everything and help her understand just what it was going to mean to them. But was it fair to burden a ten-year-old with the details of adult problems? Decidedly not. On the other hand, Thalia had a right to know what was happening with Gladiator.

Her stomach souring at the realization that this was the hard part of having a child grow up—you couldn't protect them from everything—but she was going to try. The greatest joy in her daughter's life was that darn horse. She was not going to fail there, too. Maybe she could convince the owner to let them stable the horse at another place. Or at home. And maybe Earl's would at least let her ride at the stable in exchange for the chores. That could work, if the owner would accept it. She could build a nice cozy little barn and paddock here—or convert her old shop into a barn. But then she couldn't do that, could she, because she needed to start doing her work here once she got her equipment home.

So much to do she didn't know where to start.

She looked up and met Thalia's expectant gaze.

"I asked you a question, Mom. What happened that Milan cancelled?"

Masking her emotions, she picked up the fork Thalia had set for her and stabbed at Thalia's heap of fettuccini noodles, twirled the fork and popped them into her mouth. Unlike the night before, they tasted like sawdust. She chewed.

"Well, a question came up about my designs. They haven't said anything yet, but I think they're going to pull out of the deal."

Thalia nodded and kept forking food in like the growing kid she was. If the kid wasn't careful, she was going to surprise herself and finish off this pile of food.

"So they haven't actually said they were cancelling? That's a good thing, right? Maybe they won't." Thalia cut another piece of veal and popped it into her mouth. Nodded.

"Maybe. It would be great if they didn't." Reggie looked at the fork in her hand and set it down. The one mouthful she'd eaten felt like a lump in her gut. "Listen, I'm going to be doing my work out in the shop here again. Do you think you could give Gladiator a day off tomorrow and maybe give me a hand with fixing the place up? It would mean taking a run down to Lila's to get my equipment and helping me set up here at home."

As she spoke a frown formed furrows on Thalia's smooth forehead. "But you always said that Lila's shop is way better than what you've got here. That the shop here is too small."

The shop on her property *was* small, but... "Let's just say that having my shop here gives me more control and it means that I can work whenever the inspiration strikes me instead of having to wait for a reasonable hour to go down to Lila's."

"But you said that moving your shop to Lila's was the best business decision you'd made. And your shop there gives you way more room. You didn't even have the second kiln when you had your shop here. Where are you going to put everything?"

Dammit, why was this so difficult?

"I'll get an extra table, okay? Things will work."

"But, Mom—"

"Things will work," Reggie cut the conversation off. "Now, can you come home from the barn after your chores to give me a hand, or not?"

The fork in Thalia'shand clunked against the side of the plate as she abandoned it and pushed back her chair. Her gaze flickered over Reggie's face and Reggie felt the need to look away from her daughter's wounded look and accusation.

"I'm sorry, all right? I'm just a little tense right now. This thing with Milan has got me upset and I just need time to figure things out. I need you to help out right now and not make things difficult."

Thalia was as watchful as a judge in a juried jewelry show. She swallowed and her fine, long-fingered hands caught the edge of the table, her knuckles turning white.

"This is about money, isn't it? Because of Gladiator's board. I heard about what Dietrich's doing from Lori. I guess there were a lot of people at the barn who had special deals. I just didn't think it included me, because I work for them." She nodded at the folded letter on the table with the Earl Stable crest of a dressage horse silhouette doing a piaffe, the ultimate collected trot where the horse trotted in place. "That's what the letter said, isn't it?"

Feeling a total failure as a mother because her child had partially figured out the issue, Reggie nodded and sighed. Apparently she couldn't protect her child forever, but perhaps she could focus Thalia on the board issue, because if Thalia hadn't figured out that they were in bigger financial trouble, she would soon enough. She was way too smart not to.

But if she thought that Reggie was moving the shop home to save money for the board, well, then she might not look further...

"I didn't think Aunt Lila made you pay rent for the shop at the store."

"She doesn't. It's just the time. And the gas money."

There were just too many calculations in Thalia's eyes, and clearly things weren't adding up. "Doesn't Aunt Lila want you there? Is she mad at you?"

Oh, God, she just could not do this because just starting to talk about it brought all the pain to the surface. Reggie stood up and went to the counter, replaced lids on leftover containers and placed them in the fridge.

"Of course she's not mad. We just made a mutual decision that for the next little while we should be less connected."

Pasting a smile on her face, she turned around and braced herself on the counter. "Now, are you done with your dinner? Because if so, then maybe you can give me a hand cleaning the cobwebs out of the shop for a start? Okay?"

Thalia was, and together they got her dishes washed and the kitchen cleaned up. Together they stepped out of the kitchen into the lovely cool of the summer evening, with the last glow of sunlight streaming through the trees illuminating the butterflies and bees still buzzing around the purple spikes of the butterfly bush. The soft, almost baby-powder scent sweetened the air and their footsteps kicked up dust as they went to the shop.

It was a low, weathered, log structure with a peaked roof, a door, and two small windows that had once functioned as a shop for the property's previous owner's small appliance repair business. But the building's age-darkened wood said the place was older than that and Reggie had theorized that once upon a time the building had been the lone house on the property.

She unlocked the padlocked door and it swung open on its own, the building having long settled so the floor and walls were uneven. Inside lay only darkness and the musky scent of mouse droppings and dust. Thalia curled her nose as Reggie reached in through cobwebs and flicked the lights on.

A line of four incandescent lightbulbs bloomed on the ceiling, filling the single room with bright yellow-white light that still couldn't fully dispel the shadows from the room's corners.

Cobwebs was right. In the four years since she'd moved her shop down to Lila's, neither she nor Thalia had had any occasion to come in here. Now long streamers of dust-covered cobwebs hung from the dark ceiling and caught in the rough finish of the log walls. More cobwebs shifted in the breeze from the door as if the little building breathed around them.

"That's kinda gross," Thalia said as Reggie reached in and swiped away cobwebs from the doorway. It placed a gray film over her hand and forearm.

"I guess a broom would be better for this." Reggie agreed as she tried in vain to get the sticky strands off of her skin. She went back to the house to get one and returned with the broom and a mop and a bucket filled with pine-scented water. Might as well get as much done as possible.

Venturing in with the broom as her weapon, she swept out the cobwebs on the ceiling, leaving Thalia to follow with a sponge to wash off the counters. The first circuit around the room took them an hour and left the little building damp and, frankly, a little muddy but smelling of pine forests. Reggie dumped the grimy water and refilled it from the hose, then went back inside to mop the floor. She'd just finished and was outside the workshop smoothing cobwebs off her hair when a certain maroon sedan came crunching up her driveway to stop behind the truck.

Cesare. And her looking like some self-pitying fool—with cobwebs in her hair, no less, and mud on her tennis shoes. She squared her shoulders.

When he climbed out, she waited for him and wasn't sure why she did. Attractive? Dangerously so. Was she attracted to him? Undoubtedly, yes. Would she do anything about it? Absolutely, no. Sure, he might not be quite the lady-killer, bad-boy that she'd originally assessed him as, but he was Victoria's brother— Victoria, who immediately abandoned ship and ran when all this came down.

Still, a friendly adult face was a sight for sore eyes.

He wore tan linen trousers and a loose-fitting navy shirt of a flowing fabric that nicely showed off his hard torso. Very nice, indeed. Sauntering up to her, he moved with the slim-hipped swagger of a young James Bond, carrying a bottle of wine in one hand and a leather portfolio in the other.

"Hey," he said, stopping too close to her so she had to look up at him. He eyed the open building behind her, but then looked back to her. "What's going on?"

"Just opening up my new-old workshop. I've decided to bring my equipment home. Can't let the little setbacks stop me, now can I?" Forcing a grin she turned back to Thalia. "Thanks sweetie. That's saved me a lot of time. Tomorrow I can get busy bringing equipment home. Just pull the door to and shut the lock, would you, please?"

"*Ciao*, Thalia. How was Gladiator today?"

"Terrific! Everyone was impressed. I was telling everyone about you."

Cesare shook his head. "You be careful, little one. Your coach will hate you if you talk always of someone else who brought your horse along."

As if that hadn't already happened.Dietrich didn't have to do much more to ruin it for the kid. She led him up to the house and into the kitchen. Turning back to him, she looked pointedly at the bottle of wine. "What's this?"

"This little thing?" He held up the bottle of red wine as if it was something small, furry, and friendly that had crawled into his hand. "Would you believe that I saw it and thought of you, so I had to bring it over?"

"Uh-huh," she said, hands on her hips. "And just what about a bottle of wine reminds you of me?"

He set the bottle on the white tile counter and stood back as if inspecting a piece of art.

"Well... it has curves, as you do." He looked up at her and winked as she rolled her eyes.

"It is dark and mysterious. What lies at the heart of this woman?"

He turned the front of the bottle toward them. A small, square door was etched on the label and Reggie forgot to inhale. What the heck? She picked up the bottle to inspect the picture more closely. It just couldn't be. She twisted the silver bracelet around on her wrist to expose the door with the lintels. Holy heck—line and angle, they were the same.

§

She looked—*intontito*—dazed. In the warm light of the kitchen, Reggie Lewis's face had paled, her dark eyes gone huge and wide as they looked from the bracelet on her wrist to the bottle of wine that he had brought. It was not just any wine—it was a bottle of the reserve wine all the way from Milan, from the Angelucci winery, to be exact. He had called his old friend Aldo, the vintner who he had worked with, and had had a bottle couriered to Peachland two days ago. Why he had done so, he still could not quite determine, but it had felt right.

At the moment, however, he was not so sure.

Reggie looked like a cornered animal as she stood in her kitchen. By the newly scrubbed counters and the scent of marsala, it looked like they had just had a meal. The scent told him what they had eaten. Pity they had not eaten at a more Italian dinner hour.

"I thought the wine might go well with the leftover veal marsala." He shrugged. "No problem. It is very good by itself as well. I—I found it and thought you might enjoy it, so I bring it over with me tonight."

Thalia clumped up into the house behind them, took in the scene, and frowned as she used the bootjack on her boots. "Everything okay, Mom?"

"Everything's fine, honey. Mr. Angelucci was just showing me the wine he brought." But her voice had a tremor in it that said for her more was going on.

He felt the hard clarity of Thalia's young gaze. She might be not much more than a child, but it was very clear that these two were protective of each other.

"Reggie, I did not just bring a wine bottle to show you, I brought over documents that might help you. I thought we should discuss your case."

"Case?" Thalia asked. "Mom, what's going on?"

Thalia crossed to her mother, but Reggie would not meet her gaze.

"Mom? Come on! Team of Two, remember? That's how we do things."

Reggie's shoulders slumped and she pulled Thalia into a hug. "You are such a great kid, but there are some things I don't want to put on you. This is stuff for adults, Thalia. Just this once would you let me deal with it?"

Thalia pulled back and looked up at her mother. "Nu-uh. Not when you look so worried. Don't you always say that talking about a problem is halfway to solving it?"

Reggie nodded, but clearly wanted to keep the darkest parts of her situation from her daughter.

"Thalia, how about I talk things out with your mother. Perhaps after she has her thoughts straightened, she will feel better about sharing it with you."

For a moment, Thalia's face tightened with resentment, but then she sighed. "Let me guess. Adult stuff. Right. Fine, then. I'll be upstairs in my room reading—if you want me."

As if going to the guillotine, she stumped out of the room, her sock feet somehow able to make as much noise to show her displeasure as her set of boots might have.

The fine skin of Reggie's face seemed to have aged as she turned back to Cesare.

She shook her head. "I shouldn't have done that. I'm all she's got, just as she's all I have. We've always gotten through things together—but this just seems too big and too disastrous for someone her age."

"She will get over it. Children do."

She shook her head, her Cleopatra hair swinging around her shoulders. "That's the thing. She's not exactly a child anymore. Come to think of it, I don't know if she ever was. It's been more like she's been an adult-in-training ever since she was little. We talk about pretty much everything. I figure if I'm open with her, she'll be open with me."

"But this time is different, somehow?" He caught Reggie's arm and eased her into a chair at the table.

"I guess."Reggie shoved her hair back behind her ears. "Yeah, I guess it really is because for all the challenges we've had before, we've never been this deep in trouble."

He mimed opening the bottle and Reggie pointed at a drawer. He pulled it open and found the corkscrew, pulled open the bottle of wine, and found two wine glasses in the cupboard where he'd seen them when he'd made dinner, then settled at the table with her. Poured.

"You two have been on your own for a very long time."

"Since Thalia was born. Her father died before I ever had the chance to tell him I was pregnant."

"You were married, then. Very sad."

She sampled her wine and smiled. "Very nice. Like cherries and smoke, with a peppery finish. And no. We weren't married. It was still very sad, though. We loved each other very much, or thought we did. Thalia has his coloring and his sunny temperament. I see him whenever I look at her."

A soft flush seemed to run through her skin and she finally raised her gaze to his. "So what is it you've brought me that was important enough to come see me this evening when you could be relaxing with friends?"

She reached for the leather folder and he blocked her hand. "All in good time. First let us enjoy the wine. You know how to taste it; now is the time to savor." Just like he could savor her, even with cobwebs in her hair. She was strong and passionate—at least she was about her jewelry and her daughter—perhaps she would be in other ways, too.

And that was the kind of thinking his sister thought him solely capable of. It was how Reggie thought of him as well, and he was determined to disprove it. Reggie, with all she was going through, was not a woman to be toyed with.

"So. Something else has happened, I think. Beyond the legal suit from Italy."

Her gaze went dark and distant, but he held on tight and would not let her go. Finally she shook her head.

"Money problems. Nothing you need to understand."

"Tell me. It is not need. I want to understand." And, *Madre di Dio,* perhaps he lied. Perhaps he did *need* to understand. When he looked at her so dejected, it filled him with emotion. His hand tightened around the wine glass. That someone would hurt Reggie this way... he would stop it!

Sighing, she took another sip of the wine. Another, and closed her eyes perhaps to savor, perhaps to avoid his gaze.

"It's like this. Thalia has only been able to keep Gladiator at the stable because she works there and works off seventy-five percent of her board. I pay the other twenty-five percent—that'sthe equivalent of his feed—and more for her weekly lessons. At least that was the deal with the Earls, who own the place. I think the arrangement was partially possible because Lori, the Earls' daughter, is Thalia's good friend. But now, with Liz just recovering from a car accident and Dietrich here, the Earls have handed management of the barn over to him. I got this today." She slid the letter over to him and gave him a rueful smile. "Letting you read my mail is getting to be a habit."

"It has not hurt you yet." He unfolded the letter and read, while he sipped the wine. It really was the most glorious of wines, full-bodied, but not overblown. No, this one had a nose of sweetness, the flavors Reggie had mentioned, overlaid with the sweet flavor of sunlight with the very faintest hints of the iron of the good Italian soil underneath.

"This Dietrich—he has singled your daughter out?"

"No. You heard him last night. I think the Earls had a number of side deals with people in the area. Horse board is expensive. Some people would trade for their board. The barter system. You know."

He nodded. "It was how things were done in Southeast Asia. I would trade labor with others to get my tavern built. In the camps it was the only way."

"The camps?"

Merda, he had not intended to mention them. They were the past, though his tavern still raised money for the school he had built there.

Another sip of the wine, then he looked at her. "I volunteered at a hilltribe refugee camp in Thailand. Those poor people were driven out of Myanmar by war with the government. They were persecuted in their country. Aside from direct warfare, there were rumors that the Myanmar government had gone so far as to use HIV infected medical equipment on the people in hilltribe communities." He shook his head, not wanting to talk about it further, because the inactivity of the west and the lack of media attention on such tragedies filled him with ire.

He met her gaze over the edge of her wine glass.

"It was a long time ago, but I still think of the people I met. I wonder how they are doing. If they have been successful in trying to immigrate to countries like this one."

She looked like she was considering. Then she nodded. "You surprise me, Cesare Angelucci. The man your sister described would not volunteer for anything. And yet you're here."

"And I volunteer to help again. This Earl Stable, it is the only place for Thalia and her horse?"

"The only place close enough and the only place we could afford. Gladiator is only on lease, too, and that means we have to keep him at an approved barn. What with the mortgage on this place and having to set up my shop here and the decrease in income I'm going to face, I wasn't sure we could afford it even with Thalia working there—but this."

She held up her hands and her eyes began to fill, until she averted her gaze and she swiped the tears away. This one—she did not like to be vulnerable.

"I'm sorry, I'm not usually like this, but that horse is everything to Thalia. You saw. She'd do anything for that horse, and I have to do the same."

He caught one of her narrow hands and squeezed. "You are allowed to feel emotion, Reggie. Anger. Frustration. They are normal. They are all too familiar to me. The question is how we use them."

Eyes searching his, her hand shifted in his. Held on.

"So what do you think I should do? Tell Thalia she's losing her horse—or might be? I thought of going to see Liz Earl, the stable owner, but then I thought about how that would affect Thalia's coaching relationship with Dietrich. He hasn't been here in Canada that long. He came to Earl's to open his own business and it was an answer to Liz's prayers because her physical situation wasn't letting her be as active in the horse business anymore. I thought of talking to Dietrich, but, well... I just didn't think it would help anything. For a man who has almost entirely female clients, he doesn't seem to like women very much—except for their checkbooks." She shook her head. "Sorry. That was sort of sour grapes on my part. The man has a business that he's trying to run. It just all seems so hopeless." She looked up at him, her expression apologetic. "I'm sorry. I think you've caught me wallowing in self-pity."

He arched a brow at her. "Then perhaps now is the time to show you what else I have brought you."

Chapter 13

Cesare pulled a sheaf of papers out of the leather folder and slid them to her, face side down. The smoke taste of the wine warmed her mouth and seemed to flood down her throat and out to her limbs so that she felt half-drunk even though she'd only drunk half a glass of wine. But it was good, very good, just like—against everything she'd expected—the man across from her was good also. More than good. With his tumble of black curls and his tiger eyes, his dark good looks could almost overwhelm her good sense; but instead of hitting on her, he sat there waiting just like he had the past few times she'd met him. One hand sat empty on the table, the other held his wine glass as, through the open kitchen window, the faintest light of sunset caught his profile. Of course, the fact he was here at all said that he was interested and she was okay with that.

Odd. Usually, if anyone showed interest, she got nervous and made sure there was no opportunity for them to be together.

She looked down at the sheaf of papers on the maple table, the scent of Thalia's marsala supper still lingering in the kitchen. She flipped the stack of papers over.

A letter on the top was addressed to Lila Weber and signed by someone named Sophie Vinge. She didn't recognize the name, so she scanned the letter.

This is to confirm that on or about August 8, 2010 I purchased a necklace and earrings from

This and That jewelry store. The necklace and
earrings were sold to me as original Regulus
designs and were signed by the artist.

What the hell?

Clipped to the letter was a photograph of a necklace and earrings that Reggie vaguely remembered making back in the early days. The necklace was made of a series of waves that had represented the mysterious wave action seen on Okanagan Lake that was attributed to the mythological lake monster, Ogopogo— alleged kin of the Loch Ness monster. Hidden amid the silver wave-shaped links was a single 8 mm black pearl to represent that which disturbed the lake. The earrings had a single, wave-shaped V with tiny black seed pearls at the nexus of the V. Now she remembered it all as if it was yesterday. All of the information she had squirreled away—except these came from before she started her filing system.

She looked up at Cesare, then back at the stack of papers. Turned over the next letter and it was of a similar nature. Attached was an image of a pendant she had made and sold through *This and That*, this one a sterling silver cornucopia filled with tiny clusters of garnets, amber, carnelian, and moonstones representing the cherries, apricots, peaches and apples the Okanagan was so famous for. The piece was a tad more colorful and more lifelike than the more abstract work she preferred now, but still lovely. Still hers.

"I don't understand," she said, flipping through the stack of letters and attached images. There were at least ten letters there. All with photos. All pieces she had made. All showing the Regulus design look.

"Do you not?" Cesare placed his splayed hand across the letters. "You are not alone, *cara*. There are many people who know and admire your work. Some even collect it. But the greatest friend you have is Lila. She has spent the day combing store records, contacting the purchasers, and asking them to send letters and images of the pieces they purchased. This is just those who got back to her today."

Her head felt thick and muzzy and she knew she was being stupid not grasping what he was saying, but all she could think of was: "Lila?"

"She is still at work in her offices or she would have come with me. You are not alone in this, Reggie, though you may feel you are. Events have not conspired to leave you abandoned. Lila is helping, regardless of the legalities. Your friend Chloe, as well— she reviews her records to try to recall the provenance of all the stones." He caught her hands. "I am here, too. I saw your passion for your work. Your passion for your daughter. You are not the type to steal designs and claim them for your own. No, this is a grave miscarriage of justice, and I will see it undone."

They were helping her? Cesare? Lila and Chloe were still with her? But...

"I don't see how this helps. Sure, I might be able to show that I made these things, but that doesn't prove that I didn't steal the most valuable—all the designs meant for Erminio's line—other recent pieces." She scrubbed at her face. "I don't even know what they're claiming because I haven't received anything from them yet."

Cesare reached over and tapped the side of her head. "You miss the point, cara. This is intellectual property and it was from your brain these pieces flowed. All we must prove is that you reasonably came up with the designs yourself. Your inspiration. Your stones. Your design arising from what inspired you and what you had to work with, *capisci?* We show them how your work has progressed. There is a certain something about your work from what I see in those photos. Something *certo*—unmistakable. If I can see it, so will any judge or jury."

It was too much. All this confidence in her. Yes, she knew that the work was hers, but as with all artists, her work was influenced by the work of others. Sitting here like this, his trust in her weighed like a million pounds on her shoulders. She shoved up from the tableand went to the sink, poured herself a glass of water because her head was swimming, her body too hot.

"Lila's risking too much. That house is everything to her."

She turned to find Cesare right behind her—too close. Too tall, too careful not to touch her, and yet his gaze said he wanted to.

"I'm not used to people helping me," she said, feeling suddenly nervous. Her fingers worked the bracelet—until Cesare stopped her. He lifted her wrist to study the links.

"All this misfortune. Did you ever think that perhaps these difficulties stem from this? Jas Stone and Danny Forester seem to think it has almost brought disaster on each of its wearers. This could be yours."

He spoke softly, as if he was afraid to startle her—didn't he realize she was made of sterner stuff?

"Each of their disasters stemmed from a man they had newly met." She met his tiger-eyed gaze and dared him. If he was the source of this misfortune, then she could—would—face it. Even if she suddenly felt smaller than she ever had.

Gently he turned her wrist over and again tried the clasp, but the small, ornate key refused to go through the keyhole that would unlock the band. He shrugged and met her gaze. "I had to try. Jas said that for one of you the bracelet just came undone."

His gaze still held hers and it felt like all the air had left the room. "It was the man they were supposed to be with who opened the bracelet—when both parties realized they were meant to be a couple."

"And I suppose it took time for them to come to that conclusion."

Cesare seemed to loom closer and she couldn't move. Didn't want to move because this man obviously wanted her and it had been a very long time since someone wanted her around just for her—not because she was a mother, not because she was Reggie Lewis of Regulus designs.

She went up on her toes and kissed him on the corner of that roguish mouth. Hard-soft lips that quirked in a smile under hers. Somehow the guy had managed to turn his face to catch the kiss full on. His hands slipped up her arms to her shoulders to steady her, and then he pulled back, pulled her into his chest, and rested a cheek against her hair.

"I'm sorry. I shouldn't have done that," she whispered into the silence.

She heard the low rumble of his chuckle through his chest.

"I wanted to do that from the first day I saw you, the mysterious Reggie Lewis." His hand sleeked down her skull. "Why is that, do you suppose? Is there something to this bracelet that draws the right man to it?"

She pulled back enough to look up at him, trying to be saucy. "You're the right man, now? Not just a convenient set of strong arms?"

He tipped her head back and took her mouth. Hard, deep, and passionate, then pulled back again so she remembered to breathe.

"So? You tell me?" His brow cocked in a question.

Holy mother of God, the man could kiss. Every part of her tingled, every hair on her body was on high alert, and she was pretty sure her knees would have given out if he hadn't been holding her up. Just momentary lust or something more? At this particular moment, she didn't care.

"I think I need another kiss to make up my mind."

"*Con piacere, cara.*" With pleasure.

His long fingers ran through her hair and turned her face to him. His lips found her eyes, her forehead, and slid down her left temple to the lobe of her ear. Kissed her there and then trailed along her jaw to her mouth again. Tender kisses that turned harder and left her breathless and wanting. Her hands slid up his body and around his neck to hold on. God, she needed to hold on, because at the moment he was the most solid thing in a world where everything was shifting sand.

When he lifted his head from hers, the hard glint of his tiger eyes had gone soft. He shook his head as if he could not believe something.

"What?" she asked. "What is it?"

"Strangeness. That is all I can say. There is something about you that speaks of destiny. A foolish thought, I know, but it is something my heart knows. We were meant to meet, *cara.* You and your silly bracelet. We were meant to come together—why else would I have come to Peachland to meet you?"

"Um... maybe to try to talk your sister into something?"

He shook his head and released her to refill and retrieve their wineglasses. "But is it not an odd chance that has brought us together at this exact time, when I am ready to help and you have need of assistance?"

Clinking glasses, he looked down at her with a gaze that had gone darker and considering. "It is as if events conspire to move us around."

Holding her bracelet-bound wrist up again, he considered. "It is strange enough that the Angelucci winery doorway is miniaturized in this."

He slid the links around until the little door with the lintels faced him.

"But stranger still is the fact that as a boy, I heard old legends from my nanny. She was a gifted storyteller, and one of the stories she told was of—what is the word? Lovers like Romeo and Juliet?"

She thought a moment. "Star-crossed?"

He nodded. "That is the term. Star-crossed lovers with a talisman that was the sign of their love—a bracelet it was. The story is a sad one. It tells that the woman was so beautiful that she was stolen away." His regard slipped from the bracelet to her. "As beautiful as you, perhaps."

His fingers toyed with strands of her hair until he must have seen her discomfort. He released her, stepped away, and checked his watch. Outside the kitchen window, the sky was dark.

"I think it is time for me to go and you to sleep. I can let myself out."

He softly brushed her mouth with a kiss and let himself out, while she tried to regain herself.

No! She wasn't going to let him just slip away like that. Not after all the support and kindness he'd shown her and Thalia, even if he hadn't fixed her problems.

She sprang for the door and out into the still-warm breeze of an Okanagan night: shifting air, the damp feel of irrigation on her skin, the scent of poplar, ponderosa pine, and heated summer hay. Moths battered themselves against the porchlight as the door slammed behind her and she leapt, barefoot, down to the gravel.

"Cesare? Wait!"

It was stupid and impetuous and utterly ridiculous to do this when she had so many problems. Wouldn't a man in her life just bring more complications—especially a man from Italy?

All those reservations she set aside when he turned to meet her as she ignored the sharp gravel and threw her arms around him in the welcoming warmth of the darkness.

§

To Victoria Angelucci, returning to Milan was usually like sinking down into the comfort of an ancient Roman bath. The cool breezes off the mountains, the energetic hum of the sprawling city so like her life blood, the rumble of traffic that beat with the rhythm of her heart. She loved Milan—loved the whole feel of Italy's second city with its many graceful cathedrals and the quaint, curbside restaurants and cafes that decorated the *piazza* and small side streets of its nine *zonas*. Which made it strange that today the city filled her with trepidation.

Usually she loved the sense of discovery as new places bloomed in the dark cracks of the old part of the city, and what had once been old warehouses became the new spot for nightclubs and trendy new clothing designers. Today it just made the city untrustworthy, which was a foolish thought if ever there was one. This was *her* Milan. She loved the many small clothing shops with their so-hopeful young designers.

Once she had planned such an opening for herself—something small, herself a sole proprietor who would design her clothing and make her beautiful creations to measure for the wealthy fashionista who discovered her boutique. But then her father had introduced her to an established designer he was sponsoring—Erminio. That had been fifteen years ago, and as the years had passed her designs had been set aside and she had become his right hand. Her need for that small shop that was wholly her own and filled with her own creations had passed. Or almost.

Spending time with the small *This and That* shop had reminded her of what a woman, or three women, could do on their own.

Until disaster struck.

That disaster seemed to threaten even in the spreading shadows of Milan's venerable Duomo—the fourteenth-century gothic cathedral that graced the city with its amazing confection of flying buttresses, spires, statues, gargoyles, and pinnacles. She should feel blessed to be back in its presence. Instead she found herself looking up to the gilded copper statue of the *Madonnina* atop the cathedral's highest spire. The statue overlooked the city and hopefully blessed Victoria's mission, for how Erminio would deal with news of the lawsuit against Reggie Lewis was anyone's guess.

Though older, Erminio was a passionate man—she knew, for she had had her small affair with him when she was newly his apprentice. But he was also a man of tempers, and that same temper had sent her away from him, only returning for what she could learn and because her father expected it of her. Today, she must manage Erminio's temper—or simply brave it.

Around her was the city's central square, the Piazza del Duomo, the grand, paved pedestrian square that housed so many layers of Milan's history: the Duomo, the *Palazzi dei Portici,* the single Triumph arch, the central statue of King Emmanuel II, resplendent on horseback.

As a young girl newly minted into adulthood, she had spent many hours here, seated at a café table nursing her espresso and watching the Milanese people and the tourists passing through, absorbing the trends, the grace of the people, as well as the grace of the broad arcades of the buildings and the grand Belle Epoch splendor of the arched-glass-roofed arcade of the Galleria Vittorio Emmanuel II, high above its marble floor. That was her destination. The Galleria was the heart of many flagship fashion empires and, after years of work, was the location of Erminio's newly opened flagship store—and apparently where Erminio was located this morning. Odd, given fashion week was fast approaching and the usual fever pitch of activity had been present in the designer's warehouse workshop this morning.

The oddity of it only increased her worry. Something was happening here over which she had no control—Erminio held a fairly tight rein—and over which she'd had no influence given she had not been in Milan when he had made decisions. All she knew was what Liza, at the warehouse, had said that Erminio had been strange, secretive, and had set out on some secret project that had him leaving the workshop at this time when they needed him the most.

Stepping out of the direct sun into the shadowed Galleria sent a shiver up her spine and her skin turned to gooseflesh. The sunlight here was refracted into a dimmer space, stirred by cool cross breezes flowing between the Piazza del Duomo and the neighboring Piazza della Scala that housed the famous La Scala Opera House. The rich scent of espresso from the nearby café called to her, for she still nursed a jet-lag headache from her trip home. She had forced herself out of her broad white bed this morning, had dressed in flowing cream trousers and short sleeved tunic of her own design that clung to her body in all the right places, and gone out to the securely guarded warehouse where Erminio's designs were being created.

He should have been there. She'd gone out there, planning to discuss the Reggie Lewis situation with him.

Around her, the marble facades of the Galleria boasted the who's who of the fashion industry: Versace, Armani, Gucci, Prada, Louise Vuitton, Valentino, Dolce and Gabbana. Their windows boasted the ice-cream-colored leather and silk and linen of a Milan summer or the vivid swirl of the Mediterranean coast. At one side, where a small café had once been, was the glass storefront that boasted "Erminio" on a discrete bronze plaque set into the marble stone. The window displays were covered with white plastic that blocked all view of the store within. When she tried it, the glass door—also blocked with white plastic—was locked. From inside came the horrible whine of—saws.

For a moment she felt stymied. The store wasn't supposed to be closed. There were certainly not supposed to be saws. This close to the end of summer, there was always a surge of patrons who wished to replace their summer frocks for the latest fall fashions. It was an awkward time of transition and Erminio's cadre of customer service staff were skilled in helping customers through it.

Bare knuckled, she rapped on the heavy glass door and it rattled in its frame. She tapped her toe waiting, but no one came. She rapped again—harder, and stepped up to the edge of the door.

"Erminio! It's me, Victoria. Let me in." She rattled the door again.

There came the truncated whine of a saw cut off and she heard the faint sound of movement and then the plastic guarding the doorway twitched. Erminio's dark countenance peered out at her. For a moment his strange, almost angry expression appeared to not recognize her. Then his gaze cleared like a cloud uncovering the sun.

"Aah! Victoria. *Bene!*" Almost as if he expected her.

He reached through the plastic and unlocked the door and opened it for her. The odd brew of sawdust and wood glue and cold espresso met her nose. Erminio caught her shoulders and bussed her cheeks.

"Come in. Come in. I did not expect to see you. I thought you still lost in the wilds of Canada."

Erminio Biondi was a small, dark man not much beyond Victoria's five foot six. He had a narrow face that was taken up by large luminous eyes that his followers said allowed him to see beyond the ordinary and find the beauty in all women. That saying had become the fashion house's motto: 'Beyond the ordinary, there is beauty in all women.'

Usually his slightly rotund body was clad in simple black-on-black tie, shirt, and suit, but today he wore jeans and a rugby-style shirt—in black, of course—with the sleeves pushed up on his hairy forearms.

His gaze ran up and down her. "You look lovely. That outfit—it should have graced our runway."

Victoria bit back the fact that she had asked to include a small number of designs in his last show and this had been one of them, but the request had been denied: "No need to dilute the Erminio line yet, cara." So she had had the design made for her alone and had accepted it as the lines of the piece crept into Erminio's designs.

"*Grazie. Figurati.* Just the first thing I put on this morning. I am still jet-lagged." She rubbed her eyes to demonstrate her fatigue, careful not to smudge her makeup.

"I am *pazzo!*" Erminio slapped his forehead. "Come. Come in." He tugged her past the plastic. "Come into my disaster." He grinned. "But it will not always be so. My disaster has methods in it. Now you wait here and I will get you a coffee."

He scuttled off, leaving her there at the door.

What had once been a coffee shop turned into one of the marble-floored inner sanctums of fashion was now a disaster. The flocked golden wallpaper, carefully chosen to give an opulent feel, was covered in sawdust. Racks of high-end clothing were covered in sheeting and pushed to the rear of the room. Counters had been uprooted, leaving scars in the floor that a workman was on his knees fixing, and new glass display cases had been installed in the center of the room. It would take at least a week of cleaning and organizing to get the place back in operation again.

Erminio came scurrying back carrying a small espresso cup and saucer and eased her out of the way of the workmen who were busily putting the finishing touches on the new displays— long, curved counters that flowed down the center of the room with discretely locked glass doors guarding the black-velvet-lined area inside.

She accepted the coffee and sipped to steady herself. "What is all this? I don't remember any plans to refurbish the store— especially not now, in the middle of one of our best sales seasons."

Erminio dispelled her question with a wave of his hands. He looked around proudly. "It is almost done," he said, his Italian filled with satisfaction as he scanned the store. "It was, what is the word in English? *Un lampo di genio*—a brainwave. I had it as you left, when I received notice of Reggie Lewis's lawsuit and an offer to sell the designs to me."

His grin was like a playful child's; the same impish grin that, at close to fifty years of age, had Erminio still being considered one of the young bucks of high fashion. It was a cross he had had to bear all his life and often a point of frustration as he sought to become recognized like Prada and Versace and the other great fashion house icons of Milan.

"I bought them, of course. And now that the designs are mine, I have arranged manufacture of them. And *voila,* the store shall be ready for them." He did a little one-two shuffle of glee. "Always we have had only our fashion and a few belts while the others have had their jewelry, their watches, their perfume. Now we shall have our original jewelry to go with the fashion we sell. Impressive, yes?"

Her espresso cup rattled in its saucer. Victoria set it down on one of the countertops and sought desperately for a place to sit down.

"What are you thinking, Erminio? Are you a fool? As far as we know, those designs belong to Reggie Lewis. Why would anyone who has created such loveliness sell their designs to you or to anyone? She would not do so."

Erminio caught her hands and steadied her when she thought she might stumble.

"*Bella! Cara mia!* I am not a fool. I saw the proof this man had—all he will need to win in court against the pretender. That woman—she should be arrested for the ruin she would have brought to me with her stolen designs. But he wants to see the designs ornament high fashion so he brought them to me."

She had to take a deep breath. Had to force herself not to grab the collar of his shirt and shake him. She had had similar urges so many times in the past, mostly when he had refused to allow her to create a line within his, while his designs had taken on so much of her work's aesthetic. Why she had stayed with him, she wasn't sure—except her father had clearly preferred his daughter working for Erminio instead of striking out on her own.

"Interesting," she said. "Interesting that of all the designers in Milan, he comes to you first—almost as if he knew that we needed those designs and had places for them in our shows. Had he spies who had been watching us and watching Reggie Lewis?" But why in the world would anyone do such a thing? Why go to so much trouble?

"Perhaps his people watched Reggie Lewis and decided they must stop her before she sullied the house of Erminio with stolen work." Erminio shrugged. "Either way, a disaster has been averted and you have no reason to worry."

But if that was the case, why had he not called her back from Canada? In fact, why did he seem so surprised to see her? Everything about this was most unusual—not the least being his almost mad appearance.

He made as if to usher her to the door again, but she stayed where she was. Shook her head. "No. There is something wrong here, Erminio. Reggie Lewis is a creative genius. I saw it in her work. I saw her creation in action when it came to designing the last few pieces. She draws her inspiration from the world around her, from the air she breathes, not from stealing someone else's designs."

"Stop. Just stop." Erminio placed soft fingers over her mouth. "I know you think I cannot make a decision without your help, but in this you are wrong, even if you are like my right hand. The owner of the designs is a most important man. His agent came to me because of exactly the fact that they knew Reggie Lewis had done me harm. They wished to make sure that her duplicity caused as little harm as possible. She is a sick woman, apparently. So they brought the designs to me."

It made no sense, but dared she question him? "Who is this benefactor? I do not understand."

He shook his head and eased her toward the door again. Unlocked and opened it so the echoes of foot traffic and voices, and the espresso and spice scents pressed in from the Galleria.

"Go back to the warehouse, Victoria. See to the designs and I will take care of things here."

"Erminio, think a moment. If this mysterious man plays you for a fool, think what you could lose. If they truly are Reggie's designs and you use them, she could sue you for everything."

"*Non.*" He shook his head. "It will not happen. This man—he has a most excellent reputation. He is very important, but not in fashion. It is a hobby for him, nothing more, but such genius he shows."

As usual, he would not listen. To him she was just a woman—perhaps, as Cesare had said, a talented woman whose ideas were to be mined for Erminio's own purposes. And now he would steal from Reggie Lewis, as well. She thought of the prototype designs Reggie had made based on their brainstorming sessions at the jewelry store before everything had fallen apart. Those she would keep secret from Erminio at all costs, given this was happening.

"Fine," she sighed when everything about this said to confront him. But there was something else going on here. Something else that went with the foreboding she had felt all morning "I will go to the warehouse. But tell me, please—who is this paragon who sells you his designs?"

Erminio smiled. "In truth it is not a man so much as a corporation. They sell the rights because the man himself prefers to remain unknown."

"The corporation, then. What is it?" Erminio was almost pushing her out the door, and in frustration she clung to the edge of the frame to stop him. "Why is it so urgent that we act now, Erminio? Why not let Reggie Lewis and this other person have a court make the decision?"

"And why are you blocking me, Victoria?" The use of her name stopped her. To Erminio, she was always *cara* and *bella* and other nameless endearments, just as he spoke to all other women, and she realized it left her not trusting him.

"Not blocking. I would never block you, Erminio. I never have, never will," she soothed. "You will always do as your conscience dictates to you." For good or bad, as long as it was good for Erminio. At least that was what she was coming to understand. "Now the name, please? If it is such a reputable company, surely that is no problem to share."

She stepped outside and turned back to him. Erminio rolled his eyes heavenward, his narrow face full of exasperation.

"*Schwarzenacht*. The *Schwarzenacht* Corporation. Now go on with you."

He shushed her away with his hands as if she was an annoying dog and for a moment she was tempted to tell him just what she was coming to think of him. Instead she turned on her heel and marched out of the Galleria. In the full light of the late morning sun in the Piazza del Duomo, she peered up at the *Madonnina* and prayed for the strength to do the right thing.

Chapter 14

The welcome armful of dark-haired woman Cesare had not expected. At most he had thought their kiss might have her think of him fondly until the next time they met. Perhaps dream of him as he had of her: for all her strengths, a damsel beset by monsters and he the warrior come to help her.

But now the night around Reggie's home was warm, the breeze softly soughing in the pines and poplar leaves, the night insects singing and, from down the hill came the hum of evening traffic on the highway. The air carried the warmth of orchards and vineyards heated in sunlight, but that was lost in the lure of sweet herbs and iron, and the luxurious softness of Reggie's skin and midnight hair.

The way his blood hummed in his ears. The way his heart beat a tattoo. And she was warm and alive with her strong jeweler's arms around his neck, the soft skin and muscle of her back under his hands as he found her waist, smoothed his palms across the gap between her cargo pants and her sleeveless t-shirt as he reeled her into him.

Eager, soft lips found his and he was looking into the darkness of her eyes. Drowning in it more like, and there was emotion there: fear, determination, and perhaps infatuation—*or the dawning of something stronger?*

"*Cara,*" he whispered it into the darkness under her hair as his lips traced the contours of her jaw, the soft swoop of her neck, down to the strength of her shoulders. His hands traced up her sides, felt the side swell of her breasts, but did not go further. This was too soon. So soon, that too swift an action might scare her. Might scare himself, for when had his heart ever pounded like a fist fighting to be released from his chest?

Never. And never had he ever met a woman who had captured him like this.

"I want you," she said. "I want to know you. All of you."

Her words aroused him. So did her smooth skin over the steel of muscle. She was not some 'pretty china doll' woman—this one would match him in intelligence and power. A scary thought, but it also promised possibilities that had never been there before.

And he was not sure that he could believe her change of heart. She was a woman under extreme pressure. She was seeking comfort and release and he could provide both.

The question was whether he wanted to, given he was intent on proving that he was a changed man.

With a sigh, he lifted his head from the damp tenderness under her hair, grazed her parted lips, and pulled her into his chest. He would comfort in her hour of need—not take advantage.

"I am here for you, Reggie." He stroked the smooth fall of her hair and inhaled her faint scent and felt his heart catch a little. What was it about this woman? "I will help you get through this."

Her muscles tensed under his hands. She pulled back in his arms and shook her head. Her eyes were dark pools that caught the porch light and the light from the three-quarter moon overhead.

"I don't want comfort." She met his gaze with steady darkness, while her hands tugged up the tails of his shirt and found his skin. Her palms were callused, warm, her touch like feathers teasing his skin.

"Do you know how long it's been since I was with a man? Do you know how much is knotted inside me that needs release? I need—" Her gaze dropped away to his chest for a moment. Then she inhaled and met his gaze more—this time with a steely determination. "I need someone to help me forget everything that's going on at the moment. I want that someone to be you.

I'm not stupid. I know it's just a roll in the hay—but will you help me?"

The way she swallowed and the slight tremor of her voice said this was not an easy request. He eyed the house. Thalia was there and he did not fancy making love with a teenaged girl in the next room. A house as old as this one would have thin walls and he did not want to stifle the sounds of their lovemaking.

Reggie looked up at him, pupils wide and waiting. The alcohol, perhaps? Or was it something else? Something darker? His gaze glanced down to the bracelet on her wrist and then back to her questioning gaze. He would be a fool to turn this lovely woman down, though he feared what it could lead to.

He leaned down and caught her mouth with his and she met him fiercely, up on her toes to press into him, her urgency setting his body aflame. Pulling back, he caught her face in his hands. "You are sure?"

"Very." She nodded.

"Where?"

Still in his arms, she considered. "The old shop? It's not perfect, but I just finished cleaning it."

That explained the cobwebs in her hair.

Without waiting, she turned and come-hithered him with her head, then led him up the shop porch where she unlocked the padlock and let them inside. The open door revealed only darkness until she flicked on the lights. Three bare bulbs hung evenly spaced along the ceiling, a narrow counter ran along one wall, and what might have been a workbench—now empty—filled one end of the room beneath a time-warped window. The wood gleamed with the soft patina of years and recent cleaning and the air carried the scent of pine cleaner. The space was small but he could imagine the orderly lines of Reggie's jewelry-making tools.

"Will it do? I know it's not a king-sized bed with a mirrored ceiling."

At that Cesare had to smile. "It has been a long time since I slept in such a place."

Pattaya in Thailand to be exact—the place that had changed his life when he had realized what he was becoming.

Pulling her into his arms, he kissed her right back. "It will be fine. It will be you. It will be me. That is all that is important."

She seemed to still for a moment, really look at him. Then she ran her palm down his cheek almost as if she was sad. "Hang on a minute."

She dashed to the house only to return with a blue plaid blanket, and caught his hand to lead him inside.

The cleaning fluid scent overlaid the musty-sweet of old rodent droppings and the older iron of forge coal. The lights placed hard shadows over everything, until Reggie hurriedly unscrewed two of them, leaving only the light at the far end of the building. In the dim light she returned to him and tugged her singlet up over her head so she faced him in a surprisingly feminine black lace bra that looked erotic and absolutely fitting with the exotic look of her black hair and the kohl-black thickness of her lashes.

He unbuttoned his shirt, shrugged it off, and tossed it aside as she unhooked her bra closure, then let it slide off her shoulders.

Her breasts were perfect globes, dark nipples erect and aroused, and she looked up at him through lowered lashes as she undid the closure to her camo pants.

"*Madre di Dio*, you are beautiful."

Her pants slid down off her slim hips and she stepped out of them in only black lace panties.

His body responded as it had to, to all that lovely smooth skin, those taunting breasts. This unpretentious strip tease without touching was possibly the most erotic thing he had ever seen— ever done. He kicked off his shoes, unbuckled his belt, and slipped his khakis down, leaving him in boxers—and clearly aroused.

She stepped up to him, then, running her hands over his chest, over his shoulders, and down his sides—sending pleasurable shivers down his spine as she explored, as her hands caught the elastic waist of his boxers and shoved them down. She stepped back from him then, head cocked as if to study him. Then she met his gaze.

"You're beautiful, yourself. Strong. Confident in your masculinity. Perhaps I'll use you as a new inspiration."

"And you are the very essence of *tentazione*—temptation, Reggie Lewis. Standing there with the light gleaming on your skin. Come here."

She did and he ran his hands down the smooth of her back, down her shoulders to stroke her sides as she stood immobile in his hands, her flesh quivering, her gaze on his face. He leaned down to kiss her as his palms grazed her nipples and she gasped. It had been too long for Reggie Lewis. This must be done in a way that welcomed her back to the world of loving and living.

He shifted his mouth to her neck, to her throat, down to the temptation of her breast. Kissed its top and she trembled. Breathed on the nipple and watched it pucker. Licked and she moaned and arched her back. He snaked one arm around her to steady her as he took her in his mouth, his free hand teasing her other breast so she moaned and her arms came around his head, held. Held as a hand around her back tugged her filmy panties down and cupped the softness of her hindquarters, explored her from behind.

Her breath came in tight little gasps as he lifted his head, kissed her mouth again and then went to his knees, trailing kisses down her chest, tending to her breasts, down the light down of her taut belly to the narrow strip of fur between her legs. Tongued her and she groaned.

Suckled there and she staggered. He caught her hips with his hands and lifted her up to the counter behind her. Spread her thighs and knelt to kiss their silken inner length until he reached the core of her. Found her sweet spot and she moaned and arched her back, her flesh rippling in pleasure.

Then her eyes flashed open. Lust shone there, but also denial. She was a dilemma, this woman.

She shook her head. "Good yes, but not what I want." She hauled him to his feet. "I want you. I want this—inside me."

She stroked him and pressed her dampness against him. "Take me somewhere."

Anywhere but here said the desperation in her eyes and Cesare moved to obey.

§

She was an idiot, a fool, because this would solve nothing. A roll in the hay never did. Just brought complications.

She met the gaze of the man between her thighs. He was cast in shadows in the low light of the shop and yet his smooth olive flesh and tiger eyes were so present, so alive and intent, that they gave lie to the tawdry surroundings of the newly scrubbed workshop. Like the purity of a beautiful votive candle in the darkness of a coal mine. His light gave her hope, made her believe perhaps there was still life out there after all of this.

Of course, their surroundings made it more like they were kids in high school, sneaking around behind their parents' backs.

His hesitation asked her whether she was sure, so she leaned up to kiss him and twined her legs around his hips.

"A moment," he said and found a condom in his discarded trousers. Thank God he was thinking because she was way past being cautious. She helped him roll it on in the most exquisitely sensual motion she had ever done.

His entry was one long smooth stroke that arched her back and left her gasping. It had been so long since she had taken a lover she had forgotten the ultimate pleasure. He shifted inside her and she groaned, opened her eyes, and wanted to blush at the way his tiger eyes roamed her face.

"Okay?" he asked, his voice deep and sexy with the Italian accent.

Still finding her way through the sensations, all she could do was nod—and tighten a few little muscles herself.

The golden flecks in his gaze seemed to flare and a wicked smile curved his lips. He settled himself between her thighs, caught her hips, and began to move. Slowly at first, each slow withdrawal leaving her more desperate for his presence, each slow, hard filling pushing her closer to an edge.She wanted more, wanted now, but Cesare just chuckled deep in his chest when she tried to increase their rhythm.

Slowly, slowly sensation stole her body. There was nothing else, just this man and his movements and the heat he evoked. It flared in her belly, it burned in her wrist and in the tattoos that encircled her arms as she clung to him. He smelled of dry grass and tasted of cinnamon. He gripped her hips and steadied her and the shift of his hips and hard buttocks sent scorching sensations through her thighs as he held to the slow, easy strokes that sent small jolts of pleasure screaming through her veins, pinwheeling pleasure in her brain. Breath came in small, desperate gasps as he guided her gaze down between their bodies to the slick length of him and their joining.

It was one of the most sensual things she had ever seen. She met his gaze and he smiled, dipped his head and took her nipple in his mouth and bit. Softly, teeth gentle on her nipple, then harder as she groaned and his tempo increased. She caught his hips and held on, driving herself into him as he drove into her. Deeper than before and deeper again, but she still wanted more. Wanted all of him—this man inside her, with her, comforting her.

In one swift movement he had her up and pressed into the wall, spreading her wide around him, he drove into her and she opened. Opened as wide as she could, holding on for dear life to his shoulders, her heels urging him on as they plunged together, and the room shrank around them, shrank more and there was only this moment in time and this man and this pleasure and the rest of the world was gone and didn't matter and tomorrow was another day, but for this moment there was only Cesare.

Only Cesare.

"Cesare!" It came out as a shout as she came apart inside. As his body pulsed inside her and waves of pleasure sent her under. She went limp in his arms as they tightened around her.

"*Bella*! Reggie!" he groaned into her hair and braced himself against the wall. Then he lifted her away and down to the blue plaid blanket still spread on the floor. Laid her there and stretched himself beside her, stroking her skin, his gaze roaming her body.

"*Moltobello*." His fingers smoothed molten pleasure down her side, rose up to graze the underside of her breasts.

"You're pretty *moltobello* yourself," she said, running her fingers down his chest and tweaking the nubbin on a rock-hard pec. Swallowed when his body stirred at her touch and the heat pulsed through her once more. She could make love to this man again and again, and next time she would give as good as she got. It might have been a long time, but she remembered things. How to pleasure a man.

And what was this? She wasn't the kind to be dwelling on erotic thoughts. Her hand went to the bracelet on her wrist. It was warm, hot even—as hot as the chemistry she felt with Cesare.

"You have plotting in your eyes," he said, smoothing her hair back from her face.

"Plotting?"

"As if you have things you think of."

She felt her cheeks heat and she looked away. "Actually, I was thinking of you. What I would do if this happened again." She waved down at the two of them. "It's not like me, you know. I don't do this sort of thing. I'm a mom. I do mom things, but now my world is turned upside down."

He smoothed a hand up and down her arm to settle his fingertips on the tattoos around her arm. "Tell me, why do you have these?"

Feeling shy again, she shrugged. "That's easy. I had them done as a reminder to be strong and a warrior. It's the only way to get what you want. I've had to fight for what I want all my life—my daughter, my work, my independence."

"Then there is no wonder you are amazing. Never have I had to live such a battle."

The bracelet jingled on her wrist and she brought it up between them. "They say this thing has been responsible for some pretty good rolls in the hay. I guess I'm a believer now." She smiled, feeling suddenly shy. "I guess I'll have to do better next time."

He caught her wrist gently and turned the bracelet this way and that to catch the light. "A pretty enough bauble, but it is not the thing that gives me pleasurable thoughts. You are the beauty here, but I am happy to hear you consider a next time."

She looked up at the ceiling. "Maybe some place a little different... Better."

"There is no place better than when we are together."

"And that is the Italian speaking, because this place is pretty bad," she said and waved at their dingy surroundings.

In response he shifted and took her nipple in his mouth, one hand slipping expertly between her legs to strum her like a guitar string so her body hummed.

Well, maybe the place wasn't all that bad. If this was the bracelet at work, maybe—maybe this was something worth pursuing.

In answer she caught him in her hand, stroked him as he hardened. She pulled up to kneel over him, kissing his length, taking him in her mouth, feeling the heat rising through her. Yes, they could do this again and again and for some reason with this man the prospect of a long future seemed sweet and promising.

Then a noise stopped her.

Footsteps on gravel. A voice in the driveway.

"Mom?"

Chapter 15

Erminio's warehouse sat in a rundown district, not far from the abandoned distillery that the Prada foundation was turning into an arts center. Prada's white, nine-story tower and the gold-leaf covered buildings stood out above the other low-roofed buildings in the area like harbingers of the change that was coming. Erminio already had realtors looking for another suitable space for his design studio because with the opening of the new arts center, there was no question but that this was going to be another trendy neighborhood that would bring rising rents and too much chance of design secrets getting out. Plus, Erminio felt it like an almost personal affront that he had to have the success of Prada rubbed in his face every day.

Victoria climbed out of the taxi that had brought her and stood before the familiar warehouse door. It was an unremarkable door, marked only by a simple, framed metal plaque that advertised House Erminio. This same door allowed access to some of the world's supermodels. It had given access to some of the world's rich and famous who loved Erminio's sleek designs—well, maybe more her sleek designs as adjusted and marketed as Erminio's.

She clamped down on that thought. That was Cesare's opinion.

But it was true enough—if she was honest. Erminio took advantage of her, and now did the same to Reggie. So now Victoria must do something about it.

Her stomach tied up as if she was about to open the *vaso di Pandora.*

Yes, that was it. If she stepped inside that warehouse and did what she had come here to do, it was possible she would unleash all manner of ill things upon the world.

But not to do it—to simply step back and become blind to how Erminio was profiting from what that company had done to Reggie Lewis...

Could she do that? If she was truthful with herself, she had allowed exactly that all these long years, because Erminio had done it to her over and over again and she—*idiota*—had accepted it as if Erminio was her father and she must do as he said.

Madre di Dio, she was better than this. Pushing her hair off her face and squaring her shoulders, she used her key and stepped out of the afternoon Milan sunshine into the musty cool of the warehouse.

The place always surprised her. From the outside, the building was rusted metal and concrete, but inside Erminio had had the place completely refurbished into a space suitable for the five-star clients he sought to cultivate. Since the birth of the British heir to the throne, certain royalty had breathed the air perfumed with lilies in a huge white vase while they waited on the plush white couches in the reception area. Movie stars and the *straricchi*—the über rich—had bided their time, dazzled by the original framed charcoal and watercolor art of Erminio's clean aesthetic designs that decorated the walls. They would have been dazzled by Reggie Lewis's jewelry, too. If Erminio had anything to say about it, they still would—just with the name Reggie Lewis excised.

Not fair. Not fair, by far.

Nodding acknowledgement at Lucia, the receptionist guarding the white waiting area at the front of the building, Victoria strode through the door to the inner sanctum of design studios, sewing rooms, and wardrobes as well as her and Erminio's offices.

Beyond the door, the environment changed again. Yes, the walls were still clean white, but the air buzzed with frantic energy and smelled of fabric, dust, heat, stale espresso, and—faintly—of small engine oil, from the sewing machines frantically working in the bowels of the building. Amazingly though, today the hallway was almost silent.

The short hallway connected the front office with the inner workings of the design studio. To one side a narrow door gave onto the viewing and fitting area, where clients came to choose their designs or have them made for them. On the other side of the hallway were the two doors that gave onto Victoria's and Erminio's offices. At the other end of the hall was the true heart of the business—the design studio where designs were transformed into works of art brought to life on the backs of the living.

There was no one else in the hallway, so she ducked into Erminio's office and stood there, back against the door to steady herself. Her heart beat *rapidamente* in her chest and she felt like she had just run a great race—or was being forced to start one.

The room was an opulent one that fit Erminio's personality but was the antithesis of his designs. Dark, wood-paneled walls had built-in gilt niches that held original modern art pieces, both paintings and sculptures. White crown moldings frothed around a ceiling that a poor but talented Milanese painter had painted in Erminio's own version of the Sistine chapel. The image was of a naked Erminio apparently receiving a gift from God. A huge, ornately carved black desk filled half of the room, with two comfortable chairs facing it. The rest of the room held a faux Louis XIV couch for when truly important guests came to this sanctum of sanctums. When asked about the opulence in comparison to his designs, Erminio would always smile and say it was because he was a complicated man. Perhaps that was true, or perhaps this room more truly represented the man while the designs he'd shown the world these past eight years showed a different sensibility—hers.

Teeth clenched as years of swallowed resentment came unswallowed, she crossed to the desk. For all he was a thief, Erminio truly was anything but complicated. After all these years of stealing from her, he likely did not expect anything to come back at him.

She tried the desk drawers and found only pens, note paper, and a sketchbook of drawings that, if created, would take the house in a very different direction of frothed lace crinolines that reminded Victoria of designs she had seen from the early 1980s. Nothing she would wear. Nothing a lot of other women would wear either, but interesting in that these were Erminio's drawings and matched the overblown office to a tee.

She set the sketch pad back in its drawer and scanned the room.

Cosa stofacendo? What was she doing? This was Reggie Lewis' problem, not her own. If Erminio found out, she would lose everything; all of her years here, the career she had built for naught.

But it was the right thing to do, and truly, as Erminio's assistant, she had no career, only a shadow to walk in.

She had no doubt that Reggie's designs were here somewhere; the question was where. Along the lower wall behind the desk and built into the wall were a series of lateral file drawers, the most functional part of the office. Reggie's files had to be in there somewhere.

Victoria had to work fast, because you never knew with Erminio when he would decide to come back to the office from his refurbished store. Leaving her purse on the desktop, she went to the first of the file drawers and pulled it open: accounting and tax filings for the past ten years. She rifled through to make sure there was nothing else tucked in and pushed the drawer closed. Erminio might be a heel in his business dealings with younger designers, but surprisingly he was honest with the government.

The second drawer revealed designs from past seasons. The third held designs from the current season. She rifled through it, searching, but there was no sign of Reggie's design files, or at least what she understood them to look like from her discussions with Lila.

The next drawer held model files—those he preferred marked with small gold stars like one might find in a child's classroom book, those he had booked for the fall show brought to the front of the line. All normal. All as they should be.

She pulled open the second to last file drawer and found it crammed full of files in hanging folders that she did not recognize. It could not be, could it?

Hands shaking, she pulled out the first file. A photo of a silver pendant shaped like an angelfish, with its long, graceful fins creating a circle around the diamond-shaped fish form. She recognized the pendant. It was one Reggie had brought with her to Milan and was part of the planned fall show. Beneath the photo lay a series of other documents. Silver analysis. Provenance of the fish's gleaming blue sapphire eye. A design sketch. Notes about the inspiration of the design and the piece of clothing it was intended for—all in Reggie Lewis's looping script.

She placed the file on the table and grabbed another from the drawer. A piece that had impressed her very much—a pendant shaped like a three-and-a-half-inch-tall Rococo design door, with ancient Roman glass for window panes and two small window earrings to match. It went with the angel fish file on the top of Erminio's desk.

A chain-link bracelet with a fringe of beads that went with a matching torque and large, hooped earrings.A sun and moon pendant. An abstract pendant encrusted with swirling designs of garnet and sapphire. A slave bracelet of silver, with moonstones gracing the fingers and the wrist and small silver bells at the closure. That was Reggie—her work was not only a beauty to the eye, it was interactive, a joy to touch and to the other senses. Playful. The perfect counterpoint to clothing that was elegant for its simplicity.

Each she stacked on the desk, but there were far too many files in the drawer for her to be able to just take on her own.

She pulled out the last drawer on the wall and found it filled with similar files—all Reggie's.

"*Chepalle!*" What a pain in the ass.

A soft knock came at the door and Victoria jerked upright, her heart about to escape her chest. Mercifully, not Erminio. Instead Antonia, one of their interns from Milano Fashion Institute, stuck her dark head in the door. Her hair was pulled back into a high ponytail that showed off her classic features. She wore a simple, sleeveless, cream silk blouse and high-waisted trousers of a flowing black wool crepe that had been Erminio's favored design two seasons back. Victoria doubted that any student could afford such clothes new. Either she had been lucky in end of season sales or she had a very good eye for recycled clothing.

"Erminio?" Antonia stopped, her eyes widening. "Victoria. They said you were away. I was looking for assistance on a problem with Erminio's last-minute addition to the show. The lace just is not fitting the way it should."

Lace? There was no lace at all in the new spring line.

Victoria stood. "He is at the store. Let me see if I can help you, but first give me a hand and shift these old files to my office. Erminio asked me to fax them to a supplier."

She shoved the drawers closed and tried not to regret all that they still held. At least she had the files for the pieces most at issue.

Good intern that she was, Antonia bundled up an armful of files and between the two of them, got the files into Victoria's office.

Her space was the antithesis of Erminio's. Simple glass-topped desk. Functional file cabinets and stacked boxes of samples, catalogues, and media announcements. All the things no one had time to find a permanent home for, Erminio banished to her office. On the walls were framed copies of designs that had inspired her as a young woman worn by some of the most iconic of women—Grace Kelly, Coco Chanel, Jacqueline Kennedy. Their fashion had incorporated the clean lines and classic nature that was everything she would aspire to.

"Let me start faxing some of these," she said to Antonia and set the contents of three files in her fax/scanner machine and looked up Lila Weber's number. She dialed and then waited for the indication that the other end was receiving. When she was certain the documents were transmitting, she turned back to Antonia. "So show me what the problem is?"

Reluctant to leave the documents in her office, she really had no choice, so she followed Antonia down the hall and through the second door into the pandemonium that was the design studio. It was a long, narrow room with a high ceiling dotted with skylights that Erminio had paid to have installed for the natural light that flooded the tables below. The floor space was taken up with table after table, some full of design sketches that were being translated into muslin patterns, others with fabric laid out for cutting, still others with rolls of wool in silver grey, maroon, and navy, and sample swatches of alpaca and cashmere knits, and fur skins under consideration for specific garments for the spring show. Counter-intuitive to most people, at the moment the company was putting the final touches on the pieces for the fall show that would showcase spring designs, while now, in the heat of the final days of August, they were working on designs for next spring's show of fall clothing.

At the far end of the room, another door led to the production room, but even with the baffling Erminio had had installed, the low hum of industrial sewing machines in production spoke of the manic energy it took to get the designs from idea to reality. The air tasted of machine oil and the incense stick that Erminio had established as something that *must* be lit when anyone was working in the production room. He said that the sweet myrrh scent calmed the high emotions that existed in the midst of such creation. To Victoria's way of thinking, it was simply another one of Erminio's impositions of authority.

She stopped, for a moment shocked by the level of resentment she must have been harboring for a very long time, and by what faced her in the room.

At the moment the broad space echoed with voices raised in crisis. Seamstresses and design assistants gathered like a flock of pigeons around a model wearing the newly made test garment of Erminio's last-minute addition to the show of designs for spring.

Except there shouldn't be any last minute changes in the show's lineup. There had been long discussions before she left for Canada and agreement on everything down to the shoes the models would wear and their hair styles. The order of the show had been carefully constructed by herself and Maria, her assistant, and approved by Erminio.

What had changed was apparently the monstrosity the room fluttered around.

"What is this?" she demanded of Antonia.

The garment on the model was nothing that fit with the simple, sweeping lines of the designs planned for the spring line. This—this was—as overblown as Erminio's office. Layers of soft, gauzy fabric had been gathered together at shoulders and waist to create something that, to Victoria's eye, looking like nothing more than a balloon that had had three days to deflate. On the one hand, the fabric was light and gauzy, but on the other, it was too heavy for such a construction. The top drooped and shapeless, the many-layered knee-length skirt drooping, too.

She stepped up to the model, fingered the fabric, and shook her head. "This is not working. Not at all. Where did you get such a design?"

Antonia looked at the floor and shrugged. Maria, the iron-fisted manager of the design team, shouldered through the other design staff and caught Victoria's hand. She was a woman of about forty, with black hair pulled back in a tight bun, who dressed in stylish silver-gray suits on most occasions. Today she wore her usual armor with a violet shirt that reminded Victoria of the lavender room at Lila's.

"It happened the day you left," Maria said, edging Victoria away from the group of people around the model. "I—I should have forwarded Erminio's changes to the lineup to you, but in the mad rush to get the new garments made, I forgot. I'm sorry."

"Garments? He has more new pieces?"

Maria looked away. "He has six. He struck out most of the latter part of the line and inserted these new pieces. Like this one."

She turned a noncommittal expression Victoria's way, but the studied neutrality of her gaze said exactly what she thought. Maria had been in the fashion industry for twenty-five years as a fashion assistant and to hear her tell it, that was the best job in the world, rather than the most thankless.

The latter part of the line were the pieces that most reflected Victoria'swork and her vision—the clean lines that had built Erminio's house name.

And now he was intent on ruining that name with something like this. She strode over to the model with the mock-up garment.

"What fabric is this? Who chose it?"

The group of fluttering designers went silent, gazes traveling one to the other.

"Let me guess—our illustrious leader."

Maria nodded slightly.

"Well. You can see it does not work. Do you want to show it to him like this or can you tell me a fabric that might be suitable to his vision?" Though she might no longer give a damn about Erminio, she did care about these people. If the house went down, it would impact all of them.

That got the assistant designers—men and women—arguing, but at least they were discussing how to fix this mess. She gestured to the model, "Get this rag off," and imperiously turned to Maria.

"I want to see the revised fall lineup." With that she marched back to her office to collapse into her chair behind her desk. The first batch of Reggie's file material had transmitted. She hurriedly set a second batch to send and stuffed the contents of the first files in their folders, then dumped the samples out of one of the boxes that filled the corner of her office and stacked the files inside.

A knock on the door and Maria stuck her head in. "I have the fall lineup," she said with a hint of apology.

"Come in, come in. Show me the changes and tell me how it happened." Victoria sat back in her ergonomic chair and gestured to the chair across her desk. Maria laid a file carefully on the desk and sank down in the chair.

"As I said, it was a total surprise to us all. Who throws out beautiful, completed designs in order to insert what you saw? They are an entirely different direction. They do not fit."

"To Erminio, they do." Victoria scanned the revised lineup and sighed. It was as Maria had said. Everything that was Victoria's was gone. She shook her head. "But why? How did it happen?"

"It was the day you left with the jewelry designer, that Reggie Lewis. Erminio had a visitor—a man I am not familiar with. He was tall, well-built, and wore an expensive suit and shoes. According to Lucia at reception, she thought he was German, though he had almost no accent. I asked her his name, but she could not remember it and had not written it down. Very strange, given our Lucia always pays attention to details. When the man departed and Erminio left his office, it was like he was a changed man. There was a light in his eyes I had not seen before—something I did not like. He demanded the lineup file and, right there, slashed out the items he did not want and gave us the six designs, the first of which you have seen. The others are in production, but Erminio has not been here to oversee them. I cannot vouch that they are any better than what you saw today."

Having finished her speech, she collapsed back in her chair as if now the problem was Victoria's.

"Did anything else happen during my time away?"

Maria shook her head, then stopped. "There was a shipment. Lucia said they were documents and she installed them into drawers in Erminio's office."

She stopped, eyeing the stacked folders on Victoria's desk. "Are these..."

Trust her? She had known Maria for a very long time. The woman had taken a very young Victoria Angelucci under her wing and had helped her develop the confidence to stand her ground with Erminio and anyone else, for that matter.

"If they were?"

Maria frowned. "I would wonder what the files have to do with you, I suppose."

"And if I told you they were evidence that Erminio is claiming ownership of designs that belong to someone else, what would you say?"

Maria's dark brown eyes grew cautious and she sat forward in her chair as if she wanted to leave. "That such a claim is hard to believe. I have worked with Erminio for twenty years now. We have labored hard side by side."

Victoria nodded. "I agree. I find the thought repugnant, and yet—there are these." She laid her palm on top of the files, then flipped the top one open and removed a photo. "Do you recognize this?"

It was a necklace of large rough stones of amethyst and amber hung on large sterling silver links.

Maria frowned. "Was that not the piece that Reggie Lewis brought here for the grey tunic suit?"

"Exactly. She brought it here. While she was here, someone broke into her workshop and stole all of the files she creates to document each of her pieces. Those files are now in Erminio's office and people back in Canada have received notice of legal action claiming that she stole all of her designs from someone else."

Maria's fine olive face had paled as Victoria told her story. She shook her head.

"Surely he does not know this. Surely it is a mistake. Perhaps he intends to return the files to her—has simply recovered them for her."

Victoria shook her head, though truly she did not want to. Who wishes to admit that someone they have always respected is the cheat and liar Cesare always claimed Erminio was?

"He has redesigned the main store with jewelry cases. Clearly he expects to sell something, and what else does he have?"

Maria looked worried, but still not fully convinced. "It is hard to imagine our Erminio doing such a thing."

"And yet you said yourself that he had seemed changed somehow."

"I did." Maria frowned. "As if there was a ruthless side of him beyond the demanding prima donna we have seen so many times before." She smiled an apology for speaking ill of the man who was such a big part of both their lives.

Victoria straightened and stood, her hand still on the files. "Then I fear that I must be ruthless, too. I won't involve you in this. Go back to the workroom and make sure that a suitable fabric is used for each of Erminio's pieces. How do they say it? We will make a silk purse out of a sow's ear so that the pieces do as little harm as possible to the fall show. If Erminio explodes, tell him you were following my orders."

"He will be furious."

"No more furious than I am at the moment that he would ruin House Erminio's good name. That, I must deal with." Victoria nodded to the door. "Now go."

With a last hesitation, Maria went.

When the door closed behind her, Victoria hurriedly faxed the remaining file contents to Lila's office. Then she boxed the files, called a cab, and walked out of the office and out past Lucia at reception. There were still almost two full file drawers of Reggie's files back in that office, but she couldn't risk trying for more at the moment. She climbed in the small silver car with the yellow taxi lamp and cradled the box on her lap. She gave the driver her address and the cab pulled away just as Erminio's chauffeur-driven sedan pulled up. At her house she had the taxi wait as she repacked her suitcase and taped the box shut.

Then she headed for the airport.

Chapter 16

"Mom?"

Reggie froze.

The workshop that had seemed like a safe, secret haven with Cesare suddenly sprang into tawdry relief—old wooden walls that no amount of scrubbing could truly get clean, the tangled blanket, and the naked man she knelt above like a harlot. Her daughter needed her and she was here, rutting like a—a—she couldn't come up with a bad enough word. Because he offered to help her?

She yanked up and away from Cesare and his golden body that had made her momentarily forget all the troubles she had to deal with. The air reeked of his musk and of their sex, and outside in the driveway, Thalia's footsteps crunched toward the light she had to see through the wavy shop window.

Reggie leapt to her feet and grabbed her clothes. Felt foolish and filthy as she hauled her camo trousers up, her singlet over her head and stuffed her bra and panties in her pocket, just as guilty, just as cheap and stupid, as she had been when she was a teenager facing her parents after almost being discovered *in flagrante delicto* with her first serious boyfriend.

Thalia's footsteps mounted the two stairs to the workshop porch. Reggie turned to Cesare, just pulling on his shirt, his trousers slung low and sexy on his narrow hips, and she felt the betraying need of him all over again. Barefoot, she got to the door just as Thalia pulled it open.

"Thalia! Hi!" She grinned and finger combed her hair—a ratted mess, no less. She glanced over her shoulder. "I was just showing Cesare the shop to get his opinion on moving my stuff back here."

Thalia's fixed stare held on Cesare a moment as he tucked his shirt in and then swooped to the blanket on the floor. The blanket. Oh, God. Thalia's look changed to one of confusion, then comprehension, then hurt and anger, before settling on disgust as it returned to Reggie.

"Mom?" She backed a step.

"Honey, I can explain." Reggie went after her.

Thalia shoved her away and almost fell down the steps, then she was gone, running for the house as Cesare came up behind Reggie. She felt his heat tingle down her spine, in her arm, before he touched her, but it couldn't begin to warm the cold fear that froze her flesh.

"What have I done? What have *we* done?"

"Nothing wrong, *cara*. Only what is natural between a man and a woman." Cesare's strong hands tried to pull her back against him.

She yanked away and spun to face him. "Natural for you, maybe. Falling in and out of bed with women. But not for me. I have a daughter to raise, and now I've just shown her that her mother's a—a—there aren't words bad enough for what I am."

She set off across the driveway feeling totally like the fool that she was. She'd known this could happen and she'd still let it happen. Hell, she didn't *let* it happen—she started it. All the places Cesare had touched her felt like scarlet brands on her skin.

"Reggie." He caught her arm, stopped her, and forced her to face him. "This was not just a falling into and out of bed with someone. Not with you. Do you understand? I will not be gone tomorrow. I will be with you now as you face Thalia."

"No." She pulled her arm away. "You said earlier that you just wanted to help. Well, helping right now is leaving and understanding that I haven't any place in my life for you. Please understand, I've been a fool and let my emotions wreck things with Thalia. Now let me deal with the shambles I've made of my life and my relationship with my daughter."

She strode for the house hating herself, because of Thalia, because she left Cesare behind. His gaze was a flame on her back as she climbed the porch stairs and closed the door solidly between them. She had to fight to stop from crying.

The floor joists above the kitchen creaked at Thalia's angry movements in her room. How the heck Reggie was going to deal with this, she didn't know. It was one of the reasons she never brought men home and rarely dated. How did one have a sexual relationship with someone around a precocious ten-year-old?

Well, it surely wasn't how she'd done it tonight.

So how did she explain it all to her daughter?

Pressure? Too much wine? She looked ruefully at Cesare's three-quarter-empty bottle. That might have been part of the problem, but was she going to tell Thalia that her mother was a drunk who slept with anyone when she'd been drinking?

Well, maybe not just anyone. It was Cesare.

Explain that sex was what happened between two people who cared for each other? That would never fly when she'd known the man for such a short time. Would it?

Still uncertain how she was going to explain, but praying that the strength of the Team of Two was in their ability to communicate, she climbed the stairs and knocked on Thalia's bedroom door.

"Go away."

The angry voice said this wasn't going to be easy.

"I'm your mother. I live here, so I'm not going anywhere."

"Well, go be someplace else." Thalia's voice was thick with tears.

Reggie had always believed that Thalia should have her personal space, but desperate times required desperate measures. She tried the door. Not locked.

She pushed it open a few inches. "Thalia, honey, we need to talk."

"No. We. Don't!" The girl was across the room in a flash and shoved the door closed in Reggie's face so the door seemed to quiver under her hand.

"Thalia, I'm sorry, all right? It shouldn't have happened."

"Oh, right! So, what? You're going to tell me it was an accident? Like maybe your clothes just fell off accidently and then someone held a gun on you to make you—you do whatever it was you were doing?"

From inside the room came the sound of something clattering across the floor. Her My Little Pony garbage can, Reggie'd lay money on it. The girl was seriously angry, but what could Reggie do?

She sighed and, back to the wall, slid down to the floor. Her camo pants and singlet top chafed her skin with no underwear or bra. "Thalia, I'm not going to lie to you. No one forced me to be with Cesare. When you get older, you'll understand that sometimes there's chemistry between a man and a woman when you least expect it. That's the case here."

There was moody silence from beyond the door, then: "So you're telling me you don't even love him? Geeze, Mom, do you do this with every cute guy you meet? Or was this just because he was *my* friend?"

She stood and chewed her lip, trying to decide what to say. "I guess I deserve that. To tell you the truth, I don't know what I feel about Cesare, but he was kind and caring when I was feeling really bad. Sometimes—sometimes an adult just really needs to connect with another adult. It still wasn't okay what I did, but it's done now. How do we put the Team of Two back together?"

She grabbed the door knob and found it locked. "Open the door, Thalia. Please."

She felt sick to her stomach, repulsed by what she'd done, and yet another part of her said sex with Cesare was natural between a man and woman. Just how long *had* it been since she'd been with a man she cared about?

"Why should I? So that you can get all preachy on me that I should just understand? So that you can tell me that you're a grown-up and someday I'll understand? I'll tell you what I understand, Mom. You stole my friend when you didn't even like him, and now you're making me give up Gladiator, too!"

Thalia's shout carried the pain of so much betrayal Reggie felt all her denials fossilize in her chest. For a moment she couldn't breathe, couldn't find words or air to tell her daughter the truth. When the air returned it was in one big sobbing breath.

She lay her forehead against the door. "Honey, you're wrong. I'd never do such a thing."

"Liar. I heard you talking to Cesare. You've lost Gladiator for me. You can't afford the board and I can't work it off and there's no other stable close enough and Gladiator can't just stay on our property because of the lease agreement."

A foot impacted the door and it rattled in its frame. Inside Thalia's room something breakable smashed to the floor and then all Reggie heard was sobbing.

"Let me in, Thalia. We'll figure this out together. We will. We've always found a way before."

"You don't care about me. All you care about is Cesare. Why don't you go find your lover again, Mom?"

Reggie drew in a deep breath against the dagger in her chest. Just how did kids know how to say things that cut the deepest? The hallway held the aroma of water evaporating from the shower in the bathroom, and the dust in the corners of the hallway because she just never found the time to keep up with all the housekeeping. The house felt old and sagging around her, just like her own shoulders. She ran her palms down the old wood of the door that kept her from her daughter.

So what should she do? Thalia clearly wanted nothing to do with her and sometimes she'd found that giving her daughter the space she wanted was exactly what she should do. On the other hand, walking away would only be proof that she was walking away from her daughter. If she did that, it was only going to prove all Thalia's suspicions, even though they weren't true.

She kept her eye on Thalia's door as she retreated to her bedroom, with its pale blue walls and deep blue bedspread, with its sunny yellow pillows and vintage dresser with the beveled mirror. The mirror distorted her face slightly, making her nose longer, her jaw more pointed. A witch if ever there was one, and right now she felt it.

She dragged the duvet off the bed and back out into the hall. The heartbroken sobs still came from the locked room.

She slid down the wall again, this time across from the door, and pulled the duvet around her shoulders.

"I'm sorry, baby. I'm so sorry I can't give you everything you want, be everything you want me to be, but I can't. Somehow it's all beyond me. But I can tell you that what happened with Cesare won't happen again. I'm here for you when you want to talk—when you want to figure out how to deal with this Gladiator thing."

Her hand worried the stupid bracelet as the house ticked around her, and from out on the road beyond the trees came the sound of traffic, but the driveway was quiet. Cesare was gone and the ticking quiet was a perfect metaphor for what her life was going to be here on out. Just focus on her daughter—her career was over. Her attention had to be on repairing things with Thalia after her own ridiculous lapse in judgment. She had no time for romance even if she did wear the bracelet.

§

Although the house where Cesare enjoyed Corporal Jasper Stone's hospitality was just across West Kelowna on the water side of the highway from Reggie's small hideaway, guiding his rental car down the hill and through the peach orchard and vineyard-scented night, he felt like he was abandoning something that should instead be held precious and close to his heart.

He had gone to the house only to offer hope and support. That was all.

The road bent across the benchland amongst a small group of houses overlooking night-drenched orchards that rolled down toward the dark waters of the lake. He pulled the Camry into the curb in front of what looked like a low-slung bungalow but was actually Jas's house with the vaulted ceilings. He climbed out into cool. The gentle hiss, hiss, hiss of irrigation from the orchards pulsed with the cricket song, and the air smelled of water and the dry hillside and pine beyond. Something—perhaps bats— fluttered through the darkened sky. Pulling his house key from his pocket, he walked the driveway to the house and let himself in. The stone entryway was dark, but light came from the living room on the floor below.

"Cesare? That you?"

"*Si*. It is me."

Cesare leaned over the railing that looked down over the large living room at the front of the house. The leather couch faced the huge stone fireplace that was hung with the massive Zanzibar door. A leather Swedish-modern chair sat to one side, a single side lamp that arched over the chair pooling light over Jas Stone and the book he appeared to be reading.

"There's a beer with your name on it in the fridge, if you want," Jas said.

He'd come home thinking only of being alone and trying to solve the problems of Reggie Lewis, but perhaps talking to someone—a *polizia* even—might help.

"I thought you would be with Chloe," he said as he came down the stairs.

Jas looked up. "She's got a healing tomorrow and wanted to spend the night centering herself." He hooked his fingers around 'centering,' but by his expression it wasn't meant unkindly—only that he did not fully understand all the mysteries of his woman.

Shaking his head, Cesare claimed the promised beer from the fridge, cracked it open, and drank. It was another of the rich dark beers that Jas had served him before. Rich with barley and hops with a hint of sweet, almost like molasses.

"Interesting beer," he said, examining the label as he settled on the couch and blew out a breath.

Jas closed his book and set it on the floor at his feet. "More interesting look on your face, my friend. Let me guess: you were with Reggie."

Cesare shook his head. "In all ways possible."

Jas cocked his brow. "Now that *is* a surprise. Reggie doesn't strike me as the kind to fall into bed with just anyone. She's pretty focused on her business and her daughter."

All too true, Cesare nodded and sipped his beer. "I spent today working with Lila and trying to get in touch with the lawyer for the claimant in the lawsuit. There was no luck contacting them, but Lila got in touch with many owners of Reggie's jewelry pieces. They sent photos of the pieces and letters recounting little stories of what they were told when they bought the pieces. I took them to Reggie to show her that all was not lost."

Sighing he stopped his story and took a long pull of beer. "Tell me, do you really think that bracelet is responsible for bringing you and Chloe together?"

Jas shrugged. "Sorta. It did have a door that matched the one above the fireplace. And it did come off once we realized what we'd found in each other—and accepted it. Believe me, that wasn't an easy place to get to."

"I do not think it will be so easy between me and Reggie."

Jas started to chuckle. "Easy? Chloe wouldn't give me the time of day. She wanted nothing to do with men and for some reason I, in particular, rubbed her the wrong way. But we sort of got thrown together because of a theft at the store and, well, somehow we worked things out. If it's any consolation, it was worth it."

"You did not have another person to contend with." Cesare met Jas's momentarily puzzled gaze. "Her daughter. Young Thalia. I thought that being friends with her would not be hard and we were. I even helped her with her horse, something I have not even thought of in many years. But I thought she could be an ally with her mother."

He shook his head, the rich molasses and barley rolled down his throat too smoothly and he could feel it in his head. Feel his tongue loosen around his story.

"Reggie was upset when I arrived. It seemed she had had a bad day, had perhaps given up." He told about the letter from the stable and how Reggie's money situation was not adding up.

There was no way she could manage the stable fees for Thalia's horse and that put the lease agreement for the horse at risk.

"I brought wine for the victory I hoped we would win, but she was feeling the weight of everything on her shoulders so I showed her the letters Lila had collected so far. Somewhere in there, I kissed her."

The room was quiet, the house's location far from even traffic noise. Backed by the darkness over the lake, the broad glass wall at the front of the house only reflected the room back at him and he felt foolish and perhaps even scared at what he had done. Jas just leaned back in his chair and reclaimed his beer. Sipped.

"I kissed her and it was good and I knew that if I stayed any longer something more might happen. I knew she was vulnerable, so I left." He met Jas's thankfully nonjudgmental gaze. "She came after me in the driveway. She kissed me so hard, so hot, I thought—what is the word?—steam would rise." He shook his head. "It was very good. We used her old shop. It seemed things were finally right between us—but then her daughter found us."

"Crap." Jas sat forward. "Thalia *saw* you?"

"The aftermath at least. We had our clothes on, but by her face, she knew what had happened. She was not happy." He told how she ran to the house and how Reggie reacted. "All the good that was there between us was gone. Thalia is everything to her. For her daughter she will give up what might have been."

He shook his head and drained back the beer. "And now it is time for me to go to bed and forget her."

He stood.

"Not going to happen, brother. If you were going to forget her, you wouldn't be sitting here looking like a—well, like you're looking right now. I know what you're going through, but these strong women—they're worth fighting for. Chloe was, and a woman like Reggie, who wears strength like a badge in those tattoos of hers—she'll come through this, too. Just give her time."

Cesare shook his head sadly. "Time is what I do not have. The deal in California is time sensitive. If I want the vineyard, I need to get back there and close the deal. To do so, I am going to have to prostrate myself before my father to gain his co-signature." He crossed over to the night-blackened window and peered out onto the deck and the breeze-tossed tops of orchard trees with the glimmer of waves under the young moon beyond. "This is a good place. I will be sad to leave. For many reasons."

"Cesare, I'm gonna speak frankly. You strike me as the kind of guy who has always got what he wanted with women: you're good looking, confident, athletic, and you come from money. A babe magnet if there ever was one. Ever think that maybe the one worth getting is the one you have to work the hardest for?"

Cesare turned back to him, smiled. "Every day since I met Reggie. She is worth the work. But I cannot plan my life around a woman who might be—I must plan for my life. The winery in Napa is the result of a long search for the right property. Affordable land is not easy to find."

"Is your heart set on Napa? You ever think of opening a winery here? There're some good wineries hereabouts. Chloe's brother Brett is part owner in one. If you like, I can hook you up. Maybe he can show you some properties here. It can't be as expensive as in Napa, but the wines are good."

Cesare shrugged and turned away from the window. "It would be a good thought if Reggie gave any sign that I had a reason to stay. But now I will say good night."

He headed for the kitchen to put the beer bottle with the recycling.

"You know, you're walking away from this conversation just like you walked away from Reggie tonight. Didn't you walk away from your career and your family, too?" Jas looked at him from his spot in the chair, his dark hair and brow shadowing his eyes. Then he shrugged. "Just sayin'. Chloe mentioned that your sister had said it. I guess I'll see you in the morning."

The words stung like stingray venom and he'd had personal experience on the beaches of the Indian Ocean. Feeling chastened, Cesare climbed the stairs to the second floor that held the bedrooms. Below him, in the living room, Jas reclaimed his book from the floor and settled back in his chair.

The hall was dark as he let himself into Jas's guestroom. Moonlight gleamed through the sliding glass door that gave onto a small balcony overlooking the downstairs deck and the view of the orchards and lake. He slid the balcony door open and stepped outside into sweet air barely cooled by the night. The rhythmic hiss of the irrigation in the orchards set a lulling beat, but it couldn't stop the turmoil of what Jas's words had set in motion. Had he walked away from everything and everyone like Jas had said?

He had walked away from his father, sure. The man could be a tyrant sometimes and having him look his disapproval over everything Cesare did was not how he planned to live his life. So he'd left. Anyone would have. And now he planned to crawl back and ask for his father's help.

A whoosh of wings swept by overhead and Cesare ducked but couldn't see what it was. Owl perhaps, seeking prey amid the trees. It would be something alone, venturing forth to find food, possibly for its young. The strike would be fast and whatever mouse or vole it was, would be taken from its kind for a meal, either for the owl itself or for its youngsters, if they were still fledging. He didn't know enough about owls to know which it was.

Just because he'd walked away from his father and his law degree didn't mean that he was walking away from Reggie. She had asked him to leave, had refused his help and his comfort. About the only thing she hadn't done was accuse him of just wanting sex with her.

And now he'd had sex with her and had, by his action, by all accounts, walked away when she was still under tremendous pressure.

As if events conspired to leave her alone at the exact same time that, according to the story of the bracelet, she was most vulnerable. As a matter of fact, the whole thing with the theft of her files and the legal action threatened against Lila seemed set up to drive a wedge between Reggie and the others. According to conversations with Jas and his partner, Danny, the strength of the friendships of the women was one of the things that had protected them in the past.

And now she was totally alone.

He would fix things with her. He would. And if, by some miracle, his overtures worked, perhaps he could take up Jas's offer and look at wineries in the Okanagan. His dream was not tied to Napa, it was tied to a vision of the future that involved vineyards and long rows of vines so rich with grape that you could get drunk from the sweet scent of their juice. There would be a low stone building with stout wooden doors like the old house on his father's vineyard, but this one would house a restaurant and, behind it, his home. And in the house or the restaurant, or in the shop he would build her, there would be Reggie. Designing and making her jewelry, eating meals with him, and in his bed. Out back there would be a barn, a riding ring, and a smiling Thalia.

He closed his eyes and relived the memory of Reggie's silken skin, the feel of her around him.

Yes, he would apologize tomorrow. In the meantime he would sleep. Back inside he lay down on the bed with the dark green duvet and soon gave up on the notion of sleep. His head was too full of ideas—some good, some bad. At two o'clock he gave up on sleep and, hands behind his head, stared up at the ceiling making plans.

Chapter 17

A crick in her neck woke Reggie. She still sat on the hallway floor across from Thalia's bedroom door, the old wood floor hard under her. The blue duvet she had brought from her bedroom was still pulled up to her chin, but her head had sagged, kinking her neck so that straightening it sent pain shooting down her shoulder.

She groaned, pulled her knees up to her chest, and tried to work the crick out of her neck and the ache out of her shoulders. It didn't quite work, but from her open bedroom door spilled morning sunlight into the gray recesses of the hall. She'd guarded Thalia's door all night to no avail. Thalia hadn't relented in her anger.

In some ways she could understand it. The poor kid was having the most important things in the world stripped from her because of her mother's incompetence. If she'd only copied all those files electronically, then the theft of the files wouldn't be so bad. And the fact she'd lost the files meant she was ripe for a lawsuit, and the fact she had the lawsuit to deal with, though no formal papers had come for her, meant that the store couldn't afford to sell her jewelry no matter what Lila might say. And not selling her jewelry and not having the overseas sales as a result of Milan meant that there was no way at all she could afford even the current partial board for Gladiator, let alone the full board that Dietrich was now asking. So it was her fault that Thalia was losing her horse.

Hers and hers alone.

Groaning, she stumbled to her feet and leaned on the wall for balance. Everything ached as if she'd been put through a meat grinder. Her head ached, too. Or maybe that was her heart.

No, she wasn't going there. If her heart ached it was for Thalia. Cesare had only been a one night stand. They'd had it, so now they both could move on and she should treat the whole episode as what it was—a stress release and attempted escape into sensation. Done and over and now she had to get on with dealing with the problems in her life instead of seeking escape.

First on the list: Thalia.

By the angle of the light through her bedroom door, it was still early. Seven o'clock at the most. She'd make breakfast first—something Thalia liked. Maybe she could tempt her to come out and they could talk.

She went into the bathroom—sunny yellow paint and fixtures that might have gleamed white once, but were now the dull yellow-white that came when the glossy enamel wore off. Sort of like her honor. She got the water running in the old shower and stepped in to wash away the remains of last night. Unfortunately, it didn't completely work. The sluicing water reminded her of strong hands smoothing her flesh. She felt raw and ready for more of Cesare's touch. Heat flared out of the bracelet and down to her core.

No! No! No!

She leapt out of the shower onto cold tiles and tugged at the bracelet—no luck, still apparently locked forever on her wrist unless she took the bull by the horns and cut it off. Maybe she would. She scrubbed herself dry with a rough, sun-dried towel and contemplated her pale face with the high cheekbones and dark circles under her eyes in the smoky bathroom vanity mirror. Quickly, she slicked her hair back into a ponytail and pulled on clean clothes—jean cutoffs and a black t-shirt with the sleeves cut off. She contemplated throwing away her usual camo gear, but finally settled on the laundry hamper. Then she headed down to the kitchen.

Pancakes were Thalia's thing, so chocolate chip pancakes it was. She hauled out her extra-large red mixing bowl because the only thing better than fresh-off-the-griddle pancakes were cold ones eaten with cold butter, sugar, and cinnamon. Perfect snacks for a growing girl coming home from a day of hard labor at the barn.

She set to work, humming and mixing flour, sugar, salt, and baking powder, then stirred in the milk and stirred the mass together. When she was satisfied with the lumpy consistency, she added handfuls of chocolate chips and then ladled the batter into the pan to form perfect round discs. The room filled with a faint sizzle and delectable scent.

While they were cooking, she put water in a pot to heat and set the maple syrup container in the hot water to warm. Cold butter on the table and she set two places, then she turned the pancakes and moved the cooked golden discs to the oven to stay warm. She kept cooking.

Twenty minutes later she'd finished the batch of four-inch pancakes and the heaping platter was overflowing in the oven, but there was still no sign of Thalia.

She grabbed the broom from the corner and used the handle to thump the ceiling three times, their agreed upon signal that a meal was ready. Still no response.

Her heart did a little thu-thunk. Thalia *had* been upset. Maybe she didn't sleep well and was just sleeping in. Or maybe she was still refusing to acknowledge her mother. Could be, but Reggie was pretty sure she hadn't heard any sign of stirring.

Concerned, she headed back upstairs to Thalia's room.

"Sweetie?" She tapped on the door. "It's eight-thirty. I've got breakfast made—chocolate chip pancakes in case you couldn't tell. They're all warm and gooey and waiting."

The dark hallway ticked around her, the sound of traffic from the road and a magpie chasing the sparrows in the yard the only sounds. Light through the open door to her room lit the far end of the hall, but it was dark where Thalia's door blocked the light— and kept her out of Thalia's life at the moment.

No kid was ever this quiet. Not even when she was playing hide and seek. There was something about her living and breathing that let Reggie track her wherever she was. But there was no sense of another living being beyond the closed door.

"Thalia?" Swallowing back the copper taste of fear, she tried the door. The knob jiggled in her hand, still locked. "Damn it, Thalia, answer me. You're making me afraid!"

Still nothing, and the heat of adrenaline filled her. She was getting into that room. Had to.

Tried the door again and the knob still wouldn't turn. Key. There had to be a key. When they'd first moved in there had been a set of old keys that came with the house.

In a scramble she was down the stairs to the kitchen again. Every kitchen has a junk drawer and hers was no exception. She hauled it out and set it on the table, shoving the breakfast table settings aside. Rifled the contents—take-out menus, kitchen hammer, duct tape, string, the neighbor's key for when she was house sitting, old horse show programs. In the back corner of the drawer was a loop of keys.

Clutching them and kicking herself for a fool for not having thought of this last night, she took the stairs two at a time back to Thalia's door and fumbled the keys one at a time in the lock. Finally one turned and she shoved the door open.

Empty.

Thalia's room was typical of a girl who loved horses. Pictures taken from horse magazines had replaced her childhood fascination with cute pictures of baby pigs. Dressage rider icons in top hats on perfectly groomed mounts floated in extended trots across dressage rings—Thalia's dream for the future. A near-perfect specimen of horseflesh trotted at liberty across a green field. Taped beside it was a small photo of Gladiator in almost the same position.

She couldn't look away from all of Thalia's dreams on the walls. If she kept her attention there, she could almost make herself believe that Thalia was sprawled on the bed rereading her favorite childhood novel, *The Island Stallion*. The kid was always up for adventure.

Reggie stepped into the room and forced herself to look. Bed still made, but it looked like Thalia had lain on the top. The dresser that she and Thalia had refinished into a lustrous maple glow stood with one drawer partially open. Feeling cold as if winter blew right through the room, Reggie crossed to the dresser and pulled the drawer open. Girly underwear with flowers. Training bras. The corner was empty and her legs went weak. The corner was where Thalia kept her special wallet that held the money she earned as allowance and doing grooming and braiding for other people at horseshows. She'd been saving for a new double bridle for Gladiator, a good German one with extra padding on the nose and brow bands and crystals on the headband. She had to have close to seven hundred dollars saved toward it. She could get a long way with that kind of money.

Reggie sagged onto the edge of the bed, noting Thalia's missing backpack, the way the sunlight gleamed off the line of horseshow ribbons and trophies set on shelves by the closet. Riding boots that usually sat in the corner were gone. Reggie eyed the pile of discarded shoes that Thalia only ever seemed to get as far as outside her closet. Her favorite purple sneakers were gone.

Had Thalia sat here, crying, making up her mind because not only was she losing her horse, her mother was off throwing herself at a man—the same man Thalia had dubbed *her* friend?

And Reggie hadn't seen it—seen the crisis her daughter was in, was going to be in, because she, Reggie, was too tied up in herself. She'd totally ignored the Team of Two philosophy that they worked together through the hard times. She'd left Thalia to hear the truth by eavesdropping, instead of being truthful with her from the beginning.

Sure, protecting her daughter might have been her motivation, but she'd messed up, big time.

Climbing to her feet, the room spun around her, and she grabbed the dresser edge to steady herself. She needed to call the police—or Jas Stone, at least. He'd know what to do.

She wobbled down the hall to her bedroom and grabbed her cell phone off her bedside table and finally sank down on the bed. She felt like she might never get up again.

She stabbed Thalia's number and the phone buzzed the call signal. No one picked up, so Thalia was refusing to take her calls. Her fingers were blocks of ice she could barely get to work. She kept missing Jas's number and finally dialed Chloe instead. The phone rang once, twice. Click.

"Hey Reggie! How are ya today?" Chloe's deep musical voice came through the phone.

How did she answer that? Numb. So afraid she could barely move?

"Thalia's g-gone." It was all she could manage.

Silence a moment. "What'd'you mean, Thalia's gone? Doesn't she go to the barn every morning?"

"Her backpack's gone. So's her money. We had a fight last night because she heard me tell Cesare that it was likely we were going to lose Gladiator." She scrubbed her free hand over her face and into her still-damp hair, releasing the ponytail. Damp strands fell around her cheeks and she probably looked just as messed up as she felt.

Tell her? This was Chloe, one of their original threesome of Reggie, Lila, and Chloe.

"I—I did something really stupid last night. I—I slept with Cesare. Except it wasn't sleeping with him. It was sex, plain and simple, and Thalia caught us."

"Oh. My. God. How'd it happen? Were you in the house?"

Wincing at the memory, Reggie told her the sordid details. "Thalia must have heard us talking in the house—before. She stewed on it, probably waiting until she thought Cesare had left, and then she walked in on the two of us scrambling to get our clothes on."

She hung her head. "She wouldn't talk to me, Chloe. For the first time, my baby wouldn't talk to me. She was so angry she just locked herself in her room. I camped outside her door, hoping to catch her when she came out. I guess sometime overnight she went out her window after I fell asleep. I tried calling her on her cell, but she wouldn't pick up."

The weight of talking about it seized in her chest. She couldn't talk, could barely breathe, and tears ran down her cheeks. She had made such a mess of her life and now she was ruining Thalia's, too.

All the media stories of the horrors facing young runaways filled her head like too many newscasters talking all at once. She hunched at the edge of the bed and thought she might be sick. Then she realized Chloe was talking.

"Reggie? Reggie, you still there?"

"Uh-huh." Words felt like they clogged her throat.

"Reggie, I'm going to hang up now. I'm going to call Jas and we'll both be right over. Lila, too."

"No! Don't call Lila. I've caused her enough trouble. If you could call Jas, that would be great, but I don't want you to come, either. Just Jas. I need to grow up and solve my own problems. All right?"

"Not all right. We're best friends, Reggie. You, Lila, and me. We stick together."

"No. Not now. Not when my trouble can impact you both. Lila could lose her grandparent's house in litigation. You're her partner. You could lose everything, too. It's better if you stay away for now."

There was silence a moment. "Reggie, you know you're wrong or else you wouldn't have called me. You're going to have to trust Lila and me to do what's best for us. Now I'm going to hang up and call Jas. He and Danny will know what to do."

The cell went dead in her hands and she set it on the bed beside her. Thalia. Where would she go?

The barns? She was upset about Gladiator. There was no way the girl wouldn't go see her horse and she had taken her boots with her.

From somewhere she found a reserve of energy and hope. She grabbed the phone and tucked it in her pocket, pulled on some sneakers, and ran down the stairs. The aroma of pancakes turned her stomach as she went through the kitchen to outside.

A brisk wind from the north blew down the lake, carrying the breath of fall cool that could sometimes come in late August. In only her shorts and t-shirt, her skin turned to gooseflesh. She ran for the truck, but a maroon Camry came up the driveway, spraying gravel. It skidded to a halt beside her, a cloud of dust settling like a pall over everything.

Cesare climbed out.

Not what she needed at the moment. She hit the button to open the truck door, fumbled it open, but before she could climb in and slam the door, Cesare caught her shoulders.

"Reggie! I heard from Jas. You are all right?"

She yanked away and climbed in the truck, but dropped her keys. Dammit, what was the *matter* with her? She had steadier hands than this. She bent to retrieve them, but Cesare was faster.

He dangled them in his fingers, but held them away from her. "You are in no condition to drive."

His tiger eyes were fierce this morning, as if he demanded control. Well good for him, but it wasn't going to work. She had to find Thalia. Having Cesare around would just muddy the waters.

She shook her head. "I have to do this alone. It was seeing you and me together that spooked her. I'm not doing that—it—us—whatever that was last night again."

Grabbing the keys, she climbed in the truck but Cesare didn't move. His handsome body blocked the door.

"I'll just drive forward and close it anyway," she said.

"Reggie, *per favore*—please, I am sorry for what happened last night, but we did nothing wrong. Thalia's reaction has spooked you. She might think it was wrong, but you did not—until you saw her. It—it was good between us and I want the chance for it to be good again."

She couldn't look at him, just tried to insert the keys in the ignition, but her shaking hands made it impossible. Finally she just grabbed the steering wheel and hung on.

"My daughter is missing, Cesare. This is not the time to talk about a relationship that I'm not even sure exists."

His hands covered hers. Squeezed. "That is good to hear, for I feel the same. Now come. You are in no condition to drive yourself and I have a perfectly good vehicle available."

He nodded at the Camry and smoothly freed her resisting hands from the truck's steering wheel. She swallowed and closed her eyes. Just having his hands on hers made her skin tingle. Just inhaling his scent of cut grass and verbena made something clutch in her core, and the bracelet seemed to radiate heat into her frozen arms.

She pulled loose of his touch. "Fine, then. Thank you."

Avoiding him, she climbed down from the truck, closed the door behind her. Square-shouldered, she preceded him to his car. Unfortunately he stymied her attempt to climb in on her own because he had to unlock the door. He held it for her, like some apologetic, old-fashioned gallant, then closed it when she was settled inside.

Smooth leather. Pristine clean. Though it was just a Camry, she could imagine him driving something equally pristine in Milan. Lamborghini, probably. It would suit him.

He climbed in beside her and confidently took them down the driveway, the sunlight through the trees flashing over the windshield like she was inside a movie screen. The confusion on the screen was a perfect metaphor for her messed-up insides.

"I blame this on me, not you, just so you know. You were leaving. It was my fault I came out to you. I just couldn't let well enough alone, I guess."

She felt his glance, though she kept her gaze forward.

"Or perhaps it was that I wished you to come out to me. Wishes can be powerful things."

"Yeah, right. If that was the case, Thalia and I would be at home having breakfast and laughing and I wouldn't have some flipping lawsuit hanging over my head like a guillotine. Turn left at the road. We're going to the stable."

He obeyed her directions and they cruised down the road, the stable and its pastures spread below them to their right.

Such a pastoral place of green grass and white buildings. Usually peaceful looking with its glossy, grazing horses.

Except they weren't this morning, and by this time Thalia had usually fed everyone and had started turning horses out. They'd be out in the fields, bucking or dropping and rolling or nipping at their buddy.

She frowned as they turned in at the long, white-fenced driveway. "Something's wrong."

It was easy to see in the way riders milled at the entrance to the barn and no one was riding. When they pulled up and she leapt out of the car, there weren't even any horses in cross-ties being readied.

Reggie pushed past the milling riders and ran down the breezeway to Gladiator's stall. Empty. The stall door open. Cesare came up beside her just as Thalia's friend Lori arrived.

She was a fine-boned young thing, with glossy dark hair pulled back in a ponytail. She was all legs in her navy breeches and graceful arms that looked more like a dancer than an equestrienne.

Reggie caught her arms. "Thalia? Have you seen Thalia anywhere? She's missing."

Lori's eyes widened and her tanned skin paled. "Mrs. Lewis. Um, can you come with me? Mom wants to talk to you."

Not now. She couldn't deal with the financial issues right now. But she nodded because it was Lori, and Thalia's best friend. Maybe Thalia had come running to them last night. Maybe she'd bunked with Lori. Holding to that hope she followed Lori, but not to the big white and stone house—Lori led them past horses hanging their heads over stall doors along the breezeway and then inside the partially open sliding door to the indoor arena.

Reggie ducked through the narrow opening Lori had passed through and stopped. No one was riding, but the large space echoed with Liz Earl's soft crooning to a horse that was frantically trotting the length of the arena. Big, brown, the horse was saddled, but sans rider, with reins dangling loose from the bit in his mouth.

By the small white star and strip on the nose and the two white socks on his hind legs, she recognized him.

Gladiator.

§

Cesare saw Reggie's legs start to crumple perhaps before she was even aware that they did. He caught her elbows and turned her to him. Held her up, as the dark-haired girl called to her mom in the dimly-lit arena.

Reggie shook under his hands and he held on tightly as the long-legged woman in jeans and designer-look jean jacket abandoned coaxing the horse to limp across to them.

She was a young woman, mid-thirties by the small lines that had formed around her hazel eyes. Unlike her daughter, she had fly-away blonde hair escaping from a quick twist of hair at the crown of her head. She nodded at Reggie and then stuck out her hand. Deep circles under eyes and the stoop of her shoulders said she was exhausted.

"Liz Earl. You must be the friend Thalia brought around the other day." But her gaze said that she was assessing the relationship between Reggie and himself.

He met her hand. "Cesare Angelucci, family friend."

"Where's Thalia?" Reggie asked.

Liz's gaze widened. "We wanted to ask you the same. The middle of the night I got a call from neighbors that one of our horses was loose. We went looking and found Gladiator like this, running down the road. We managed to herd him into the arena, but we still haven't been able to catch him."

She motioned at the horse, who reached the end of the arena and wheeled back to canter back the way he'd come. His sides were drenched with lather.

"Something has spooked him big time and he can't get past it. We've tried buckets of grain. Treats. Even getting a group of us to herd him into a corner, but nothing works. He gets terrified and bolts right through us and that's totally unlike Gladiator."

"But where's my daughter? That's her horse and her riding equipment." Reggie's voice rose an octave.

"We went looking for her last night, figuring maybe she fell off in a ditch. There was no sign of her anywhere. That's why we didn't call you then. We figured maybe some kids had gotten into the barn and taken the horse, that's why we went to wake up Dietrich in the apartment above the barn—to ask whether he'd heard anything and why he hadn't done anything about it. He wasn't there and we haven't been able to get in touch with him."

Reggie seemed to freeze in his arms. Then she placed her palm on his chest and pushed herself free of him. The panic she'd displayed had been replaced by dead calm.

"You're saying that man has disappeared and so has my daughter?" She looked at the horse, her throat working. "Doesn't that disturb you? Who is this Dietrich? What kind of references did he even have before you put him charge of my daughter?"

Her voice was escalating and Liz's look of contrition said every word of Reggie's was too true by far.

"Reggie stop. Please," Liz Earl said. "We need to figure this out together. I didn't know Thalia was missing until just now."

"If you'd wanted to know, you should have phoned me."

Things were going to get bad before they got better. Cesare stepped between them. "Perhaps now is the time we need the police, no? Reggie, why do you not contact our friend the detective and ask him to meet us here? Then we can speak with clearer heads."

Reggie, blocked from her recriminations, pulled out her smart phone and dialed. In the meantime, Cesare walked Liz out in the arena. "Let me try something, yes? You still have the bucket of grain?"

She nodded toward a lone metal bucket in the center of the tanbark footing.

Cesare collected it and strode out into the arena. Gladiator had slowed to a trot along the wall as if seeking a way out. He was smart, this one, the way he craned his head sideways so that he did not become entangled in the dangling reins—reins that suggested the rider had taken a fall. Not good, but he would not think the worst.

At the far end of the arena, he placed himself right in Gladiator's path. He leaned against the wall and began a slow shake of the bucket so the arena filled with the soothing sound of grain slipping together.

Gladiator reached his end of the arena and Cesare hummed. The horse's ears twitched as he wheeled back and trotted back the way he'd come. He wheeled back from the far end of the arena again and trotted back toward Cesare.

He repeated his bucket shake and continued humming. This time Gladiator slowed a little, watching Cesare before he wheeled and was gone again.

The circuit repeated three more times, but on the fourth Gladiator stopped five paces in front of him, head down, nostril's wide, sides heaving.

Cesare didn't move, except to keep shuffling the grain in the bucket. He shifted his hum to a low-voiced conversation.

Gladiator's ears twitched, but they focused on him. One step. Another.

"Good man. You are a good man, aren't you, but something scared you very badly. No one is angry at you, old man. No one will hurt you."

Another step and Cesare held his breath and shuffled the grain bucket.

Gladiator seemed to make a decision. The big horse sighed and took the last step, burying his nose in the bucket to snuffle up grain.

Cesare carefully snagged the reins and gently patted the great sweating head and neck.

"You see? You are actually very brave to trust an almost stranger like me. But you are going to have to cool down before you will be allowed to enjoy your breakfast in peace. How about if we let a nice young woman lead you around for a bit?"

He walked the big horse across the arena to where Jas and Danny had just arrived to speak to Reggie and Liz.

"That was amazing," Liz said. "We've been trying for the past three hours to catch him."

Cesare shrugged. "He needed to decide to come to you. He finally did. I suggest your youngster here walk him out for a while."

He handed the reins to dark-haired Lori and went to Reggie. Raised his brow in question.

She nodded. "I'm okay. Thank you for slowing me down a little. My head was spinning so fast I wasn't thinking. Liz, I'm sorry for accusing you."

"Perhaps what we need to do is go someplace quiet and put the pieces together?" Jas Stone offered.

With his red-headed partner, they took control of the situation and Cesare stepped back, ensuring he stayed by Reggie's side. This was not going to be easy. Thalia was everything.

Liz led them to an upstairs glassed-in viewing gallery where everyone could sit. Reggie repeated the story of what had happened last night except for the part about the sex—just that Thalia had discovered the two of them together and been upset— about the horse and her perceived betrayal.

Liz then told the story of receiving the phone call about a loose horse at two in the morning and how they'd called Dietrich to help them catch the animal, only to discover he was gone. It had taken them most of the night to corral Gladiator and search the ditches to find the rider. In all the fuss they'd neglected to call Reggie—or anyone else, for that matter. They were just trying to deal with the horse.

Liz sighed and sagged in the lounge chair she perched on. Her eyes were almost as haunted as Reggie's.

"I'm so sorry." Liz caught Reggie's hands. "It all caught me so off guard. Thalia's such a wise kid I would never have thought she'd leave in the middle of the night. I thought it was more like Dietrich got it in his mind to go for a midnight ride, got thrown, and the fool was too stupid or too smart to come back and face the music." She shook her head. "Between you and me, I wouldn't be unhappy to see him go, even if he's the big-name German coach everyone's been looking for. There's just something about him that seems off. I've even had a few comments from customers that he creeps them out."

Reggie sat up straighter, nodded. "I thought it was just me. Something about his eyes…"

Then she scrubbed her face with her hands. "Oh, God, I trusted that man to be around my baby."

"Hold on, everyone. We don't know that this Dietrich had anything to do with Thalia's disappearance." Jas intervened. "Now let's calm down and answer some other questions. First off, what's Dietrich's last name?"

"von Byer. Dietrich von Byer. He had a file of recommendations from German riding schools. That's why we hired him."

"Have you got copies of those recommendations?"

Liz nodded.

"Did you contact those schools?"

"Only one of them." Liz shook her head.

Cesare kept his hand on Reggie's shoulder. Here was this powerful woman still trying to be strong when he could feel her trembling. She looked up at him, her face deathly pale, those midnight eyes of hers lost, her expression broken.

"I think I will take Reggie out for some air. We will be back shortly."

It was telling that she didn't resist when he helped her up, led her like a child to the door, down the stairs and out. Meek. That was the word, and Reggie Lewis was never meek.

"Come. Walk. You need to get your blood moving."

She pulled loose of his hand—good, at least there was some fight there.

"What do you know about it? You haven't lost a child."

"I could say that I've lost a woman who has lost a child—but we do not know that Thalia is gone for good. I think it would be more to your advantage to be ready to act—to search for her. Now tell me: When did you last eat?"

Her dark defiant gaze met his, but then she had to look away. "I—I don't know. Yesterday morning, maybe. The night before for sure."

"*Basta*—that's enough! How silly are you? You cannot live and be strong like that!" He grabbed her arm and led her to the

Camry. "Get in. I'll take you for food. Wait a moment and I will let the others know."

He leaned in to kiss her softly and she did not resist, but her lips tasted of iron and her flesh was too cold.

"It is a wonder you have kept going so long."

She only looked at him as he squeezed her hand and turned back to the stable. Behind him he heard her phone ding.

Chapter 18

Everything was a fog as Cesare walked away. A white pall seemed to cover the day, milking out the color of the fields, the barns, the life, the sky. She was floating in that fog as if she was floating on water, and the sweet smell of hay and horse that would always signify Thalia was slipping away, just as her daughter, her life was. She had to find her, make sure she was safe. But how was she to do that when she had no clue where Thalia had gone? She knew in her heart that it was Thalia who had taken Gladiator. There was no question of that.

But something had happened to separate her girl from her horse. The only thing that could do that was something bad. Thalia would never abandon her horse to run down the road, let alone in the middle of the night. The fear that knowledge brought made whatever Cesare had planned a lesson in futility. There was nothing she wanted to eat, let alone leave the farm to find something. There was even less possibility that she'd keep anything down. Her mouth tasted like ash and that was all that her life would be if she didn't know that Thalia was safe and sound. And happy. She had to be happy.

Tired beyond exhausted, she leaned her head against the window and closed her eyes.

Her phone buzzed in her pocket. She hauled it out—it was—Thalia!

She stabbed the receive button. "Thalia! Honey! Where are you? Are you okay?"

Silence at the end of the phone and then a voice. Male. Older, by the sound of him, and so cold and clinical the world went truly white around her. There was only the voice.

"I have your daughter. I will make you a trade of the bracelet for her life. Come to the cross-country ski site on Glenrosa Road. Come alone. Do not call the police or you will never see your daughter alive again."

"Dietrich, is that you? Don't hurt my baby, please. I'll do anything. We'll find a way to cut the darn thing off." Her hand, if she had to. Just save Thalia's life. The phone went dead in her hand and all she could think of was the odd look she had seen in Dietrich von Byer's eyes the last time she'd been at the barn. And now, though it had been his voice, it had also been something else. As if something worked his vocal cords like a puppet master worked the strings.

Fingers numb, she fumbled the car open and stood. She couldn't wait for Cesare. She needed her truck and her truck was home.

She abandoned the car and started up the driveway. Not a long walk to her house: it was a walk Thalia did every day. Thalia, her baby.

Adrenaline flooded her and she started to jog. Made it down the long driveway and was halfway down the street to the turn to her house when a car engine came roaring up behind her and stopped.

Suddenly Cesare was beside her and caught her wrist. "What the hell is this, Reggie? I leave you for a moment and you run away?"

He towered above her and his tiger eyes flared anger. She shook her head and tried to pull loose. This time he wouldn't let her.

"I have to go. If you care anything for Thalia or me, please let me go."

He kept hold of her arm, but his anger softened.

"What's happened, Reggie?" Soft. Dangerous.

"I—I got a phone call from Thalia's line. It was Dietrich, I'm sure of it, and yet not him." The icy fear was enough to almost leave her immobile, but she had to find Thalia.

She held up her free arm, the bracelet feigning innocence as it gleamed in the sun. "It's about this. All of it is. I'm sure of it. He says he wants to trade it for my daughter. I'm going to give it to him."

She tried to twist free, but Cesare held on.

"Please. She's my daughter, Cesare. I have to do this."

He stepped into her and enveloped her in strong, comforting arms. "Of course you do, *cara*. I will come with you."

"No!" She ripped away. "I have to go alone. You can tell Jas and Danny, but only after I have a head start."

"*Basta*, Reggie! That is garbage and you know it. I will not let you do something so stupid."

She glared at him, knowing they were in a standoff and that Cesare was nothing if not stubborn. After all, he had pursued her even though she refused him.

"Listen to me, Cesare. This isn't about doing something foolish. This is about getting Thalia back. If I have to give him the bracelet to do it, I will. It's only a bracelet. Can that be so bad?"

"I thought the bracelet did not come off. Jas told me."

"Only because no one has tried to cut it off. No one has wanted to injure this stupid precious thing, but I will. I'll take a pair of tin snips to the damned thing if it will save my daughter. Hell, I'll melt it down if that will save her."

His tiger gaze searched hers as if seeking the lie. He didn't know everything. Didn't need to know that no one even knew if it was possible to cut the silver links that would not come off her wrist.

Then he sighed and she knew she'd won.

"Where are you going?"

"To the old cross-country ski area up Glenrosa Road. Jas and Danny will know it. Everyone does."

She stood on tiptoe to graze his lips with a kiss and dashed away up her driveway.

The truck stood like a sentinel in the dusty sunlight, her small house like a mirage of what happiness had once been, the workshop a reminder of her sins. She pulled the keys from her pocket and fumbled them trying to find the lock. Damn hands were shaking too hard. So were her knees.

Food, Cesare had said. She felt weak enough maybe there was something in his words. She went to the house and the smell of her homemade chocolate chip pancakes still permeated the air. She grabbed a handful from the platter cooling in the oven and then rooted around in the kitchen junk drawer seeking an old pair of tin snips that she'd kept for rough work at home. She came up with them and was out the door again, stuffing her face with the ashen taste of Thalia's favorite breakfast.

Mashed pancake with her teeth and swallowed the tasteless mess down. Lead in her stomach, but she forced herself to eat another as she finally got her keys in the lock and climbed in. Tossed the snips and the other pancakes on the seat beside her and got the engine started and the vehicle in gear. Gravel crunched under her tires as she turned the truck around and headed down the driveway. When she hit the road, Cesare's Camry was thankfully gone. He'd tell the others and help would come after everything was over and Thalia was free.

Glenrosa Road sat between Peachland and West Kelowna. The paved road led up past the town's Lumber Mill and through a housing development, up into the folded mountains toward the Crystal Mountain Ski Resort.

Reggie turned the truck off the highway onto Glenrosa and accelerated up the winding road through the suburban housing development. Then the road narrowed as the landscape changed, the road following a narrow valley with larger acreages complete with lounging horses and here and there even a sheep farm. The truck's motor roared as she pushed the old beast up the straight sections. The rear wheels squealed as she took the corners too fast. She could feel the rear end slipping, but it didn't matter. Thalia had been in the hands of this monster for at least twelve hours. There was no telling what he could have done to her. Her heart pounded in her chest as the adrenaline pumped through her. She'd get her baby back if it was the last thing she did.

Gradually the number of houses decreased and the forested hillsides ran down to the road. Higher up from the lake, the ponderosa pine were interspersed with fir and huge red pine. Poplar and cottonwood trees towered along the watercourse of highland stream. The air through her open window smelled of water and pine and underbrush heated by the August sun. Sunlight gleamed on tall, yellowed grass between the trees and on glimpses of water.

The old cross-country ski area sat in a flat-bottomed valley where the land broadened back from the road. A small manufactured building served as a lodge in the winter, selling hot chocolate and hot dogs to skiers escaping the cold. During the summer the place looked abandoned except for a grey Suburban parked in the shade of the building.

Reggie slowed to study the scene: no Thalia waving to her. No man holding a knife to her daughter's throat, either. Over the rumble of the truck's engine she couldn't hear much, so she cranked the wheel and pulled into the parking lot and cut the engine.

Robin-song and the rapid tap-tap-tap of a woodpecker came from the woodlands. Insects hummed in the grass that covered the open valley floor. From far away came the rumble of the highway and the hum of suburban lawnmowers. The dry ground was crisscrossed with vehicle tracks following the ski trails— probably motocross riders and ATVs.

She climbed out into the heavy silence of the late morning, the sun almost directly overhead and pouring down heat.

"Hello?" she called. "Anyone here?"

Silence ached back at her; even the woodpecker had gone elsewhere.

"Mom!"

The call quickly cut off. Reggie spun around. The sound had come from the wooded hillside. Grabbing the pair of snips from the truck, she cut across the flats, the tall grass running across her bare lower legs, late summer grasshoppers leaping before her. At the forest edge, she stopped.

"Where are you?" she called.

There was no answer, but she thought she heard something—a rustle in the brush that was more than the wind. Perhaps a murmur or order. A whimper.

Thalia.

She set out, directly into the thick brush under the trees, ignoring how branches tore at her legs and bare arms. It was hard work, but she pushed, shoved, and dragged herself up through the trees and came out on a loop of the ski trail. Where to now? Left or right?

"Where do I go now?" she called. Surely Dietrich could see she was alone.

She was met only by silence and the hush of the wind in the pine boughs and the rattle of poplar leaves. Again, there came a slight disturbance in the forest. Something to her left and higher up the slope as if something larger pushed through the underbrush, but there was also a rustling lower down and behind her as well.

The larger noise had come from above and that was more certainly where Thalia would be if Dietrich was trying to ensure that they were alone. She turned left and followed the trail up the hill.

It looped around and back in a switchback, taking her up the steep mountain slope. It would be a good downhill glide in the winter months. In the summer it was just a reason to sweat and get out of breath. She was puffing by the time she reached the top—a viewpoint where she could overlook the valley and the not-quite-a-lodge below. In the winter it would probably be a welcome sight and a call to come in for some hot chocolate. In the summer it just looked desolate.

She never saw him coming.

Suddenly she found herself slammed into the ground, barrel-chested Dietrich holding her down with his weight. Before she could shield herself, his fist came up and he slammed her in the face.

Darkness.

§

Cesare shoved through the underbrush trying in vain to keep silent, when woodcraft was not his forte. He was an Italian city boy who had managed to acclimatize to third world countries, but always in the city. This thick forest was definitely beyond him.

But for Reggie and her daughter he would find a way. Carefully, he pushed branches aside. More carefully he watched where he stepped, trying to avoid the crack of the tinder-dry branches that littered the ground from the pine trees that had branches turning red. He'd read somewhere it was the Asian pine beetle killing the BC forests.

When Reggie had refused to let him come with her, he had done the only thing he could think of—had gotten in his rental car and driven while she ran to her house. He had followed the map he pulled up on his smart phone when he searched for cross-country skiing in West Kelowna. He'd driven until he saw someone riding a horse and had asked for directions, had driven past the flat-bottomed valley and found a place to pull over and park. Then he'd phoned Jas Stone and told him what was going on, hanging up when the detective started to swear.

He had left his car higher up on the road beyond the ski area and had crept through the underbrush and waited until the sound of an engine roaring had said that Reggie approached. He'd watched her then, had heard the call from up in the woods and had begun this long, circling exercise through the woods seeking her and the man who held her daughter. He would kill Dietrich if he hurt either of them. Might do it anyway for the fear he had bestowed on them.

He came out at the trail one more time and paused. Sweat ran from his hair into his eyes. His grey polo shirt was sodden. There was only the forest silence of birds and groaning tree trunks in the wind, the pulsing hum of cicadas. Noonday sun burned through blue sky so he missed the umbrellas and curbside tables of Milan plazas. How easy it had been to sit there with his espresso or Campari, choosing his next conquest from the flocks of well-dressed women.

And now he was here, risking himself to save a woman who was unlike any of those he had ever sought before. As strong as he was—stronger, perhaps, for what she had overcome. Nothing had come easy to Reggie Lewis, and that had made her stronger.

So what was he? Dilettante, raconteur. Cad. Lazy, good-for-nothing eldest son. Even his little foray into business seemed like nothing compared to what Reggie had done—forged a career and raised a daughter out of sheer talent and determination. He wanted that kind of determination. Was going to prove that he had it by finding her and making sure she and her daughter were safe—even if she was still determined that there was nothing between them.

But first he had to find her.

Listening gave no clue. There was only the lulling wind through the branches and the croak of a huge black bird. Raven, maybe. Laughing, probably, at his efforts to belong in this country.

He scanned the trail, but there were only scuff marks and the dried-in-mud tracks of all-terrain vehicles. What he wouldn't give to have one of them right now. He chose to go left because surely he would have heard her above him if she had gone that way. Not too far along, he found a single clear footprint in the dust. Long slim sneaker footprint and he knew he was right. He lengthened his stride up and around the curve of the trail and was faced with a steep incline that just made him sigh.

A noise stopped him and made him step off the trail into brush and tree shadows.

The rattle of brush and he was sure someone or something was up there, just over the crest of the hill. He started up, trying to be as silent as possible and just before the crown of the slope, he stepped upslope into the masking trees. Higher up like this the tree branches were more thickly matted together, the brush thicker, making passage difficult—and noisy, because he could hear whoever was up here moving through the forest.

Cesare eased through the trees, because he was pretty sure that whoever was here was unaware of him and that was his only advantage. If it was Dietrich, he was confident enough that he was alone to disregard the noise he made. Making that amount of noise, he wouldn't be as likely to hear Cesare behind him.

He sped up, shoving through the branches, trying not to cause the shotgun sound of the shattering of dead wood that came through the trees from whoever he pursued. Cesare angled right, eventually finding the marks indicating someone else had passed this way. He stopped and hauled out his phone and punched in Jas Stone's number, imagining the man's curse when he saw the caller ID.

Someone picked up.

"Where the fuck are you?"

Not Jas. Danny, his red-headed partner.

He cupped his hand over the receiver and his mouth. "I'm up on the mountainside above the cross-country ski lodge. Reggie was above me, but I think she's either met someone or something has happened to her. I followed her up the trail, but then there was crashing through the woods. I am following the sounds."

"We're at the lodge now. How far up the hill?"

Too hot and sweaty by far, was his first thought. "I crossed the trail once before I found her footprints on the second loop. I followed it eastward toward the lake, but it turned back on itself and took a steep climb upward. At the top is where I heard someone. I followed them and they are going farther up the hill through the brush."

Ahead of him, the noise of the other person's passage had stopped. How long had the silence held?

"Shit," he whispered into the phone. "The noise has stopped. He might have heard me."

"You've got to be very careful, Cesare. If this is like the other times, this guy is dangerous. He wants that bracelet and he'll do anything to get it."

"Reggie said she would cut it off and give it to him for Thalia's return."

The airspace pulsed empty for a moment. "She might say that, Cesare, but we don't even know if it's possible. In the past, he's said that the only way to get the bracelet off the woman's arm is for them to be dead."

Suddenly the shady forest on the hot afternoon was cold.

"Dietrich said this?"

Another beat. "Not Dietrich. The thing that's inside him at the moment. Whatever it is, it can force him to do anything. I know. It was inside me, once."

Cesare looked at the phone, still not believing their story. But Reggie had hinted at strangeness, too. No wonder Reggie was frantic for Thalia. In the hands of whatever this was, there was no knowing what it would do.

And it had Reggie now.

The fear that had kept him moving tightened into a cold stone in his belly. Was that what he'd heard above him on the road? The fatal strike? Was Reggie gone? If only he'd gone up to the crest of the hill, he'd at least know if there was blood on the road.

The phone was droning at him in Danny's voice. He hit the off button and started through the brush, vigilant about the sound he made.

A sound like a muffled shriek brought him upright as he was ducking under a tree. He banged his head on a branch, cursed once colorfully out loud, then swallowed the pain.

The forest had gone watchfully silent. The cicadas had stopped, so had the little birds' songs. But through the still forest, along with the wind, a predator came stalking—he was sure of it—and what it was stalking was him.

His flesh cold, he ducked under the trees and off the path to the right of where it ran. There was an area of pine-beetle-killed trees, and their sagging red branches allowed more space between the bases of the trees. He loped silently up through the graveyard of forest, praying Dietrich, or whatever it was, hadn't seen him. Then he angled back to his left and started down the hill again. It couldn't be far from here that Thalia and Reggie were held. It couldn't be far and maybe, if the guy was out looking for him, he'd find them alone and could free them.

At the moment that was all he could come up with for a plan.

Away from the beetle kill, this high on the slope the ground was bathed in shadow. In the gloom there was no way he'd find

Reggie and Thalia. What was the saying?—a needle in a haystack, only in this case, the haystack was a mountain.

He slowed, picking his way through the trees, straining to hear anyone who might be stalking him. Maybe Dietrich had given up. Maybe he was already finishing what he'd started and Reggie was already dead. Thalia, too.

It was not possible. He would make it not possible, no matter what Jas and Danny said.

Ahead, a beam of sunlight cut through the gloom and the sound of water trickling tinkled in the air. Instead of the sigh of the wind and groan of the pines, came the waterfall sound of shifting poplar leaves. Cesare slowed, the air heavy and waiting around him. The scent of old campfires reached him.

Odd.

This had to be it—the place Reggie and Thalia were held. The light would make it easier for Dietrich to keep track of his victims.

Crouching amid the underbrush, he edged forward through the trees. Something bright lavender caught his attention and he craned for a look. It was hard to tell, through the screen of brush, tree trunks, and tall grass, but he finally made out the outstretched jean-and-riding-boot-clad legs and lavender t-shirt. It had been the shirt that caught his eye—a color Victoria had always loved, but the riding boots told the tale. Thalia, for certain.

She lay unmoving in the grass and a sudden burst of panic held him where he was.

Was he too late? Had Dietrich truly killed both Thalia and the woman he loved?

Loved?

No time for silly thoughts. Where was Reggie and where was Dietrich? If Thalia was here, he couldn't image Reggie being too far away, so where was the man who held them?

There was no sign of him in the clearing.

Cesare edged closer to Thalia. If he could get close enough, he could free her—if she still lived.

He shifted closer.

Was it supposed to be so easy? Could it be a trap? He sat back on his heels, listening. There was no sound of anyone in the woods, so Jas and Danny hadn't caught up yet. Wait for them?

This might be the very best chance he had to get Reggie and Thalia to safety. He had to take it.

Hunkered over, he crept farther into the clearing. Thalia lay there, her eyes closed, her blonde hair tangled around her face, but still breathing.

Where was Reggie? He scanned the area.

Something lay amid the trees on the far side of the opening. A cruel place to put her—so close but so far from her daughter.

He crossed to her, chancing the open area, and with sun on his back, knelt beside her. She lay bound and gagged and stretched out. Her hands and legs tethered to trees so she couldn't move, but she was still alive. That was what mattered. Her midnight eyes widened when she saw him, her hair a wild tangle in the grass around her. She'd fought. She had, but a spreading bruise and a cut on her brow said how she'd been brought down.

He held his finger to his lips. "A moment and I will free you."

She shook her head, "no," which made no sense. He slipped the gag from her mouth.

"He's looking for you. He knew someone was there. Go. Get help."

"And leave you both here? I do not think so," he said softly.

Her bonds were thick rope, skillfully knotted. He set to working at the loops of braided nylon horse rope that held her wrists. Finally he freed the first loop, began worrying the second.

"Cesare! Watch out!"

His head came up in time to see the thick-set man lunging toward him with a stout branch ready to crush Cesare's skull.

Cesare threw himself aside. The blow struck the earth at Reggie's side. Cesare rolled and came half up to his feet, but the branch was whistling through the air toward him again. He stumbled sideways and put a tree between himself and his assailant. Dietrich, but not the man he'd seen at the stable. This man was haggard, wild haired, and wilder eyed. His mouth was stretched in a vicious grin as if he enjoyed the possibility of spreading someone's brains all over the rough ground.

"Dietrich, what are you doing? You are a riding instructor, not a kidnapper or murderer."

The other man lunged to get around the tree and Cesare leapt away again. Came up behind Reggie and yanked on the last loop of her bonds.

They pulled loose, but she stayed down as the man came after Cesare. Dietrich's eyes seemed to flare red in the sun and his features flushed dark.

And then suddenly he wasn't there—had turned and leapt across the clearing to Thalia. He hauled her up off the ground until she hung in his grasp, still unconscious.

"No!" Reggie screamed and fought with the ropes around her ankles.

"Put the girl down," Cesare said. "She has done nothing to you."

In response, Dietrich dropped the heavy tree branch and from somewhere produced a knife.
"You will sit down beside the woman and retie her bonds. Then you will tie your legs."

Cesare hesitated.

"Do it, or I will use this on the girl." He brandished the knife, so sunlight caught its edge.

"She's a child!" Reggie screamed, her hands frozen on the ropes. "She's done nothing to you."

"But she means much to you." Dietrich's eyes flashed as the knife pressed into Thalia's pale throat.

Anger, fear, and frustration tangled in Cesare's chest. He could not let this happen, and yet what choice did he have? The knife was too close to Thalia's throat, and if they lost Thalia, it would kill Reggie.

He knelt beside Reggie. "Lie back and put your hands behind your back."

Her dark eyes were huge in her pale face.

"It will be all right," he said. "We will get free. All of us."

She didn't look like she believed him, but she stayed silent.

He tied her ankles first, looping the ropes around them but leaving the knot loose. Her hands he did the same, tying them behind her back but using his fingers to show her that they would be easy to release.

Then he sat down beside her and did the same to his feet, using a simple ground line hitch to make the knot look secure.

"Sit with your back to the tree," Dietrich commanded.

Cesare squirmed into position and Dietrich dropped Thalia as if she was nothing. The girl sprawled on the ground. He approached cautiously as if he did not trust Cesare. The grass rustled around Dietrich's legs and Cesare tensed.

This had to work. There was no telling whether Jas and Danny would get here in time.

The man smelled of horse and ash, like the remains of a fire in a burned-out building—what he had smelled when he first entered the clearing. Dietrich knelt behind Cesare to tie him. To tie the knot, Dietrich would have to put his knife down. Cesare expected it.

Uno. Due. Tre.

Chapter 19

In the dappled light of the poplar clearing, Cesare yanked his hands away from Dietrich and threw himself sideways. In the process, he grabbed the end of the hitch on his legs and tore the rope free. The sky was blue, the air heavy with dust. Then Dietrich was on him, knife plunging toward his chest.

Reggie screamed.

Cesare grabbed the knife arm and tried to twist it aside.

The man was stronger than Cesare had expected. He stank of fire. His flesh was hot. He straddled Cesare's hips and used his weight to press the blade down. Cesare braced against him, but the man had the laws of nature on his side. The blade sank closer.

He could fight the slow, inexorable descent of the knife or he could truly fight. He released one hand and gouged Dietrich's eyes and wrenched himself sideways. Dietrich fell and Cesare scrambled away. Was barely up on his feet when Dietrich slammed into him again. He tore away and felt the slice of metal into his side. If he hadn't moved, the blade would have found his heart.

"Run," he shouted at Reggie. She had freed herself and stumbled to Thalia.

Blood ran warm down his side as he turned to face the armed man. Dietrich circled him and Cesare circled with him, then suddenly the riding coach plunged away toward Reggie and Thalia.

Cesare leapt after him, tackled him from behind and together they went down, but Dietrich twisted in his hold. Kicked Cesare in the temple and the day went dark. He couldn't move. Then he could and rolled away and was up.

Reggie had Thalia by her shoulders and was dragging her away.

Dietrich, knife ready, was almost on her.

Cesare sprang one more time, tackling the armed man to the ground. Dietrich's elbow connected with Cesare's injured head. The world spun, he caught a glimpse of light on steel and managed to roll. Heard a scream as pain fountained through his chest and then Dietrich was on him again.

§

Blood! There was blood covering the front of Cesare's gray shirt and Dietrich was killing him—still had the knife, and was trying to use it again. Somehow Cesare was holding on, had braced the knife away from a second plunge into his chest, but for how long she didn't know.

He needed her help, but she had to get Thalia away.

Sunlight through the trees made the scene a terrifying patchwork of light and shadow, sunlight gleaming wetly off the vivid red soaking Cesare's shirt. He was going to bleed to death.

He was doing it to give her and Thalia a chance to escape.

She couldn't let this happen to him—but she had to.

"M-mom?" Thalia's groggy voice cut through her terrorized debate.

"Thalia! You're awake!" She hugged her daughter so hard that Thalia protested.

"Mom! Untie me."

Reggie checked over her shoulder. The two men were still struggling. She set Thalia down and untied her arms.

"Honey, I have to help Cesare. Untie yourself and get out of here. The trail's that way. When you reach it, follow it down and you'll come to the cross-country ski lodge. Here's my phone. Call 911."

She didn't want to leave her daughter, but if Cesare went down, Dietrich would be after Thalia again.

Reggie pulled all that amazing young girl warmth into her arms. "I couldn't bear it if anything happened to you. Understand?"

"Go, Mom. Help Cesare."

Reggie turned and ran.

The two men grappled, the knife still in Dietrich's hand, but the distance between Cesare's chest and the blade had shrunk by half. She had to do something. She looked around for the stout branch Dietrich had used on Cesare. There—across the clearing. She leapt through the rough grass. In her hands it had a good heft, like a tire iron, and her muscles felt ready, like she was facing a forge and this was her hammer.

So far Dietrich hadn't noticed her. He was too intent on finishing Cesare.

Tree limb raised like a bat, she crept through the grass. The two men grunted with effort. Dietrich growled low like something demented. Sunlight flashed on the blade he held and the clearing reeked of flesh forged hot as heated metal. The bracelet was hot on her wrist as she raised the club higher.

A branch snapped underfoot and Dietrich sprang up to face her, his eyes red pits in his skull as he stepped toward her.

"I should have slit your throat when I struck you, but I knew someone else followed."

His voice was Dietrich's accented English, and yet not. There was something wrong with him. Something that made the words issue from his mouth out of sync with his lip movement. A shadow shifted around him, like an extra cloak. He held the knife before him, the blade already stained red.

Behind him on the ground, Cesare struggled to rise. It wasn't working too well. Loss of blood, most likely.

Dietrich advanced, the knife ready, his eyes flaring red, deep in his skull.

"You're—you're not Dietrich, are you? You're something else."

Dietrich's lips stretched in a mannequin smile. "Something strong. Something powerful beyond anything you can imagine, and yet you are foolish enough to resist when it is futile."

Keep him talking. Maybe it would give Cesare a chance to get up and escape. Every moment she kept him talking was another moment help had to get here.

He lunged at her and she swung the branch. Heard it connect with the knife arm and heard bones crunch. Dietrich's flushed face paled. He changed knife hands and lunged again, his broken arm flopping sickeningly. Lunged again. Again. She swung her club each time but missed him and he drove her back, back, back until her spine came up against a tree trunk.

"The bracelet is mine. It was stolen. I want it back," said the thing in Dietrich's body.

Keep him talking. Get as much information as she could. "When you tried to get it the first time, you told Chloe it was only a trinket, a bauble with purely sentimental value."

The man-creature before her snarled. He lunged at her before she could swing the club and the knife was at her throat, cold steel slicing her flesh, his stench of burning metal and ash stealing her breath. She was going to die and Thalia would grow up without her mother. Team of Two would be over and she would never again tell her baby how much she loved her. Would never see her married with babies of her own.

"Long ago I rid myself of a problem with that bracelet—or thought I did. Now that problem threatens again—and will, as long as the bracelet remains in the hands of you and your friends. That ends now."

Tears filled her eyes as she looked into the swirling darkness of the creature before her.

A crack like an explosion filled the clearing and Dietrich's eyes went wide. He stumbled against her, the knife searing her neck. Warm blood blossomed and poured down her chest.

And then Dietrich crumpled to his knees; the knife fell from his lax hand. The angry red darkness of his eyes still swirled in front of her as a cloud of something dark and reeking of burned-out buildings rose from his body. Heat like a furnace made her shield her face. It rose up and up in a column like flames and then, whether it was the wind or the thing's will, it came apart into fine gray particles like ash that whipped away above the trees and eastward, though there was no breeze.

She collapsed to her knees, Dietrich's body before her, a bloody wound gleaming red beneath his left shoulder blade.

"Mom! Mom!"

She clamped a hand on the awful warmth of her neck and looked up in time to see Jas Stone and Danny Forester and four uniformed officers push into the clearing. Then Thalia burst past them to throw her arms around her mother.

One armed, Reggie clung to her—never wanted to let her go—but she had someone else to check on.

"Help me up." Thalia and Danny did. He checked her wound and from somewhere produced a dressing for her to hold against the cut.

"You'll live," he said. Then he checked for signs of life in Dietrich. He shook his head.

But Dietrich didn't matter—except that he was no longer a danger. Leaning on Thalia's shoulder, she stumbled over to where Jas Stone knelt over Cesare. She went to her knees beside him.

Cesare's usually handsome, olive tan was far too pale. The gleam of his tiger eyes was dulled by pain, but he smiled as she caught his hand.

"Thank you. Oh, my God, thank you," she said.

She leaned down to kiss him on the mouth. Softly. Tenderly, and his hand came up to cup the back of her head.

"This is not how I imagined our next kiss, *caramia*."

Her eyes filled. "Damn you, Cesare Angelucci, you made me cry. You better darn well live because we've got some talking to do."

At that his brows raised in question marks and he winced.

Paramedics came through the trees and Reggie was shoved aside once they had checked her over and bandaged her neck wound. Holding Thalia's hand, she and Thalia followed Danny through the woods to where the ambulance had somehow managed the grade of the cross-country ski hill. They loaded Cesare and ground down the hill. Reggie and Thalia followed, helped by Jas and Danny.

As they started down the last loop of the ski trail, the sound of ambulance sirens retreated down the hill toward Kelowna. Jas came up beside her.

"You okay?" He motioned at the bandage on her neck.

"It's Cesare I'm worried about. Will he be okay?"

Jas shrugged. "Knife wounds are always ugly, but he was in good shape and I'm hoping that there was no serious injury to internal organs. It looked good from what I saw." But his expression was grave.

She squeezed her eyes shut. Cesare had all but given his life for her and she'd treated him so poorly—had almost run him off her place when he'd come to help her look for Thalia.

"We never would have survived if not for him. Dietrich would have killed me for sure, for this stupid bracelet, but he heard someone else coming. He must have thought the bracelet wouldn't come off easily so he had to finish Cesare first to give himself time."

Jas looked down at the bracelet as if considering. Then he met her gaze. "So have you found your matching door yet?"

She shook her head, refusing to think of the door on the wine bottle. "Why? You actually think it's going to signify my soul mate?"

He shrugged. "No reason. I just sorta thought..." He shook his head. "It's nothing. Guess you'll have to wear it a while longer, then."

Danny drove her truck back to her house while Jas transported Reggie and Thalia to Kelowna General Hospital. Thalia kept protesting that she was okay, Dietrich had just knocked her around a bit—but there was no way Reggie was buying that. Her spritely daughter's pale face and over-large dark eyes suggested she was still in shock.

They wound down out of the hills and onto the highway, past the turn to their place, and through the old town of Westbank that all the new folks in the myriad new housing developments had voted to rename West Kelowna—much to the dismay of the old-timers. The strip malls and big box stores had eaten up the orchards. Retirement condos had devoured the grassy benchlands until there was nothing but rooflines to see down toward the lake.

So much was changing and Reggie wasn't sure it was for the better. She slung an arm around Thalia's shoulders and pulled her baby into her side.

"Team of Two," Thalia murmured.

Reggie kissed her hair. "Always."

Chapter 20

Jas Stone's front room ticked silence around Cesare. Sure, there was the sound of distant traffic from the road, and through the open door to the deck in the two-story glass front wall of the living room. There was also the hum of insects in the orchards along with the distant voices of the pickers come in for the harvest, but the house itself was silent. At the moment he didn't want silence. He wanted distraction from the corkscrew of his thoughts.

The room was wood and stone with modern furniture, the black leather couch and Jas's favorite low, black, leather chair set before the floor to ceiling stone fireplace with the antique, iron-bound Zanzibar door hung above it like the mystical entrance to some Middle Eastern potentate's fortress. As usual, the sky outside was blue, the clouds as fluffy as froth on a good beer, and the sun far too hot for a man just released from the hospital. Thankfully Dietrich, or whatever he had been, had not been proficient as a knife fighter. It was one thing to slit the throats of a woman and a girl he had trussed and tied. It was another to actually stab to kill a man who fought back. Dietrich, for all that something else had looked out of his eyes—perhaps the man himself had not wanted to kill.

Cesare worked his shoulder against the tight muscles and the bandages that bound his side and chest. The chest wound had been the worst looking and it had gone deep, but had—praise

God—missed all the organs and arteries. Truly a miracle. The wound on his side, however, had sliced deep into his trapezium muscle and was as painful as hell. They had bound his arm to his chest to give the muscle some chance to heal instead of being torn open by movement, so he was left wandering around the house with an open shirt thrown over his shoulder as if he fancied himself an Italian supermodel.

Victoria would laugh—had laughed, actually. His sister had shown up at his hospital bed, worry on her face and a shake of her head as if this was the kind of end she expected him to have. Damnable woman had still not discussed his request with their father, either, and the time to finalize the Napa deal was slipping away.

He should be making calls himself—to lenders, to the land owner—asking for more time. He could even contact his father himself, but something stopped him. He kept thinking of the lovely, rolling Napa farmland just waiting for someone to lay out the vineyard and plant the fledgling vines and watch them grow.

The trouble was, every time he visualized the winery to be, a Cleopatra-haired woman somehow entered the picture and would turn to look at him with Reggie Lewis's eyes.

Could he leave her behind? Ask her to come with him?

It was a conundrum he wasn't sure how to fix. He could not imagine Reggie leaving her friends, her home, and dragging Thalia to California. This was their home.

Besides, he had not seen the woman since she snuck inside to thank him in the emergency room bay where he was being worked on. She had been pale over the bandage on her neck; her eyes dark wells of emotion under the deep blue bruise on her temple, her hair pulled back in a ponytail somehow made her more exotic and yet more vulnerable. She'd still had streaks of dirt on her face from her ordeal. The doctors had apparently kept both her and Thalia overnight at the hospital out of concern for concussion, while him they had sent packing after stitching and once the scans proved that he had suffered only tissue damage.

He wondered how she fared. Jas had casually let drop that both Reggie and Thalia had been released to their home this morning, as if he somehow knew the information was important to Cesare.

With a sigh, he padded into the kitchen for another of Jas's most excellent beers. He opened it and headed for the deck and the chairs there. If nothing else, he could renew his tan while he decided on his future, for that was what he was doing. This time, after all the years of making decisions without ever looking back, whatever he decided would be a turning point.

He had just stepped out into the hammer-heat of near noon and was settling himself in Jas's newly acquired patio lounge that had been bought with Chloe's urging, when a faint knock on the front door stopped him. Groaning, he struggled to his feet and returned to the high-ceilinged living room.

Not that sitting was comfortable. But then neither was standing or lying down.

He limped up the long flight of stairs and reached the door just as he heard a car engine start with a familiar rattle. He yanked open the door and stepped outside.

Cream-colored truck, faded. Reggie at the wheel, turned to look over her shoulder as she backed out of the driveway. She glanced back at the house and the truck lurched to a stop and then pulled forward again. Stopped and the engine cut off.

She climbed out and smiled shyly in his direction. "I didn't think anyone was home. No one answered."

Cesare shrugged and wished he hadn't. Winced. "I was out front. It took me a little time to get to the door. I am slow at the moment."

He glanced ruefully at his shoulder. "You are well? Your concussion is not so bad?"

She smiled, her dark eyes lustrous under midnight bangs. "A little headache, and that's fading."

"And Thalia?"

Her smile broadened. "Fine. She's down at the barn regaling everyone with her adventure and patting Gladiator. Apparently the horse knew something was wrong with Dietrich when he appeared on the road when she was trying to run away. She tried to make Gladiator do what she wanted—in other words, trust Dietrich, but Gladiator was too wise. When he wheeled away, he unseated her. She hit her head then and didn't wake up until Deitrich had her in the woods. He apparently hit her again after he got her to call me and didn't come to until I was dragging her out of harm's way. She needs to go in for more tests, but so far everything looks good." She studied him a moment, but then her gaze fell to her feet.

"She wanted to come to thank you and make sure you were okay, but I said we had a few things to discuss privately."

The sun burned down on them. The slight breeze picked up her hair, and the neighbor's sprinkler went spss-spss-spss across sunburned grass.

"Do you want to come inside?" he asked feeling more awkward than he ever had in his life. "We can talk."

He held the door for her and let her enter ahead of him so he caught a whiff of her scent of baby powder and iron. He didn't know if that scent would ever leave him. It made him think of a certain night in a certain dusty workshop. Oh, for the time to luxuriate in this woman.

He stepped in behind her and closed the door.

"I don't want to keep you from whatever you were doing," she said and looked around the entryway. It had an exposed aggregate floor and railings that allowed a view down into the living room.

"You are not keeping me from anything." Because had he not just been thinking of her? "I was having a drink on the deck. Would you join me?"

Reggie looked at him and checked her watch. "A little early for me, but I guess."

"Would you like something to eat? We can make something of this—a picnic? That is the word?"

Her full lips curved in a smile as if she appreciated this reprieve from whatever it was that had brought her here. "Sure. I can give you a hand."

In Jas's small kitchen that sat back beyond the stairway to one side of the living room, he and Reggie pillaged the fridge and found the makings for chicken sandwiches. Reggie set to work buttering and mayoing the bread, while Cesare fumbled his way through one-handed carving of chicken off the small carcass. A little lettuce and salt and pepper and Reggie carried two plates with sandwiches while Cesare brought her beer out onto the deck.

They didn't look at each other as they settled in chairs around a small glass table under a patio umbrella. This was harder than he had thought it would be, given he wanted to talk to Reggie. He clinked her bottle with his.

"To survival. We both did. And Thalia. All is good."

She gave a quick nod and then looked down at her food. "Thank you for lunch."

Unable to help himself, he reached for her hand and ran his thumb over the smooth skin on the back. The bracelet lay like a beautiful silver shackle against her tan.

"I am truly glad that you are safe. The cut on your neck—it is not so bad?"

Her free hand came up to touch the bandage still in place. "It's fine—not too sore. I've only kept the bandage on because I plan to work in the shop a bit today and I want to protect the wound from the grime. The doctor says I'll barely have a scar."

"That is good news. I would hate for this lovely skin to be marred."

An attractive blush rose up her shoulders and she avoided his gaze. "You see—you talk like that and you're just like all those Italian guys in the movies with all their compliments that make a woman uncomfortable."

"And it is a shame that you think that, for the compliment is well deserved." He squeezed her hand. "Reggie, I was terrified something horrible had happened to you. Jas and Danny told me more of the history of this bracelet and the attempts on your friends' lives."

Not releasing her hand, he slid his chair closer to hers to better study the bracelet.

"Did I tell you that this is a most amazing piece of work?" He released her hand to examine the links of the bracelet one by one. "Each of them is so exact. So precise in the way they are made. So much detail, as if they had real life examples to be modeled from."

His finger came to rest on the small door shaped like his family's winery door. The same image that decorated the winery's best wine's bottles.

"This one. I know you saw the wine bottle, but that door is more than simply a label. Let me show you something." He pulled his wallet from his hip pocket and thumbed through an inner pocket to pull out a precious old business card. This he slid across the tabletop to her and waited, holding his breath.

§

The warm breeze on the sunny patio suddenly felt cool in the umbrella's shade. The scent of the chicken sandwich overlaid the fragrance of ripe peaches from the orchard and the hops scent of the beer, but most of all she was aware of Cesare's scent of verbena. It was more intoxicating than the beer. So were the gold flecks in his tiger eyes. His gaze was so intense she almost couldn't look at him because her body reacted like some silly schoolgirl.

She could throw herself at this man all over again and that was—well—stupid. Look at the trouble it had got her and Thalia in the first time. She didn't need more of that.

The sad thing was, she was pretty sure she needed him. Was almost positive the way her skin tingled and flushed when he touched her hand. Even the stupid bracelet turned warm in Cesare's Italian heat.

To avoid letting him read her reaction to him in her eyes, she eyed the card on the table. Faded, well-worn at the edges as if he'd carried it in his wallet for a long time. The paper was white, or had been, but showed the sepia discoloration of long handling so she could almost imagine Cesare sitting for many hours considering that card between thumb and forefinger.

Embossed black lettering spelled out *Cantina Angelucci* in an old-fashioned script and underneath it the name Renaldo Angelucci, *Vinaio*. From what she knew of Italian, that was

Angelucci Winery, Renaldo Angelucci, Vintner. To the right of both names was an ink drawing of a door, one she'd seen before on a wine bottle but tried to ignore. Tall, narrow, and plain, an ornate lintel over the top. This time she couldn't ignore it.

Holding her breath, she picked up the card and held the image next to the small link on her bracelet. Line for line it was the same.

"What is this?"

"My great-grandfather's business card. He was the vintner of Angelucci Estate Winery. As I told you the other night, the door is the front gate to the cellar where the wine is still made."

His picked up the card and his thumb automatically ran over the image as if it was like Braille to him—a way to read the world.

"This was the place I was happiest in the world as a young man. All the places I have been, I still have not been able to find that happiness again—until now." He shook his head as if he could not believe it either. "You know you are a very difficult woman, and yet I keep coming back to you as I did to that winery cellar. I loved that place."

His words hung as he caught her wrist again and peered down at the offending door. His touch was warm and tingles ran up her arm. The silver warmed on her wrist. "So why has this bracelet been made to look like my grandfather's winery?"

She didn't know what to say. Instead she turned her hand in his and linked their fingers. "That's the strangeness of it, isn't it? I had no intention of becoming involved with anyone, and yet here we are after all this trouble."

He shook his head and used his other hand to awkwardly lift his sandwich. He winced at the movement but still bit in. "Good." He nodded.

Reggie grinned. "Yup. That's me. I'm good at chocolate chip pancakes and chicken sandwiches."

He looked at her from the tops of his eyes. "You are very good at many things."

A ridiculous flush flooded through her and the heat told her the color showed in her cheeks.

"Yeah, well, thank you for that, I guess."

"I think this beautiful woman does not know how to take compliments."

Darn it, didn't he realize how hard it was to keep herself together in the face of such outrageous comments? Much more and she *was* going to throw caution to the wind and make love to him, and that was just craziness.

"Um, Thalia and I were wondering if you would like to come over for dinner? We both wanted to thank you."

He cocked his head at her, those tiger eyes intense. "I would be honored. Tell me, is that what you came here to say?"

Oh, God, he knew there was more. She felt like a kid in high school again because she still didn't know how to do this well.

"Look. I know Thalia and I put you through a lot, and I know I acted like a real bitch practically the whole time you've been here, but—well—" Come on, Lewis, cough it up. Get it out there. You practiced it the entire drive over. "Okay, I'm just going to say it. I liked what happened between us. I wondered if you wanted to go out sometime."

His expression at least said he seriously considered her words as he took another bite of his sandwich and chewed.

The birds warbled laughter, the orchard irrigation went tsk-tsk-tsk and she realized she sounded like a totally desperate woman. It was so not her style, it was pathetic.

She tugged her hand away, pushed back from the table, and stood in one smooth motion. "Listen, I'm sorry I've made you uncomfortable. Me and mine have caused you enough pain already. I'll just get out of your hair and let you get on with your life. The last thing you need is a woman with encumbrances messing up your plans." She nodded at the half-finished sandwich. "Thank you for the lunch."

And turned to go.

"Reggie, no." His chair scraped across the wood decking and suddenly he was up behind her, his good hand covering the Celtic knot tattoo on her left arm. "I would like to come to dinner with you and Thalia. I would like to continue to represent you in dealing with this lawsuit. Most of all I would like to go not on just one date, but on many dates with you."

She swung around to look up at him and his hand came up to smooth away the hair the breeze had plastered to her cheek. He looked as solemn as if he were at a funeral.

"There is just one problem that makes it all impossible. I must return to Napa this week if I am to purchase the land for the winery."

He glanced back to the table, to the card still between their plates, and her heart fluttered and something broke. Swallowing back the flood of emotions, she nodded and forced a smile.

"Well, I guess that's it, then." She stepped from Cesare and held out her hand. "You'll still come for dinner of course, because Thalia wants to thank you as well. How does tomorrow night sound?"

Her voice almost sounded normal—not as strangled as she felt. She looked up at him for a nod—something—anything to indicate what he was feeling, but it was like he was frozen.

Then his good arm snaked around her and pulled her into him, his lips sought hers. Heat, passion, and one armed, he held her firmly as if afraid she would escape him.

His mouth trailed kisses along her jaw line and under her hair. Kisses down her collar bone, shoved the strap of her shirt and bra off her shoulder and heat flowed from those kisses, from the bracelet, and flooded into her.

"Oh, God, Cesare, I want you." And she wasn't ashamed that she could want anything quite so much.

"Come with me." He caught her hand and abandoned the food on the patio to lead her into the house and up the stairs to the hallway that gave off of the front door foyer.

Down the hall through a doorway into a plain room of queen-sized bed, cast-off maple dresser, and blind-covered windows that filled the walls with slatted shadows and light. A chair sat beside the bed and had a single small suitcase, open, but neatly packed. The closet stood empty. She'd bet the dresser drawers were, too. He was leaving this small cell of a room to get on with his life.

"You've packed to leave," she said.

"I was going to buy tickets for the day after tomorrow."

She turned to him and slid her arms up around his neck. "Then we have this afternoon." And maybe tomorrow, but she would not be greedy.

He nodded and leaned down to kiss her.

Gently she slid his shirt off his shoulders and pulled her shirt over her head. She stepped out of boots and let her camo plants slide down her hips to the floor. Stepped out of them and stepped into him to unbuckle his belt. His gaze was like a brand as she unbuttoned his shorts and set them sliding off his hips. He was already aroused and so was she. She pressed herself against him and his good hand pulled her face up so he could take her mouth.

Hungry, like they were both starved. He shoved her backward onto the bed and she pulled him down on top of her.

"Let us get rid of these, shall we?" With a flick of his fingers, her bra was undone. Her panties he shoved down her hips. She helped him with his boxers and divested herself of underclothes and then it was just flesh against flesh, nothing between them except Cesare's bandages. His hands stroked her flesh and heat roared through her body. She explored him with her lips, kissing and loving and then she helped him pull on a condom and straddled him, took him in and then they rode together, his good hand on her breasts, in her hair, sliding down to her hips. Her fingers found the small nubbin on his chest and gave pleasure there.

She arched her back and drove herself against him, accepting him deeper than she had ever taken a man. Too deep. Could she leave this life behind for Napa? Could that be her future?

No, don't think about that. Think of only now. That was all there was—the moment you were in and the person you were with. She would give all she could and love with all her might and when it was over and he was gone she would have that to hold to.

She brought her hands up behind her head and worked herself against him. He freed his injured arm and held her hips to set their rhythm. His eyes were darkness with swirling golden flecks and she might never see them again and it broke her heart at the same moment that he filled her up, set her emotions, her body, the world exploding around her.

She came in a long shuddering convulsion that rippled up through her skull. She threw her head back.

"Cesare!"

"Reggie! *Cara!*" One armed, he hauled her down against his chest so she felt the wildness of his heart at the same time as he pulsed inside her.

He held her so tightly that she could not move, just close her legs around him when he rolled them onto their sides. She would not release him from inside her and she peered up into his gold-flecked eyes and felt like crying. She wanted to have those eyes look back at her always.

Emotions strangled her and she pulled away, didn't want him to see, pulled the tangled duvet between them. If she did not touch him, it would be easier to say goodbye.

"I—I guess I should go." From in the house she heard the sound of footfall. Jas's steady tread, she was pretty sure, and she was mortified that he'd caught her in a bootie call.

"You are not going anywhere. I have you in my bed and that is where you are meant to be."Cesare dragged her back against him.

"But you're leaving in two days. This is stupid—stupid to get involved. I—I don't think I'm made of the stuff that can just do this for the sex, Cesare. I'm all about attachments and emotions. I realize that. It's why I haven't had any casual sexual relationships all these years. And I didn't have a place for more attachments, what with Thalia and all."

His palm smoothed her sweat-matted bangs off her brow. "And yet now you do. Things can change, *cara*. For the right one, things can change."

She didn't know if it was true, but as she kissed him, she hoped it was.

Chapter 21

They didn't have dinner at Reggie's. When she and Cesare finally came out of the guestroom, Jas had left again and had left behind a note that Chloe had phoned him and there were plans for a big celebration down at *This and That*. Thalia was invited, for a barbecue was planned and she could also go to the beach if she wanted.

The sun had reached the tops of the western hills above the lake when Cesare's maroon Camry pulled into Reggie's yard. She watched him from the kitchen window as he climbed out of the car, looking like an Italian movie star with his jet black curls shoved back behind his ears, and a long-sleeved shirt worn loose, with the cuffs turned back on his muscled arms. He stood in the golden afternoon light, the dust motes playing around him, and her whole body tightened with desire for him. Right here, right now, in this kitchen. It pulled her thoughts from drain-circling around the lawsuit still pending. What was happening with that?

"Hey, Mom. Cesare's here." Thalia scooted into the kitchen, dressed in knee-length cutoff jeans and a sky-blue t-shirt as Reggie turned back to her. "Oh. I guess you saw."

Her head cocked as she looked Reggie up and down. Her eyes narrowed. "You're all dressed up. You look real pretty."

Reggie groaned. She hadn't been going for all dressed up. She'd been hoping for casual good looks even though she'd spent what felt like ages choosing what to wear tonight so that Cesare could see that she wasn't just someone who lived in singlet and camo pants. The man had to have standards. After all, he *was* Italian.

She turned back to the window. "I just went digging in the back of my closet and found this. I thought it might as well get worn."

"Nuh-uh." Thalia came up beside her to watch as Cesare headed for the kitchen door. "You like him. You like Cesare."

It was a little bit gloat and little bit question.

Reggie sighed. "I'm afraid that I do. A little more than I wanted to."

Thalia glanced back out the window. From somewhere Cesare had produced a bouquet of flowers. "I think maybe he likes you, too." She grinned impishly up at Reggie and then ran for the door.

She threw it open as Cesare climbed the stairs.

"Are those for me?" She grinned back at Reggie as Cesare seemed to waver.

"Rotten child. Those are for me, I think. Cesare, come in. You really shouldn't have."

He stepped into the kitchen and she accepted the flowers, perhaps the biggest bouquet of pink and white lilies, white roses, and baby's breath she had ever seen. Their scent flooded the room as she trimmed the ends and set them in water in a large crystal vase that she placed in the center of the kitchen table.

"They are truly beautiful." She leaned up to kiss him lightly on the mouth, a test for her and for Thalia. Thankfully, Thalia didn't fall apart or exhibit disgust, and Reggie—well, her heart beat a little too fast and her skin tingled at the nearness of him.

"Only the beautiful for a beautiful lady."

"How is your chest—the wounds?" she asked.

"Healing." He worked his arm on the injured side. "It will get better. I decided to set aside the sling."

His gaze skimmed over her, touching off small fires of desire and igniting the memory of his hands on her.

She wore linen, wide-legged trousers that flowed around her thighs, and a sleeveless navy silk oriental-style tunic that hung close to the body and buttoned on one side. With plain silver hoop earrings three inches round, and a simple silver chain with a wider circle of silver as a pendant, she was actually as dressed up as she ever got.

"Mom says it's just some old thing she pulled out of her closet, but I think she got dressed up for you," Thalia said with a cheeky grin at Reggie's dismay.

"And that, daughter of mine, is enough to tempt me to pull out your baby pictures. In particular some of you running around with a scarf stuck in your panties pretending you were a horse."

Thalia's eyes grew round with horror. "You wouldn't."

"Keep it up and see what happens when you have a boyfriend. Team of Two, remember?"

Thalia did a mock salute and turned back to Cesare, who was amusedly watching their interchange. "Let me know what you need to know and I'll give you the lowdown," she stage-whispered to him.

Reggie threw up her hands and together they filed out to Cesare's Camry for the short ride to Peachland, Reggie carrying the special salad she'd made of romaine, avocado, green onion, and mandarin oranges, with butter-fried almonds and sunflower seeds and a slightly sweet dressing. Even balancing the bowl on her lap the whole way there, she was too aware of Thalia in the back seat and of Cesare's presence so close and of her desire to touch him. The one good thing was that her feelings were a distraction.

The afternoon light placed a faint blush on the glossy white paint of the *This and That's* siding. The small discreet sign in the store window said it was closed. No one sat in the wicker furniture on the porch. They piled out of the car and Cesare produced a carefully wrapped bottle of wine and another bouquet of flowers of orange lilies and purple iris and lilac. Pretty, but not as knock-out gorgeous as the bouquet he'd brought her.

"So that's what you do, buy out a flower shop?" she asked, dropping back to walk beside him around the side of the house while Thalia ran on ahead with her bathing suit. She took the wine and flowers from him to give relief to his injured arm.

"The truth is that I went in to buy flowers for Lila for this evening, but I could not leave without something beautiful for you, too." The fingers of his free hand trailed down her cheekbone and he leaned down for a light kiss on her lips. Groaned. "Do you know how much I would just like to turn you around and take you home with me again? To be with you?"

"The thought had crossed my mind."

His brow arched and he leaned in to kiss her again. "Then hold to that thought, *cara*. We will find a way."

"Reggie? Cesare?" Lila's voice preceded her around the corner of the house as if to give them warning and Reggie stepped back, but not before Cesare caught her around the waist and dragged her into his side.

"There you are!" Lila wore a rose-colored, sleeveless summer dress that hung straight from her shoulders, its shapelessness made up for by the womanly shape underneath. Her long curls were coiled on the top of her head and held in place by a set of silver chopsticks. Dangly, silver chain earrings almost touched her shoulders. She caught their arms and walked between them, chattering about the menu for dinner—fresh sockeye salmon cooked on the barbeque with white wine and dill, and roasted vegetables to go with it.

"Chloe made the most fabulous looking dessert of raspberries and blueberries in a trifle-like concoction and your sister has been busy all afternoon making a perfect Tiramisu. Kylee and Brett brought wine to go along with yours and a platter of cheeses and crackers, and Danny and Jas brought souvlaki lamb skewers. We will feast in celebration."

They came around the corner to the rear patio. Kylee and Brett were taking care of drinks, pouring white wine for everyone from a chilled cooler Brett had provided. Jas and Danny were tending skewers of lamb on the barbeque. Bowls of tzatziki and small rounds of pita waited on the table as well as Kylee's platter of cheese and crackers for appetizers. Chloe looked chic in a long black caftan that was slit up the sides to expose black leggings on her legs. She still wore necklaces of jet beads, but this time they were interspersed with yellow amber. Victoria reclined on a chaise, her blonde hair pulled up and pinned on the top of her head, a diaphanous robe over top of a form-fitting white mini dress that showed off all her attributes—attributes that Danny couldn't seem to get enough of, given he eyed her like the wolf with the three little piggies.

"So—uh—one thing I'm not clear on—just what are we celebrating?" Reggie asked as she found herself amidst the people she treasured most in her life. Thalia was caught up in conversation with Jas and Danny, and Cesare and Brett had joined their conversation. Thalia didn't look at all like the manic preteen who couldn't wait to escape her elders for the lake. In fact, she looked like she fit right in.

"Well, for one, the fact you two and Thalia escaped the bracelet demon." Lila led them to two chairs left free by the table. "For another, Cesare's sister. Victoria came back to us, but she didn't just bring herself. Come on."

Leaving Cesare with the men and Victoria, Lila led her into the house and through the kitchen with its clutter of kitchen cooking and the various courses ready for eating. The room was redolent with garlic and coffee and berry and lemon and dill.

"I think I could gain five pounds just standing here inhaling," Reggie said as she hesitated before following Lila. "Where are we going?"

"The office."

Lila's heels tapped as she climbed the stairs and then they were in Lila's office where she kept the books for the store. Whereas usually the place was a pristine temple to organization, at the moment the place looked like all of Lila's carefully kept files had exploded.

"What the heck happened here?" Reggie asked.

Lila shrugged. "You knew I was attempting to get in touch with purchasers of your pieces, because often you gave them the design sketches to go with them as a memento of your design process. I wanted to see if we could collect any of them to help refute the accusations against you."

Reggie shook her head. "That's a lot of work to go through when I haven't even been served with anything. This whole situation has been positively weird."

"It's been like whoever it was, was trying to cut you off from all of us. I mean, that was my first reaction—I had to protect my assets in this house. Then I realized that an attack on you is an attack on me and everything we've built. I was all over this." She waved a graceful, long-palmed hand at the stack of files in her office. "There were actually a lot of people who still had your sketches. They've been outraged at the suit and have all sent back whatever they had from you. A few have even sent testimonials to sitting down with you to design a piece for them. But that's not what I wanted to show you."

She picked up a file box from beside her desk. "Victoria brought this home for you. Check it out."

Reggie hesitated.

"Go on. It won't bite." Lila nodded at the box and Reggie opened the lid.

Files in plain vellum stuck inside hanging folders. It took a moment before she recognized them. She riffled the files, then did a detailed check. "But how? This is the entire collection that had been planned for the Milan show."

Lila nodded. "You'll have to talk to Victoria for the details, but she found all your files in Erminio's possession. This was all she could manage to get out when she left, but they might be the most important part. If Erminio was planning on using your pieces in his show, now he's out of luck, and from what Victoria was saying, it looks like he had more than that up his sleeve. She indicated that it looked like he was planning on mass producing your pieces for sale."

"What? He can't do that!"

"Well, he could have tried. He can't now." She patted the box. "Let's just say that the phone lines have been burning between Milan and here. Things aren't totally settled yet, but they're looking good. Cesare has been a godsend. Let's just say that if the plan with the lawsuit had been to separate you from your friends to make it easier to take the bracelet, well then, the plan failed."

Reggie threw her arms around Lila and gave her a hug. "Thank you! Thank you so much. I can have my life back."

"You can." Lila fended her off. "So a question for you? You and Cesare finally worked things out?"

Reggie winced at the subject. "We did. As much as we could. He's leaving for Napa, but we've got the next thirty-six hours to be together." She swallowed back the emotions that flooded her, but apparently not well enough, for Lila pulled her into an embrace again.

"Oh, honey, I'm so sorry. I've been hoping things would work out. The way he looked at you, it was like he was smitten from the start."

"The worst part is, I like him back a little too much." She shook her head and looked at her friend—Lila, ever calm and cool and collected and not bothered by something as mundane as romance.

"Men and women are built to like each other. Then it's up to said men and women to find a way to make it work. Maybe you have to visit him in Napa."

"Maybe."

Feeling glummer than the box of files should leave her, she followed Lila back to the party. Brett and Cesare were deep in conversation over the merits of various grapes, while the others were caught up in their various conversations. She wanted to thank Victoria for what she'd done, but not here—not now, when it would become a big scene.

"Victoria? Can I steal you away for a moment?"

Victoria stretched like a cat and abandoned her chaise. "What can I do for you, Reggie?"

"Maybe we can talk on the front porch? I want to check on Thalia. I take it she's gone swimming."

"Of course. Though I don't want to get too close to her splashing."

Reggie shook her head. "Not close at all. We'll just go around to the front porch. I should be able to see her from there."

Victoria followed her around the house and they settled on the wicker loveseat with its cushions of turquoise and tangerine. Out past the copper planters with their load of heliotrope and petunia, on the lake it was a typical summer late afternoon. The air hummed with cicadas. Canada geese floated past in phalanxes of almost fully grown ducklings. Kids were getting in their last swim of the day, while families had their portable propane stoves set up either on the beach or on picnic tables. Dinner was being readied, but a few preteens were out having a splashing battle. Thalia was demonstrating that she was particularly good at it and a couple of the boys took after her and pulled her under, much to Thalia's squeals of protest.

"Look at her. Were we ever that young and carefree? Two days ago she was a hostage. Today you'd never know it. Oh, for that resiliency." Reggie shook her head.

"I remember being young and swimming in Lake Como, but it was never with the abandon that these children have. There is something about this place, Reggie. The blue water and sky, the hills that are so strong. There is still a wildness to it that runs in the blood of this place. It is like there are possibilities here that you never find in a place like Milan."

Reggie frowned and looked from the familiar blue lake that always seemed to fill her with cool. Wild? She'd never thought of it that way. "Maybe it's because everything isn't developed. There are still possibilities."

"That may be it." Victoria nodded.

"Listen, I wanted to thank you for bringing back those files. I can't believe that Erminio had them, that he would work in such bad faith with me."

Victoria shook her head. "There is something wrong with Erminio. When I saw him, his eyes were not right and he did not smell like Erminio—he smelled of smoke and yet there was none. He had all your files, Reggie. File cabinets full of them, but I did not have time to get them all. I grabbed these as most important and took them from his office to my apartment for my bag and to the airport."

"He must be furious."

In the lake, two of Thalia's friends had been called away to dinner. That left her and one boy and a girl. They splashed to shore and threw themselves down on towels.

"It is more than that, Reggie. I am finished in Milan. After what Erminio is saying about me, no one would even think of hiring me."

"Oh, my God, Victoria. That's a huge price to pay."

Victoria waved her words away. "Not so big. I realize now that I was not so happy. Perhaps Cesare was right that all these years Erminio mined me for ideas, but never gave me credit. I think perhaps it is time for me to try things on my own. Lila and I are discussing opening a clothing store in some space down by the bakery café."

"You'd stay?" Reggie grabbed Victoria's hands and gave her a hug. "That would be marvelous. Another woman in the pantheon of talented women! If that can come out of this horrible business, then at least something good has happened."

"Surely that is not all the good that has happened?" Cesare's voice floated up to them as he climbed the porch. He followed Reggie's gaze out to Thalia. "Still safe, I see."

"I was just thanking Victoria for bringing back my files."

Cesare eyed his sister, nodded. "It was a good thing. Very good. Enough to allow us a countersuit, I think."

He settled himself on the loveseat arm next to Reggie's shoulder. "There is something else I need to discuss with you—something else that can be very good."

He slid down to the wicker chair beside Reggie and pulled the chair around to face her.

"Reggie, there is a chance—a chance for us. My heart had been set on a winery in Napa, but since meeting you, I have had my doubts about that dream. I want to be with you, but your place is here. I cannot see you in California. Your place is this lake and these mountains and these people."

He was so earnest, clutching her hand as if he would not ever let go. Victoria had gone still and was pressed back in her chair as if she could not believe what she was seeing.

"What—What are you saying?" Reggie asked.

At first he would not meet her gaze, then he did and the amber in his eyes flared and sizzled like lightning across her skin.

"It is very sudden, I know, but your friend Brett has just told me of an opportunity. His partner is an older man who would like to retire. He would like to sell his half of the winery. Judging by the vintage that Brett has provided for dinner, he is making very good white wines, but there is another set of skills to develop good reds. There is the possibility that I could purchase half of the winery and have my dream here. He is even interested in the idea of opening a winery restaurant, at least during the summer season. Together we could bring that vision to fruition."

He met her gaze. "What do you think?"

"Oh, my God, yes! Oh, Cesare, then we'd at least have a chance to find out if this works." Heat flared through her and she threw her arms around him. Something thunked to the floor as she kissed Cesare. When she pulled back, Victoria had already scooped up what was fallen.

Silver links and doorways. The bracelet draped over her wrist.

"Don't!" Reggie yelled, but it was already too late.

Victoria had set the small key through the lock, a pleased smile on her face as she jingled the infernal bracelet into place.

"What is the matter? It looks nice, does it not? I have admired it ever since I first saw it on your wrist."

Reggie sighed and caught Cesare's hand. The saga of the bracelet might be over for her, but it wasn't done yet.

Not by any means.

Epilog

Five days of running through the cracks and fissures of the earth, and the thing that sometimes occupied the head of Johan Fehr hung in an ashy fug in the Berlin park across from Johan Fehr's apartment. It was night and it was raining and the water placed an oily slick across the linden leaves and on the pavement of the road that gleamed in the headlights. The traffic hissed in the night like ill-tempered snakes. He could relate to those snakes, could taste the warm blood on the wind. Human. Male. Coming in this direction.

Five days of burning in hot, forest fire winds, of blowing over cold peaks under a too bright sun. Always there were people and animals talking, whining, howling at the moon. Always the wind hummed and roared and ripped at his form, tore pieces away, until finally, finally he had found a crack in the earth that led down into the darkness and silence where there was only the grumble and moan of stone.

He had settled there, resting, coalescing into his natural form. It had been eons since he flickered and burned as his own essence of smokeless fire that the ancient humans had named him. They had known enough to fear him, too. Hunter, trickster, the source of bad dreams. The thing travelers feared to meet on their journeys through the lonely desert lands. The evil that mothers tried to save their children from.

The ancient power that Acacius, the tinsmith, had attempted to thwart for the love of a woman. All for naught. The man had fought back, 'twas true. Acacius had twisted the powerful curse that had imprisoned him back on its maker.

And as result he was here, in the rain instead of standing before the windows of his penthouse apartment planning his next move. He needed to get back to Johan before the man was discovered as the driveling madman he was without the intellect that usually rode in his brain. The trouble was, the sudden end of his host and the unlocking of the fourth door of the bracelet had left him weak—too weak to converge and take control of another unwary life-form. He'd been forced to snake his way under the oceans and through the cracks and tunnels and ancient caves and coal mines of Europe to reach home, slowly gathering strength as he went. Berlin with its swirl of nightlife. Its corporate powerhouses. Its Janus faces of world leader in humanitarianism and nascent totalitarianism. If he could breathe, the evil undercurrents would long sustain him.

And yet those blasted women had somehow outwitted him, and they had drawn other women to them as if the bracelet wielded some influence over them and the world around them. Was that even possible?

Acacius had been a most troubling adversary when he was alive—pardon—make that when he had been a man. Young, handsome, too certain of his own prowess and determined to hold to the woman he loved even though Acacius had stolen her right out from under his master's nose. As if their love gave Acacius the right to keep the beauteous Laelia to himself when prophecy surely said she was meant for someone else. Someone greater.

And so the master had reclaimed the woman and destroyed Acacius in a most delicious way. But during the destruction, lovesick Acacius had somehow trapped much of his master's power in the bracelet. Now that power bled away, as each lover found their doorway.

And what had seemed like a well-conceived plan to drive a wedge between the women had not worked. Instead it seemed to have acted in exactly the opposite way. There had to be some way to address this—to isolate the next woman wearing the bracelet.

Perhaps he had gone about this all wrong. He had focused on masculine force. Perhaps there was another way to bring about ruin. Perhaps all these years had dulled his thinking, for was it not said that the more dangerous of many species was the female? The female praying mantis and the black widow spider came to mind. They loved and destroyed at the same time.

He would take a lesson from them.

The sound of footsteps on rain-sodden pavement came from down the path just beyond the sodden shrubbery and flower gardens. By the weight of the footfall, it was male. On a gust of wind he roiled up using the strength he had gained on his long journey home. A young man clad in the black uniform of a Berlin police reared back and went for his gun.

No use against a cloud of ash and invisible flame that swirled around him, that entered through eyes, nose, mouth, and ears to coalesce in the back of the brain.

The night was dark as he used his little-recovered strength to work the fists and shoulders of this new host. Strong—stronger than Johan Fehr by far, but physical strength was too limiting. He set out walking, ignoring the rain that beat on his head and shoulders. He stepped down into a space in the traffic and jaywalked the street to the glassed-in foyer of the residential tower. Didn't bother stopping for the concierge, just stabbed the button of the elevator.

It arrived with a ding and the annoying hum of Muzak. Inside, he hit the number for the penthouse and the elevator started its swift ascent.

Yes, he was coming home, not a victor, but having damaged the women's place in their puny little world. There were still lawsuits to pursue that would keep them distracted. And while they were distracted, he would strike again and leave the bracelet-wearer on her knees.

Before he killed her.

It had been just so with Laelia.

About the Author

Karen L. Abrahamson is a well-traveled writer who has explored cultures and countries around the world, but south central British Columbia, Canada is one of her favorite places to come back to. She is the author of mystery, romantic and fantasy fiction including the highly regarded Cartographer fantasy series. She lives on the west coast of Canada with two Bengal cats that aren't quite as well traveled as she is.

When she isn't writing she can be found with a camera and backpack in fabulous locations around the world.

If you would like to get an automatic e-mail when Karen's next book is released, sign up at her website:
www.karenlabrahamson.com.
Your email address will never be shared and you can unsubscribe at any time.

A Special Request from the Author:

Word-of-mouth is crucial for any author to succeed. If you enjoyed this book, please consider leaving a review at Amazon, Barnes and Noble, or any other e-tailer, or on Goodreads; even if it's only a line or two, it would make all the difference and would be very much appreciated.

To find more of her writing, visit

www.twistedrootpublishing.com.

KAREN L. ABRAHAMSON
UNLOCKING
HER CHANCES
Unlocking Saga, Book Five

Unlocking Her Chances

Prologue

The thing that was Johan Fehr hung up the telephone in his Berlin office. He felt weak, the physical strength of the Johan Fehr body not enough to overcome the disquiet he felt.

His desktop was empty save for a computer screen and a single file folder—opened. It contained everything he knew about the blasted women in Peachland. Four. There had been four! But no longer, apparently. Somehow they managed to draw others into their infernal cabal.

The office air held the chill odorless mechanical tang of air conditioning, but not enough to mask the burning scent that increased with his anger. The walnut paneled office walls held the carefully collected remains of two lifetimes—photos of Johan Fehr with various dignitaries, at construction site inaugurations and political events in Germany and beyond. There were photos of Johan's father as well. Guided by the thing which had inhabited him, Heinrich Fehr had risen quickly in the military and then with his business in the heady days of the rebuilding of Europe. Medals and commendations as well as letters of recognition from the Allied occupiers and the *Bundestag* all framed and mounted, commemorated the Fehr contribution to the rebuilding of Germany. Shelves of law books and the classics were built into the walls—not that he had any need to read them, with teams of lawyers to do his bidding and no interest at all in human literature.

And all of it was worth nothing if he did not develop a plan to deal with the situation!

Afternoon sunlight filled the tree-lined streets far below his window. The sun glared off of the glass of the other downtown towers like sunlight on shifting water and for a moment he was amazed at what the humans had done. It was a far cry from the towers of Babylon or Giza's ancient pyramids. This was the true wonder of the world—that humans had created such a thing.

And since when had he admired anything about these lesser beings?

Johan Fehr shivered. The disquiet he felt had to be because of the abrupt ending of his last effort to reclaim the bracelet. The body had been killed while he had still controlled it. In his already weakened form he had been left to coalesce as best he could. That had not occurred for eons—not since most humans had forgotten that they shared this earth with other beings. In the past he would simply have taken another nearby human, but the opening of the fourth door of the infernal bracelet had stripped him of too much of his power. It had left him restless and weak, the need for revenge coiling in him like a fire about to leap between buildings.

It had taken all his strength and five days to find his way back to this body again. The fourth door of the bracelet opened by the fourth couple forming and vanquishing the power that had long ago been stolen from him and locked in the bracelet. Only three doors remained—fewer than half of the seven—over half of his power lost forever.

The body's hand closed into a fist. Those infernal women— they'd bested each of his emissaries. Perhaps that was the problem. Newly snatched bodies were not fully cooperative. Humans hired for their skills at killing had to be trusted to know what they were doing. The trouble in each case was that the body or the emissary were unable to get close enough to do the job—or too incompetent to finish it. There always seemed to be something that stood in the way of the woman trusting him—usually that something was the man she was meant to be with.

The man. Now there was an interesting consideration...

Chapter 1

"Victoria! What have you done?"

Victoria Angelucci, late of Milan, Italy, looked up from the lovely silver bracelet around her wrist. Cleopatra-haired Reggie Lewis wore a worried expression on her flushed face—the flushing the product no doubt of the expert kiss of Victoria's one and only scoundrel brother, Cesare, who sat on the chair arm beside Reggie.

"Done? I am sorry. I simply try your bracelet on? It fell from your wrist, you know?" In the shadows of the broad front porch of the stately old red and white house she angled her wrist this way and that, admiring the seven small silver doors. Angled sunlight filled the early evening and patterned the waves on the huge lake across the street with the same patina of silver. Okanagan Lake, Reggie had said, was over eighty kilometers long, running north and south between ridges of low mountains.

"Is this one of your making, too, Reggie? I have admired it since I saw it in Milan."

Reggie Lewis had come to Milan at the invitation of fashion designer, Erminio Biondi, who had planned to use Reggie's jewelry for his Fall and Spring clothing lines. Unfortunately the deal had fallen through due to a variety of circumstances. It had led to them seated here, on brightly cushioned furniture on the quaint front porch that extended the breadth of the old house in the sleepy Okanagan town of Peachland. The deep indigo of

Okanagan Lake and the red-gold gilding of the evening sun on the sun-baked dry mountains across the lake sent a momentary pang of homesickness through Victoria. The scent of sun-warmed water was so like Lake Como in Italy and yet the dry hills were so not like the hills of her home.

Though there were copper planters on the broad front porch overflowing with red and white geranium and purple heliotrope, it was not the lovely bougainvillea flocked with pink, purple and white blossoms that in some places around Lake Como covered entire estate walls. There was none of the thick dark green pine on the mountains across the lake—these were barren, the product of a forest fire a few years back she'd been told, though hints of green said new life was coming back. There were none of the graceful old towns that had slumbered by Lake Como for hundreds of years. No here, there was a straggle of small shops, a bar and a string of small beach bungalows gradually being replaced by condo developments and million dollar monster houses that destroyed what might have been the feel of the town.

Reggie pulled away from Cesare. "Let me see," she said and grabbed Victoria's wrist most unceremoniously.

She flipped Victoria's hand over to expose the closure—a most clever ornate keyhole that a small key slid through. Reggie tried to slide the key back through the lock. It did not work. She tried again. And again and released Victoria's hand to slump back, eyes closed, in the loveseat next to Cesare.

"Oh God. It's happened again."

Victoria shielded her wrist with her other hand feeling momentarily hurt by Reggie's response. What was the problem? "I am so sorry, Reggie. If I had known that trying on the bracelet would upset you so, I would not have done it. Here. I give it back to you." She slid the bracelet around so the closure was on the back of her arm. Tried to slide the key through the key hole.

It was as if, at the last moment, the key grew too large for the opening and confused her fingers. The closure refused to open. She frowned. "*Cos'è questo*? What is this? It was so easy to close."

Reggie's jaw was a rigid line, her knuckles white as she clasped Cesare's hands.

"Reggie. Please. Forgive me this. I did not understand this piece was so important to you."

But Reggie was shaking her head.

"It is not the bracelet, *Cara*," Cesare said, his dark hair falling charmingly over his eyes. "Or perhaps it is. The bracelet is the source of trouble here in Peachland. Reggie wore it all the time because it would not come off. It was like you find it now—locked on her wrist."

"But why? How? The key fit through the lock. It must fit in reverse." She tried the stubborn bracelet closure again, but it still resisted.

"*Che palle!*" In disgust she shook her wrist and the silver doors tinkled together most prettily. It really was a lovely piece even if the fact it would not come off was a pain. "But Reggie, it just came off your wrist. And surely you can cut it off and repair it with no sign, yes?"

Reggie Lewis was a well-known jewelry designer on the verge of becoming internationally well-known if not for Erminio's actions in Milan. A little snip and a solder. Surely that would do the trick.

But Reggie was shaking her head. "I didn't wear the darn thing because I wanted to. I wore it because someone had to and it wouldn't come off. There's a story attached to that bracelet, Victoria and it's not a good one. I guess with you back and forth to Milan no one told you about the trouble that darn thing has caused around here. It's what led to the attack on Thalia and me." Thalia was Reggie's ten-year-old daughter. "'Course it also helped get Cesare and me together."

She looked up at tall Cesare who draped his arm around her to pull her into his side. It was still a surprise seeing him like that—yes, Cesare had had many women in his life, but Reggie Lewis was different. Not a flighty jet-setter, and not some random girl he had picked up off a beach. Reggie was an artisan, a business woman, and a partner in the jewelry store called *This and That,* which occupied the front of the main floor of the white and red house. She was also the mother of the very active Thalia who was currently splashing in the lake across the street under Reggie's watchful gaze. Aside from the fact that Reggie was unusually beautiful with her black Egyptian haircut and her thickly lashed almost black eyes, she wore her difference from Cesare's other conquests in the two Celtic knot tattoos that encircled both her biceps. Both were visible in the sleeveless navy silk tunic blouse she wore with wide-legged trousers. It was a simple design—something Victoria herself could have designed—if she hadn't wasted her entire career letting Erminio rob her of her ideas.

Victoria sighed shook her head. "I am sorry. I do not understand. It is impossible that a bracelet will not come off and must be worn."

"Not this one," Cesare and Reggie said in unison.

"You need to understand," Reggie followed up. "The bracelet isn't any design of mine. It came to *This and That* in a box of jewelry from an estate sale. Kylee found it and was the first one to put it on."

Kylee Jensen, the little blonde who was a marketing genius for the store.

"Someone tried to abduct her to get the bracelet. It only came off when she and Brett finally accepted that they were to be together. Chloe was the next. She put it on sort of like you did—not knowing. It wouldn't come off her wrist, either. She was attacked, too, and things were really touch and go until she and Jas Stone finally realized they were right for each other. Ally was next—that's Allison McVay, the international photographer. She was visiting and was nearly killed in a diving accident. It came off for her when she and her old flame Seamus worked things out. That was when I put it on. I knew what I was getting into, but there was no one else. You know what happened to me."

It had been a very near thing indeed, with Reggie's daughter abducted and both of them and Cesare nearly killed. Cesare still favored his side from knife wounds.

The air was suddenly chill even though it was a warm evening with barely a breeze off the lake. Victoria's arms turned to gooseflesh. The sweet scent of heliotrope seemed suddenly smoky and the golden light on the mountains seemed to dim. She did not like the idea of an attack on her life. Not at all—and to have the bracelet only release when she had found her love interest—that was ridiculous surely.

"But you can cut it off, yes? I do not fancy being a target." Sighing, she jingled the bracelet on her wrist again. It might be lovely, but she shivered with a fear that matched what she'd felt when she abandoned Erminio in Milan and brought back a box full of Reggie's designs that he had stolen. She'd been brave then, but she was not stupid.

"I'm not sure it can be done," Reggie said with a shake of her head. "More importantly, I don't think it *should* be. You see, there's something else. I don't know what it is, but there's something that wants the bracelet. If you talk to Danny Forester he'll tell you that whatever it is, it's like an alien in your head. I think it was controlling Dietrich when he tried to kill Cesare and me. When he died it was—" She looked at Cesare. "It was like something came out of him. A huge grey cloud like ash that the wind swept away. Did you see it?" she asked him.

Cesare shook his head. "It seems that I was too busy convincing myself that I was not going to die."

"I'm a little happy that you didn't." Reggie leaned in to give him a peck on the lips that swiftly became something more. "Make that a lot happy."

And the thing of it was, by the look on Cesare's face he was happy, too. The happiest Victoria had ever seen her older brother, and he was making plans to get on with his life—to work. To do something instead of wandering the world and wasting money— all that he had done for the past five years ever since he began his feud with their successful industrialist father. Seeing his happiness, for a moment she felt envy.

But the bracelet... She looked at Reggie and felt a little baffled resentment. After Victoria had risked everything to get Reggie's files back was removing the bracelet so much to ask? It was so typical of so many people. They used you and you could not trust them.

"But I cannot wear this thing if it brings danger. I cannot. I refuse." She stood up. "I will go speak to Lila and she will help me if you will not." Or she would cut it off herself. After all, in this world there really was no one else to depend upon.

She abandoned them on the front porch of the house and went down the porch stairs to circle around the side of the two-story house to the flagstone patio in the rear.

It was a festive place: Lila Weber, the tall, willowy, auburn-haired owner of the house had decorated the patio with tea lights set in the broad kitchen windows across the rear of the house and small white lights hung in the maple tree in the garden corner and on the eaves of the low-slung building that was Reggie's work shop. A stainless steel barbecue smoked with the scent of skewers of tender lamb, and an aluminum foil packet that must hold the salmon Lila had said she was going to cook.

Petite, blonde-haired Kylee looked up from her seat on a turquoise-cushioned chaise with tall beach-boy blonde Brett at her feet. Kylee frowned as if she read something on Victoria's face. Her concern must have registered, for the two other women on the patio, Lila and Chloe Main, Lila's other partner in the shop, both turned in Victoria's direction. All three gazes fixed on her wrist and the happy conversations sputtered out.

"Victoria? Oh my God?" Kylee sputtered. "How did the bracelet get from Reggie to you?"

How? How? "It was a mistake. An accident. Cesare came to the front to tell about possibly partnering with Brett in his winery He and Reggie kissed and the bracelet fell." She told how she saw the bracelet fall and picked it up. "It was so pretty that I draped it across my wrist. Then I could not resist closing the clasp."

"And now it won't come off," Kylee said, scrambling up to catch Victoria's hands and lead her to a chair. "Sit. You look like you could fall down."

Feeling numb, Victoria sat and met the gazes of the people on the patio one by one. There was concern there and pity, expressions she was not used to. Lila found a lovely soft ivory pashmina that matched the flowing pantsuit Victoria wore. She draped it around Victoria's shoulders but it couldn't seem to dispel the freezing cold she felt. She didn't need this. She had enough problems—her career ruined and her name as well—at least in the Milan fashion industry—Erminio was seeing to that. Her father—always concerned for the Angelucci reputation—was furious. She already had two stormy voice messages from him, but had held off returning his calls. Her 'theft' to reclaim Reggie's files from Erminio's office likely meant she couldn't even go home to Milan without facing arrest, even if the files had been originally stolen from right here in Peachland.

And now this. A bracelet with some wild story attached. But there was no denying that the silver-door bracelet would not come off. She scanned the faces of those around her, but could not bring herself to ask for help. Too many people had always thought she was no more than her father's coddled daughter. Kylee looked anxious. Lila reserved, but concerned. Chloe was clearly afraid for her. Brett held Kylee's shoulders protectively as if he would stop her from getting involved. Jas Stone, the detective in the Royal Canadian Mounted Police and Chloe's lover, standing in reserve—help when needed. He had been there for Reggie, too.

And beside him stood the last of their number, Jas Stone's partner, Danny Forester, though the diminutive name did not suit him. He was a big man, like Jas, just as broad of shoulder, but instead of dark, almost Italian good looks, Danny was every inch a Nordic redhead, with the high cheekbones, square jaw, and rugged good looks of Vikings. He wore a faded green polo shirt that brought out the colour of his eyes. All evening he had stayed beside the barbecue tending the skewers. Danny Forester who Reggie said knew about whatever wanted the bracelet. In the light from the barbecue flames, his watchful eyes glowed red.

Chapter 2

In the tea-lit back yard amidst the bevy of beautiful women, Danny kept his attention on the sizzle and pop of the lamb skewers he was tending—or tried to. It should be easy. He was a flexible guy. Easy going—that was his motto. In the often tense world of policing, that was the only way to get by. And this was a social event with people he liked. Throw in a little humor and easy-peasy.

The air was cool, the soft strains of classical music—something like Appalachian Spring—came from the speakers on the corner of the flagstone patio. As the sun fell over the mountains behind them the dusky sky had darkened toward night and from the street came the sound of voices calling—the beach was closing down and people were saying their goodnights. The breeze carried the scent of the lake, the heated sage of the hills, and the sweet of the petunias planted in pots around the garden.

He used barbecue tongs to turn the skewers. He'd volunteered for the job first of all because he was all about the grill and the meat. In fact he'd made a bit of a study of it this summer on his long evenings at home alone and wanted to show that he could cook lamb without creating leather. At home there might not be someone to cook for, but he could experiment and it was a safe enough hobby. A hobby he could focus on while he tried to come to grips with exactly what had happened to him in June. Because he might be easy going, but having something take over your flipping body was not something you could be easy going about. Besides, he was a police officer—a detective in the cop television jargon—and he prided himself on cool logic, attention to detail and dogged determination in order to solve his cases. He and Jas as a team had an incredibly high clearance and conviction rate for their cases. All good, but that time in June when something had entered his brain and had him doing things that he would *never* do—well that tended to put all his beliefs about himself in question.

The second thing that kept him focused on the juice-laden lamb skewers that he'd marinated all afternoon in lemon, olive oil and spices, was the latest addition to their little enclave of friends here at *This and That*. Beautiful women had never scared him off and the first time he'd seen *This and That* when he was his own man and not some automaton driven by an external force in his brain, he'd looked forward to opportunities to come back. He liked women and beautiful women most of all and *This and That* had no shortage of them. Oddly, although he liked to think of himself as a bit of a ladies' man, he hadn't hit on any of the women here. It was the conversations that he'd had with the women and the friendships that he had with their men that had drawn him the most.

Until tonight.

Somehow while everything was happening between Cesare Angelucci and Reggie, he'd missed meeting the gorgeous blonde that was Cesare's baby sister. A cross between Brigitte Bardot and Angelina Jolie with thick blonde hair and a figure that made his mouth go dry; he'd had a tough time finding the words to do more than greet her with hello when they'd been introduced. And he'd stumbled over that and managed to cover it with a cough—he hoped.

Good going, ya idiot. Impress her all to hell and stand like a nimrod next to the barbecue all evening. That'll get to know her.

'Course now that she had the bracelet on and was surrounded by Lila and the others, maybe he should just pack himself up home and to bed, because he clearly wasn't good for much around here.

There'd be some knight in shining armor sweeping in to save the glorious Victoria from whatever threats came her way and that would be the end of his chances.

"You're being awfully quiet, friend. No quips? No mention of the fact that there's a good chance she'll meet her soul mate?" said Jas, out of nowhere.

Danny stiffened at the way the words reflected exactly his thoughts, but that could happen with police partners. Jas had sidled up beside him, from where, Danny couldn't say and if that wasn't a sign of being outta sorts, well, what was?

"Got to tend to this meat. It'll burn if I don't. But then, perhaps you prefer shoe leather?"

He couldn't help himself—he glanced over at Victoria as Lila and Chloe and Kylee fussed over her. When he looked up at Jas he found his partner studying him, his expression almost gloating.

"What? What's the problem?"

"Hey! Nothing, man." Jas held up his hands. "Just thought I saw something. Clearly I didn't. Damn bracelet, though. I swear it knows just when there's a new wrist to climb onto."

Danny snorted and raised his brows. "You're believing an inanimate object has intention, now, are you?"

Jas shook his head. "After the past few months I'm open to just about anything if it will explain what's been happening. I mean shit, Danny. It's been a month and we aren't any closer to solving this whole thing. We've got bupkis except crimes— attempted abduction, break-ins, stolen files. The break-in at *This and That* and the attack on Chloe, we've got a 'file closed' stamp on, but we both know that's not really the case because the perp was 'effin' possessed at the time. We'll never know if the others all were. At least the guys who tried for Ally and Reggie had links to Germany. That at least puts their origins as the same country as our mystery man, Johan Fehr, but it still doesn't get us either Johan Fehr in custody or a better understanding of why *This and That* seems to be the eye of a storm."

Danny grabbed a plate and began shifting the skewers onto it. The foil-wrapped package of salmon he slid onto a platter. "That was a mighty big speech there, partner. You're sounding a little frustrated."

"Aren't you? I don't like that this is happening. It's wrecking our clearance rate and I really don't like not understanding what's going on. Why the hell this bracelet? Why the hell now?"

Danny sighed and met his partner's gaze. Jas was as solid as a cop could get and yet he'd put aside his own 'show-me' approach to life to believe in a crazy-ass story about possession because Danny had said that was what was happening. Of course, the fact that there had been suicide notes and two perps in the psych ward all talking about aliens in their heads had helped, too, but Jas had believed Danny when he could barely believe it himself.

That kind of partner was something you couldn't put a value on.

"And now we've got another woman vulnerable."

Jas thought a moment. "We could put a watch on her? Maybe we'd be able to pick up the bad guy before he had a chance to take action." He nodded. "That could work. What'd'ya think? You up for a little surveillance?"

Jas turned and Danny followed his gaze to the blonde goddess on the chaise. It looked for all the world like the others were her handmaidens. It would be an excuse, wouldn't it? A valid excuse to be around Victoria Angelucci. There were a hell of a lot worse ways a red-blooded man could spend his time.

"I could do that."

Jas chuckled and elbowed his arm. "I'll just bet you could, old man."

"What the hell's that supposed to mean?"

"Not a darn thing—except you've avoided her like the plague since you met her this evening and that ain't like you. Not when the woman's that good looking."

Damn. The last thing he needed was Jas Stone laughing at him. Laughing at a partner's romantic pursuits was more his own department.

"She looks like a lot of woman." Someone far too far above him—hell she was almost Italian royalty.

"Yup."

"The high maintenance kind." Perfect manicure, perfect hair, perfect clothing while he was more the throw on what he found on the floor that morning kinda guy. If the tie didn't match the shirt, well, what of it?

"Yup again."

"She sorta dazzles the eye with that high fashion thing of hers."Just the graceful way she brushed a hair from her perfectly made-up face could take his breath away.

"She does that, too."

"What the hell am I going to do, Jas? I don't know if I can even talk to her." Danny stopped. Had he said that out loud?

A clap on the back said he probably had.

"Welcome to my world, ya poor bastard. Welcome to the lightning bolt."

§

Victoria sipped the glass of cool white wine that Kylee had given her, but her fingers felt wooden and her hand actually shook. As a matter of fact, her whole body felt wooden. It did not help that everyone—Chloe, Kylee, and Lila were acting as if she had just been struck down by a serious illness. Was it truly that bad?

"But this is craziness, surely? It cannot be true." She held up her arm to examine the offending bracelet. A series of seven small doors made up the links, each one unique. A small arched door had what looked like small vines coiled around the arch. One looked like a mysterious North African door of heavy wood bound in iron. Another was a simple door with a gargoyle knocker and still another reminded her of the entrance of her family's musty old winery entrance. Another had ornate metal hinges over wood like a door from a fairy tale complete with a padlocked chain , while another had hinges shaped like leaves. The last, and the one that charmed her, looked like a classic Dutch door of plain lines. It was even made of two pieces, top and bottom cleverly fastened together by what looked like a small iron bolt. Charming. Utterly charming and yet—not.

Given everything she had been told, the fact the piece of jewelry sat on her wrist terrified her. She might be bold in her meetings with Erminio and clients, but the prospect of physical danger—well, that took her from her fairytale world of fashion and design to somewhere real that she did not wish to go. Especially not with the tales of aliens and demons they had told her. It was against—against all her good Catholic upbringing.

Now there was a laugh. She might have been raised Catholic, but when was the last time she had gone to mass and meant it? The confessional?

Could the priests protect her? Perhaps they could get the bracelet off?

"Victoria? Is she okay?" Reggie rushed up to her, her daughter and Cesare in tow. Ten-year-old Thalia was wrapped in a bright blue and green beach towel, her blonde hair matted to her head and smelling of lake water. Cesare stood behind them like a protector—something Victoria had never seen before. Perhaps it was true—he had finally grown up and found what was important to him—this dark haired woman with the concerned eyes. Was that the bracelet's influence?

Victoria caught Reggie's hand. "I am well. Fine, as you say. Just surprised and a little overwhelmed? Is that the word?"

Reggie nodded. "Overwhelmed is the perfect world. It's exactly how I felt when I put the bracelet on."

"That goes double for me," Chloe said.

"And me," Kylee chimed in. "I really thought I'd done something wrong because Lila had asked me to sort through the stuff in this shipment, not try stuff on. And then the darn bracelet wouldn't come off. I was mortified."

"Mortified." Victoria tried the word out. Yes, it fit. She had been so stupid putting Reggie's bracelet on. "I just don't know what came over me to put it on. It is yours. It should never have occurred to me, given it is not my possession. It was like a small voice in my head told me to do so." She shook her head. "Silly, I know."

Reggie shook her sleek black head. "The bracelet doesn't belong to me—to any of us really. I think it came to us for a reason. Chloe talks about fate. Well, I think this was fated. Me. The bracelet. Meeting Cesare. The others and their partners. It's all worked out and now it's your turn."

"If it's any consolation, I remember that little voice in my head, too," Kylee said with a self-effacing shrug.

"My turn to meet a man and fall in love?" Victoria frowned and shook her head. "I am too busy—have too many other things to worry me. Men come and go. You cannot expect anyone to be there for you. Besides, why should I wish to settle down now?"

Reggie gave her the once over and shook her head. "Sorry, Victoria. Ally was way more committed to having and discarding men and now, after wearing the bracelet, she's back with her first love. I expect we'll be invited to a wedding sometime in the next year." She looked meaningfully at Chloe and Kylee and their men. "Maybe more than one. Who knows? The point is that you can't just kiss off the power of the bracelet. It won't let you."

"Won't let me? But it is a bracelet—not a thinking being."

Reggie shook her head. "I guess you're just going to have to live it. The big thing is that you need to be very careful."

"That's what concerns me," Jas Stone interjected. A *molto bello*—very handsome man, he commanded attention even standing back by the barbecue with his equally good-looking, but silent, partner. "Whatever is after the bracelet, the attacks on the wearer of the bracelet have become increasingly deadly. The attempts are escalating as if the perpetrator is becoming more desperate. I don't understand why that's the case, but it means that whoever is wearing the bracelet has to be extremely careful. Victoria, I hate to say it, but you probably shouldn't go anywhere alone. Up to now the attacks have been subversive and opportunistic—catching you when you're alone and taking advantage of opportunity—until the last one."

"What he's saying is that he—it—whatever or whoever is spearheading these attacks took a different approach with Reggie—he abducted Thalia to force Reggie to come to him and he had a weapon." Jas's partner assumed the story, his intent gaze a heated weight on her skin.

"None of the others did that," Danny finished. He shrugged in his slightly rumpled looking shirt.

The way he kept looking at her she couldn't meet his gaze. What was it about him that made her a little weak and a lot uncomfortable? She had never had difficulty dealing with handsome men before.

"No. Thank you for your concern, but I am a private person. I will not be accompanied by someone everywhere I go. I will not be a burden. It is enough that I impose on Lila's hospitality." Her fingers strayed to the bracelet; the silver now warm as if it felt her discomfort.

"You're absolutely no imposition," Lila said. "You fit right in and besides, we were going to explore the possibility of opening a store. I want to show you the space that's come vacant in the little line of shops by the bakery café. I'll bet you could do a very good business given Peachland is becoming a bit of a destination place for restaurants and jewelry. If you're interested we could work together on it while we sort through this whole mess with Reggie's lawsuit."

Someone had stolen the files Reggie kept to document her jewelry designs and then had claimed *she* was stealing the designs for her jewelry. The files had turned up in Victoria's employer's possession and he had planned on selling jewelry made from the designs as his own. Victoria had stolen the most important files back for Reggie, effectively ruining her career in Milan.

She shook her head. "It is a lovely idea, Lila, but is it even possible? There are Visa issues and so on, surely. My brain is too full with all these stories and this silly bracelet that will not come off..." She scrubbed at her forehead. "It is too much to think about. Where does such a thing as this even come from?"

Lila shook her auburn head. Tonight, as in every moment Victoria had known her, Lila exuded an effortless beauty that Victoria could only wish to aspire to. All the careless beauty Victoria showed to the world took hours of careful attention: the makeup, the hair, just the right clothing.

"That's what we've been trying to figure out," Lila said. "We know the previous owner, a British colonel, found it in the North African desert when he was a lieutenant during the Second World War. He called it his luck and from the moment he found it his career advanced quickly. He did well in business once he retired. Apparently he asked about the bracelet's provenance in Egypt, but experts there said it wasn't Egyptian and looked more like Mesopotamian, or something from the eastern Mediterranean."

"I got the test results back from the university," Reggie said, standing up from Victoria's side and accepting a wine glass from Cesare. Their fingers lingered as they touched. There was clearly something powerful between them—something that Victoria had never experienced because she had always been too busy.

"Sorry. With everything that's happened I forgot to tell all of you," said Reggie. "The metal analysis suggests Italy—northern Italy to be exact."

The patio's gathering of people went silent except for the sound of the grill.

After a moment, Danny turned to platters he had filled and shifted them to the table. "Food's ready everyone. Dig in."

Dig in, indeed. Food was not something to just be dug into. It required the right wines and a table set for friends. But aside from Danny, everyone on the patio was looking at her and at Cesare.

"I told Reggie that there was an old tale of a bracelet that our nanny told us when we were children," Cesare said, filling the pause in conversation. "*Ti ricordi,* Victoria? Do you remember?"

Victoria frowned. She remembered the nursery where she and Cesare had spent too many days as children because they had been too much trouble for their busy father to deal with. Their mother had long been dead and so *Bambinaia* Maria had been the mother to them, fixing their cuts and scrapes, kissing better the wounds of their father's inattention. She had been a gentle woman of the Milanese countryside, with dark brown hair always drawn back tightly to a bun at the back of her head. It had been a severe hair style, one their father demanded, but her eyes had always been laughing. Though she was long ago retired to a small pension near Lake Como, Victoria visited her regularly. She needed to tell Maria what had happened. The elderly woman would be distraught if she heard only the stories from Erminio that the Milanese media would convey.

But Maria had told stories when they were children—the best ones in the world about Kings and Ravens and men turned to stone, and singing waters and talking doves. There *had* been one about a bracelet, too.

She looked up at Cesare. "I remember. It was something about lovers and an evil King who wanted the woman."

"That is the one. I remember it, too, but I don't recall the details," Cesare said.

"Are you telling us that there might actually be a story that will tell us what we're dealing with?" Kylee asked.

"A fairy story?" Danny was handing out plates while Lila opened the foil wrapped salmon, releasing a luscious, lemon-scented steam.

"Fairy and folk tales often hold a core of truth, whether as a teaching tale or a remembrance of history—at least that's what I've read," Chloe said, returning from the kitchen with Reggie, both bearing salad bowls.

Lila opened another foil packet to reveal dill and garlic-scented roast vegetables. A bowl held fresh sour cream and another fresh salsa of local peaches, blueberries, red onion and cilantro and everyone began to fill their plates. Thalia ran and changed to khaki shorts and a blue t-shirt inside and then disappeared again to eat while watching the television in Lila's reading room. The low drone of the television came from the window at the far end of the house.

"Victoria, I think we need to know more about that story. Can you remember it?"

She thought a moment and shook her head. "Not details. It has been a long time. Perhaps Maria still remembers. I can give her a call."

"That'd be easier than all the reading it took to go through the colonel's journals. Aside from telling us where he got the bracelet from, he didn't have much for us." Kylee said. "I really don't fancy having to read all of Italy's fairytales."

"Could you give her a call, then?" Lila asked.

"I would be happy to." Victoria sliced through a piece of the skewered meat. Not what she was expecting. Given the grill mark and char she's expected to have to saw into saddle leather. Instead, the meat was tender and the flavor was a lovely Grecian mix of lemon and licorice.

She looked up and found Danny watching her, his green gaze expectant.

"*Bene*! Good. Very good in fact." She nodded in his direction and the compliments started flowing to the cook, but Danny had already sat back as if the only comment that mattered was hers. He started eating, chewing methodically, as if he ate the way he might conduct an investigation. Was he like that in all facets of his life? That could be—interesting. Or perhaps not. His rumpled shirt suggested that he did not pay attention to details and in affairs of the heart details were everything.

No Signor Danny might know how to cook, but that did not mean he was good for anything more, and what was she doing thinking of him at all? He was not her type. Handsome, yes, but a Viking polizia? A rumpled one, at that. He showed none of the *passione* for life that was so a part of Italian life. This man hung back silently. Talking to him would be like talking to an echo. Where would be the vibrant arguments? The passionate embraces afterwards and the claims of undying love? No. A quiet man like this Danny was not for her and where the thought had even come from she was not sure.

The food was very good. The salmon cooked perfectly on a bed of lemon and herbs, with more lemon and herb stuffed inside so the tender flesh was succulent with it. The salsa was a perfect crisp counterpoint to the salmon's richness and the vegetables were tender, but not overcooked; tiny sweet onions, vibrant green beans and whole baby carrots and small yellow pattypan squash all roasted and steamed with olive oil, garlic butter and fresh chives over top. But it was the lamb that was the star, outdoing even Lila's salmon. The heaped skewers quickly melted away as the crowd devoured them. Even Victoria split a second skewer with Lila.

They drank Brett's chilled white wine and Cesare's red brought all the way from Milan. That got her brother and Kylee's Brett into deep conversation about their plans for Elkhart Winery. Jas Stone and Danny spoke quietly together, but the way they kept glancing in her direction, she was certain she knew what they conversed about—and she was not having any of it.

She stood up and went to the two handsome polizia, catching them both by the elbow to lean over their shoulders as they stood over the now empty grill.

"What do you plot about, you fine men?" And they both were fine. Strong muscles in both their arms that pleased her. A clean scent of soap, water and sunshine from Danny. A simple man of simple tastes.

"Plot? We don't plot!" Danny protested, but by the look in his eyes she had caught them.

"We're concerned about you, Victoria. It comes with the job and with what we've seen. The bracelet is bad news in so many ways and Lila and Chloe say that it clouds the wearer's judgment. All we want to do is keep an eye on you."

"An eye? Yours?" She gave Jas a once over. "Or perhaps yours?" She turned to Danny and a dark flush ran up over his fair redhead's skin.

Oh ho! So that was the way of it then.

"No. I will have my privacy and you two brave men will fight the evils in the world. If I have need of you, I will call. Yes?" She patted both their cheeks and turned, smiling, as she left them speechless.

These North American men had met their match in Victoria Angelucci.

Look for *Unlocking Her Chance* coming January 2016.

**Romance, Mystery and Adventure
from Twisted Root Publishing**

If you enjoyed this book, you might enjoy other
titles available from Karen L. Abrahamson in
your local bookstore or wherever e-books are
sold.
www.karenlabrahamson.com

Romantic Suspense   Mystery   Urban Fantasy